THE TEMPLE SCROLL

(The Temple - Book 2)

Set in the present day, this second novel in The Temple series follows young church minister Helen Johnson and archaeologist Sam Cameron as they continue their struggle against evil in their quest to solve the mystery of the missing Templar hoard.

D. C. Macey

Also by D. C. Macey
The Temple Legacy - published August 2015
The Temple Covenant - published August 2017
The Temple Deliverance - published April 2019

THE TEMPLE SCROLL

(The Temple - Book 2)

Butcher & Cameron

D C MACEY

Published by Butcher & Cameron
Copyright © D C Macey 2016
ISBN 9780993345852
ISBN: 0993345859

Chapter 1

MONDAY 5TH AUGUST

The little blue and white passenger ferry circled round the island to set up its line of approach to the jetty in the north bay. On board, Sam Cameron braced his legs and gripped the handrail to steady himself as a wave caught under the turning bow. The engine seemed to growl just a little harder as it pushed against the waves, then it eased back to a purr as the captain guided the ferry into the lee of the island and towards the jetty. Two fat grey seals snorted and honked disquiet as they slipped off the rocks and disappeared beneath the water. A great bull seal held his ground, huffing and puffing; he glowered at the approaching ferry, nothing was going to move him until he was ready.

The engines went astern and the sea churned around the propeller as the captain took the way off the boat, drawing it to a halt exactly at the jetty. A complex and well-practised manoeuvre so skilfully executed it seemed effortless, child's play.

As the crew tied the boat up, the captain called through to the passenger lounge. 'If you want to get off and look around, now's the time. You've got about an hour and a half. Be sure and return to the jetty here for four o'clock. We'll be back then and won't be able to wait, the tide will be turning and that'll be the last pick-up of the day.' Several elderly tourists sat tight, sticking with the shipboard

1

experience. A little group of tourists lined up behind Sam and they all funnelled down the gangway, off the boat and on to Inchcolm Island.

Ashore, Sam spotted the rangy figure of a man standing a little way up the path. Each waved an acknowledgement to the other as Sam approached.

'Pete, how you doing?'

Pete Summers grinned at Sam. 'Can't complain, this place keeps me busy,' he said. They shook hands as the tourists strolled past them.

'What a great place to spend your summers, I'm jealous.' Sam let his eye scan across the little island. Slim at the middle, broadening out at either end - like a distorted dumbbell. From previous visits, he knew it would take little more than half an hour to stroll right round the shoreline. They stood at the island's pinch point. Directly behind him was the north bay where the now departing ferry had landed its passengers. In front of him, and no more than twenty paces ahead, was the south side bay. Much more erosion and the two bays would meet, cutting the island in two.

Pete pointed to the eastern part of the island where his office and workshop were housed in a green coloured building that merged into the scenery. 'I've got something for you to see in there. But come on; let me show you the source first. Based on what I've been hearing lately, it's right up your street these days.'

Sam nodded and was happy to follow Pete who set off at a quick pace. They headed west across the waspy waist of the island. Directly ahead, Sam could see Inchcolm Abbey. Tourists were wandering amongst the medieval ruins, which stood imposing and solid in their calm isolation; unflinching in the face of a thousand years of history, it was a survivor of wars, invasion and political turmoil.

Further off, Sam could make out the occasional concrete structure - gun mountings, the evidence of responses to a succession of threats thrown up over the generations: Napoleon, the Kaiser, Hitler. The island and the abbey had come through it all - seen them all off. Beyond it and across the water, he could see the Forth Bridge, iron red and imposing, dwarfing the boats that passed beneath.

After graduating and a period of sometimes challenging military service, Sam had opted for an academic career. On the other hand, his friend Pete had always been a bit of a loner and favoured the practical world. People skills had never been Pete's strong point. Eventually he'd worked his way into his perfect job. Summers on the island: thinking, digging, conserving. Winters in the Historic Scotland Workshops at the Granton Depot in Edinburgh: researching, analysing and preparing for the next digging season.

There were a couple of seasonal staff based on the island too, really only there to help and support the visitors. Pete didn't bother anyone and nobody bothered him.

'Well, are you going to tell me?' said Sam. They were weaving through the ruin now. The faded gold and grey shaded stone construction was impressive but Sam had visited several times over the years. Right now, he wanted to know what his friend thought so important.

'This way,' said Pete, 'nearly there.' He led Sam across the site, weaving between walls, under archways and amongst a succession of stone-floored spaces. Some parts now lay open to the sky, where the roofing had long since collapsed.

Pete stopped abruptly and pointed down to a weathered slab of stone. Sam saw his knowing smile but was none the wiser.

'It's a slab,' said Sam. He looked around and saw several similar candidates within stepping distance.

'Yes,' agreed Pete. 'But not just any slab. This one's for you.'

'Well,' said Sam, 'why?' He knew Pete was not the strongest communicator but he was well grounded. Whatever reason Pete had called him out here for, it would be solid.

'It's a grave slab,' said Pete. 'Though some of these stones have been moved around, maybe a bit of grave robbing in centuries past, we'll never know. What I do know is there is nothing under the stones; I had them up three or four years ago. But interesting for you, this particular area is predominantly fourteenth century. Very old. And back then, burial slabs like this were used for only the most important of people.'

'Yes,' said Sam. 'So what have you found?' The fourteenth century had been occupying a lot of his thoughts this summer. Ever since his discovery of a Templar dagger in the Fife sand dunes had dragged him and his friends into a web of murderous events. Thankfully, the threat had passed once the police had caught the gang concerned.

Pete waved his arm round embracing a whole collection of slabs. 'These slabs are all so worn, if they were ever engraved, the messages seemed lost to time long ago.' He crouched down beside the slab and stroked it, then glanced up at Sam. 'You know what I'm like, I need to know and don't like to give up. I thought I could just about make something out here, just didn't know what it was. See, here.' He traced his hand across the stone.

Sam looked carefully. If there was anything at all, it seemed like mottling, little more than natural variation in the stone. He knelt down. 'What is it, Pete? I can't see anything.' Sam's hand followed the route Pete's had traced across the stone. He felt nothing.

Pete laughed and stood up. 'At first, I was like you. Didn't consider there was anything there to see. But the more I dwelt on it the more I began to wonder. There are several stones like this. Here and there, just the slightest hint of a blemish, shades of something, perhaps. So I did what I do best. Thought about it, worried over it and then stewed on it for a while longer. Then, a couple of weeks ago, I had a piece of kit shipped over from the Granton Depot. A portable scanner. It's a step up from the raking light source technique we used before. I just knew there was something inscribed there. A gut feeling, you know? So with this scanner, I've imaged the slab's surface and you're going to love it. Let's go see.' He stood and nodded towards his workshop base at the eastern end of the island.

Sam knew there was no point in pressing Pete. His friend would reveal the answers when he was ready, that was just how he was. The pair walked off towards the workshop.

Perhaps it was the tranquillity of the little island, perhaps the permanence of the buildings, whatever, Sam relaxed, couldn't help it. So close to nature and the unmoving stones of the ancient buildings, it was just peaceful. Heavenly. Helen was returning from the States tomorrow. He was sure she would like to visit here once she'd had a chance to settle back in.

Sam did not notice the tourist wandering through the building after them; didn't see him meandering across the floors, looking here, looking there. As if by chance the tourist stopped where Sam had stood, looked down at the stone slab, thought carefully then took its picture from several angles. Then the man headed east, making for the little gift shop set beside the staff workshop.

• • •

'Well, what do you think?' asked Pete.

Sam looked at the computer screen. He gave a nod and stroked his chin. He had to agree the scanner had done a good job. 'What a great piece of kit you've got here, Pete.'

'I know. To be fair, it's really just refining a well-established process: recording the shadow patterns generated when a light source is shone across an ancient stone surface. It's hard to appreciate just how sensitive the scanner is, until you see the results. But it works on the standard assumption: long worn away engravings still leave miniscule edges and depressions, imperceptible to the naked eye, but shine a bright light from exactly the right direction and those edges cast tiny shadows; shadows that can be recorded and seen - revealing the eroded message.'

'Right. I think this is interesting, though in isolation it makes no sense,' said Sam. A little niggle of worry started to rise; something that had faded during recent weeks came creeping back.

His finger ran across the screen, tracing out the familiar shape of a Templar cross. This was not just any engraving of a Templar cross; it was a perfect likeness of the cross that was engraved on the dunes dagger they had unearthed earlier in the summer. This was *their* Templar cross.

'There is no record of any Templar involvement here. There should be no such artefacts,' said Sam.

'That's what we thought, but what do you make of this?' Pete reached across to the screen and swiped, dragging the image off screen, replacing it with a second scan.

...e Be...
Ex Deo natus est
Vir pugnator
Filius Lindum

Sam took a moment to review the inscription. It was such a rare find, pretty well unique. 'This is tremendous. Both the cross and inscription are definitely from the same slab?'

'No doubt, look, I can shrink the images, and you'll see the juxtaposition of cross and text. Problem is they have weathered slightly differently. Each section needs a different angled light source to show at its best. So I have to capture the engraving as two separate scans, otherwise one or other part of the image is scarcely visible. I'll merge the two images into one when I get time.'

'Why would it have weathered differently? It's the same stone.'

Pete gave a shrug. 'Can't be sure. My guess is moss or lichens grew on different parts of the stone at different times or perhaps the stone was partly covered for a time, maybe when the original roof came down.'

'Or natural variation in the stone, even?' said Sam.

'Could be that too. What I do know for certain is we have a Templar grave marker and an inscription. Neither of which should be here, and knowing your interests, I thought you were the man to speak with first. What do you think?'

Sam translated the text, reading it aloud in English. 'The top line is hard to read, the beginning and end are lost completely; I don't have any idea what it says. The rest is clearer though. This line reads, Child of God. Then, Man of war or perhaps it means warrior. Finally, at the bottom, Son of Lincoln.'

Pete nodded. 'That's about where I got to. A warrior's epitaph that's for sure. But this is an abbey, a place of peace. It's just the wrong place; why it's here is beyond me. And what does it represent? The Templars are your baby, Sam, what do you think?'

Sam would have to work up an answer. Could this be another strand of the Templar mystery he had been grappling with all summer? It was certainly contemporary with their previous finds, and the cross was a perfect likeness. The niggle of worry grew - then he gave himself a shake, there was nothing to be concerned about. The police had broken the gang who had hunted them earlier in the summer and their leader was in custody. Perhaps this gravestone would be a clue to help him solve the riddle of the Templar daggers.

• • •

Her last day at home in the States had Helen Johnson sat snug behind the desk in her father's study. She pulled her eyes away from the window and a scene that had been the backdrop to all her early life. She didn't need to look to see it; she knew it so well, it was always with her. Outside the window, the neat and ordered houses of her hometown filled the foreground. Beyond were gently rising hills, thoroughly greened with a blanket of trees.

The harmony of the tranquil scene was broken only by a gash in the trees, creating space for pylons that carried the power lines down into the town - and even this harshness carried the comfort of familiarity. Idly, she watched a solitary car as it progressed up the road that ran parallel to the power lines - up hill, out of town. It disappeared over the brow of the hill and the scene lapsed back into stillness. Tuning out the road and pylons, she could focus on the surrounding untouched green, the natural America. She liked to tell herself it looked just how the land had looked before her ancestors came.

Her parents were out for the morning, some church business, leaving her free to catch up on her own affairs. Turning her attention to her phone, she began to scan her messages. They all seemed routine, nothing that couldn't wait until she went home tomorrow. Helen stopped herself. Wasn't this home anymore? Edinburgh really had grown on her. She thought of Sam and smiled, then laughed to herself. Well, as they say - absence makes the heart grow fonder. She'd see him tomorrow, looked forward to it.

More than a month's break, spent here with her parents, had restored her, normalised her again - jaunts out, visiting family and friends, keeping busy doing nothing. And now it was time to go back. The gang who had threatened them and caused so much suffering was gone, its leader locked away. Peace had returned. Peace and a treasure hunt to solve. This time Edinburgh was going to be exciting for all the right reasons.

An email caught her attention; she did not recognise the sender's name. Having scanned it quickly she stopped and made herself start again, this time reading it very carefully. The author's first language was not English, but a closer reading made his meaning clear enough. Helen's spine tingled with excitement, a little fear, mistrust, a bit of everything. The author seemed to be offering a gift horse, or perhaps he was a Greek bearing gifts? She didn't reply straight away, needed to think.

A little while later, she referred back to the email, checked the phone number it gave and called it without any hesitation. The call took a moment to link through, then a continent away it started to ring - at least the number wasn't a hoax. After several rings, the phone was answered but nobody spoke.

'Hello,' said Helen. 'Is anyone there?'

Silence. It seemed to stretch for a long time.

'Hello, this is Helen Johnson, you emailed me earlier. Can you hear me?'

'Helen Johnson. You got my message, that's great,' a young man's voice, sounding at once cautious and relieved.

'You must be Erling then,' she said, struggling for the right pronunciation.

'Ja, oh, yes, I mean yes. I'll stick to English for you. That's probably best, yes?'

'I guess so, if you don't mind. Norwegian is not my strong suit. In fact I don't understand it at all.'

'English it is then and thanks for calling me. When I contacted your church's email address, I didn't know if it would reach you or not.'

'It's fine. One of the elders forwarded your email to me. I'm intrigued by your message; do tell me more about yourself, about your find.'

'Intrigued?' said Erling, puzzled.

'Oh sorry, I mean interested, I need to know more.' Helen switched her phone to speaker mode and grabbed a pencil and pad so she could make notes.

'Ah, yes. Well, you already know I'm Erling, that's Erling Karlsen. I saw the pictures in the newspapers last month and then I knew you would want to speak with me.'

Helen's thoughts flashed back to events earlier in the summer and the danger she and Sam had faced. She shivered as images of the brutal murders that had centred on St Bernard's, her parish in Edinburgh, scrolled through her mind. Memories resurfaced of the heartless slaying of Sarah MacPherson and her husband - Sam's boss at the university. The poor couple had died awful deaths simply because MacPherson had custody of the Templar dagger that Sam had discovered in the dunes. The dagger was one of a set, which somebody else wanted, wanted very badly.

She and Sam had identified four daggers from the set. First the dunes dagger and then a dagger in the National Museum of Scotland - both of which the killers had ultimately taken, using the cruellest of methods. Then she had inherited the St Bernard's parish dagger, the key dagger, from her mentor John Dearly. Another shiver ran through her body at the thought of his suffering, but he had not given up the parish dagger, had been strong to the end. She'd inherited more than just a dagger, responsibilities and wealth too - she had spirited the dagger back here to the States for safekeeping. And fourthly, there was John Dearly's friend and ally Xavier, the old Catholic priest - his dagger was kept hidden in Sardinia.

There were more daggers to find; each blade with its own unique, engraved pattern, and how they would be combined remained unclear. Xavier had been on the periphery, responsible for just his own dagger he only knew part of the story, but he insisted the daggers were a code, perhaps to the lost Templar treasure. John Dearly, the keeper of the key dagger, was the one man who had known all the answers - now he was dead. So many deaths, and for what? She forced the vivid images from her mind; they all died for no reason - their friends and so many others, all dead. Thank God, with the killers caught they could now solve the puzzle without threat.

The reassuring image of DCI Wallace flitted through her mind. He had proven to be a good policeman; she still felt guilty about not having given him all the facts at the time, but circumstances had made that impossible. So she had been delighted when he finally got his man.

She recalled the conversation she had with Sam the day before leaving for her holiday break. They had decided to give DCI Wallace a photograph of the dunes dagger. It was the blade that seemed to have sparked the killing spree. Sam had handed it in.

Wallace had been delighted that the Scottish police had something to put out to the media. He just wanted to be sure whoever now had the dagger would not be able to sell it on. If nothing else, releasing pictures of the dagger might reduce the original's commercial value to zero - no sane person would touch it with a bargepole. She and Sam had not thought it likely the original dunes dagger would ever go on the market, but if it helped DCI Wallace, it was worthwhile. And now, here she was speaking to an earnest young Norwegian, Erling Karlsen.

'Go on,' said Helen, hesitantly.

'Well, this will be hard for you to believe. I promise you it's not a trick. A hoax, you would say. Yes?'

'Well?'

'Like I said in my email, I have the same dagger as in the police photograph.' Erling stopped talking, waited for a response, an indication of Helen's thoughts.

'You said that in your email. But why are you telling me? Surely you would want to inform the police?'

'I know. I know I should. But the police won't give me money.' The young man sounded almost embarrassed in revealing his motivation.

'I see. And why do you think I might give you money?'

'Because you are with the church and your dagger was originally found on the skeleton of a Christian knight, a Templar. I know, I've read all the coverage. In the papers, online, everything. And my dagger has a church link too.'

Helen tensed; this was suddenly on the money. Perhaps there was something in what Erling had to say. 'Erling, what do you mean, your dagger has a church link?' She made her voice sound calm, almost disinterested.

'My uncle was a pastor, in Oslo. He was killed in a coach crash, maybe three years ago. He and many of his congregation were on a trip. The driver lost control; they went over a cliff edge into a fiord. Nobody survived. You might have seen it in the papers?'

Helen made a sympathetic sound, sucking a breath in between her teeth; she said nothing. Something about the event did trigger a distant memory, another sad story, a fleeting news item almost buried somewhere in her subconscious. She wasn't sure, but didn't want to explore the accident now - it would divert Erling from his main story.

'The investigation was inconclusive, maybe the driver just lost concentration, we'll never know for sure. Anyway, that was that. Afterwards, we were all a bit surprised at how much money our uncle had in the bank. He had no children so it was all split between his nephews and nieces. As well as the money, his nieces all got to choose bits and pieces from his home. His nephews too, but my brother Jan and I were the only male inheritors so we got the man things. He got an old gold signet ring and I got a silver dagger. That's the dagger I'm calling you about.'

Letting the pencil go, Helen snatched up the phone and switched from speaker mode back to handset. Forcing herself to talk in a calm tone, she asked him to repeat what he had said. The story sounded plausible, contained elements that the teller had released quite innocently, clearly not appreciating how each successive snippet of information supported the whole. Could one of the daggers have travelled as far as Norway? And more importantly, since DCI Wallace had not released information about the signet ring, Erling couldn't have begun to guess about that.

A short conversation established that Erling needed money quickly - quite a lot of money. His share of his uncle's inheritance had been frittered away on fun and holidays, and too much gambling. His pregnant girlfriend wanted him to settle down with her, get a job, and make a life together. She was right; it was time. But first, he had to put his financial affairs straight. His father had died the previous year, but had not been a wealthy man. The brothers had inherited his house in Sandefjord and little else. The only way to get on a level footing was to sell the family house or sell the dagger. No choice really, if he sold the house their plans for a family life together would vanish.

So he was selling the dagger, and he hoped Helen's connection might be able to help him find a good buyer, maybe even the Church - he'd pay her a commission. Helen smiled to herself, thinking of John Dearly's bequest, her trust fund. Never mind a commission, if anyone was going to buy it, she was. She decided to act at once, to secure this dagger now, while the opportunity presented itself.

Helen was wealthy, very wealthy. It had come as a shock to her when John Dearly, her mentor and the previous minister of St

Bernard's, had nominated her as his beneficiary, but with his wealth came responsibilities and she had to live up to them. Instinctively she pressed her hand to her breast, felt the heavy gold chain and the hardness of John's signet ring - the symbol of her inheritance and responsibility.

By the time she hung up, plans were in place. She dialled the airline, switched her tickets. The change wouldn't even add a day to her journey back to Edinburgh. And what was that if this lead proved to be right? She sent an email to Erling, confirming her travel plans and then settled down to write a message to Sam. He'd understand the urgency of her response to Erling's offer.

Tonight there was a leaving party in the community hall. Family and friends; it seemed half the town was coming. Tomorrow morning she would be gone.

• • •

At the jetty, Sam shook Pete's hand and then stepped aboard the ferry. He entered the passenger lounge, sat at a window seat and looked on as the crewmen cast off and the ferry started to pull away. He waved farewell to Pete then watched, startled, as his friend was almost knocked into the water by a late arriving tourist who rushed past to leap the widening span between boat and shore. The tourist was grabbed and steadied by the crewmen, their expletive laden greetings made clear what they thought of the man's timekeeping. The tourist gave a shrug that could mean anything the viewer wanted it to, from sorry to get lost.

From across the passenger lounge, Sam watched as the tourist stepped inside and selected a seat. The man sat and let his heavy rucksack slide down between his feet as he leant back and relaxed. Sam turned to look back at the island. Pete was still visible, now standing at the top of the slope above the jetty. A hand rose in final salute and then he turned and walked away, back into his private world.

Sam knew exactly what Pete would do now, what he did every day after the tourists had gone. He'd take a careful walk around the island, do a visual inspection of the ancient ruins and then finish up at the residents' cottage in time for his tea, prepared by one of the seasonal staff. After that, he'd read the papers delivered earlier in the day by the ferry. Finally, he'd return to his office to squeeze in a couple of hours' work before turning in.

Sam suddenly felt as though he was being watched and turned towards the lately arrived tourist. The man averted his gaze. Had the man been watching or was it just his imagination? Sam put it from his mind; he had a new mystery to consider now. What did the Templar inscription mean?

• • •

Pete Summers settled behind his desk. The quiet of the island's evening always carried him close to nature. It was almost perfect; the gentle lapping sounds of the sea were carried up through his open window and punctuated by an occasional seabird's shriek or the distant snorting and puffing of grey seals, beached and heavy with a summer of feasting.

Pete leant down to switch on his computer. Nothing happened. Surprised, he tried again, dead. He checked the power supply, active, tried the power switch again, nothing. Bending under the table he looked at the box and suddenly felt a twinge of puzzlement, the casing's access panel was ajar. Had he or Sam kicked it by accident earlier in the afternoon?

Getting down under the desk he pulled open the access panel and found the problem - he didn't need to be an IT expert to recognise it. The hard drive was gone and the insides of his computer had been butchered in the process of extraction. He leapt up, rushed out of the office and headed for the cottage to confront the seasonal staff. Neither knew anything. Pete was not good with people but even he could tell they were genuine.

All three went back to his office to inspect the damage, and the speculation began. There were so few plausible explanations, none in fact, and they quickly ran dry. Pete traced the day's events. At first, nothing came to mind. Then he finally focused his thoughts on Sam's departure from the jetty. That late coming tourist was a possibility. The man had jostled and pushed him aside in his rush to leap on to the ferry. His rucksack had been heavy, clearly too heavy for just refreshments. It may have held camera kit; it may have held *his* hard drive. But why?

If it had been the tourist, he would be long gone. There was nothing of any real value on the computer, just admin files, his research and, of course, his scans. Nothing secret or confidential. Anyway, he had it all backed up. That comforting thought suddenly prompted him to action and a fit of nervousness; he tensed and pulled open the desk draw. He relaxed. The little external hard drive was where it should be, all his information was safely backed up. Why his computer had been damaged was beyond him; he'd need to start keeping doors locked while tourists were on the island. Now he would phone the police station at South Queensferry.

• • •

The day had come and gone in a rush. Now, in the still of the evening, Cassiter sat quietly looking out of his office window. Being held on remand had been an inconvenience. But it had provided the time he needed to think through exactly what had happened and how he should respond.

Cassiter had been a little surprised that it had taken quite as long as it did for pulled strings to have the desired effect. But here he was, free. The procurator fiscal had finally decided there was not enough evidence to bring against him: the case was dropped.

It had proven unfortunate for the procurator fiscal that both his desire to one day stand for the Scottish Parliament and his unwholesome interest in boys scarcely out of school had come to the attention of Cassiter's research team. It had taken them a while to capture recordings of the necessary evidence, but a little patience ensured they did get what was required.

Once the fiscal had been presented with the video evidence of his personal predilections he quickly became Cassiter's man and had been equally quick to discover weakness in the prosecution case. In particular, he suddenly found little strength in the key DNA evidence. Yes, it was Cassiter's DNA on the blood-splattered handkerchief found on the church path beside the murder scene. Happily, the procurator fiscal had now decided it could have been dropped anywhere, then carried to the scene of the crime by a gust of wind.

When Cassiter's team had insisted the fiscal say exactly where that physical evidence was being stored, it was only a matter of time before it disappeared. Humans were weak and Cassiter's team were experts at finding the weak spots.

Today, he was out, a free man, an innocent man. Collected in an anonymous black Land Rover, he had been whisked directly to his office. Tinted windows afforded him some privacy as a sour faced woman delivered a backseat briefing on the various projects he was working on.

By lunchtime he was on top of things, happy his teams had been working correctly, he knew who was where, who was watching whom. The required monitoring and information gathering had continued in his absence. All but one of his projects had been running smoothly - the one that had forced him into the open and into contact with the police, it was the one he intended to drop, but it just wouldn't lie down and die.

He had just taken a call from Parsol, one of his bigger clients; it was Parsol who had originally commissioned Cassiter's team to hunt down the Templar daggers. Today Parsol had virtually begged him not to drop the troublesome job, and had offered silly money for Cassiter to stay on it, a fortune. Finally, Parsol invited Cassiter to his chateau for a council of war, the invitation so rare it could not be declined.

Anyway, Cassiter reflected, perhaps it might be in his interests to have a little patience, to ensure the job was put to bed properly without any loose ends. He'd accepted Parsol's invitation, agreed to keep the contract live for a little while longer. After a month in gaol, a couple of days here or there would not make any difference, one way or the other.

In the meantime, it would remain business as usual on Parsol's contract, until a decision to the contrary was reached. The reports involving Norway were very interesting. The email intercepts his team had continued to harvest in his absence made clear there was something important there and now the Johnson woman had booked a flight to Oslo. That situation was going to need some special attention, fast.

It would also be interesting to review whatever it was that had drawn Cameron out to Inchcolm Island. It may be of relevance, it may not - he'd know all about it soon enough.

Chapter 2

TUESDAY 6ᵀᴴ AUGUST

DCI Wallace kicked the wastepaper bin. It flew between the desks and nobody moved to pick it up.

'What the hell is going on?' said Wallace. He looked around; half a dozen pairs of eyes desperately scanned the floor tiles, detectives wishing they could find a gap to slip into. He growled, turned and for a long moment looked out of the window. Then he turned back to face his team.

'Well? Who's going to tell me? I put things in order, go on holiday and have to come back to this disaster. Somebody tell me who caused this mess. And where's DS Brogan? Why isn't he here?'

Three weeks holiday had done wonders for DCI Wallace, his health and his disposition - a happy wife, happy teenagers: happy family. Two minutes back in the office and it was as if he'd never been away.

'He hasn't come back from his own holiday yet, boss. He's sick. Got a virus or something when he was away. He's been off as long as you have. May not be back for another week,' DC Grant chose to answer the easy question, hoping somebody else would pick up the trickier parts.

Hell, thought Wallace. This is such a cock up. He was annoyed, needed to understand. 'Well, Grant, what happened?'

Grant shifted uncomfortably. 'Boss, there was nothing we could do. Pretty well as soon as you were away on holiday, headquarters started to push the idea that the whole business around St Bernard's parish, the killings, everything, was all caused by those two we found dead in the car up at Silverknowes.' The others nodded their heads in support but kept silent, forcing Grant to continue. 'Word is the chief constable himself wanted this tidied up quick and clean, wanted to give the media a positive news story.'

'Yeah, apparently the top brass liked the idea that the pair rounded it all off with a murder suicide,' said an unidentified voice from a little way behind Grant.

Grant was emboldened. 'Then out of the blue the procurator fiscal just dropped the case anyway. He said the DNA evidence wasn't enough. Apparently, our suspect liked to do cemetery walks, could have dropped the evidence at any time. Or someone might have stolen it and dropped it there - as if anyone would want to steal a bloodstained handkerchief. Anyway, with headquarters pushing the murder suicide pact and the legal boys suddenly deciding our evidence didn't stand up, we had to let him go. The file's sitting there on your desk, ready for you.' Grant reckoned he'd done his bit now. One of the other guys could finish off, he hoped. They stayed silent.

'When did you let him go?' Wallace fixed Grant with an accusing glare.

'Yesterday morning. At least he won't have had time to do much harm,' said Grant, searching for something, anything that might ameliorate the appearance of their position.

'Have we been watching him? Watching his office? What's been happening? Did we inform the church folk that he was out?' said Wallace. The team shuffled, but all noted the use of *we*. Wallace was slipping back into harness. For all his shouting, it was clear from the team's demeanour that they were glad he was back. In his absence, and for whatever reason, the powers that be had destroyed the case. Wallace was the man to bring some sanity to the situation.

'We've been told not to bother the suspect again, boss. That includes his office and staff. If any new evidence comes to light we have to run it past the police HQ and the fiscal's office before doing anything.'

18

'I see. Well they can stuff that for starters. And again, did we inform those people from the church that he's been set free?'

The team remained silent as Grant shook his head slowly. Noting the signal, Wallace growled and purposefully walked across to the battered wastepaper basket; he retrieved it and placed it back beside his desk. Stepping back, he took a run up to the basket and kicked it as hard as he could. It flew, hit the ceiling, the wall and finally stopped behind the door.

'Whatever you do, whatever you don't do, never leave the civilian population exposed, ever. Protecting them is our first and last task. Anyone who can't buy into that get out of this office now.' He retrieved the fatally distorted wastepaper bin and placed it by his desk. It rocked gently on to its side and Wallace finally sat down. Welcome back, he thought.

'Somebody fix me an appointment with that girl from the church, Helen, Helen Johnson, as soon as possible. Somebody get me headquarters on the phone. Somebody, I want a coffee. And Grant, call DS Brogan, tell him I need him to be fully recovered by tomorrow, regardless. The rest of you look lively, this isn't over, not by a long shot. Get on top of whatever else you're working on, and then get the decks cleared. Let's be ready to act if, when, things happen.'

• • •

There was a fast train link to Sandefjord from Oslo's Gardermoen Airport. She had taken a taxi - an hour's drive, but after a transatlantic flight, it gave her a bit of privacy and some time to decompress before her meeting. Helen hardly noticed the Norwegian landscape flash by. Having first worked through her texts and messages she then turned her attention back to the coach crash that had taken Erling's uncle, the pastor; searching the web with her smart phone to revisit the material she had viewed the day before. A cautious streak had grown inside her over the summer and it demanded she scour the available information. Anything linked to the daggers called for care. But there was nothing, it really did seem to have been a tragic accident. Finally, just as the taxi drove into Sandefjord, she put her phone away and sat back to take in the view.

The taxi swept past a big hotel and along the seafront to a huge roundabout. Turning off to the left, the taxi passed what she thought might be the town green and then the taxi slowed as it merged into a light traffic flow. It passed a mix of modern commercial buildings and older traditional properties, some of which might once have been homes. She squinted up. Perhaps above the ground level some still were.

The taxi stopped outside one of the older buildings, now a café. She got out, smiled thanks to Knut the driver. He nodded an unspoken understanding and pointed across the road to an empty parking bay. She stood and watched the car steer into the space, it stopped and Knut settled down to read his book. He was on the meter for the day - easy money.

Helen paused outside the café and for just a moment looked back at the taxi, her lifeboat if things went wrong. The cost was worth it, just in case, and anyway, she didn't need to worry about money anymore.

She entered the café; it was clean, functional and seemed to be aimed at the quick drinks and snacks market. Low cost value. The only customer was a young man, not much more than twenty. She guessed, correctly, that he was her appointment. Helen walked across and introduced herself.

Erling was delighted to see her and insisted on buying her a drink. She settled for orange juice, thanked him and then asked for proof of his identity. He seemed surprised but after a moment produced an ID card. She looked at it closely, checked the picture and was almost satisfied.

'Have you anything else?'

Erling looked slightly puzzled but produced a bankcard, worn from too much time in a back pocket, it was going to break soon but his name was clear enough.

Helen handed back the cards and nodded acceptance of his identity. She took a sip of orange and looked more closely at Erling. He had an open face and under other circumstances was probably fun to spend time with. But the furrow in his brow showed he had worries. He had already told her he had money problems. It showed.

'Don't you want to see my identity?' she said.

Erling shrugged. 'You've come to meet me. If you weren't you, you wouldn't be here.'

Helen was startled at the naivety of the reply. Erling was clearly an innocent. He had no idea of the danger owning such a dagger would have put him in, even just a few weeks ago. She spent a few moments exchanging small talk but it was quickly clear both parties really wanted to get down to business.

'Well, I think we should push on. I need to see the dagger and to know how much you want for it,' she said.

Erling lifted open the mouth of a plastic shopping bag that lay on the table beside him. Something bright glinted in the café's electric lights. Something familiar, Helen knew exactly what it was. A tension in her stomach, the thrill of discovery, this was easy. Too easy? She leant forward slightly, looked at the point of the dagger, could clearly see the engraving, saw the Roman numeral five. That number alone was enough to convince her - they didn't have a five yet, this was the real deal. She did not try to touch it, leant back and looked at Erling.

'How much?'

'500,000.' A slight variation in his tone told her that Erling was not at all sure of its real value. She was taken aback at the scale of the request, tried not to show it. But her surprise must have leaked.

'Kroner,' he said, quickly. 'Norwegian Kroner.' Then, almost pleading. 'The silver's metal value is probably that alone.'

Helen fixed a non-committal expression as she nodded acknowledgement. Then she pointedly took her phone and searched out a conversion rate. Erling watched anxiously. In moments she realised he wanted less than £50,000; this was something she could manage.

'You're right. I might be able to manage something today, but I will need a little time,' said Helen.

Erling looked relieved then shifted in his seat. His expression became anxious again. 'My brother Jan owns the big ring. Will you buy that too? Same price. Cash, please.' He pulled his clenched fist from his jacket pocket. Opened it to reveal a Templar signet ring. Helen recognised it instantly, it was identical to her own ring - she had to have it.

'Same price? Are you sure he wants to sell it? I should meet him first.' Helen could tell Erling was desperate for a deal, for cash. It seemed his brother was too. She reflected that she could easily have haggled the price down, but why should she? The deal was affordable and the boys were just innocently doing the best for themselves. She might even have been tempted to pay a bit more had they asked; after all, they were only trying to get by.

Helen left the café with an agreement to buy, a slip of paper with Erling's address and an arrangement to meet there two hours hence. He promised his brother would be there too. In the meantime, she needed to phone Franz Brenner, her private banker in Switzerland, to confirm access to the money. Franz was custodian of her trust fund; she had inherited him from John Dearly along with the Trust. While Franz could do his bit from afar, she had Knut drive her to the local bank where she would make use of the local banking connection Franz had established for her.

When she reached the bank, the manager was polite, almost deferential.

'Please, call me Oskar,' he said. 'I understand you are a very valued customer of our friends in Switzerland. Please, my office is your office. Whatever you need, just ask.' He whisked her past the serving counters and into his private office, fine coffee and delightful pastries following directly behind. Then he left her to do what she needed.

First, she phoned Franz who promised to contact the bank manager immediately to confirm her cash requirements. Then she took the time to call Sam. They speculated on why DCI Wallace wanted to visit her. Sam had fixed a meeting for the following afternoon. They swapped news about the epitaph engraved on the Templar gravestone and the Sandefjord dagger and ring, and looked forward to linking up later in the day.

• • •

Knut drove Helen beyond the outskirts of town. The taxi turned into a little lane, both sides of it deeply bordered with thickets of trees. The roofs of traditional houses could be seen, dotting away into the distance; spaced well enough apart to provide privacy, near enough to maintain a sense of community. They passed a smart

SUV driving out of the lane and then, bang on time, the taxi pulled up outside Erling's home. Like every other, it was neat and well presented. It was a lovely home; she could understand why Erling's girlfriend would want to raise a family here.

There were two cars parked in the driveway, blocking access. The taxi parked in the lane at the foot of the driveway. Helen hopped out, clutching the neat little briefcase full of money she had been given at the bank. Twenty paces and she was at the front door. She tapped, received no answer.

A distant siren broke the still suburban air. She tapped harder, still no answer. Puzzled, Helen peered through the little sighting window set immediately beside the door; she could see no signs of life and wondered if Erling was round the back. Stepping off the porch, Helen started to make her way round the house. The siren was louder now, sounded like more than one vehicle.

Helen passed the front windows, paused to look in. She guessed this was a lounge, spacious, but everything was cluttered as though tossed and turned. Then she noticed there was somebody lying on the sofa, Helen tapped on the window. No response.

She looked again and tensed, peered in carefully. It was Erling and it was clear why he was not moving; he was dead. She scanned the room, and then instinctively stepped back in shock. Inside the room and immediately below the window was a second body. It lay face down, bloodstained puncture wounds across its back showing where this young man was mown down - probably making a dash for the window.

She looked again at Erling, looked more carefully. His injuries were suddenly painfully clear. A bloodied mouth. The lips broken and torn and she could clearly see dark gaps in his tooth line, gaps that had not been there that morning. The bloodied gaps that told of teeth pliered out. A little bloodstained patch on his shirt, over the heart, marked his end. Helen gritted her teeth; it had started again.

She backed away, looked about; nobody was in sight. Without another glance, she turned and walked briskly back to the taxi. The sirens were louder now. She knew exactly what they were wailing for and she had no intention of waiting. She jumped into the back of the taxi. 'Drive. Drive on quickly.'

Knut had watched her movements closely, he could tell

something was wrong and turned in his seat to face her. 'What's up? What did you see?'

'Just drive, now. Quickly, we mustn't be here.' The pleasant voice that had so engaged Knut throughout their journey had suddenly acquired an edge. It was a leader's voice and he was being ordered. Instinctively he obeyed.

The taxi drove further up the lane as police cars and an ambulance screeched to a halt behind them. Lights continued to pulse out warning flashes as the sirens fell silent. Looking back, Helen could see police fanning out, weapons drawn, cautiously manoeuvring into the driveway.

'What the hell just happened back there?' said Knut.

Helen shrugged. 'I don't know but there were dead people in the house, it looked like a bombsite inside.'

'Dead people? Why didn't we wait for the police? We should go back.'

'No. There is nothing we can do. It happened well before we got there. We'd just be held up here for ages and get in the way of the investigation.'

Knut was not convinced, but recognised they might be held up. His home was on the other side of Oslo and he wanted to get back at a reasonable hour. Certainly, he did not want to be called all the way back here again as a witness, off the meter. He turned his attention back to the lane and started to accelerate away, then stamped hard on the brakes. 'Hell,' he shouted through the window. 'Are you mad?'

Helen was thrown forward between the front passenger seat and the driver's seat. She pulled herself back and up, and looked ahead to see what Knut was shouting at.

Standing in the middle of the road was a young woman, heavily pregnant, desperate, hands held up towards the car in a stop sign.

Knut was firing off a stream of Norwegian in the girl's direction. Helen could understand none of it but could sense the spirit of his message. She leant forward, rested a hand on his shoulder to calm him.

'It's okay, Knut, nobody's hurt. Take it easy.'

Knut pointed a finger through the windscreen and shouted again. Then he turned to Helen. 'Take it easy is easy for you to say. It's my livelihood, if I'd hit her I would be in trouble.' He fell silent for a moment, breathing hard. Then he shrugged. 'Well, I suppose nobody was hurt, but no thanks to that mad woman.' He pointed again at the girl who had not moved and was still blocking their route. She was in distress, tear streaked, dishevelled.

'Wait here,' said Helen as she got out of the car.

'Are you all right? Do you speak English?' she said as she hurried towards the girl.

The girl sobbed and threw her arms around Helen, leaning, finding support. 'Ja, ja, I speak English. Help me please, they have killed my boyfriend.'

Helen didn't need to ask who her boyfriend was. 'Come on, let's get in the car. Take it easy now. Is the baby okay?' She guided the girl past a scowling Knut and eased her into the back seat.

'I think so,' sobbed the girl. 'Thank you.' She glanced up at Knut who had turned to give her a closer inspection. 'I'm sorry. I didn't mean to anger you. But I had to stop you.'

Knut could see her distress, he softened, grunted what seemed a sign of forgiveness and turned away to look through the windscreen. 'Well you managed that. Should I drive on?' he asked Helen.

'Yes, let's go.'

'It might be a dead-end ahead.'

The girl shook her head. 'It's okay, keep going. You can go this way. The lane loops round and re-joins the main road further on.'

Helen had her arm round the girl's shoulder. 'So, what's your name?' she said.

The girl was cradling her bump in her hands. Avoiding eye contact, she stared determinedly down as she replied. 'I saw you arrive at the house, I was watching from up in the woods,' she paused for a moment, finally looking up to make eye contact with Helen.

Helen gave an encouraging smile. 'Why were you watching us?'

The girl's sobs became a howl of distress as she leant into Helen's shoulder for support. 'I'm Laila. Erling's girlfriend. They killed him, killed them both. You're Helen, I know, the boys were waiting for you to buy their things. Why were they killed, who would do such a thing?' She stopped talking, overcome with shock and grief.

'Which way?' said Knut as the car came to a halt where the lane rejoined the main road. He had decided it was best not to get involved in what was being said in the back of the car; best for him just to focus on the road.

'Head back into town please. Just keep moving along,' said Helen.

Helen turned her attention back to Laila. She knew exactly who would launch such an attack and why. But that threat was in the past - wasn't it? They were broken, their leader locked up. So where did this attack come from?

'Laila, concentrate, what happened back at the house? I need to know exactly.' Helen gave Laila's shoulder a gentle squeeze. 'Can you tell me?'

After a little while, Laila spoke. 'I'm not sure how it all started. I had been having a rest in the sunroom, at the back of the house, while Erling and Jan played some computer game, waiting for you. Then there was shouting and fighting, lots of men. I peaked a look through the serving hatch, maybe four men, guns,' she shivered and sobbed again as her mind revisited the scene.

'I heard them demanding the dagger and the boys wouldn't tell. Jan made a break for the window and they shot him', another heaving sob, she rubbed her swollen belly. 'They just shot him.'

Helen pressed her hand on to the girl's hands; it wasn't much of a comfort, just a gesture of support. 'What then?'

'Erling told them the dagger was in a carrier bag, but when they looked it wasn't there. They got really angry. You see, I had taken the dagger out of the bag and carried it through to the kitchen with me. I had decided to give it a polish, so it would be nice for you. They started to hurt him and I was afraid. So I sneaked out of the back door and hid in the woods behind. Then I called the police on my phone.'

Helen cradled the girl, supported her and felt sick inside herself. More killings, more brutality. That was all meant to be over now, in the past. She should have completed the purchase earlier when she first met Erling. He and his brother were dead because she had not moved quickly enough. And the dagger was lost. She needed to call Sam; warn him it was all starting again.

'I told the emergency service telephonist there were armed robbers in the house, she told me to get away,' said Laila. 'She said the police would come quickly. I could hear screaming from inside the house, they were hurting Erling. More shots, then just silence. They left in a big black car and then you arrived.'

The taxi was driving through the town now, Knut needed instructions. Helen told him to keep driving round in the traffic flow for a little while, until Laila had settled a bit. She also needed to think, she had let a dagger slip through her fingers. Would it always be like this? Always on the back foot?

'They killed the boys for an old dagger. Why? What can it be worth to do such a thing?' said Laila.

'Mad people do bad things,' said Helen.

Knut had been trying to tune out but enough got through for him to have a grasp of the key points. 'You're well out of it. If they want it that bad, best they have it.'

'They don't,' said Laila. She swung her shoulder bag round and pulled out a rolled up polishing cloth. Unwrapping it, she let Helen see the dagger.

Knut spotted it in his driving mirror and immediately started shouting in Norwegian again. As before, Helen had no difficulty in grasping his message. Laila shouted back and for a few moments chaos threatened to break out.

'Shut up both of you,' shouted Helen. Her pulse had leapt at the sight of the dagger. The killers had not got it. How did Laila manage to get away with it? Again, she shouted, the command in her voice forced the others into silence. Then she prompted Laila to explain.

'When I'd finished cleaning it I just kept it with me, felt too tired to take it back through. I knew Erling needed to sell it to you, for us, for the baby, so I just wanted it to look nice for you. When I ran, I took it - I didn't think. I didn't realise what they would do to him.' The crying started again.

'You did what you thought was right, that's the best anyone can do,' said Helen. 'It's no consolation, but I think they were both dead the moment the men walked into the house. If you'd gone back you would be dead too.'

Knut's voice rolled in from the front. 'Hey, you did well, girl. You saved your baby.'

Helen nodded. 'Yes, hang on to that. Now, what to do with the dagger?' Her question was rhetorical. She knew what she wanted to do. Leaning forward, she told Knut to make for the bank.

Laila was happy to relinquish possession of the dagger. By the time they arrived at the bank Helen had given her the briefcase, for Erling's baby, and established that Laila had family near Oslo, Knut would take her there today. Both agreed for their own safety that they must never talk of this to anyone.

Oskar was not surprised to see her return to his bank. Helen's original plan had been to leave the dagger at the bank after she had bought it. It would attract far too much attention at airport security. He took it without comment; then she stopped him and produced her phone to take pictures of the dagger, carefully recording the patterned markings on the blade. Those would keep Sam going until they could access the dagger again. It had been arranged that the bank would hold the dagger in safekeeping until Franz organised an interbank transfer to move it safely to Switzerland.

And as Franz had pointed out earlier, she was supposed to have visited them in Switzerland already. He needed her to visit to complete certain transfer protocols for her trust fund and now she would have her own reason to call at his bank too. She had promised to travel as soon as possible. Conservative, sure footed, in his impeccably polite way, Franz left her feeling that at least this task would work out according to plan.

Having checked local flight schedules she realised she could fly from Sandefjord's Torp Airport to Edinburgh and there was a flight due out quite soon. Back in the car, she encouraged Knut to hurry; she could just about make the next flight from Torp if he got a shift on. She knew his view of her had changed over the course of the day, could sense the growing respect and the slightly nervous looks he gave her. There was an increased deference in his voice, and she suspected he was quite keen to see the back of her. They made the airport in good time.

Helen gave Knut a very generous tip and again confirmed the arrangement that he would take Laila straight to her mother's home outside Oslo. After ensuring Laila knew how to get in touch in the event of an emergency, Helen left the taxi and allowed Knut to transfer her suitcase from the boot on to a trolley. She walked into the airport pushing the trolley with one hand while reaching for her phone with the other. Sam needed to be updated.

Helen had not noticed the black SUV that had rolled into the airport drop off zone just as Knut's taxi pulled out.

Chapter 3

WEDNESDAY 7ᵀᴴ AUGUST

Helen studied Sam across the breakfast table. She had returned to Edinburgh with mixed feelings. On the one hand, delighted to be with him again after what had felt like a very long break; on the other, sick to her soul that all the trouble from before was re-emerging. She had anticipated that her return would herald an exciting hunt to unravel the mystery of the daggers; there was nothing exciting in this. They had shared their news the night before. Now, in the light of day, plans needed to be made - made fast.

'I've been thinking, Sam, we need to let the guys know what's happening: Elaine, Grace, Francis, Xavier and Angelo too. If this is going the way it seems then they are all at risk again.' She waited for Sam's reply as he swallowed a mouthful of cereal. Her experiences in Edinburgh had forged close bonds with a mixed bag of people. People who, but for the recent killings, might for the most part have remained little more than acquaintances.

The common link between them all was John Dearly, and he had been killed for that link. Elaine, the senior elder at St Bernard's, had survived - though she had suffered cruel torture at the hands of the gang. Her daughter Grace was involved, young, loving life and always game; and Helen too, she bit on her lip. All three of the women now lived with the knowledge that they had seen the killers' faces, seen them in action - a shared hell. Then there was Francis, priest of the local Catholic parish, he'd been John Dearly's long-standing friend.

Finally, there was Xavier, the charming and enigmatic old priest from Sardinia. He at least had some knowledge of the real value of the daggers, and of the forces that seemed to be emerging once again. And always at his side was Angelo - a young assistant priest and his protector.

All together, they had faced evil before and against the odds come through. Now the friends needed to be warned that it was not over.

'Yes. We should warn them today. But what about the problem itself, what do you think now?' said Sam.

'Our original plan had been to solve the mystery of the Templar daggers and then expose the whole story to the public, a fait accompli. If the whole world knows the whole secret, it's not a secret anymore and there is nothing left to kill for. You and Xavier reckoned that was the only certain way to stop these lunatics. I think you were right then and, with the threat coming back, I still think you are right now,' said Helen.

'I know. We had planned to go after this secret hoard, or whatever it is, once you came back from the States - search it out in our own time. All I see now is it's just become an urgent activity. No - the only activity. We will need to devote everything to solving this now. I'm not expected on campus too much for a while. Other than the workshop I'm booked up for at Bristol University early next week, I should have a good deal of time to focus on this. Perhaps your church work will need to take a backseat too.'

'Agreed, I don't see this threat sitting back and giving us the time to sort things at our own pace. We need to step it up again. Anyway, judging by the emails Elaine has been sending me while I was away, the Church has still not set a date for the reopening of St Bernard's. So I don't think I'll have much on for a while.'

'I wonder what DCI Wallace wants. Perhaps he can shed some light on why this is all blowing up again,' said Sam.

'Perhaps that's why he's coming. I'm seeing Elaine at teatime, getting up to speed with the parish news. I'll warn her then; if Grace is around, I'll tell her too. If not, Elaine will tell her later.'

Sam stood and carried plates and mugs towards the dishwasher. 'Francis is coming round to visit this evening, we can update him then and I'll give Xavier a call after we've spoken to Wallace. Are you going to tell Wallace about Norway?'

'Not unless he asks. I am just pleased we didn't get embroiled with the Norwegian police; otherwise, I might still be stuck over there while they try to solve the killings. And you know what? I'm not sure they will. The killers over there seemed every bit as ruthless and professional as those over here were.'

'I'm sure the Norwegian police will be able to work something out for themselves eventually, ours did. I don't think you should worry about them, it's not as though you were actually in the crime scene or left any evidence.'

'You think?'

Sam tried to move the conversation on. 'Come on, DCI Wallace is calling round to the manse at three o'clock. I want to spend some time trying to match up our blades with the picture of the dagger you took in Norway. You never know, we might get lucky.' He had spent many hours studying the patterns engraved on the daggers that they had recovered during the summer; trying to understand their meaning. To date he had not made a breakthrough and was hoping the Norwegian dagger might help.

• • •

Cassiter sat motionless in the back of the limousine. It had collected him at Montpellier and set off at once for Parsol's chateau estate. Other than confirming his identity, the driver had made no attempt at conversation. That suited Cassiter; nothing annoyed him more than idle chatter. He was content to sit back, watch the scenery pass by and think about recent events. The journey had taken them about 40 kilometres out of town. With every passing kilometre, the driver seemed more dominant, more possessive of the road they travelled.

Gradually the main road whittled away until it was little more than a single metaled track that traced a route high along the remote valley side. All around, the grey white stone had weathered in extremes of sun and cold. The gnarled and stunted trees seemed to have weathered in sympathy with the rocks. Yet still the grasses and shrubs remained determinedly green in the face of the summer heat. It was a beautiful yet inhospitable environment.

Suddenly, the car swung off the road, it nosed down a lane into the valley below. Ahead he could see an old stone bridge arching over what was currently little more than a stream, the long drop from bridge to water level indicating that at times the stream could swell dramatically. A tight cluster of buildings stood on the far side of the bridge. There were perhaps twenty or so houses, a little chapel, a café and two or three commercial buildings - possibly barns or warehouses. Every building looked as though it had been old long before Napoleon's time. The lane wound amongst the buildings and the limo slowed for children playing in the road outside the chapel. The driver sounded his horn and waved two young boys down from their perch on the chapel's Mary Magdalene signage. Then the limo pulled away to emerge from the village and follow the lane as it snaked up the opposite valley side.

There, perhaps two hundred paces above the village, a high wall marked an estate boundary. The lane continued to work its way up the hillside, following the line of the wall until it reached a pair of ancient stone gateposts that supported very modern gates. The gates opened automatically as the limousine approached. Cassiter wondered whether the limo had a remote control or if the gates were under the control of a surveillance camera operative. He spotted a couple of men patrolling through the wooded grounds within the walls; his money was on manned surveillance control. It was clear that even here, in the rural wilds, Parsol left nothing to chance.

The limo raced along the private estate road and as it pulled clear of the woods Cassiter saw a broad and perfectly maintained lawn, in its centre an ornate fountain playfully jetting out a plume of water. Beyond lay the chateau, a broad set of steps accessed a raised terrace that seemed to run right round it. The limo followed the driveway as it skirted the lawn round to the front of the building; there it drew to a halt at the foot of the steps leading up to the grand entrance.

Cassiter travelled light but did not get a chance to carry his own bag. Four men appeared on the steps as he got out of the limo. Two hung back, guards, fit, strong, always alert. Cassiter thought back to the guards that had died in Edinburgh. These were equally as powerful, as were the others he'd seen dotted about the grounds. It seemed as though Parsol had a little private army. The other two men approached him. The first took his bag and retired back up the steps. The second, older, greeted him. Was he a butler or a lieutenant? Cassiter decided it didn't matter; the man clearly held station above the guards.

The older man informed him that Parsol was currently busy. Cassiter could settle in and they would talk over dinner - they ate early in the chateau.

• • •

Helen opened the manse front door to find DCI Wallace on the step. DS Brogan stood immediately behind him.

'Good afternoon officers, come on in,' she greeted them both with friendly smiles, hoped they had something positive to say. Though in the light of recent events, she and Sam were becoming increasingly concerned about the visit.

The policemen funnelled past her into the hall. Helen noted that both men threw glances towards the kitchen door as they passed it. Like her, they had been privy to the horrific events in their earlier in the summer.

'Take a right, Sam's in the study, we'll join him,' she said from the back. She followed them into the study, allowing her hand to stroke lightly against the kitchen door as she passed.

During her break back home, the church had replaced the whole kitchen and redecorated. It was the place where she had shared so much time with John Dearly and she remembered the laughter, the chat, the friendship; it would always be a special place. But the refresh had somehow made it easier to use the kitchen again.

Wallace shook Sam's hand and then took a seat, as invited. He wasted no time with pleasantries. 'Bad news, I'm afraid. The leader of the gang behind all the violence, the one who claimed his name was Innes, and by the way, I'm still convinced he had a false identity, I'm afraid he's gone. Been released,' his voice was level, matter of fact.

'Oh, no! I thought you had it all wrapped up,' said Helen. Sam stood up and crossed to stand beside her, his hand rested on her shoulder, provided a comfort.

'How could this happen?' said Sam.

'Well, all I can say is it's not what we planned. Sometimes the legal system just throws up outcomes that defy logic or the common sense of ordinary folk; that and the fact that a key piece of evidence is not to hand anymore.'

'What do you mean, not to hand? Is it lost?' said Helen.

Wallace shrugged, clearly couldn't and wouldn't explain the loss. 'We have no evidence to press charges now and it turns out that even before the DNA evidence disappeared, the fiscal was having second thoughts. Apparently, there are other equally as plausible ways the DNA evidence could have arrived at the scene. Ways that are unrelated to the crimes.'

'I'd like to hear them,' said Helen.

Wallace shrugged again. 'It's for the fiscal to weigh up the evidence. You should know the police now officially consider that the whole affair was perpetrated by the two scumbags we found dead in their car up at Silverknowes after all the killings.'

Helen felt sick in her stomach, she knew who had been involved but had been obliged to keep quiet at the time to protect her friends. She couldn't now provide the information without landing them all in trouble, and probably prison, for withholding evidence. The face of the man Wallace had just let go was etched behind her eyes. She had seen him in action. He was evil personified and now the police had freed him.

'So, who killed the pair in the car?' said Sam. Helen noted how calm he seemed in contrast to the emotions boiling inside her.

'Murder, suicide,' said DCI Wallace.

'Really? Do you actually believe that?' said Helen.

'That's how the evidence is being interpreted. Senior police, the fiscal, everyone seems to see it that way.'

'You too?' said Sam.

'The important thing is to ensure you are all safe. The man would be a complete fool to try anything now, and be assured he is no fool. Even so, it makes sense for all of you to take care, for your own piece of mind if nothing else. But I am pretty sure you are safe here. He wouldn't be stupid enough to try anything now.'

'Pretty sure?' Helen forced herself to remain calm. 'Would you be happy with *pretty sure* for your family?' She turned to Brogan. 'Would you be happy with it for yours? What's your take on all this anyway?'

Brogan gave a noncommittal shrug. 'I think what the DCI thinks,' he said.

'Don't press him,' said Wallace. 'He follows my orders. Look, I know it's bound to be distressing for you, but you should know I've put the man under surveillance. He left the country, so you can relax. I understand he's in France. And when he comes back to Scotland we'll pick him up again.'

Shortly afterwards, the police left. Wallace had agreed that panic buttons would be installed in the manse, both her and Sam's flats and the senior elder's home too. He had argued with Helen that the latter was not necessary but had conceded under pressure.

Closing the front door, Helen leant back on it, fixed Sam with a worried look. 'Well, what do you think?' She closed her eyes and breathed out long and slow. Then, feeling Sam's arms around her, she responded, hugging him back.

'Like you said before, I think we need to warn everyone, right now. Wallace might be saying there is no problem, but I don't buy it. That business in Norway, it had all the hallmarks, and he is out free right now. But how did they know you were there? Have they started spying on us again?'

'We'll have to ask Elaine to have Scottie do another security sweep of the buildings.' Helen was starting to feel annoyed. Who were these people to forever push and pry into their lives?

• • •

From her vantage point, just inside the entrance to St Bernard's church, Helen saw Elaine at the head of the centre aisle. Given the distance, she could hardly make out the injuries the senior elder had suffered during the assault earlier in the summer, though it seemed that she was on the mend. With a wave, Helen walked up the aisle towards Elaine. Sam followed behind carrying a load of empty cardboard packing boxes that Elaine had asked him to collect. As the distance between them closed, she could see Elaine's marks and scars. All the medical supports had been removed now but Elaine was disfigured; there was definitely more rebuilding to do.

Helen hugged Elaine and Elaine allowed her arms to circle Helen in response. Helen felt her friend's hands lightly rubbing and patting on her back. Then Elaine pulled away. This was as much intimacy as she could tolerate and certainly nobody other than Grace, her own daughter, would be allowed so close. As Elaine stepped away, Helen gripped her arm, allowing it to slide through her hands, before gently holding her wrist. She made herself look at Elaine's hand, inspecting it to see how it was healing now the tortured finger had been removed. The surgeon had done a good job, very neat. Elaine's hand looked in far better shape than her face.

Helen looked up at Elaine; saw a warmth of welcome in her eyes that was not obvious in the woman's stern and now broken features. They headed for the office. To get there they had to walk through the vestry, the scene of Elaine's suffering. Helen watched for a reaction. Nothing. If Elaine could cope, then so could she.

Once in the office, Sam dropped the boxes and made his excuses. Leaving the two women, he went back to the nave and sat in one of the pews near the front where he spent a little quiet time reviewing the pictures Helen had taken of the Norwegian dagger.

Finally settled in the office, Helen wondered why Elaine was engaging in any church work at present. She really needed to recover properly, see to herself first. With a wave of her arm, Elaine swept the observations away. The church had yet to reopen and pastoral visits were shared out amongst the other elders. She was taking it easy, but James Curry, the presbytery clerk, whom Helen had clashed with before, had summoned Elaine to the Edinburgh Presbytery's office in Manor Place - specifically her. She hadn't known why: now she did.

'James Curry intends to close the church down completely,' said Elaine.

'What? He can't do that, can he?'

'Well, no and then again yes.'

Helen squinted at the contradictory answer. 'It can't be both.'

'With membership falling everywhere and presbyteries required to submit forward plans, it's obvious one of the churches in the city will have to close, that's just the pressures of life. It was talked about by James Curry's predecessor, so it's no surprise. Should it be St Bernard's? We don't have such a big membership anymore, but there are few churches that do. I could point to several that are in a worse state than us.'

'So why us then? Can't we fight it?'

Elaine nodded. 'Of course, and rest assured I put down a marker, he knows I don't agree. Though he has made a strong hand for himself.'

'Oh?'

'Changes like this are meant to be negotiated, consensual; he's taken advantage of there being no minister at St Bernard's, and my being off after the attack, to do his listening and consultation in a hurry - I'm not sure how he's managed to get it all concluded so quickly. I think everybody outside the parish may be quite keen to see St Bernard's swept out of the spotlight as soon as possible after what's happened.'

'Is that possible?'

'It seems that way. Maybe anything's possible if nobody challenges him. He's arguing that recent events in the parish will always be a focus for media attention and that will detract from our Christian message both here and in the wider presbytery. Apparently, if St Bernard's continues, then it might attract a ghoulish element that can only make things worse for everyone. He's arguing that events have created a stigma around St Bernard's that brings the whole Church into disrepute.'

'Rubbish.'

'I know, but the numbers don't lie. Economics dictate that at least one Edinburgh parish will have to merge with its neighbours. And let's face it; none of them will be turkeys voting for Christmas. We are suddenly the obvious and maybe the popular candidate for closure. In the meantime, he's suggested that we don't resume services. Rather just continue to support members in attending at their next nearest parish church until a final decision is reached.'

'It sounds like a decision has already been made,' said Helen, throwing her hands up in despair. 'And what about his thing for rules and procedures, surely there is a process to follow.'

'Yes there is. It's all meant to be by mutual agreement. The individual parishes do have a lot of independence, but he's guided the presbytery to take an emergency decision in the interests of members of both this parish and the whole presbytery. There are lots of steps to go through but, apart from us, who is going to stand up?'

'Where does this leave us?' Helen had other battles to fight, but the parish had become dear to her and the people here were her people now.

'In a difficult position...' Elaine's voice trailed off.

'Well?' said Helen. 'I can see there is more bad news, you may as well get it over with in one go.'

'The Church will probably want to sell the parish property. There's always a demand for development property in the city. James Curry thinks they will get a good price. It seems he's asked the Church's General Trustees to back his disposal proposal and...'

'And what?'

'He wants to sell the manse too. He wants vacant possession ASAP so the estate agents can start marketing it. The elders, which really means me, are to give you notice to quit the manse. Incidentally, I could tell he really enjoyed having me pass that message on.'

'It's only a few weeks ago that I was asked to move in. The police recommended the manse be kept occupied. Doesn't he remember that?'

Elaine nodded. 'Of course he does. I think he wants to cause you as much discomfort as possible.'

'Well he's done a good job of that.'

'No, there's more. Since there will be no parish, there will be no parish assistant. You are to get a month's notice. He thought you could help prepare the parish for closure before leaving. And you'll need to give back the keys to your own church flat too.'

A silence fell. In a world of threats and surprises, all this was the very last thing Helen had expected. 'The tunnel. What about the tunnel? We can't give that up. Oh, what is that man doing to us?'

She and Sam had planned to explore the secret tunnel that ran beneath the manse. If James Curry's plans to sell were implemented, they would lose access to the tunnel - disaster.

• • •

Relaxing in the comfort of an opulent chateau bedroom, Cassiter was feeling very pleased with himself. His research team had come up with something very special. He looked again at his laptop screen, watched the loop of video as it continued to display footage extracted from Edinburgh Airport's security archive.

The camera caught the glistening high spots of reflected light as a polished plate, cup and cross all sat proudly on the check-in counter. Framed behind them was Helen Johnson's smiling face. Beyond her, just in the edge of the frame, were her friends. These recorded images had been found and extracted by his team. It had taken them a while, they had a myriad of different sources to search, running facial recognition and comparisons, but steady work pays rewards.

It was clear the girl was going away, and he could just make out a United Airlines logo on the ticket in her hand. It had been easy enough from that clue for his team to find out exactly where she was going and why. And now he was very interested in what she was taking. The St Bernard's communion set. He remembered it from events in the vestry when he had so nearly come a cropper. Watching the video loop play through again, he wondered what was so important about the communion set. Then, in a flash of inspiration he knew, recognising it for what it was. He paused the tape, zoomed in on the cross and after careful consideration gave a grim smile of satisfaction.

He called a number on his mobile phone and waited for an answer, it came quickly.

'Excellent piece of work with that security footage, well done. Now, there's more to do. But first, who have we got on the Eastern Seaboard right now?' he said. Acutely aware that this chateau wasn't his place, he was careful with his voice projection and the words he used. Parsol would have the room bugged - it would be negligent not to. He waited for a moment while sour face got the information he needed.

'Good. I am going to send you some instructions; they must be acted on at once. Ensure it is understood they must overcome any resistance; they will only get one chance at this. Is that clear?' A few moments later, he hung up, still very happy. He typed up instructions and sent them back to his office. Once the instructions had been sent he deleted them and then wiped the video too.

Cassiter looked out of the window, allowing himself a moment to appreciate the beauty and scale of the chateau gardens; he thought he might take a stroll around before meeting Parsol at dinner. Then he noted more guards patrolling in the distance. He reckoned there were always at least two teams on the move. This was a serious arrangement.

• • •

By the time Helen and Elaine emerged into the nave, Sam had put away his phone and was sitting, gazing almost absently at the glass in the windows behind the communion table. He recalled, before the summer he had thought them quite distinctive, still did now.

With just a friendly wave towards Sam, Elaine left Helen and hurried away.

Helen selected a place at the front of the church and paused for a minute's quiet prayer. She thought of all the people who had served here, prayed here, thought of all the secrets that had been kept and thought again of the horrific violence and killings she had witnessed. This was not the quiet little parish church it seemed.

Finally, she stood and headed towards Sam.

He pointed up beyond the communion table. 'That's an unusual window you've got there. I've not really registered it before,' he said.

'Yes, it is,' she said, turning to look at it.

'It's quite a mix of styles; the old Scottish churches went for just plain glass, quite austere. But this one has a series of small images dotted across the plain glass to depict various scenes. It's a real jumble,' said Sam.

'Right… John Dearly explained it all to me. Apparently, they're very old. They are out of scale with the window setting because they all came from the original parish church long ago. That building was much smaller - they were installed here when this one was built. And even this is an old building now,' she stopped for a moment. Thought again of John Dearly, remembered his warmth and kindness and his cruel ending. She shivered, and then continued. 'I'm sure I made a note of it all at the time he told me. I haven't the foggiest where it is now though. I'll see if I can find it.'

'No hurry, I just thought it looked interesting. I recognised the burning bush in the middle, but as for the rest, biblical imagery is not my strong suit.'

'Well we know that, Sam Cameron. And don't think I won't be working on it one day. But yes, you're right, that is the burning bush. It's the Church of Scotland's symbol. John did say it also represented the parish for some reason. I can't recall exactly what. Some of the other images are a bit obscure though. I'll try to look the note out.'

They locked up the church and headed back to the manse.

• • •

Cassiter and Parsol ate in an intimate dining area. It lacked the palatial splendour of the grand dining room he had noted earlier while wandering round the chateau's more public spaces. Nonetheless, the food was excellent and the swift, hushed table service made clear that Parsol's home base ran on the strictest of hierarchies. The heavy silver cutlery and crystal glass spoke of high values whilst the elaborate coat of arms engraved on each piece spoke of something else. Embedded within the heraldic symbol was a tiny shape, a cross, one that Cassiter had seen frequently during recent weeks.

'I am so glad you could spare the time to visit me here,' said Parsol.

'Least I could do,' replied Cassiter. 'We do need to wrap up this project. I told you the other day that I intended to close off my group's involvement completely. You asked me to continue and I have, pending this discussion. Now, I think you need to tell me why I should remain engaged. After all, my own base in Edinburgh has been compromised and we're in the process of relocating. That doesn't matter of itself; one base is as good as another. But in the short term, it has disrupted workflows, to say nothing of my personal living arrangements. I like Edinburgh; it's a comfortable place to live. Now, I have to move, at least for a while.'

Parsol tutted in sympathy. 'Yes, it's unfortunate. I regret that it all spiralled out of control. Yet, you seem to have reasserted yourself. And you are here with me now.'

Cassiter was mindful of why things had spiralled out of control. Ultimately, it was because Parsol had arrived in his theatre of operations and insisted, against Cassiter's advice, on accelerating recovery of the daggers. He now took the opportunity to make his views clear to Parsol.

Parsol listened carefully then glanced around, gave the slightest of hand signals and immediately a steward arrived from some unseen quarter, topped up their glasses and retired.

'I accept, with hindsight, that your more measured approach might have proven more productive in that instance. If you agree to continue, I agree not to interfere operationally in the future. Cassiter, I need to acquire the missing daggers. I have all the assets to support that goal, plenty of manpower to call on. Every resource you could ever want, but I must have the daggers.'

'I recognise your urgency but I have my own team, my own network of resources; my own contacts in high places,' said Cassiter.

'Yes, yes, I know. And very accomplished they are. I know it is your team's expertise and skills that can resolve my problem. Though, while they may be experts, they are small in number. I simply meant I have the manpower to support you, whenever you need it, wherever you need it.'

His elbow on the table, Parsol raised his hand, one finger gently pointed up, describing a little circle in the space above them. 'And yes, you have contacts in high places; but I *own* high places. Right now, I need your specialist skills. Work with me on this and I can guarantee that you'll never need to worry about local police in future. Given a little time, I can cut away any pressure, from the top down. No authority will ever want to challenge you again.'

It was an interesting concept; Cassiter tilted his head back slightly, nodding, listening, not quite persuaded. He had always been a lone wolf. But these were turbulent times; he was at least prepared to consider the advantages of the pack - at the very least, be seen to consider the offer.

Parsol let his hand drop. 'Europe, the Americas, the Antipodes: wherever you have one business relationship I have a score of friends, more even. Let's work together. I will reward you handsomely, whatever you want. You want a nice island home to retire to one day? I will get you the whole island. Tell me your price and it will be met, anything. I need you and your team's intelligence network. I have the numbers, the brute strength to complement your stealth. Nothing must block achievement of the goal. Nothing.' Parsol's normally calm, expressionless delivery had risen very slightly as he finished talking.

'But what do you want, exactly?' said Cassiter.

'I want the dagger from St Bernard's. I want the other daggers, all of them.'

'All of them? How many are there?'

Parsol fixed Cassiter with his cold unswerving stare and was suddenly slightly unsettled. Perhaps for the first time in his life he found it mirrored back at him. 'I am happy to tell you, but there are some things you can only know if you commit to us completely and you should understand, once in, if you step away from us, there is only death.'

Cassiter gave the slightest of nods accepting Parsol's warning.

'There are nine daggers. I have one, my family's. We also have those two you retrieved for us, the dunes dagger and the one from the museum.' Parsol paused for a moment, gathering his thoughts; he sipped from his glass and then continued. 'Of course, by rights, I claim them all as mine and I need them all to solve an old mystery - a family mystery.'

Cassiter could tell the daggers were important to this wealthy man, more important than anything else. Yet he felt he was not quite getting the whole story. Again, he nodded encouragement for Parsol to continue.

'I must have them all. But most important is the dagger from St Bernard's. Where they hid it I don't know, but it is the key to everything. I cannot stress enough just how important it is. Merde!' a little bit of French fire finally slipped out as Parsol banged his hand on the table. 'Those women, they blocked us before, it must not happen again. Get me that dagger. And one day I want you to destroy those churchwomen, sweep away everything. Leave nothing behind. But for now, I think we should give them a little rope. It seems they were looking for the same thing as us before. So let them search. Keep close behind and if they do find something, we can just take it like sweets from a child.'

Cassiter acknowledged Parsol's goals before indicating he would need a little time to consider circumstances and plans, and then he steered the conversation on to more general topics. The edge slipped out of the meeting as dinner progressed to a natural conclusion. Cassiter asked about the little cross on Parsol's family crest, without ever receiving a direct answer. He did learn that Parsol's family were survivors: wars, revolutions, republics - nothing moved the Parsol family; they had held their land and estates for a very long time.

Both men retired early. Cassiter had a long journey ahead of him next day and a good deal to think about. He knew of a dagger in Norway, corralled in a bank vault, he had people working on that. Now, thanks to a video loop and a flash of insight, he had finally worked out where the St Bernard's dagger was and he had that in hand too. Perhaps he should have mentioned these things to Parsol. Not yet, he decided. With so many secrets ghosting around, it might be sensible for him to hold one or two of his own, at least for a little while. And once the plans he had set in motion earlier in the day were executed he would be in a more secure position.

Tomorrow, he planned to stop off in Paris. Spend a few days at his French connection and satisfy himself that the work transfer from Edinburgh had gone smoothly, that everything was as it should be. It would be his main base for a while so things had to be right. And from there, back to Britain. He planned to take the ferry, slip across unnoticed - just one more pedestrian traveller on a busy route.

Chapter 4

FRIDAY 9TH AUGUST

Francis leant across the table, eager to top up the wine glasses. Gathered around the restaurant table with him were Helen, Sam and Grace. It was a welcome home night for Helen and a chance to get out and enjoy a break in each other's company, and with the Festival under way there was a real buzz about the city. Elaine was missing, she was not up for late nights at the best of times and certainly not while recuperating from the injuries she had received earlier in the summer. Xavier and Angelo were missing too. They did not intend to visit from Sardinia for another week, by which time the Festival would be in full swing.

Excuses for more nights out during the Festival weren't needed and they had all just blanked out another couple of dates in their diaries to accommodate the Sardinian priests' visit.

Helen picked up her glass as soon as Francis topped it up. As the bottle continued its journey from glass to glass, she looked at the company. Smiling faces, laughs and jokes, they were all enjoying the moment, seizing it, making it good. Tonight should have been a proper celebration, a reunion, troubles behind them and an exciting mystery to solve ahead. Instead, she knew the happy faces were superficial, smiley masks determined to banish thoughts of the threat that had returned.

Arms stretched out and glasses clinked - she reached out and joined the toast. Their waiter arrived, a weathered, experienced Italian. He balanced a row of soup bowls along one arm; plates of garlic bread defied the laws of physics to remain attached to the other. As he distributed the food, he smiled and joked. Finally, in an audacious move he gently touched Grace's cheek with the back of his hand. Declared she was the most beautiful girl in Edinburgh and he must sing a song for her. Then he looked at Helen and gave an apologetic shrug; if she weren't taken, there would have been a song for her too.

Helen laughed with him, insisted no songs and joined Grace in shooing him away. She wondered when it had become so publicly obvious that she and Sam were an item. And she noted he had not demurred. Then, smiling to herself, she had joined in the chatter about the stand-up comedian they had just watched. He was rude, raucous and funny - one to recommend.

Francis was in charge of the tickets and the schedule. He was consulting a note he had made and trying to keep everyone up to the moment. 'After dinner, there's a play starting at nine-thirty, should be fun, it's only two minutes' walk from here, though the venue might be a little cramped. Then it's up the mound into the Old Town and just time for a quick drink before moving on to a satirical revue.' He shuffled through the sheaf of tickets. 'I've heard it's really funny. A bit naughty though,' he looked a little sheepish.

This was Helen's first festival. She understood now why her parents had always tried to visit. The city was full, alive with the hustle and bustle of good-natured crowds out for fun and entertainment. And everywhere were enthusiastic performers mixing with the crowds, promoting their shows; all decked out in a selection of mad, weird and occasionally outrageous garb.

It was well into the early hours by the time the night out ended. Back at Sam's Marchmont flat, Helen opened a bottle of wine and they settled down to relive the laughs of the evening. Finally, as the sky was just starting to lighten, they crawled off to bed.

Chapter 5

SATURDAY 10TH AUGUST

Peter Johnson was woken by the ringing phone at the side of his bed. He groaned and peered at the digital alarm clock on the bedside cabinet, made out a blurry green glow and his hand scrabbled out for the glasses he kept there. Pulling them on brought the green light into focus, 04.13. He groaned again, calls at this time were always bad news, he wondered which member of the church needed him.

'Hello, Peter Johnson speaking. How can I help you?'

He listened to a man's voice as it delivered a crisp message; this was not what he had expected. It was the security company and the church's silent alarm was sounding. As key holder, could he respond? The mobile patrolman would meet him there, but he was in the next town up the coast, it would be around thirty minutes before he arrived.

The church was literally across the road and the alarm had not triggered in years. Peter got out of bed and peered through his bedroom window. He could see the church and everything seemed quiet.

'It's probably a false alarm,' said Peter, into the phone handset. 'I'll get dressed and go have a look. See if it needs reset or something. Should be fine.'

'Are you sure you wouldn't like to just wait at the premises and link up with our patrol when it arrives, sir?' asked the security controller.

'No, I'll be fine. It'll just be a fault.'

'Okay sir, if you are happy with that. I should say from our records you are in a low crime zone, so it may just be a fault. I also see your system is overdue an upgrade. It's very old now.'

'Yes, I think it's about done. We've certainly had it a long time, I can't remember exactly when it was installed,' said Peter Johnson.

'Perhaps you would like to call me once you've scouted around, sir. Then I can sign off the incident. Shall we say call back in twenty minutes?'

Peter Johnson agreed, hung up and got dressed as quietly as he could.

Joan Johnson stirred. 'Who was on the phone?' she said, sleepily.

'It's nothing, just the alarm sounding in the church. I'm going over now to reset it.'

Joan sat up quickly. 'Are you sure it's okay?'

'Don't worry. The system should have been upgraded years ago. Probably just worn out, I'll be back in a few minutes, you get back to sleep.' Grabbing his walking stick, Peter Johnson headed out of the bedroom.

His wife's voice followed him down the stair. 'You be careful, Peter. Any sign of trouble, come right back and we'll call the police. I don't know what that alarm company is thinking of, letting you go over there.'

Peter Johnson paused at the front door and called back up the stairs. 'Stop fussing, Joan. I know everyone in this town; nobody is going to break into my church. You get back to sleep.'

He pulled the front door shut and headed down the path for the front gate. Directly across the road he could see the church, dark and still. Pausing at the kerb, he half turned and waved his stick up at the darkened bedroom window. He couldn't see her but he knew Joan would be watching, wouldn't turn in again until he returned.

Crossing the road, he could see the church's front doors were firmly shut. He gave the handle a little push to be sure - locked solid. Peter walked round the side of the church, lost sight of his home but was quite comfortable. These were shadows he had walked in a thousand times over the years. He checked for broken windows as he went. Nothing.

Reaching the end, he turned the corner of the building and continued his quiet inspection. At any given point on his walk round, he could picture exactly what lay on the other side of the wooden walls. This had been his place for too long to think about.

Turning the next corner, he was heading back towards the street: would soon be out of the shadows. As he approached the church's small side entrance door, he paused for a moment. Had that been a flash of torchlight inside? He shook himself, don't be an old fool. He passed the suspect window and tried the door handle. To his surprise it gave. The door opened without a sound and he stepped inside.

The little room was still and silent. Peter scolded himself for forgetting to lock the door - perhaps Joan was right, maybe he was getting a little forgetful after all. Well he'd come to check things out, might as well take a look round. He flicked a switch and the room was flooded with light. He squinted, the sudden brightness hurting his eyes.

Everything seemed in order and he crossed the floor towards an open door that led into the big meeting room where many of the church's group activities took place. His rubber-soled shoes silent on the wooden floor, the only sound the tap, tap, of his walking stick - but the door ahead of him should certainly not be open. Never mind security, he knew he closed every internal door, drummed the importance of doing so into the congregation at every opportunity. A closed door held back fire, every moment mattered in an emergency. Peter started to wonder; perhaps things weren't as they should be.

Stopping at the doorway, he looked in, peering round the meeting room. Lit by the light from behind him, he could see it was empty - as still and silent as the smaller room that he had just passed through. Chiding himself again for being so silly, he felt down the doorframe for the light switch and lit the space properly. Again, nothing lurking in the corners, the moment of worry passed. He crossed the room, made straight for his office. It was one of several doors letting off from the opposite wall. His journey was again heralded by the tap of his stick.

Half way across the room he paused, finally convinced things weren't right. His office door was ajar; forget all the other signs, this would never happen. That's where all the church's confidential papers were kept, locked safely away. For just a moment he wondered if he should retreat, call it in. But there was no sound - if there had been an intruder, he was long gone. The sooner he found out what had been going on the better.

He pushed open his office door and saw the contents of the room were scattered every which way. The shaft of light from the meeting room crossed the office and settled on the security cabinet set against the far wall, it was open. His heart sank. 'Oh no,' he said and hurried across to the cabinet. Helen's communion set was stored inside.

He scanned the nearly empty shelves of the cabinet, checked the things strewn on the floor beside it. Odd, the cashbox was still there. So was the old wooden box that contained the communion set Helen had entrusted to his care, but it lay open, silver glinting up at him. For a moment, he thought it was all right, the set had not been stolen. But as he checked more carefully, he realised only the plate and cup remained, the cross was gone. He felt sick. He had let his daughter down - her secret was lost.

How the crooks knew about the cross and its secret, he didn't know. He and Joan had told nobody. But right now, he needed the police to close the road out of town. There might still be time if he acted quickly.

He stepped over to his desk and picked up the phone, dialled 911. Before the call could be answered, there was a ripping sound and a great shape of a man rose from behind the desk. In one hand, it held a telephone cable, a loose end ripped from the wall socket. In the other hand, a cross, Helen's cross.

There was no time for fear and he wasn't giving ground to any hood. That was his daughter's cross; he was taking it back.

'Put that cross down,' he shouted. Leaning one hand on the desk edge to take the weight off his bad leg, he raised the stick to swing at the intruder.

The man ducked as the stick whizzed above his head.

Peter gasped at the exertion and raised the stick again. 'You won't get away with it. The police are coming.'

51

'No they're not, old man. That was the call I just killed. Now, maybe I'll do that to you too.' The shape was fully upright now and moving round the desk. 'You're on your own here. Best lie down and I might just let you be.'

The stick swung back towards the intruder's head. A strong arm rose in an attempt to block the blow and there was a gasp of pain. Peter smiled to himself - contact.

He tried to pull back for another stroke but couldn't, his arm was grabbed by the intruder who had thrown himself across the desk towards him. Dodgy legs didn't equal weak arms, and an active life meant Peter's were as strong as any. He reached with his free hand to grab the cross, they grappled for a few moments but finally the intruder's upper body strength began to prevail. He pressed his body over on to Peter's and their combined weights bore down on to his bad leg. It collapsed and both men fell to the floor.

Peter's arms were trapped under the weight of the intruder's body, giving the man free hands to work with. He raised one, formed a fist and brought it down into the side of Peter's head. The blow stunned Peter and he was still for a moment. Satisfied the intruder made a noise somewhere between a grunt and a cry of victory. He raised his hand again and Peter could only watch as the fist came down hard on his head.

Struggle over, the man stood, brushed himself and looked down. 'You done now?'

Peter's mind was coming back into focus but not his eyes, his glasses were lost somewhere on the office floor. He looked up at the figure standing over him and knew, for his daughter's sake, he must not quit. A boot thumped into Peter's shoulder; instinctively he grabbed it and twisted, unbalancing the man.

The man threw out a hand as he started to topple, grasping on to the desktop to break his fall and Peter held on tight to the boot. The man loomed over him, balanced on one leg, a hand on the desk's edge, the other still holding the cross.

'You've done it now old man, I could have let you live. But you' just gotta go.'

Peter saw the man's hand swing under arm towards him. Saw the cross coming towards his head, a bludgeon to break him. He managed to get a hand out to ward off the blow. It grazed his forehead, opening the skin, producing a flood of blood but the main force of the blow was deflected and a great clang rang out as the cross smashed on to the metal leg of his desk.

Amidst a torrent of curses from above, Peter realised he had lost the grip on the man's leg. As his assailant started to raise the cross to deliver a second swipe, Peter made a grab for it, got a hand on the base and held on tight. The man jerked up hard against the strong grip of Peter's hand, half lifting him from the ground. Then, as they struggled for possession, the cross separated into two parts. Free from Peter's weight the man's hand soared up as Peter, clutching the base, fell back, crashing his head against the metal table leg.

Through blood-filled eyes, Peter saw the blurriest vision of the man; he seemed to be looking at his own hand in surprise. Peter saw the man's expression change to pleasure as he realised his mission was accomplished - he had the dagger. Then, finally, defenceless, Peter felt a boot crack into his face. Again, his head banged against the table leg, and finally, beaten, he slid away into nothingness.

• • •

Helen sat at the breakfast table nursing a sore head and sipping coffee. Enviously, she looked across at Sam. He seemed quite impervious to the after-effects of alcohol. His assertion that she felt three times as bad because she drank three times as much was probably true, but of little consolation right now.

Tomorrow he was flying down to Bristol to attend a three-day archaeology workshop at the city's university. In the meantime, she was annoyed that this day was not being spent as she had planned. The wine had spoilt it. She decided to go for a shower and headed for the bathroom. He seemed happy enough, busy studying the pattern on the Norwegian dagger; intently cross-referring between photographs of the various blades, twisting and manoeuvring them around into different combinations, the perpetual puzzle that could always be counted on to fill any spare moments he might have.

Perhaps she would feel better once she was cleaned up. Then they could do something together in what was left of the day. Maybe even check out the secret tunnel beneath the manse that they had first encountered earlier in the summer.

Standing under the stream of warm water, Helen promised herself she would ease up on the wine. It had been creeping up on her over the summer. Something she would need to cut back, especially with the troubles coming back. Stepping out from the shower, she grabbed a towel, dried herself down and wrapped it around her. She lifted a hand towel and wrapped it round her head - now she needed orange juice.

Sam was on the phone as she entered the kitchen. He looked at her, and at once, she could tell there was trouble. He held the handset towards her.

'It's your brother Steve,' he said, with the slightest of grimaces.

Serious faced, she took the phone. 'Steve, what's up?' She was quiet for a minute taking in what her brother had to say. Then she cut in on him. 'Hold on a moment.'

She looked across at Sam. 'Can you turn the computer on please? I need to book a flight right away. Pop's in the hospital, he's in a bad way. Attacked at the church, the cross has been stolen.' She turned her attention back to Steve while Sam hurried towards the computer.

Chapter 6

SUNDAY 11ᵀᴴ AUGUST

Helen slumped into the sofa. 'Well, it looks like he's going to get through this okay, Mom.'

Joan Johnson nodded and Helen slid across the sofa to reach a comforting arm round her mother's shoulder.

Steve and Chris, Helen's older brothers, crossed from the kitchen into the open plan living area. They brought cold drinks with them, handed them out to strained smiles of thanks and then sat in armchairs. Her two sisters had decided to stay on at the hospital a bit longer, familiar faces on hand should he wake, allowing Joan the chance to get home for some rest. She had been at the hospital for the best part of 24 hours.

'Okay, Chris and I've talked it through,' said Steve, glancing towards Chris, who nodded acknowledgement. 'Helen, we don't understand why our parents were hiding this stuff for you. We don't understand why it was being kept here if it's so valuable. But we're not stupid. We've seen the news reports; know what's been going on over there in Scotland. If it's anything to do with what happened at your church, you should never have brought the trouble back here.'

'We all love you, but this is too much,' said Chris.

'It's got to stop right now. What were you thinking of?' said

Steve.

Tired as she was, Joan sought to exert her influence; the home was her territory. 'Okay boys, just cool it. Your father and I knew exactly what we were taking on. It's not Helen's fault, it was your father's idea to bring her things back here to store. And we'd do the same again to help her. We'd do the same for any of you.'

Steve was not happy. 'Well none of us would have such a prob-'

'Steve! Right now, I need you to be supporting your sister, not falling out. What's done is done. We stand together, okay?'

Steve looked carefully at his mother, glanced ruefully towards Helen and then nodded. 'Okay, Mom. Whatever you want. But how do we keep you safe with all this going on? I'm in New York and Chris is in Chicago. What can we do from so far away?'

Helen stood up. 'I'm sorry guys. Sorry I ever brought this home. Sorry it got pop in the hospital. All I can say is, whoever attacked him got what they were after. They have no reason to return.'

'And what about that?' said Steve, pointing towards the battered communion set box which rested on the low table set in the space between their seats. 'They didn't get that.'

Helen followed the direction of his point and then nodded her head in agreement, the movement morphed into a headshake.

'That's not what they wanted; it's only purpose was to conceal the dagger. It has no value now. Worthless.'

'Are you sure?' said Steve.

'Well if they'd wanted it they could have taken it, couldn't they? They took what they wanted and left.'

'No, they beat pop around the head, took what they wanted and left,' said Chris. 'And it's not worthless, that's still one big chunk of silver.'

'That's just my point,' said Helen. 'If they were after material value, it would have gone too. They weren't interested in dollars.'

'Okay, that's it. I said I didn't want any arguments. What's happened has happened. Now let it go. We need to think about your pop now; think about what's best for him and what's to happen next. Not what has been. But Helen, I think you should take that away. I know you say they don't want it. I guess you're right. But it's a reminder of what happened. I don't want your pop worrying about that too. Can you find somewhere else for it?'

'You bet she can,' said Steve. Then fell silent under his mother's gaze.

'I'll take it back with me,' said Helen. 'It's not a secret anymore.'

'Well, still be careful. It may have lost its big value, whatever that was, but I'll bet there's plenty of other folk would like to take that lump of silver off your hands. Put it in the bank, or sell it, just don't keep it lying about,' said Steve. Chris nodded agreement.

Chapter 7

MONDAY 12TH AUGUST

Sam looked out across the water. The sky was shading to dark now. He noted how much earlier darkness fell in the south at this time of year. Back in Edinburgh, it would still be daylight. Still, the streetlights were on and things were bustling here at the quayside. The old industries and environment were gone. The docks had been refreshed, reinvented, and now everywhere teemed with people out for a good time as they dotted between the restaurants, bars and clubs. Dozens of little dinghies and pleasure boats were moored to pontoons that floated against quaysides where once the world's merchant ships had tied up.

'Lovely place,' said Howard Vance. Tall, slim, grey haired, a worn tweed jacket, corduroy trousers and open necked shirt; he was every inch the off duty academic. The professor from Lincoln University was participating in the same workshop as Sam.

Sam nodded agreement, pointed towards a table outside a pub. 'What do you fancy to drink?'

'A pint of larger for me, please,' said Howard, taking a seat.

'Right, back in a moment,' Sam disappeared inside to get the drinks.

A couple had been strolling arm in arm behind the two men; they chose to settle at a nearby table. The man disappeared into the bar behind Sam and left his partner to lookout across the water.

Sam emerged with drinks and sat opposite Howard, smiled and raised his glass. 'Well, cheers, and here's to a great workshop. If the next couple of days keep up to this standard we're in for a great time.'

Howard raised his glass too. 'Cheers. Yes, it's got off to a good start and there are a couple of sessions I am really looking forward to tomorrow.' He paused to take a drink.

'Sam, I've been thinking about your little problem,' said Howard, pulling from his pocket the printout Sam had given him that morning. He spread it on the table between them and traced out the cross with his finger. 'As you've already noted, Templar, and quite late in style.' He looked at Sam. 'We're agreed there I think.'

'Yes, though it's your period, I'm happy to take a lead from you.'

The older man smiled. 'No need for my input there anyway, you're spot on.' His fingers slid down the page and lightly stroked the text, almost a caress. 'And you say this was found on Inchcolm Island? In the abbey? You're quite sure about that?'

'That's right. I hadn't really reached any conclusions about how it came to be there. But it's the inscription I was really hoping you might be able to shed some light on.'

'Well, your guess is as good as mine over the burial site. There would have been no safer place to inter a body than an isolated island abbey. As I've said, judging by the style of the engraved cross it must have been near the end of the Templar period. Perhaps he was an important man and they just wanted to put him somewhere safe. We may never find out for sure. But certainly, the Church always needed money. If your Templar's friends had enough of the shiny stuff, anything's possible.'

'Yes, I can see that, but what about the inscription, does that tell us anything more about our man?'

Howard leant closer to the paper and carefully read out the inscription.

'*...e Be...*
Ex Deo natus est
Vir pugnator
Filius Lindum'

He glanced up. 'As you observed, the first line is a bit of a mess. But what about the rest? Now let me see again, what did you think?' He paused to re-read Sam's sheet. 'Ah yes, *Child of God, Man of war, Son of Lincoln*. Well, we could chew that over a bit, but on the whole, I can live with your interpretation.' He looked up from the paper. 'Well, exactly how can I help?'

Sam saw Howard's eyes sparkle, he knew something, was just going to make Sam work for it.

'Howard, you are an expert on the Templars in Britain. I've only recently taken an interest. So you are miles ahead of me on this. The inscription references Lincoln. As a professor at Lincoln University, if anyone is able to cast any light on this it's you.'

'Oh, you're just trying to flatter me, Sam.' His eyes sparkled again. 'Though as some say, flattery gets you everywhere.' He took another drink from his glass, put it down and paused for a theatrical moment, perhaps collecting his thoughts.

'And?' said Sam.

'So, let's try and put some meat on these bones shall we? Not so hard really. From the design of the cross emblem we know it's a Templar grave marker. Whoever he was, the very use of the engraved stone marks him out as very special. And it's clear; his people didn't want him disturbed. I suppose it was a time of war in Scotland. Nonetheless, burying him on a remote island abbey would have cost them a fortune in fees - today we might call them bribes. And it was certainly taking extreme measures to protect his last resting place. Why? Your note says the stone had been moved so we can't link it to a particular body. If we could, we might have a better clue. In any event, the epitaph as a whole is what you might expect for a fighting man of that time.'

'Yes, Howard, but can you cast any light on it?' said Sam. 'Or are you just spinning it out to get another drink out of me?'

Howard laughed. 'No, one's enough for me these days. That's what age does to you. Anyway, I don't believe you will want to cloud my thoughts until I've told you what I think.'

'So you have an idea?' said Sam.

'Like I said, it's not so hard - maybe. Let's see what you think. So, our Templar, for all his Christianity, is still a son of Lincoln.

Unusual for an individual Templar to keep that link alive for eternity, don't you think? You came to me because it's my speciality, because the Templars were big over in the eastern part of the country, around Lincoln. It's the Lincoln connection that needs to be explored. But to do that we need to consider who our man is.'

'Agreed,' said Sam. 'But how do we work that out?'

Howard gave a little smile. 'I think I can help you there. Do you see the first line of the inscription? In all probability, that may well be a name, long worn away.' He touched the first line, read it out. '*Something, e, Be, something.* Even for a modern burial that probably wouldn't be much to go on. You'd think it a lost cause. And you know, fourteenth century wise, I think it would be anywhere else in the country, maybe all of Europe.'

'You think you have something?' said Sam.

'Well I gave it a little thought this morning and at lunchtime I called back to my research assistant at Lincoln. He spent some time following up my pointers and I am quite sure I have something of interest for you.' He paused as a group of young women went by. There had clearly been plenty of drinking and, as they headed for a bar further along the quay, it seemed certain more was planned.

'Let me tell you Sam, I'm really excited about this. If we're right, then it really opens up some new lines of thinking to develop our understanding of that era.'

'How so?'

'First of all, we apply a simple process of elimination. In our Lincolnshire records for the time, do we have any names that our letters might fit with? There's the first letter e. The ruling elite of fourteenth century Britain were pretty well all of French stock, with French rooted names. So, the e is almost certainly part of de.'

'Yes, yes I can see that. Makes perfect sense.'

Howard tapped the paper again. 'Right, but what about the *Be...*? That might seem a bit trickier. But I think we've got it for you. There is one particular Lincolnshire family that seems to have had two names. Well, one main name while a particular branch adopted a change that would have been perfect for your Templar: de Bello or perhaps it's de Bella, there's some debate over that.'

That name triggered a memory sequence for Sam - something he had heard earlier in the summer. A story Xavier had told. 'I know that name,' he said. 'Heard it recently. Of course, de Bello, Henri de Bello, he was an important Templar knight, based at their preceptory in the village of Temple, outside Edinburgh. In fact, I'm sure he was involved in some stuff I've been working on, quite separate from this inscription. Could they be linked? It's the right time and place.'

Howard raised his hands, shrugged and reached for his drink. 'There you are then, it all falls into place, I think.'

Sam's elation at closing in on an answer was tempered by the slightest nagging feeling. Did everything need to be linked to their troubles? It seems he just couldn't shake them off.

'I'm pleased you're pleased,' said Howard. 'But there's more.'

'Do go on.'

'Well, if the name is right, and I rather think it is, because my assistant could not come up with any other Lincoln names starting with *d Be* at that time - assuming we are going with the very late style of the engraved cross, it's got to be around 1300. Though we'll be checking through the records again of course. If it's right, it creates an entirely new family link and I hope you will allow my people to engage with you, supporting the research.'

Sam hesitated; only a week ago he would have had no qualms about letting Howard and his staff from Lincoln University share in the investigation. Now those sinister clouds were gathering again and he was mindful of the suffering that could befall any who engaged with their quest - knowingly or otherwise.

'What else have you got?' he said, avoiding any commitment.

Howard chuckled.' You're cautious, can't say I blame you. But if I'm right, this is bigger than you think. You'll be pleased to share the load.'

'How so?'

'The names de Bello or de Bella seem to get muddled up in the record somewhere, that's families for you. And they definitely have very different meanings - war or warlike, and pretty, or some such. You pay your money and you take your choice. But if we're talking Templar, I guess *pretty* doesn't quite capture it. Anyway, it's the other family name de Bello is linked to that interests me. So, in certain quarters, de Bello and de Haldingham are taken as interlinked. At that date, we do have a Richard de Haldingham in Lincolnshire. He would almost certainly have had a familial link to your de Bello - cousins, uncle and nephew perhaps, that sort of thing. Certainly would have been quite a close relation. You probably don't know the name but he is credited with a piece of work that you will know.'

Howard paused and glanced over Sam's shoulder. He smiled acknowledgement at somebody. Sam turned in time to see the smiling young woman sat at the table behind him glance away. She was remarkably beautiful, quite stunning - though she was sitting, Sam could just tell she was tall and shapely. Her long dark hair shimmered in the quayside lights while framing a perfectly symmetrical face with full lips and dark, dark eyes. Her boyfriend was heading away into the bar to get more drinks.

'Someone from the workshop?' said Sam.

'No, I don't know her, she sat down at the same time as we did - that's all.'

'Right. Now, you were saying Richard de somebody.'

'Ah yes. I see the name means nothing to you, just as I thought. But I know you will have heard of his work. Richard de Haldingham is generally credited with having made the Mappa Mundi.'

'What? *The* Mappa Mundi? In Hereford Cathedral?'

'The very same, it's the definitive Christian map of the medieval world. You can see why I'm interested, I'm sure. The map has some attribution to Lincoln too. I've been over to Hereford many times to study it.'

'Of course, I see.' Sam was making a series of links that went way beyond anything Howard could imagine. 'Tell me then, our Richard de Haldingham, he's the main man when it comes to fourteenth century maps?'

'Oh yes, he's what some might call the big cheese.'

'I need to see the map as soon as possible.'

'Well, I've got to know the dean at Hereford Cathedral very well; I've been such a frequent visitor, we've become good friends. I could set you up with a meeting. You can see the map anyway, it's on public display, but I'm sure Charles will give you all the background you need.'

'Would you fix it up, please?' said Sam.

Howard hesitated for a moment. 'You mean now?'

'If you could it would be a big help.'

Howard recognised the signs of an academic on a hobby horse and decided it would just be easier all round to make the call, late hour or not. 'When do you want to see him?'

'As soon as possible, I'll fit in with any time he suggests.'

'You won't want to miss any of the workshops,' said Howard. Then fell silent, it was clear that Sam suddenly didn't care about workshops. Howard pulled out his phone and made the call.

Fifteen minutes later, Sam had a meeting with the dean arranged for Wednesday morning, at the cathedral - and in return, Sam promised to keep Howard in the loop.

They finished their drinks and stood to stroll along the quayside before heading for their hotel rooms. A little way along they stopped to look at the boats. The evening was now turned to night, fully dark but still warm. All the bar and restaurant lights shining on to the water created a beautiful backdrop, perfect for courting couples. Sam tensed a little; the courting couple closing on them were becoming too familiar for his liking. They had followed them into the bar's outside seating area, had sat behind them and now were following them again. Sam had long since abandoned the idea of coincidences. He had to assume the worst.

Just to Sam's left was a little foot ramp. It sloped gradually down, dropping below the level of the quayside to where it reached a floating pontoon that ran parallel to the quayside for fifty metres or so. Along the length of the pontoon were tied small cruisers and pleasure craft. Sam watched an older couple gently guide their inflatable dinghy across the dock to reach the far end of the pontoon. He saw the man tie up the craft and the woman cut the outboard engine. They strolled along the pontoon, heading for the up ramp and a drinks date with friends on the quayside above.

'Come on,' said Sam. 'Let's go and take a closer look at some of the boats.'

'Whatever you fancy,' said Howard, 'though I'm not a big boat fan myself.'

Sam led the way down the ramp and paused at the locked access gate. He fumbled in his jacket pocket as the elderly couple reached the other side of the gate; they released the night latch and pulled the gate open. With a smile, a nod and some muttered word of thanks, Sam hustled Howard through the gate and on to the pontoon, then he slowed, making a point of admiring the assorted boats. The elderly couple let the gate close and lock behind them, then headed away up the ramp. Sam took the opportunity to glance behind. The courting couple had not followed them down; instead, they had settled onto a quayside bench, appeared to be absorbing the romantic atmosphere. Sam was still unsure.

'Fancy a boat ride?' said Sam.

'No,' said Howard.

'Come on; let's try this one out for size.' Sam stepped into the elderly couple's dinghy, taking Howard by the arm.

Howard shook him off. 'What are you doing, Sam? We can't just take a boat.'

Sam had been monitoring the courting couple as he stepped off the pontoon. They were standing now. The man was making a phone call as both walked towards the ramp.

Sam tugged on Howard's arm. 'Come on man, we've got to go.'

'It's not our boat.'

Sam pointed towards the quayside ramp where the couple were moving as quickly as they could without actually breaking into a run. 'You see them? They were behind us earlier, sat behind us at the bar. They're following us now. And it's not to get a famous archaeology professor's autograph. We've got to go now.'

Howard turned to look at the advancing couple. Sam could tell he recognised the girl, her previous smiles abandoned to reveal a hard-set face.

The courting couple broke into a sprint as they realised their cover had been blown; they came to a halt against the locked access gate and immediately started to climb over it.

'Get in, now!' Sam pulled on Howard's arm again. Howard allowed himself to be pulled on board as Sam untied the inflatable dinghy and pushed off hard with his hands. They floated gently away from the side and by the time the couple arrived, the dinghy was just too far off for a good jumper to bridge the gap.

The couple stood and glared at the receding dinghy while the man resumed his phone conversation. As Sam pulled the engine into life and headed the dinghy away into clear water, the man ended his phone call. Sam watched the pair turn and run back along the pontoon.

'What the hell was that all about?' said Howard. 'Who were they? What are you mixed up in?' He looked back as the couple reached the top of the ramp. They split up. The man ran along the quay, keeping the dinghy in sight, the woman disappeared in the other direction.

As the distance between their dinghy and the quayside widened, Sam eased back on the throttle; gunning it seemed to make no difference anyway. The outboard was so old that even when running flat out it scarcely moved the dingy above walking pace. He headed the boat over to the opposite side of the dock.

'It's a long story, and there's certainly not the time for telling it now. They're part of a dodgy group that are after some Templar information or relics. I don't know quite what our scan of the Templar grave marker means to them, but look, Howard, I'm sorry to have got you involved in all this. It's something you really don't want to get too close to.'

'What are we going to do? Shouldn't we call the police?'

Sam shook his head. 'I'm going to drop you over there,' he said, pointing at the waterfront flats ranged along the south side of the dock. As the distance closed, the domestic lights suddenly looked reassuring, safe. 'Get a taxi back to the hotel, get to your room and keep your head down.'

Sam stopped talking for a moment as he concentrated on bringing the dinghy safely alongside the quay.

'It's not good enough, Sam. Those people were chasing us. I need to know why.'

'No you don't. It's safer not to know. Look, they don't know who you are. Just slip quietly into the night, you'll be fine. I'll lead them off and be in touch tomorrow with a proper explanation, okay?'

'And what about this dinghy's owner?'

'Howard, you need to go now, before those people catch up with us. Believe me, they're a bad bunch. Look, take a taxi and get away while you can, please.' Sam almost pushed Howard out of the dinghy.

'Get a taxi and get back to the hotel now,' repeated Sam, as he started to nudge the boat away from the side. Distance ended the conversation and Sam watched for a moment making sure Howard moved on. With a parting wave of encouragement, he headed the boat away and through the docks. Glancing to his right, he thought for a moment he could make out a figure running along the pedestrian walkway on the far side of the dock. He looked more closely; there was nobody there. He told himself to get a grip; it was just his imagination running riot. Looking ahead, he focused on getting the dinghy to his planned destination.

He knew the waters of this dock well from his time teaching at the university. For two years, he had been a member of one of the city's sub-aqua clubs. If he kept going, he would soon reach their boathouse and store, where he could leave the dinghy in safe custody for eventual return to its owner.

Equally important, at this time of evening there could still be two or three of the old hands hanging about there - cleaning dive gear, swapping stories, tinkering with boats. Some of them seemed to have no existence beyond the club, and the pub. Right now, he was banking on things not having changed much since he had left the city.

Looking over his shoulder, he scanned the north side of the quay again. Suddenly the running figure appeared. There was no doubt this time; it was the man. He disappeared again behind a screen of ornamental bushes, or were they low trees? It didn't matter which, a few moments later the man re-emerged as the run of shrubbery petered out completely. The chase was on. Sam tweaked the throttle, got the engine going full out. Any increase in speed was marginal but he was not concerned, the boat's straight line course through the water would eventually outrun the man who had to follow the longer line of the quayside, and he was on the far side of the dock anyway.

Sam looked ahead again, focusing all his thoughts on how best to shake off his pursuer. The sight of the SS Great Britain's masts looming ahead flagged to Sam that a turn in the dock was coming. He guided the dinghy as close to the side as he dared. Keeping in tight beside the SS Great Britain's dock at the turn, his route would be much shorter than the long arc the running man would have to cover on the north side of the quay, more advantage. As he reached the old ship's dry dock, he gave it one admiring glance, then turned the dinghy hard into the bend, straightened out and let it move ahead into the stretch of open water.

Sam looked back, confident he had left the runner well behind on the far side of the quay. He groaned to himself, the man had stopped running. Two cars had pulled to a halt beside the man, now he was gesticulating, shouting orders to the drivers. Then, with a jabbing hand point towards Sam's dinghy, he got into the lead car. Escape was not going to be so easy after all.

Suddenly the odds had changed. Pressing on at dinghy speed, Sam knew he could not win this race; he could tell the cars were struggling to keep their speed down as they tracked him from across the far side of the dock. He did have one advantage, the cars were driving along the north side and he was following the south side. True, if they simply kept going, their paths would eventually converge at the locks. But that was not how he saw things panning out. He knew that in a few moments the road would take the cars away from the quayside. He would have three or four minutes while out of their sight to play his hand.

Here on the south side there were several inlets, wharfs that indented into the long run of quayside. One such inlet housed the sub aqua club. If he could get his timing right, he would be able to turn into the inlet and be hidden, leaving the cars to speed to the end of the dock and cross to the south side by the old swing bridge that spanned the narrow channel between the dock's inner and outer basins.

Sam swung the dinghy hard over, manoeuvring into an inlet between two wharfs. Looking over his shoulder, he watched the cars on the north side of the dock pause for a moment and then accelerate away and out of sight just as he turned to check he was on course. Directly ahead was an old warehouse. Several boats were moored alongside it. A big impressive dive boat dominated and a variety of RIBs, rigid inflatable boats, both large and small bobbed beside it. He knew the hunched shadow on the quayside was winching gear - used for getting boats into the warehouse or on to trailers. He could make out a light in the clubhouse yard; someone was still around.

Sam took the way off the dinghy and allowed it to nudge between two of the smaller RIBs. He jumped out and tied its bow mooring line to a ring set in the dockside then he turned and sprinted into the yard. The office door was open and music wafted out.

'Hello, anyone home?' shouted Sam while rapping on the doorframe.

'I know that voice,' came a cheery shout from within. A chair scraped and footsteps brought a middle-aged man to the door. Once ultra-fit, a body honed to perfection through youthful service in the Royal Marines and the Special Boat Service was now starting to run a little plump, and his long uncombed black curls were streaked with grey. 'Sam Cameron! You old reprobate. What are you doing here, Cameron? Why didn't you call? The guys would have loved to see you.' He put out a hand to shake Sam's but it morphed into a bear hug. Then, with a guiding arm round Sam's shoulder, he drew him inside. 'Come in. You'll want a drink. I know I need a top up.'

Sam allowed himself to be led inside but spoke as he walked. 'Listen, Bill, it's great to see you -'

'You too. It must be getting on for five years, more even. What's kept you away so long? And what's brought you here in the dead of night?'

'That's just it; I'm in a spot of bother, trying to give someone the slip. Thanks for the offer, but I don't have time for a drink and catch up. I need to keep moving.'

'Oh, what have you done?'

'Nothing, well…' Sam collected his thoughts for a moment.

'Bill, long story short, there are people chasing me. Archaeology stuff, if they get me it will be bad. I've left somebody's dinghy tied up outside on your wharf; I pinched it over at the Waterfront Square, can you make sure it gets back to them? But most important, is there any way I can get out of here without being spotted?'

Bill didn't betray any surprise. Perhaps it was the effect of several whiskies or just years of diving experience; staying calm and complete trust in your dive partner were essential for survival. 'How bad if they get you?'

Sam looked him in the eye. 'Terminal bad.'

Bill gave a little grin. 'I always knew there was something in that Indiana Jones stuff. Always said you'd come to no good. How far behind you are they and how far do you need to go?'

'Two, three minutes maybe, and as far as possible. What do you think, can you help?'

Bill scratched at his unshaven jaw for a moment, ran his hand through his hair, swept it back from his forehead and whistled air out between his teeth. He finished his whisky in one gulp and banged the glass down on the table.

'Oh, I can help alright. I'll want a full explanation later and a drink, lots of drink.' He crossed the room to a key cabinet, unlocked it and pulled out a set of ignition keys.

'You're going to owe me big time. Come on. And grab that lot, you'll need them.' He pointed towards a set of waterproofs. Sam picked them up and followed Bill out into the yard. Back at the quayside, Bill pointed out one of the larger RIBs. 'Take that, it's got a full tank; I've just got it ready for a dive trip tomorrow.' He passed the ignition keys to Sam. 'You've used this one before, it's old but sound. And watch out, it had a new engine fitted last year, so it's got a lot more power than when you last took it out.' He glanced at his watch. 'I heard some folk talking over at the pub earlier. Think they're planning to get out through the locks about now. If you're quick, you could get through with them. Any problem there, have them call me, but you know the ropes anyway.'

The men looked at each other, Bill stretched out a solemn hand, and they shook. 'Good luck. I wish I could come but I'm past all the action man stuff these days,' he shrugged. 'And anyway, I'll have to get another dive boat ready for the trip tomorrow, thanks to you. And here was me planning an early night.'

The sound of tyres screeching on the road behind the warehousing announced the pursuers were in the area. Sam jumped aboard and got ready to move off. Bill untied the mooring line and Sam pulled the loose end on board.

'Whatever you do, take care of the RIB. Damage it and the committee will crucify me - you're not insured for it anymore. And they're my waterproofs too.'

Sam gave a wave of acknowledgement, pulled away from the sub-aqua club moorings and headed out of the inlet and back into the open dock. He turned the RIB in the direction of the locks, all the time scanning up and down the quaysides; there was no sign of the chasing cars anywhere. He might just get away with it.

Moving steadily ahead, he steered the RIB under the old swing bridge. Beyond, at the far side of the outer basin, he could see the locks. They were open, three or four small cruisers had already entered and were waiting for a big RIB to join them - its antenna and radome radar housing marked it out from the other boats - it was kitted out for serious work. He opened the throttle, with a little bit more speed he knew he would make it. The RIB's bow rose as the propeller's thrust kicked in. Impressed at the power, he eased back a little, certain now he would catch the locks before they closed and not wanting to attract unnecessary attention by racing.

The final obstacle between Sam and the locks was the flyover bridge. As he lined up to pass beneath it, he saw her - one of the cars must have taken the outer route and dropped her there. At the midpoint of the bridge, standing on the pedestrian walkway was a young woman; she leant almost casually on the guardrail but was scrutinising him and his RIB carefully. Sam knew exactly who she was. He bent down, rummaged in a storage net and pulled out a cap, which he slipped on his head before rising. He was careful to avoid his face showing as the RIB slipped under the flyover bridge.

Passing out on the other side, he dared not look back. If she had crossed the dual carriageway to maintain her surveillance, any such movement by him would mark him out in an instant. He covered the remaining distance to reach the lock gates without incident. With some relief, he nudged the RIB into the lock and secured a line to hold his position amongst the other boats as the lock gates closed. He had made it. Slowly the water level in the lock dropped to carry its flotilla of boats down to river level.

The locks opened on to the river and Sam got the engine turning over, then released his mooring rope and pulled it in. He pushed ahead slowly, taking his turn to exit. As he left the lock, he glanced back and his heart sank. The young woman had indeed crossed the carriageway to peer down into the locks; she was scanning the boats and their crews. She spotted Sam's glance towards the bridge and focused in on him. As soon as she recognised Sam, he saw her produce a mobile phone and make a call. He knew she was calling her car back.

He was found, but he had a little time. Her car was again caught on the wrong side of the docks. It would need to double back to pick up the woman before giving chase. Calmly he headed out into the river and turned downstream towards Avonmouth.

Just as he started downstream, Sam noticed the big RIB had pulled into the riverside; it was towing one of the smaller cruisers towards a mooring. The cruiser skipper was trying to restart the engine, without any joy. Sam could see the big RIB had things under control and he was happy to pass quietly by.

The sides of the Avon Gorge rose rapidly to form a claustrophobic channel that hemmed the river. Ahead of him and high above was the Clifton suspension bridge. His RIB would pass under it in a minute; then he would start to relax. He knew it was an entirely notional boundary and offered no protection but it was a marker. From there it was only a short run down river to Avonmouth where he would berth Bill's RIB and hire a car; slip away into the night.

Looking back, he saw the big RIB was now tied up alongside the cruiser it had nursed to the side. The RIB's skipper had hopped over to the cruiser to help with the engine problem. He smiled, normal problems, luxury! Just as he was turning his head to monitor his progress downstream, another movement on the road caught his eye. The smile left his face.

A car was driving fast down from the flyover towards the riverside road. He gunned the engine, for the first time he really pushed the RIB along. With a final glance over his shoulder he saw the pursuing car had halted near the mooring, somebody had got out and crossed from the car to the river's edge and was peering down at the big RIB. Then he had to turn his attention back to navigating the river.

Two or three minutes later, he became aware of the car again. Now it was driving parallel to his RIB on the run downstream. They were too far apart for him to make out who was in the car but more than close enough for them to spot his boat. He powered on, silhouetted in proud isolation against the dark shimmering of the river.

For much of the distance between Bristol and Avonmouth the road followed the course of the river, hugging the north bank; the gorge suddenly felt more like a trap than a channel, he could never outrun a car. He knew that only on the last stretch, as they approached Avonmouth, would the road and river separate as riverside developments forced the road a little inland. Sam revised his plan again. He would leave the boat beyond the point when his pursuers were forced away from the river. Find a spot to berth on the south bank and get a taxi.

From his Bristol diving days, he recalled frequently passing a little tidal inlet at the village of Pill on the south bank: he had never stopped but remembered there were always a few boats moored there. Instantly, he knew it would be ideal. With no local access bridge across the river he could get well away before the people in the car even realised he had left the RIB. Perhaps he'd even double back to Bristol; that would throw them.

Happy with his plan, Sam relaxed and a little while later he eased back on the speed as the RIB approached the great bend in the river that came immediately before Avonmouth. Here the road and river parted company. He had to push the engine revs up again as the power of the incoming tide almost brought the RIB to a halt. While steering into the bend he chanced a look at the car and gave a theatrical wave goodbye as river and road parted. He was puzzled at the happy wave he received in response. Then the car was gone and he was alone.

The village of Pill came up on his left hand side and he spotted the inlet where he planned to moor. Just as he started his turn, some instinct made him look astern. The big RIB he had last seen up river at the locks was coming up fast. Too fast, it was not following the river rules. That could only be for one reason - it was following him. His pursuers must have commandeered the big RIB back at the mooring when it stopped to help the little cruiser. There was no advantage in stopping now. With a boat, they could be on the south side of the river at the same time as him.

Abandoning his plan, he gunned the RIB downstream again, passing under the great road bridge that carried the M5 motorway into the West Country. He could see the docks at Avonmouth ahead and pushed on harder. There was no stopping here.

He glanced back. Since he'd sped up the distance between the two boats had been maintained, perhaps even opened up a little. He'd have to get out of the River Avon and into the big river, into the Severn. Then he'd be able to throw them off once and for all. He just needed to get there. With the throttle open full, he felt the push of Bill's new engine: it was good. He killed the navigation lights as the RIB raced past the docks, beyond the mouth of the River Avon and out into the darkness of the wide Severn Estuary. He formed his third plan in less than twenty minutes. This one had to hold or he was out of options.

Chapter 8

TUESDAY 13ᵀᴴ AUGUST

The cross-channel ferry had been much slower than the train or plane but the extra anonymity was worth the time. Now, in the early hours of the morning, Cassiter stopped at the pick-up point outside the ferry terminal and glanced around. A movement caught his attention in the car park as a big man climbed out from the driving seat of his car and stood quite still, staring. Cassiter saw just the slightest movement of an arm as the big man reached into the car to flash his headlights. He had not needed the flashing headlights, even from a distance Robertson's frame was instantly recognisable - a living bulldozer.

Robertson placed Cassiter's bag in the car's boot and closed the rear passenger door once Cassiter had entered. He got himself behind the wheel and drove off immediately.

'Well?' said Cassiter.

'Cameron gave them the slip, boss. He did a runner in Bristol. That Cameron has something about him, still on the run, but the guys reckon they have the measure of him now. They'll catch up with him soon enough.'

'And the old man he was meeting with?'

'Gone. They let him run while focusing on Cameron.'

Cassiter scowled. That was an unnecessary loose end. Then he relented, perhaps it was better the other man was still alive. If questions remained to be answered after he'd established what Cameron was up to, the old man could be tracked down and he might yet prove useful.

'And?'

'Turns out Cameron had some inscription; the guys have kept you the old man's copy. He dropped it on the quayside after he'd explained it for Cameron. Anyway, the guys know the details; they'll brief you when we link up. Some of it wasn't for the phone. I've arranged to rendezvous with Collette in a couple of hours. Seems the old man set up a meeting for Cameron with somebody at Hereford Cathedral. She heard the whole conversation.'

'Really? I wonder what that will be about. Cameron has been a busy bee. We'll have to see.'

Cassiter leant back into the comfortably upholstered seat. He was unconcerned by Robertson's vague account - he was a good man and loyal but his strengths did not lie in the thinking zone, Cassiter had others for that. Robertson had different though equally as valuable skills. And one thing was certain; this whole business would be an altogether easier proposition once his team had got a handle on what Cameron was up to. He thought about the route to Hereford. With a bit of luck, there would be time for a few hours' sleep in a hotel bed.

• • •

Sam pushed the engine on a little more; he had been going easy, conserving his fuel while the flood tide in the Severn estuary carried him upstream and exactly where he wanted to go. In the black night, surrounded by black water, it was cold and he was grateful for Bill's waterproofs. Now, as the tide slackened off, he needed to power on. Avonmouth was way behind him. So was the Second Severn Crossing, carrying the M4 Motorway across the river from England into Wales. Immediately ahead, the original Severn Bridge was close. Tilting his head up he could see the headlights of occasional early morning lorries as they tracked across the bridge. He planned to run the RIB beneath the bridge on the Welsh side of the river, aiming for Chepstow and the River Wye.

The RIB sat low on the water giving him a very short horizon. There was no sign of the larger RIB - he hoped he had shaken it off but couldn't be certain. If its radar was active and his pursuers knew how to use it, they would be able to hang back, tracking his movements from beyond his limited horizon. He glanced behind, nothing. Here's hoping, he thought, as he turned the craft into the mouth of the river Wye. The night black of the river mouth was accentuated by the glow of distant shore lighting to either side.

He pushed on; the plan now was to reach Hereford by river. Years before, he and some friends had done the Wye 100, the 100-mile canoe trip from Glasbury to Chepstow. He knew the river, knew that this way he could slip unnoticed into the very heart of Hereford.

He gently motored the RIB up stream and cruised quietly beneath the imposing walls of Chepstow Castle, where he realised a thin layer of mist was forming over the river.

He watched the last of Chepstow's urban lights fade away as the RIB followed the course of the river into open countryside. He cursed his luck as the mist thickened further, filling to a fog, and finally he had to stop his regular scanning of the river behind him and concentrate all his senses on what lay ahead. Running slow, always striving to keep one riverbank in sight, he edged on as quickly as he dared.

Metre by metre he took the great horseshoe loops in the river; and one by one, they were left behind, unseen and unappreciated. For the umpteenth time he wiped the fog's water droplets from his face and eyes and, gradually, he began to relax. He must have given his pursuers the slip out in the estuary. Sensing the slightest change in the light he guessed it would soon be dawn.

It was very early to make a call, but this was the first moment he had found in the chaos of the chase to contact Helen, to flag up this latest round of danger. He wasn't even sure if her plane would have returned from the States yet, but he could leave a message. Moments later, he shoved his phone back in his pocket, disgusted, a flat battery. He would need to find a phone somewhere soon.

Continuing the journey up river, the darkness above the fog blanket began its lightening into the dawn. But the persistent fog meant visibility improved only marginally and it was still cold and wet, though he could just about make out the riverbank on both sides now. He noted a narrow band of grey muddy flank was clearly visible above the waterline - telling him he was still within the tidal range. He opened the throttle a little more, knew the tide must have started to turn in the estuary by now and needed to get away from the pull of the sea that would already be stretching its reach up stream.

The early morning sun was slowly cutting through the blanket of fog to let him glimpse hints of things beyond the riverbanks. Then, to his left hand, a dark shape appeared out of the fog. It grew, rising into the sky, floating over the fog bank. High spans of a building showed, reflecting the rising sun; then disappeared into another layer of the shifting fog only to reappear stronger, brighter and more solid before vanishing once more. Reaching up were great arches, towering walls, a majestic ruin. Tintern Abbey. Its grey stones, old before Columbus reached America, still stood defiant against the destructive efforts of time and kings.

Sam weighed his options. He should push on, get up river as fast as possible, and certainly get beyond Monmouth before people were up and about. Then he could make the gentle and anonymous run up stream to Hereford. But his first priority must be to alert Helen and a public telephone kiosk would do the trick. The village of Tintern was as good a bet as any, provided he could do it quickly before the water level dropped too much with the ebbing tide.

He eyed the banks cautiously. Here the muddy slopes were not safe to scale so he pushed on a little. Just past the abbey, he found a lighting spot close to the village car park. It would do for a little while, but not too long or the RIB would be left stranded, dangling by its mooring line against an inaccessibly muddy tidal riverbank. He nudged in and secured the RIB. With some relief, he pulled off his waterproofs and felt fresh cool air against his body. He dropped them on deck and jumped ashore, scrabbled up the bank and headed across the car park towards a pub or, no, maybe it was a café, hard to tell at first in the half-light.

Sam was focused on a familiar shape that was emerging from the shadow of the café - a public telephone kiosk. He couldn't recall Helen's mobile number so decided to leave a message on the manse's answering machine. Even if Helen did not pick it up herself, with all the carry on over getting the property ready for market he knew Elaine was there every day for one thing or another. She would make sure Helen got the message.

Call completed, Sam hung up and paused for a moment; he leant back against the clear Perspex panels of the phone kiosk and took a couple of long slow breaths. It had been a long night. The dawn chorus had started filling the air with tweets and chirps, and with every passing moment the warming sun was thinning more of the chill fog.

Then in a rush, the ancient abbey appeared in its full glory, bathed in light as the sun finally burst through to sweep aside the fog. Beyond it, on either side of the river, green wooded valley-sides now rose up. The air was still, cold and suddenly crisp in his lungs while the early morning sun warmed his face - nature at its best.

Alone for a moment in a world of tranquillity, he allowed his mind to properly take in the scene. The ruined abbey; abandoned since the closing of the monasteries by Henry VIII, yet here it still was, solid, permanent. He wondered what would remain of modern buildings if left untouched for five hundred years. Not many would match this.

His moment's peace was disturbed by a slight disruption in the birdsong, then by human sounds coming from the riverbank. Time to go he thought. As he headed back across the car park towards where he had moored the RIB, a man's head appeared rising from below the level of the riverbank. He spotted Sam and shouted a warning to somebody beneath the bank. Then he scrambled up and immediately broke into a run, charging straight at Sam.

Sam saw the man produce a pistol from his jacket and raise it, stretch his arm out and take aim as Sam turned and ran. He felt the whizz of a round passing close by, heard the crack of the shot and ahead of him heard a faint crumping sound, saw the rear window of a car frost over as it was punctured. Another round flew past him, tugging at the sleeve of his jacket. Sam darted past the telephone kiosk and threw himself over a waist high stone wall that defined the boundary between café and car park. He landed flat on the damp lawn of the café garden. Voices were approaching fast, two, perhaps three people.

Sam cursed himself; he had dallied too long. Now it wasn't just a changing tide he had to deal with. Well, he wasn't going down without a fight. He crouched low, and hurriedly followed the line of the stone wall. At the end was a gate leading back into the car park. He cautiously looked out. He could hear the men calling to each other as they started a search, but he couldn't see anyone. Knowing he would be quickly found if he stayed in the garden, Sam slipped out of the gate and broke cover, running for a higher stone wall directly ahead. It was only a few metres' distance. Before the hunters spotted him, he had covered the ground and was heaving himself up the wall.

Gunfire sounded as Sam rolled over the top of the wall and let himself drop down on to the grass below, unhurt. Getting up quickly, he glanced around and realised he was in the abbey grounds. He hurried towards the ruined buildings. Then heard a thud behind him as somebody dropped, close to where he had landed only moments before. Fast steps closing from behind, this one was an athlete. Sam was fast but was suddenly not sure he would make the shelter of the abbey.

Throwing himself over a low broken wall, he worked his way amongst the remains of worn and weathered walls, the remnants of ecclesiastical support buildings: perhaps a hospital, a kitchen, some such. Then he found himself stepping into a square of lush green grass. The shape and suggestion of privacy created by the surrounding walls screamed cloister, though any covered walkways were long gone. He sprinted across the grass making for a modest arched doorway on the far side. He could see it led into the main body of the ruined abbey; from there he might be able to slip out and away, unnoticed.

Sam didn't quite make it. Just as he reached the doorway, he felt contact from behind. A hand grabbed him round the neck, bringing him to a halt. He could sense the assailant's other hand sweeping round; instinct told him it held a knife and it was intent on meeting his belly.

Ignoring the chokehold he was in, Sam stretched out both hands in an attempt to block the incoming knife. His right hand managed to catch the attacker's knife hand and slow the impetus of its journey; his left caught up and jointly they began exerting force to stop the blade. But the chokehold around his neck meant he was weakening by the moment. With the other hunters closing in, Sam needed to act.

While his hands grappled with the knife, slowly, determinedly, he gritted his teeth and bore the resulting extra pressure on his Adam's apple as he pushed his head forward into the chokehold. Then with all the force he could manage, he jerked his head backwards to make hard head contact with his assailant. He heard the crack, felt it sore on his skull, knew it would be worse for the man's face. The chokehold loosened slightly and as it did he forced his head forward against the slackening arm, then instantly jerked it back a second time. He felt the flood of something warm running down the back of his neck and the attacker's arm slide away; releasing him as the man recoiled clutching at his nose. It was flattened into his face.

Sam stepped ahead, deeper into the doorway. Gasping for breath, he braced to fend off the attacker who had quickly regained his composure to ignore a broken face and flood of blood; the man prepared to come again with his knife. The low morning sun was now shining directly into the abbey behind Sam. It flooded through doorways and arches and poured down through roof spaces long since left open to the weather; all combined to form a backlight, to silhouette Sam in the doorway.

The attacker came again. Knife outstretched, mindful this time to ensure his blade made contact with its target; with a shout, he lurched forward, knife high, arcing down towards Sam's chest, a trajectory that Sam recognised he could not deflect. In that moment, as he braced for impact, a shot rang out. The assailant seemed to pause in mid-air as a puzzled look flashed across his face then lapsed into expressionless death. The knife dropped to the ground as the man's momentum carried him on into Sam's arms. Sam felt the man's last breath ease out across his cheek and he was supporting a corpse.

Peering over the dead man's shoulder, Sam realised what had happened. On the far side of the cloister was the gunman; he had caught up and shot at Sam just as the knifeman lunged into the path of the shot. Thank the gods for friendly fire thought Sam, as he held tight to the dead body. The gunman fired again and again. Sam felt the thud and reverberation as rounds powered into the corpse. He needed to get away before the shooter got lucky. Holding the body upright, he dragged it with him, using it as a shield as he backed away under the doorway and into the abbey. A few steps in and he let the body drop, ducked behind a pillar and ran. Suddenly, all around him were great stone pillars, impossibly high arches and thick stone walls. They bounded broad open spaces that had once housed so many worshipers - now they just defined a clear killing field. This was no place to hide for long. He heard the gunman shout and then Sam knew for certain that there was a third man, but where?

Sam slowed down, he was eager to be away from the chasing gunman but cautious not to run from one gun into another. Stepping quietly between the pillars, he took his bearings, realising he had entered the abbey near the northern transept. He suddenly felt dwarfed by the building as he moved into the nave proper and the building's imposing power struck him. Yes, a ruin, but a magnificent ruin, and he did not intend to end his days here.

Sam moved, working east along a row of pillars. His feet silent on the covering of dew soaked grass that carpeted the abbey. He could hear boots slapping on the stone steps leading from the cloister into the abbey, laboured breathing. The gunman was not so fit; perhaps he could give him the slip. Sam turned left, saw a flight of worn steps leading up to a mezzanine entranceway and took them, silently, leaving his pursuer to search cautiously amongst the pillars.

Passing through the mezzanine entrance, he came to an abrupt halt. He was on a balcony and progress was barred by a guardrail that protected visitors from an abrupt drop back to ground level. He could see the line of the river a hundred metres distant. In between were more of the abbey outbuildings, a series of smaller ruins: some half remnants, others just knee-high stone ridges, stumps of what had once been. He looked down over the balcony guardrail; it was a fair drop to ground level. Swinging his legs over the rail, he climbed down, taking advantage of stones jutting out from the fabric of the abbey, the remnants of some long demolished support building. He let himself drop the last metre down to ground level and immediately wove a course amongst the ruins, making for the river and his RIB, and all the while keeping a wary eye out for the third attacker.

The abbey grounds were shielded from the river by a hedge, a low wooden access gate set near its midpoint. Sam climbed over the gate to reach the riverbank. He could see the water level had already started to drop, and it was going down quickly. Glancing upstream, he saw his RIB at its makeshift berth. Tied to its stern was his attackers' larger RIB, sitting further out in the river flow, clear of the riverbank and tugging on the line tethering it to his own RIB. Crouching down he hurried as best he could for the boats. In only a minute or two, his boat would be completely stranded. It was only clear of the bank now because of the pull of the larger RIB behind it, preventing his from settling into the rapidly emerging muddy riverbank. No amount of tugging would keep his RIB off the mud once the river levels dropped much further.

As he reached the mooring, a shot rang out. He glanced back to see the gunman coming from the abbey. A little further distant, the third man appeared, running for the riverbank. The bow of Sam's RIB was already suspended above water level as he jumped down on to it. It bounced against a large rock that was settled into the muddy bank, and he fought for his balance. The stern dropped and the bow tilted yet higher with his weight on board. He needed to get away but couldn't outrun a gun - he'd be a sitting duck out on the river. He needed a weapon.

Grabbing the emergency kit, he pulled out the flare gun, banged in a cartridge and looked up at the bank, which was now below his eye line - nothing. Taking advantage of the lull, he worked to untie the mooring line; then heard the laboured breathing of the gunman hurrying for the bank. Abandoning attempts to free the line he straightened and aimed up at the riverbank.

The man appeared, his pistol in hand, he raised it to aim at Sam just as Sam fired the distress flare. It punched out and fizzed straight into the gunman's chest. The gunman screamed and fell, disappeared from Sam's view and the pistol dropped onto the bank. Sam turned his attention back to freeing the mooring line and quickly worked it loose.

For a moment, nothing happened. Sam looked over the side; the RIB's bow was now settled into the muddy bank, trapped. Curses from above told him the unhappy gunman had survived his flare attack and a burning jacket flew over the bank, splashed into the water beside him to be carried swiftly downstream. But no sign of the gunman - he must have been hurt by the flare.

Sam could hear more distant shouts, knew the third man would soon be arriving. He stood and carefully edged to the back of the RIB, which was still in deep water. He started to jump up and down, trying to dislodge the bow from the bank. The RIB didn't shift. He looked back at the bigger RIB, still tugging on the mooring line that tethered it to his. He coordinated his jumps with the big RIB's tugs. His boat shifted a little but still stubbornly stuck to the bank. He jumped again; it rocked, edged out a little and settled once more.

Changing tack, Sam took hold of the larger RIB's mooring line and heaved it in towards him, pulling against river current and tide. His only hope now was to jump ship. Hand over hand he pulled in the line and the big RIB edged in closer, all the while straining against the river.

A voice shouted at him from above, the third man had arrived. Sam looked up; he was out of time. The third man stooped and picked up the pistol from the riverbank, brought it to bear on Sam. There was nothing more Sam could do; he let go of the big RIB's mooring line and raised his hands in the forlorn hope the man might show mercy. A glint of white teeth behind a cruel smile told Sam there would be none. The pistol fired.

Suddenly Sam found his world in a spin, he grabbed for the side to stop himself going into the water. Loosed from his hand, the big RIB had been rushed by the current out to the end of its mooring line and come to a halt with a jerk. In turn, it had yanked his RIB hard from the bank and, as a result, the shot had whizzed past Sam's shoulder instead of planting in his chest. Now, the steady pull of the big RIB was edging his own RIB away from the muddy bank winning the fight against the sticky mud.

Sam regained his balance and looked up again; the third man was squeezing the pistol's trigger in frustration, it was out of ammunition. Further out into the flow now, his boat's stern was being tugged by the river. If he could get the engine going it might finally break free of the mud. Sam moved towards the controls.

The third man realised that Sam was slipping away and he jumped for the RIB. Just as Sam slammed the engine into reverse, a stronger tug from the big RIB behind finally jerked his RIB free.

The third man landed where the RIB's prow had been, now there was just muddy riverbank. His determined features registered horror as his boots entered the mud and kept going down. Ankles, calves, knees, all vanished. He finally stopped sinking with the mud about his thighs.

Sam heard his cry, saw the man's hand reach out for help; he ignored it. Pulling his RIB out into midstream, he took a moment to untie the larger RIB; caught by the current it moved away, quickly gathering speed on its journey downstream. Then he turned his attention back to the riverbank. He gave the trapped man a cheery wave and pointed to the bank above him where the burned gunman was slowly struggling to his feet. They could see to themselves.

Turning the RIB upstream he moved off. He had business to attend to and wanted to be beyond Monmouth before too many people were up and about. If he could manage that, he just might create enough clear water to keep himself free.

• • •

Helen walked into the manse, exhausted by what seemed like days of almost non-stop flying, she dropped her travel bag in the hall and made straight to the study. Elaine was there already and wasted no time on ceremony, just pushed the play button for Helen to hear Sam's message. Once it had played through, Helen felt Elaine's steady gaze and gave a drawn smile.

'Well, it's heating up again,' said Helen.

Elaine nodded. 'What will we do?'

Helen sank into the chair behind the study desk. Then she leant forward, placed her elbows on the desk edge and cupped her chin in her hands. She closed her eyes and shook her head gently. 'What can we do? We can't run. You see their reach, Norway, even the States. Nowhere is safe. Like we said before, the only way to stop them is to take it public -'

'And until we've cracked the puzzle of the daggers there is nothing to take public,' said Elaine, finishing Helen's train of thought.

'Exactly. We're right back to where we were before. So what are we going to do? Well, I'm going to join Sam in England. You have to stay here, Elaine. Grace is too young and Francis too old to be dragged into this. You'll need to look out for them while I'm away. And if it does all go pear shaped before we get back, you must call DCI Wallace. I know we agreed not to involve him in some of this, and telling him will certainly get us into serious trouble for holding back the things we couldn't tell him last time; but if you're caught in a corner, needs must.'

'Okay, but are you sure it's wise for you to go down south?'

'No, I'm not sure of anything just now, but Sam's on his own. His message says he's heading for Hereford. That's where I'll go. I'm going back to my flat now, to grab a shower and then get some sleep - I'm wiped out. Later on today, we can meet to discuss this business about James Curry closing the parish and maybe for you and me to catch up properly. In the meantime, hopefully Sam will get in touch. Tomorrow morning I'll fly down. What do you think the nearest airport will be?'

'Birmingham, I would think. I'm sure Hereford will only be an hour's drive or so from there.'

'That's where I'll go then.' Helen left the room, grabbed her travel bag and returned to the study. She dumped it on the desk and unlocked it. After rummaging inside for a moment, she pulled out the communion set box. Inside were the plate and cup and a very battered lump of silver, the base and stock of the cross. Without the dagger completing the top of the cross, it looked forlorn. She held it up for Elaine to see. 'That's all we have left. They got the blade.'

Elaine tutted quietly to herself. 'How is your father doing now? Your mother must have been distraught.'

'He's a tough old bird. Conscious now, talking but sore. At least all the moving parts still move. He'll be fine, thanks. My mom's upset but she's not going to let that interfere with life. I wish to Heaven that I hadn't taken this over there now, just don't understand how they found it. Could they have been spying on us again? Maybe you could get your surveillance expert friend to check it out, what was his name?'

'I'm ahead of you there. If it's any consolation, I've just had Scottie Brown sweep for bugging devices everywhere, including your flat. He found nothing. So our privacy is assured here. I'll have him check regularly in future. They must have other sources of information but I can't think what. At least we have a photograph of your blade, so its information's not lost. But Scottie did say they might be able to monitor email and web stuff too. Perhaps that's a weak spot. We'll have to be more careful.'

Helen put the base back into the box and closed the lid, then she slid the box across towards Elaine. 'I'll get going now. We need to hide this in the tunnel. Could you do it please? That's the only place we know that is really safe and secret. I just wish I'd thought to hide it there from the outset.'

'Okay, I'll do that for you. Well, I'll have Grace do it. She's coming over in a little while. She'll be sorry to have missed you. She's shown me how to open the secret tunnel doors but I'm still not up to all that stretching and twisting.'

'Oh, Elaine, I'm sorry. With all that's going on, I didn't ask how you are doing. Tell me now, how do you feel?'

Elaine waved a dismissive hand. 'Don't worry about me. I get stronger every day. I'll soon be up to speed. It's you I'm concerned about, deliberately flying towards trouble. Remember, DCI Wallace has said they are maintaining a watch up here. We should be fine. The danger is where you're headed.'

Helen gave Elaine's arm a gentle squeeze. 'Don't worry. I don't intend to let a bunch of crooks get the better of me,' she said.

'That's as may be. But Francis reckons this is not just a bunch of crooks. He and Xavier are convinced it's much bigger than that. And I don't think Sam would want you going down there. Why not at least wait until he gets in touch again?'

'Listen, it's not up to Sam to decide what I do. If he's in trouble, he will need help, and who else can go if not me? Sam and I will be back before you know it. We'll see whatever he's found out down there and then we'll all take stock together. Try to resolve the puzzle, okay?'

'Okay, but this is the last delay. If we can't solve it when you get back, I'm going to the police anyway. I don't want to see Grace or anyone else harmed. That's not negotiable.'

Helen nodded acknowledgement, then sat down at the desk again. She reached beneath it to the computer tower and pressed the power button. 'I'll just sort out my flight and hire car now so I have travel times to leave with you in case Sam gets in touch again.'

'All right. But Helen, at some point we will need to talk about how we respond to James Curry. I've been sounding people out. It's as I thought, Curry did do some fig-leaf consultation whilst I was off sick, folk didn't have the stomach for a fight after what happened in the church and he just rolled everything up. Nobody here is happy about it but I'm not finding any support in the surrounding parishes. It does seem correct that one parish has to close because of the falling membership rolls across the city. Transferring our membership amongst the neighbouring parishes will help to make all the others stronger. If we're the one to close, the others feel safe.'

'Well, I guess no one wants their own church to close, right?'

'Right,' said Elaine.

'You can't blame them. Let's talk about it later on. I've had a lot of time to think about it on all my flights in the past few days. We can try again to rally some support, but if we can't beat James Curry on this, then at least I think I might have a solution of sorts. I don't want to say much in case it spooks things.'

Elaine's face betrayed no emotion. 'I hope it's a good solution, because we are losing ground here. It's not looking good and we're almost out of time.'

• • •

'Right now, I don't care how it happened. Tell them to forget about Novack's body, just leave it. He'll be found when the tourists start to walk around. They must get themselves away from the area and keep out of sight,' said Cassiter. His calm voice betrayed none of the irritation he felt. The trace and track mission he had set his team had somehow morphed into a hunt and kill - and it was his man who was dead. 'Once they have shifted location they can let you know where they are and you can pick them up.'

Robertson nodded. 'I'll head down that way now. They said they are outside the village and with plenty of cover to hide in, close to the riverbank. I should have them picked up within the hour.'

'Quick as you like then and be careful, don't let yourself get drawn into any trouble. If it's too hot when you get there, just drive on and let the police have them, we'll sort it later.'

'Okay, I'm off. It's all quiet there now; we might just get away with it.'

Cassiter watched Robertson cross the room, open the door to his suite and walk out. The big man was halfway through the doorway when Cassiter called out and the big man paused, turning back to listen. 'And remember, Robertson, make sure everyone understands exactly, I just want to know what Cameron's doing, hang back and observe. He's worth more to us alive than dead right now.'

Robertson gave a curt nod then glanced along the corridor. 'Here's your breakfast coming, boss.'

Cassiter heard the sound of a trolley rolling along the corridor. He nodded towards Robertson and waved the big man away just as room service arrived.

Sitting at the dining table in his suite, Cassiter savoured the aroma that suddenly surrounded him as he lifted the silvered cover from his food. His breakfast looked as good as it smelled. He took a moment of pleasurable anticipation before eating.

It had been a long night. He had lost a man, which was a high cost, but he was content. Thanks to Collette's overhearing the quayside phone call, they knew exactly where Sam Cameron was going and when. He did not really understand the why yet - all Collette had been able to tell him was he had set up a meeting with the cathedral's dean. He would just let things run there for now. Pick up Cameron when he kept the appointment. See what happened then, see what was for him.

He put thoughts of Cameron and the debacle at Tintern from his mind. It would only spoil his breakfast.

• • •

Sam slowed the RIB down to a crawl and pulled it across towards the east bank. He waved a greeting to the pair of anglers on the west bank. They nodded a greeting back, acknowledging his consideration in not scaring the fish on their side of the river.

Once past, he manoeuvred back into midstream and opened up the throttle a little more. Monmouth was well behind him, passed without incident or notice. Now he was making his way through the calm of rural Herefordshire. As he powered the RIB on against the river's flow, his mind continued to churn over the early morning events. He hoped Helen had picked up his message. Hoped Howard Vance had got back to his hotel safely. Wondered what he would learn in Hereford.

Red and white beef cattle grazed happily on riverside pastures. One or two lifted unworried heads to watch him pass before returning to their grass. Tired now, he forced himself to focus on the surroundings; above and beyond the pastures rose heavily wooded hillsides, sometimes gliding smoothly down to the riverbanks, elsewhere dropping away in cliffs.

Everywhere now combined to form a green and winding gorge that the river flowed through, sometimes looping back on itself, always finding the course of least resistance. Symons Yat; the banks rising to form towering cliffs that hemmed the river, and everywhere that gravity permitted, trees gripped and grew to create a sound deadening blanket. Sam was alone with just the gentle purr of his RIB's engine and the sounds of the river. The sense of seclusion was not threatening here, just calming. He knew this place well enough from his canoeing days but today there was no time to linger and he kept the RIB moving upstream.

He passed a couple of pleasure cruisers, moored, unmanned and silent: waiting for the arrival of the day's tourists.

At Ross-on-Wye, he was more cautious. If there was to be an ambush, it could well be here. Approaching the road bridge that crossed the river, he paused to scan the parapet and banks, nothing. He gunned the engine and the RIB shot under the bridge, he followed the sharp bend in the river and immediately had to weave around some river shallows. All the while, high above, perched like a citadel was Ross, forever watching the river's tranquil flow beneath. He pushed on for Hereford.

Sometime later, Sam guided the RIB into the shallows and then drove ahead hard, beaching firmly on to what was today a sandy riverbank. Come the winter rains it would revert to riverbed but today it was dry. He stepped out, pulled the mooring line tight and secured it to a tree trunk. Without a backward glance, he climbed the bank and found himself in what seemed like a public park. A little footbridge led across the river, he took it and then, having fixed his bearings, he cut across the green, heading straight for the city centre.

A charity clothes shop answered an immediate need and he paused there to select trousers and a sweatshirt that he guessed would roughly fit. He paid for them. Then stepped to the back of the shop and, before the assistant could object, he stripped off his dirty clothes, bagged them and pulled on his purchases. Then he aimed for the nearest prominent hotel.

Inside, a slightly circumspect receptionist eyed his dishevelled appearance. For a moment, Sam thought he was going to be turned away. He explained that he had been travelling all night, his suitcase had been lost and he really needed a room to get cleaned up and some rest. He promised her he was more respectable than his worn appearance suggested. Finally, aided by sight of a platinum card, the receptionist softened, took pity on his plight and booked him in. She lent him a phone charger from the stack kept beneath the reception desk.

Before heading off to his room to get cleaned up and a quick sleep, Sam handed over his carrier bag of dirty laundry and asked for coffee and a sandwich to be sent up to his room. A little later, with his phone on charge, the sandwich remained uneaten as sleep overtook him.

• • •

Sam woke in the early afternoon, called Helen immediately and was pleased to learn she was safe and planning to travel to Hereford tomorrow. He looked forward to seeing her again. In the meantime, he wanted to see how the land lay.

It was only a short walk to the cathedral and Sam took his time about it, taking in the environment and layout. It was set amidst its own greened policies and here and there little groups of friends sat out, enjoying the afternoon sun. Around them, a steady flow of the city's residents crisscrossed the green, going about their business.

Sam wandered around inside the cathedral, admiring the craftsmanship evident in every corner. Finally, he followed the signs for the gift shop where he bought histories of the cathedral and the Mappa Mundi. Stopping at the café he bought a drink and took it out to sit in the quiet of the adjoining chapter house gardens; enjoying a few minutes of tranquillity as he browsed the books and brochures. By the time he visited the dean next morning, he would be properly informed.

Chapter 9

WEDNESDAY 14ᵀᴴ AUGUST

The assistant did not have the chance to usher Sam into the dean's office before the man himself emerged, hand outstretched and beaming smile.

'Sam, good to meet you,' he said while they shook hands. 'Come on in. I'm Charles Rodgers but please do call me Charles.' The dean stepped to one side and waved Sam through the doorway to his office.

'Thank you, Charles, it's very kind of you to fit me in at such short notice,' said Sam.

'No problem. Howard made it quite clear you were in a hurry. Now, can I offer you a coffee?'

'Thanks, that would be nice, just white, no sugar.'

The dean glanced back towards his assistant and arched an eyebrow. She nodded.

'I think I might have one too,' said the dean. His assistant smiled an acknowledgement.

Closing his office door, the dean pointed Sam towards a cluster of comfortable looking occasional chairs on the far side of the room. Sam admired how the dean had captured both efficiency and comfort in his office décor. As he took his seat, he glanced briefly at the group of framed pictures arranged on the wall beside the chairs; there was some familiarity that he couldn't quite place, he speculated they might be popular prints; anyway, they fitted in well.

'Now, what can I do for you? Howard did say your research might have established some link with Richard de Haldingham, the fellow we believe created the Mappa Mundi. It's our most prized treasure, so anything that sheds light on its origins is good for us too. How exactly can we help?'

Sam explained about the Templar's gravestone at Inchcolm Abbey, its reference to Lincoln and Howard's theory about alternative family names that might make Sam's grave find in Scotland related to the creator of the Mappa Mundi.

The dean did not understand quite what the urgency was but his friend Howard's reference was certainly good enough for him and, in any event, Sam's credentials were impeccable. 'I've made arrangements for you to speak with Simon Owens. He's our volunteer historical expert. Though don't be fooled by the word volunteer. Simon retired down here but he used to be a big noise at the Imperial War Museum. We could never afford him, but he's with us a day or so a week, volunteering. Keeping us and our band of volunteers in line and up to speed. Simon's expecting you. Let's finish our coffee and I'll walk you down.'

On leaving the dean's office, he slipped a piece of paper into Sam's hand. 'Oh, nearly forgot. In case I don't see you before you leave, I've taken the liberty of making an arrangement for you to visit one of our rural parishes this afternoon. Spoke to the local vicar and he'll be pleased to show you round. Lots of Templar types go there. I thought it might give you some local context or whatever.'

Sam glanced at the neatly written details:

Rev. Jerry Brown, St Michael's, Garway. 3 o'clock, today. There was a postcode and telephone number too.

The rest of the morning passed in a flash. Simon had shown him the Mappa Mundi. It had been a thrill for Sam; he did not know why he had never been to see it before. Standing in front of the medieval map of the world, mounted on the wall behind its protective shield, he took in one of the wonders of the cartographic world.

'You'll see the projection is very different from the one we use today,' said Simon. 'East is at the top and west at the bottom. North is to the left and south to the right. And scale, well that's all over the place, but look, they've captured so much of what we know today. There's Jerusalem right at the centre, then everything radiates out from there.'

Sam was nodding, acknowledging Simon's words as he scanned the map, searching for anything that might link with his Templars and their hiding place. Nothing.

'It's faded a bit of course. But you can see the big cities - Constantinople, Rome, Paris, London. And then look more closely - there's Lincoln, Hereford over here,' his hand traced a line over the armoured glass. 'Here, see, Edinburgh. You're on the map too.'

Sam looked at where Simon was pointing. 'Edinburgh? Scotland. That was pretty much the edge of the world then.'

'Yes,' agreed Simon. 'Though it's a Christian world map. Scotland's a Christian country, even if you Scots did fall out of favour with the pope for a while back then. I suppose it would have been a surprise if they missed it out, don't you think?'

Sam nodded agreement. 'I guess so. Is there any Templar linkage with the map?'

'Templars? Well, no. Not directly.' Simon paused and gave a little chuckle. 'The Church of England likes to keep things on the straight and narrow. Templars are viewed as a bit racy, don't you think?' His hand swept across the face of the map. 'In all seriousness, I've never identified anything specifically like that. Come on, I'll give you a copy of the map; we've reproduced a scaled down version, sorted out the colour fading and so forth. You can decide for yourself.'

Sam was disappointed. He didn't want to leave the original map. The family connection between the map's maker and their Henri de Bello had seemed to offer the best chance of finding the other daggers. Instead, it was a dead end.

Simon had walked off, still talking. His words drifted back across the map room as he headed for an opening. 'Now, if it's Templars you're interested in, you should have said. We've got plenty of that in these parts...' the sound of his voice trailed away to nothing as he disappeared from view.

Sam hurried after him, following him into a room bright with natural light. Tall rows of old wooden bookcases jutted out from either side of the room but never quite meeting in the middle, leaving space that combined to create an aisle down the centre of the room.

Fixed between each row of bookcases were benches and reading ledges. Each bookcase was laden with aged books. Almost all had covers of heavy worked leather and each book was securely chained to its shelf. A book could be lifted down from the shelf and on to the reading ledge in front of it, the reader could sit on the bench and read, but the tethered book could never leave its location. He was in the cathedral's ancient chained library.

Directly beneath the window at the front of the room, Simon was now bent over a broad and busy librarian's desk. He was scanning through lists of entries, searching. He continued to talk as though Sam was beside him and Sam caught up in time to catch the end of Simon's discourse.

'…, of course this was real border country in those days. Edward had certainly beaten the Welsh by then but it was never an easy peace. For a good part of its length, the river Wye defines the border between England and Wales. Though the border didn't always stick to the river, which didn't help local tensions as you can imagine.'

He glanced round at Sam, seeking his acknowledgement of the fact.

'And how did the Templars fit into that landscape?' said Sam.

Simon turned back to the ledger he was consulting, continuing his search as he replied. 'Well, generally speaking, we had a lot of Templar activity in this area. They had been gifted various parcels of land, farms and so forth. I don't doubt some gifts would have been to support a worthy cause. But let's face it, those land owners gifting parcels of land to the Templars knew they would be losing some income from the land they gifted, but also knew they would be getting a bunch of disciplined, principled and armoured men living near at hand. In those wild times, their presence could have been generally stabilising. Certainly reassuring to a local lord.'

'I see. So the Templars were clearly well established here.'

'Oh yes. In fact, they were even involved with a hospital here in the town. It's long gone now of course. Off hand, I can't recall exactly what their involvement was but they certainly had something of a profile here about. Apparently, at some point the Templar grand master, their leader, even came this way on a visit. Then there's St Thomas de Cantilupe of course. Cantilupe was bishop of Hereford - there are indications the bishop might himself have been a Templar.'

Simon rummaged in a desk drawer and pulled out two pairs of gloves. He straightened up, handed Sam one pair and began to pull on the other. Then he beckoned Sam to follow him as he wandered away down the aisle glancing to left and right. He stopped, stepped closer to one of the bookcases and browsed along a shelf. Finally, he pulled one book out. Its attached chain clinked quietly as he laid it on the ledge.

'What have we got here?' said Sam.

'This book is pretty well contemporary with the latter end of the Templar period. Amongst other things, it includes some records of exchanges between Templars in this part of the country with those elsewhere. Some art works and the like, quite unusual, not the normal Templar stuff at all. I am certain there are some references to Lincoln too, which is what you're interested in, I think - the Templars were big over there as well. Of course you'll know that.'

Sam agreed, he was suddenly feeling excited again. Templar art works. Could there be a link? Perhaps his trip to Hereford was not to be in vain after all.

'I'm going to leave you to it. Any questions, feel free to ask at the desk and they'll call me back. If there is anything of interest let me know and we'll see what can be done.' They shook hands and then he was gone. Sam settled down and pulled the heavy book towards him.

He slowly turned the pages, in part cautious at having such old documents in his hand, in part just amazed at the mixture of information on the pages. Here, beautifully worked and developed art; there, script packed so close the words were hard to decipher. Some pages seemed lists of facts, almost the routine of housekeeping; others were more structured and formal. He lingered over each page taking in the information, enjoyed the proximity and connection to long gone lives but not finding any references to maps or their secret. It was another dead end, fascinating but ultimately unproductive.

Sam glanced at his watch. Helen would be arriving soon and he decided to call it a morning. They were to meet for lunch and then they could go out to visit St Michael's together - hopefully there would be something of use there. He flicked quickly through the last three or four pages, mostly religious illustrations and iconography, nothing of relevance. Closing the book he reached up to return it to its place on the shelf when something about the religious imagery stopped him - a sense of familiarity, vague, unformed, yet still hauntingly familiar.

Putting the book back down, he gently opened it to the last page and looked carefully at the beautiful illustration. A tempest whipped up a deep blue coloured sea that surrounded a series of colourful religious images, cameos, little islands, all tethered together against the storm by a burnished golden vine, heavy with fruit, the vine reached out from the centre of the picture to embrace and link each of the cameos. A beautiful artwork - he knew it but couldn't place it. He shrugged to himself. In spite of a decent night's sleep, he'd not really caught up on the previous twenty-four hours' exertions. His mind was still tired; it was probably just generating false memories, wishful thinking.

Across the room, he could see that a volunteer worker was busy explaining the library's workings to a little group of tourists gathered at the chain library's entrance door. Unobserved, he pulled out his phone and took the opportunity to photograph the page. It was beautiful; Helen would be interested to see it. And she might be able to explain any religious symbolism, which eluded him completely.

He took a moment to review the photograph; happy with it, he trousered his phone, put the book away and hurried off to get ready for Helen's arrival.

• • •

Sam sat in the front passenger seat as Helen drove the hire car along narrow country roads. With every turn, the sense of remoteness increased. There were high hedges and yet higher trees whose canopies often overhung the road, all combined to create a green tunnel that she drove the car through. Occasional field gates gave fleeting glimpses of the hop fields and apple orchards beyond.

Driving into the village of Garway, she slowed the car, both to comply with the speed restrictions and to take in the idyllic setting. First some cottages, then to her left the village green where some teenagers were having a cricket knock about, to her right the village pub, the Garway Moon Inn - but no sign of a church. She stopped and asked in the pub for directions, then hurried back to the car.

'It's through the village, down the hill and take a turn on the left hand side,' she said.

'Okay, drive on slowly and I'll keep an eye open for it.'

Helen started the engine. For just a moment, she wondered about the car that was rolling into the village behind them. She was sure she had seen it before, during the drive out, but it slowed to a halt in the pub car park as she pulled away, the driver got out and headed into the pub - nothing for her to worry about.

A little further on, Helen turned off the minor road that was masquerading as a highway and drove down the narrowest of lanes. Ahead, they could see the church, set back from the lane and she gingerly drove towards it, hoping no traffic came from the other direction. Finally, she pulled into a little dead-end that ran off towards the church. Stopping the car, she got out and Sam joined her, they both looked over to the church.

'Come on, let's have a quick look round, it's not three o'clock yet. We have time,' said Sam, while walking through the gate and into an ancient graveyard that spread round the church. Helen followed him, noting that many headstones were so old the inscriptions had worn right away.

They wandered about, recognising the age of the building, and just as they completed their circuit a plump man entered the graveyard from a little side gate. He waved and beckoned, then called across to them. 'Come on over. Good to see you, Sam isn't it? The dean said to expect you. Jerry's the name. Jerry Brown. Welcome to St Michael's.'

Jerry led them back through the side gate. 'The vicarage is only a short distance away, do come and have some afternoon tea with us.' Two or three minutes' walking found Jerry guiding them into the vicarage gardens and thence inside to his study.

Judy, the vicar's wife, served afternoon tea with home baked scones while her husband told Helen and Sam what he could. 'The church here was Templar, way back when they were at their height. Of course, they had a farm and lands here then; it would have been quite a place in its day. The church has been rebuilt since then, but you can still see vestiges of the original round Templar church's foundations, and there's a defensive square tower still standing - that may have Templar roots too. Even the newer bits of the church are very old by any measure. I'll point the Templar parts out to you on the way back to your car.

'Having said that, I really don't know what the dean thought I could tell you. Oh, we get visitors all the time, Templar enthusiasts and such, but they are really just here to take some pictures and have a browse around. I'm pleased to encourage them, and they all seem to go away happy enough.'

Helen smiled an acknowledgement. 'Is there nothing that you can tell us? Some village lore even?'

Jerry Brown sucked in his lips a little and shook his head. 'Sorry, beyond the public records I don't know very much detail of the Templar history at all. Tell me though, why the big interest in the Templars? What's the big mystery?'

Helen explained as little as possible of their deeper motive while telling of their finds during the archaeological dig in the Fife dunes and their goal of finding out a little more about them.

'Oh, I know you now,' said Jerry. 'The church killings, up in Scotland. Good Lord, I'd have thought you'd want to keep all that stuff at arm's length. They got the people involved though, didn't they?'

Judy Brown gasped quietly to herself.

'Well it's quite complicated, we're trying not to get involved with all that. Our interest is to trace the origins of the artefacts Sam's students found during the dig.'

Judy was looking very anxious. 'I think I saw the police publicity photograph in the paper. A dagger, I think. Gold or was it silver?'

'Silver,' said Helen. 'But listen, if there is nothing to tell, then that's it. To be honest, it was the dean at Hereford who suggested coming here. Sam and I had not given it a moment's thought.'

The room fell into silence, nobody quite knowing what to say next. Then, Judy looked across to her husband, making a determined eye contact, questioning. 'You know, Jerry, there might be something. Oh, long before our time, of course, and we've been here fifteen years, more.'

'What's that, dear?' Jerry looked at his wife inquisitively.

'The padre. Tell them about the padre.'

Jerry sat up straight, 'Good Lord, you might have something.' He looked at Helen and Sam. 'It hadn't even occurred to me to link it till this moment. But Judy's right. There may well be a connection. Who'd have thought it?'

'Go on,' said Sam.

'Well it's an old story, as Judy says, long before our time. I can't vouch for it I'm afraid. In fact, Judy, you tell it. You are the one who picked it up at the W.I.'

'W.I.?' said Helen.

'Women's Institute. How we keep the community together. Coffee mornings, talks, abseiling, book clubs, trips away. You name it; we'll give it a go,' said Judy.

'Right, sounds great fun. How come your W.I. is involved?' said Helen.

'It's definitely fun all right. And for clarity, we're not involved in the story itself. The W.I. has another important role, one we don't put in the literature: if there's any gossip or dark tales to tell, the W.I. eventually ferrets it out. There are no safe secrets in a rural community.'

'I see, sounds like you keep your finger on the pulse. So, who is the padre?'

'Well, and I stress this is just hearsay over the tea urn. If there is anything to it and you want to know more, I'm sure we can point you in the right direction.' Judy paused, finished her cup of tea, put it down carefully then lent forward to share her story.

'Long ago, 1943, '44, something like that, I don't know. During the Second World War anyway. Well, the then vicar of St Michael's, I think his name was Roberts, maybe Clive Roberts, anyway that doesn't matter so much. He was completely moved by the young boys from the parish being conscripted, taken away to face the horrors of war. Well, I'm sure you can imagine what war's like.'

Sam didn't need to imagine, he knew from bitter personal experience, and didn't wish it on anybody.

'Well, to support the boys, he joined up too,' continued Judy. 'I think most regiments needed a chaplain of some sort; their title is the padre. Hence, *our padre*. Thing was, he didn't come home. Poor man was killed while serving with his regiment.' She sighed and looked around the company.

Sam tutted a little. 'It happens; a bullet doesn't worry what your faith is. Soldiers reckon if it's going to get you, it's going to get you.'

'That's a little fatalistic, isn't it?' said Jerry.

'And how does the padre fit into your story?' said Helen.

Judy smiled at her, glanced round at the others who all nodded encouragement. She continued. 'So, when Reverend Roberts left for the war, the parish had no vicar. At that time, the war affected everything. There was a shortage of people in every walk of life and people had to make do and mend. The bishop in Hereford had no replacement available and so the neighbouring parishes had to shoulder Reverend Roberts' pastoral duties for the duration. Neighbouring vicars shared out the workload, conducting services and so on until well after the war. There was quite a period of delay while the country came off a war footing. The vicarage here was locked up until well into 1947 when a new incumbent was finally appointed.'

Jerry leant forward and picked up the teapot. 'Let me top up the cups while Judy tells the story. More tea, anyone?' Without waiting for replies, he refilled the cups and offered round the scone plate again.

'Thank you, Jerry,' said Judy, taking one. 'Now here's the thing, it was all about the new man who was appointed to the parish back in '47. He spent the rest of his working life serving the community here. Watkins, Tom Watkins, very popular in the parish. He got married some years later and his new wife,' she leant forward again in a conspiratorial way, 'who I believe was a good deal younger than him, had the whole vicarage gutted, top to bottom. She insisted on having everything new. And you will never believe what she found, hidden away in the attic.' She stopped, left her audience hanging as she broke off for a mouthful of scone and a sip of tea.

This was a woman who could work a story for all it was worth, years of experience, thought Helen.

'I wonder what it was,' said Sam, dutifully.

'Well would you believe it? She found a silver dagger.'

'A what?' said Helen.

'Yes, a silver dagger. Apparently, it was hidden beneath the attic floorboards. Though what she was doing rummaging around up there is quite beyond me. Trust me, the attic in this house is dark and cramped and I for one wouldn't want to spend any time up there.'

The information was falling into place for both Helen and Sam. They exchanged glances as they made links with the Lincoln connection, the Templars and the mapmaker's links to Hereford Cathedral. And now, within the diocese an old Templar church and lands; and hidden in its vicarage, a silver dagger. Coincidences might happen for some people, but Helen, like Sam had come to recognise there were no coincidences where the Templars were concerned.

'That sounds like a really exciting find, what does it look like? Where did it go?' said Helen.

'Oh, I've never seen it myself. Apparently, it's very beautiful, simple, elegant even. I would imagine it might be a bit like the one you found on your expedition, but I couldn't say.'

Helen tried to mask her urgent interest. 'Did it go to a museum? It sounds just like the sort of thing Sam might like to see while we're in the area.'

'I don't know. Jerry, do you have any idea what they did with it?'

'Not the foggiest. I think everyone assumed it had belonged to the padre but I don't think he had any family. Tom Watkins and his wife might even have just kept it as a memento. Maybe they sold it. Certainly didn't leave it behind when they left, I know that for sure.'

'Tom Watkins is dead now of course,' said Judy. 'About ten years ago.' She noted the look of disappointment cross Helen's face. 'But if it's important to you, his widow is still alive, Eileen. Jerry, do you know how Eileen is these days?'

'She's still doing well as far as I know.'

'I'm sure we would have heard if something had happened.' Judy stood and went to collect her husband's telephone directory. 'I'll give her a call now if you want.'

Eileen wasn't at home. Judy promised Helen she'd try again later and would pass on a message if she made contact. If she could set up an arrangement for the next day, she would. Shortly afterwards Helen and Sam made their excuses and left. As Helen drove, Sam phoned the hotel to confirm they would like to stay for at least one more night.

Chapter 10

THURSDAY 15TH AUGUST

The steward guided Helen and Sam into the Rowing Club lounge. Little knots of people sat dotted here and there. A few chatted to those around them. Others looked quietly out through the great windows that overlooked the Wye; some of the watchers idly traced the route of a straight four that had just powered up stream past the clubhouse. Now far in the distance, the spectators watched it slow, turn and seem to pause for a moment in midstream as the rowers steadied before the pull back downstream.

Glancing round the lounge Helen worried for a moment that their appointment had not shown. Judy had phoned her the evening before to confirm that Eileen had agreed to meet them. She and some old friends met for lunch at the clubhouse once a week - Helen and Sam were invited to arrive half an hour beforehand for a short chat. So where was she?

Helen had experienced a passing pang of concern during Judy's phone call. Immediately after Helen and Sam had left St Michael's, other visitors had arrived. Judy assured her it was quite normal. At this time of year, they could get several Templar tourists visiting the church each day, especially if the weather was good. She had not spoken to them but Jerry had commented that they did not seem to fit the normal profile, just a little more 'corporate' than usual. They hadn't stayed long at all before dashing off.

A call from across the room attracted Helen's attention. Seated at one of the window tables was an old woman. She was waving, beckoning them across.

'Over here,' she said. 'Come and join me.'

They walked quickly across to her. 'Is it Mrs Watkins?' said Helen, weighing up the old woman. She must be eighty but had the bearing of a sixty-year old.

'That's me, but please, call me Eileen.' The old lady waved a hand towards the empty seats beside her, inviting them to sit. They chatted for a while about everything and nothing, Helen and Sam ensuring the older woman had a chance to become comfortable in their presence.

Finally, it was Eileen that brought them to business. 'Now what can I do for you? It all seems very mysterious.'

Helen explained their interest in the dagger and Eileen's eyes misted for a moment.

'It seems like only yesterday that we found it. But now I think, it was over half a lifetime ago. So much has happened since those days.' She suddenly looked sad. 'So much gone.'

'I'm sorry. We hadn't planned to upset you,' said Helen.

'Oh, I'm not upset. It's just unexpected. I'm a bit taken aback, that's all.' Eileen gave a little chuckle. 'Or should that be taken back? Believe me, once you get to my age it's generally a lot more fun to look back than it is to look forward.'

'So, the dagger?' said Helen. 'Can you tell us about it please?'

'It's beautiful, solid silver I believe, though no hallmarks so it must be very old. It had a Templar cross on it, the most intricate of line patterns that made no sense to either Tom or me. Oh, and there was a number eight in Roman numerals. My husband and I often wondered what it was for, never really worked it out. Mysterious, but beautiful as well.'

Helen could hardly contain her excitement; they really had found another dagger, just like that. The thrill of this unexpected success grew in her as Sam explained to Eileen that he was an archaeologist and had also found a silver dagger with a Templar cross on it - he wondered if they could make a comparison.

Eileen's face dropped. 'I can't help you I'm afraid. I don't have it any more.'

'Oh, is it in a museum now?' said Sam.

'Sadly no. We were burgled years ago. Horrid experience. The dagger went, I'm afraid, along with so much else, the mementos of a lifetime. I think it was that incident that set poor Tom on a downward spiral. He never really got over the shock. It's the intrusion you see. We weren't harmed or anything; weren't even at home when it happened, actually. But by that time, Tom's health wasn't good anyway and I think he just felt his life had been violated, couldn't get over it. Never came to terms with it, he just started to fade away after that.'

'I'm so sorry,' said Helen. 'We've come seeking your help and dredged up only misery for you. Please, accept our apologies, if we had known how painful this would be we would have acted very differently.'

Eileen waved her protestations away. 'Hush there, you weren't to know. You certainly weren't to blame. Tom and I had a long life together. There were more than enough happy memories to wash over the bad times. I just regret I can't help you. Our dagger was a mystery that always puzzled us. I know Tom would have loved to help you understand it, if he were here.'

'What do you think happened to it?' said Sam.

'I don't know, probably melted down. That's what they do isn't it?'

'Sadly, yes, that's often the case. I don't suppose you have a picture of it by any chance? At least I could study the pattern on the blade, that's one of the common elements I'm trying to understand.'

'No. Nothing at all. These days you have your smart phones and take pictures all the time. In our day, most people bought a camera spool for the Christmas holidays and maybe one for the summer, and that was it.'

Eileen's lunch partners had started to arrive; the little group of elderly ladies were now bunching up a few steps away from the table. Realising their time was up, Helen stood and thanked Eileen, Sam followed suit. As they started to move off, the old ladies swept to the table, passing Helen and Sam in a flurry of head nods and inquisitive glances.

Disappointed, the pair left the lounge and made their way down the stairs to ground level. They paused for a moment to look through the glass exhibition wall that provided a view through to the fixed rowing machines, each set in their oars-width pools of water. Empty now but Helen could imagine the energy that would be expended by the crews when training here. They started to move on when Helen heard a voice calling from the top of the stair.

'Helen? Sam? Are you still there? Wait, I'm coming down.' Eileen's voice reached them from the top of the stair. Sam immediately turned back and Helen followed behind.

'You stay up there,' called Sam. 'Save your legs, we'll be up in a moment.'

'There's nothing wrong with my legs, young man. I've always kept in good shape. I could probably still give you a run for your money.'

Helen smiled to herself as she caught up. This feisty old lady would probably be prepared to take him on if offered the chance.

'Look, I can't linger, I'll miss my lunch, but you've created quite a stir with the girls in there. They wanted to know what it was all about. Thing is, one of my chums reminded me, there is a slight chance you could get a rough idea of what the dagger looked like.'

'Oh?' said Helen.

'Yes, now I don't know if it's still there, but the dean, you've met him I think?'

'Yes, Charles, we had coffee together yesterday morning,' said Sam.

'Good, that's him, well it's not a promise, but he's a good friend of my daughter and might just be able to help. You see, the dean is my granddaughter's godfather. Oh, that sounds a bit convoluted, and doesn't it make me sound old?'

Helen assured her it did not.

'Well I happen to know, some years back, at the time of my granddaughter's confirmation, that she made him a gift of sorts and he displayed it in his office. He promised everyone he'd treasure it forever. It was certainly still there when the ladies and I got the special behind the scenes cathedral tour seven or eight years ago, I pointed it out to them all then, in his office. Do you think that might help?'

'Well,' said Helen, patiently. 'What is it exactly?'

'Oh, how silly of me, I haven't actually told you, have I?' Eileen gave a little laugh to herself and squeezed Helen's forearm. 'Old age, it can't be helped, you know.'

'You're doing fine, Eileen, but what is it?'

'It's a brass rubbing; well, strictly I suppose it's a silver rubbing, isn't it? As I said, about the time when my granddaughter was confirmed she made a rubbing of the dagger blade and her father had it framed as a gift for the dean. I thought it wasn't in particularly good taste but I suppose it did have that little cross and everyone else seemed happy enough with it. I can't promise he still has it now but -'

'He has.' Sam cut in over her. 'I saw it yesterday over coffee. It's framed, hung on the wall beside the occasional chairs.'

'That's it, just where we saw it all that time ago. Oh, the dear man, he must really have liked it after all.'

'I knew there was something familiar in that room, but it was too vague, unexpected.' Sam had spent weeks studying the blade patterns. Couldn't believe he had not recognised it in front of him - hiding in plain sight.

Helen gave Eileen a hug. 'Thank you, Eileen. You'll never know just how happy you've made that archaeologist.'

'I'm going to phone Charles now and tell him to let you have a copy of it at once. It's not the dagger but if it's of any use to you at all, you must have access. I suggest you go over there now while I call ahead. Then I'm going to have my lunch. And while you're there Helen, take the opportunity to look at the Mappa Mundi; it's quite famous, you know.'

'Oh, I know all about it, Eileen. Sam has the guidebooks and the brochures; he spent half of last evening showing me this, that and the next thing about it. But while we're in the cathedral, maybe I will go and have a look at the original myself.'

Chapter 11

FRIDAY 16ᵀᴴ AUGUST

Sam entered the manse kitchen carrying a sheath of notes, photo prints and sketches. 'Sorry I'm late; the departmental administrator phoned and asked me to call into campus. It seems I'm the go to person until a new head of department is appointed to replace MacPherson.'

Helen smiled a greeting, now the whole gang was gathered at the kitchen table.

At the far end of the table sat Xavier, to his right hand was Angelo. As promised, the two Sardinian priests had come to Edinburgh for a Festival visit, which had now morphed into a council of war. Helen couldn't help thinking these were not the circumstances anyone expected when the visit had first been organised. In the light of recent events, the two priests' plans for a fun holiday were consigned to the dump. This was now to be only a fleeting visit - one night only. Still, Xavier's presence was welcome, both as a dear friend and for the insights his long experience could bring. Following John Dearly's death earlier in the year, Xavier was the last of the old task bearers; a dagger custodian, they needed his knowledge, Helen needed his knowledge.

To Xavier's left was Elaine. Her steady recovery ensured she was getting stronger by the day but still not moving as briskly as she once had. Next to her was Francis. Opposite Francis sat Grace, Elaine's daughter. She was keeping herself occupied by determinedly speaking to Angelo who, unusually, was joining in the conversation.

'Well, here we all are and it seems the old problem has come back too,' said Helen as Sam sat in the empty place between her and Francis. 'Everyone here knows the risks; it seems to me the only difference is the net is spreading much wider now.'

'Yes, though at least DCI Wallace thinks they will be wary of stepping out of line on his patch. He did say he had tabs on them here,' said Sam.

'Uh huh, he did. But does Wallace understand the scale of the threat we face?' she said.

Sam gave a shrug. 'Probably not, but who could?'

'My friends,' Xavier's warm and confident voice caught everyone's attention. His heavily accented speech told of his Mediterranean roots. 'My friends, it is clear that the police did not manage to bring this to a conclusion before. I don't understand why, they had the guilty men and the evidence. What is clear is that we must once again try to resolve this ourselves. It seems there is little help to be found from the authorities.' His left hand rose slightly from where it had rested on the tabletop, pushing back at Helen as she started to speak, silencing her. 'Yes, yes. I know your detective is providing support here. But how far does that protection reach? The end of your street? Your city boundary? The Scottish border?'

Xavier raised his right hand to join the left; turning both palms out towards his audience as he gave an emphatic shrug of his shoulders. 'From what Sam told me earlier, they do as they like in England. Your Wallace has no say there, no?'

'Yes,' said Sam. 'But this takes us right back to the heart of the problem. If we tell the police, we put them in the line of fire. No matter what we say, they will not be able to appreciate the scale of the danger until it's too late. Everyone who knows about this is eventually eliminated. Tell DCI Wallace and we sign his death warrant.'

Francis gave a sigh. 'Don't tell him and we leave ours on the table, signed and sealed, waiting for execution. What are our options, then, if not full disclosure to the police?'

'And let's not forget, last time around, Helen, Elaine and Grace had to withhold information from the police. If we tell now, they could well end up in jail for obstructing justice,' said Sam.

Xavier pointed at Helen. 'You and I must fulfil our obligations as task bearers; we must protect our responsibility -'

'Hold on now,' said Sam. 'We've been over this last time; Helen did not know what was involved when she took over from John Dearly. You can't force retrospective responsibility on her now.'

Xavier gave a wry smile. 'I know, I know. This we have talked about before, yes?' He let his gaze range across the group, finally settling on Helen. 'Do not forget what Sam said last time the troubles came, which we all agreed. The best protection is publicity. We solve the puzzle; then tell all the people, and then these, these Mafioso, have nothing to gain and everything to lose by staying involved. My view now is that the only protection for ourselves, and the best protection for what we hold in trust, is still to solve the puzzle and then to share it with everyone.'

'I agree,' said Helen. 'If the alternative is to let these killers snatch the prize, whatever it is, then that is not fulfilling any commitment, that's just surrender. And I'm not up for that.'

'And until the mystery is solved and made public, we are still targets,' said Elaine, her gruff voice stressing each point. 'I'm with Xavier though and we are in a better position than before. At least this time around, we know there is a threat. And will have a solution if we can solve the puzzle.' She looked at Sam. 'Over to you for that.'

'So are we all agreed to try to solve this now? Or do we run for the hills?' said Sam.

'No way,' said Grace. 'After what they did to my mum before, there's no way I'm letting anything go. Count me in.'

Helen gazed around the group. 'So if we are to solve the puzzle we all need to understand where we are today and then get thinking. Sam, sum up for us. Show us what we've got so far.'

Sam paused for a moment to collect his thoughts. 'Xavier told us earlier in the summer about Henri de Bello. He was based in the Templar preceptory at Temple. It was he who split the Templar secret into parts. He had each part engraved on to a different blade drawn from a set of nine matching daggers. The daggers were then carried away by trusted knights who scattered and hid them across Europe - we think the secret is a map, perhaps to the Templar hoard. To reassemble the message and understand its secret requires possession of all the daggers.

'The first dagger, the key, was kept hidden here in Edinburgh, in St Bernard's parish. It has a blade engraved with a list of Roman numerals, one to eight; placed in a seemingly random order, but which we think may be the order that the other eight blades must be laid in to recreate the map. It has been snatched from Helen's home in the States. So we know the number sequence and now so does our enemy.' He paused for a moment and rifled through his sheaf of papers, lifting a photograph of the stolen blade and holding it up for everyone to see.

'Are we sure it was the engraving that was important?' said Francis.

'Well, let's hope so, otherwise we're stuffed.' Sam gave a rueful grin. 'I believe it's the number sequence on the parish blade that's most important, it provides a place order for the other eight daggers. Using that we can align them all together in the correct sequence to form the message or plan, whatever it is. Other than the number sequence and Templar cross insignia, the parish dagger had no features. Each of the other daggers has its Templar cross, an individual number from the sequence and a unique section of engraved pattern too. On its own, each pattern remains quite unintelligible. And each was sent away without knowledge of where the others were going.

'We have a copy of the dagger found on the dig in Fife; it's engraved with a number three. They killed to get hold of the original. We have a photo of the one we found in the National Museum of Scotland; it has a number four. They have that now and they killed to get it too.' Sam paused. He felt Helen's hand rub gently against his forearm; some comfort, a prompt to continue.

He pressed on. 'We have the dagger from Norway and once again, they killed for it, but this time they didn't get it: that's a number five and it's sitting safe in a bank vault in Norway until Helen's Swiss banker gets it moved for us. Then we have a picture of the rubbing from Hereford cathedral, which the dean gave us, that's a number eight. And finally, we have Xavier's in Sardinia:

number seven.

'So that leaves three missing daggers. They should be numbered one, two and six. To solve the mystery we need to find those three daggers - before our enemy does. And that's where our problems really start. We don't know where to look and Xavier thinks it's highly likely one of the missing daggers is held by a task holder, just like him and Helen. Someone with the knowledge, someone who wants all the daggers, that's where our threat is coming from. Even if we did know where to go to, we might just blunder into the arms of the very people who are gunning for us. And finally, even if we did have all the daggers, it's still not exactly clear how the individual markings will fit together; we've had no luck so far in piecing together the parts of the pattern we already have.'

'Well, there you go,' said Francis. 'We'll get that lot solved by teatime, I'm sure.' He looked round the table. 'Perhaps running for the hills is a better idea. I don't see how we can solve this. Not at all.'

'Let me finish taking you all through what we have got,' said Sam. 'Then you can start to worry.' He looked at Grace. 'Could you switch the TV on please; I'll show you all the picture sequences I've tried to work on, perhaps one of you will have a better eye than I do.'

Grace stretched behind her to switch on the TV. Then as Sam worked his smart phone, she slid her chair to one side, close to Helen, allowing everyone a clear view.

Sam began to guide the group through his workings, experiments and struggles to align the blade patterns. He was not confident anything concrete had been established. After twenty minutes of show and tell, it was clear that nobody had an insight into the patterns or code.

'I think that's about it, I'm afraid,' said Sam, flicking through the remaining pictures on his phone. 'None of this is relevant.' He was about to abandon his picture show when something caught Grace's attention.

'Whoa, whoa, go back Sam,' said Grace. 'There was something there I think I know.'

Sam gave her a questioning look. 'Which one?' he asked, as he started to flick back. Everyone focused on Grace's claim, wondered what it could be.

'Back again, back again,' said Grace, prompting him to scroll faster back through the images. 'There! Stop, that's it. I don't know what it is, but I know it, I'm sure.'

Sam shook his head. On the TV screen was the photograph he had taken in the cathedral's chain library. 'No, you're mistaken, Grace. I took that in Hereford, you can't have seen it. I just thought it was interesting and Helen would be able to explain the iconography. Haven't had the chance to show her yet, that's all.'

The others looked disappointed. 'It's very beautiful, Sam, where exactly did you find it?' said Helen.

'I do know it,' said Grace, staring intently at the screen.

'It was in one of the medieval books from the chained library at Hereford. It's contemporaneous with our daggers and events,' said Sam.

'Grace is right, I know it too. Just can't place it,' said Elaine.

'Well my friends, let's not argue. Perhaps if we try to understand the picture it will help Elaine and Grace recall where they have seen it before,' said Xavier.

Sam looked doubtful. 'Look, I told you I took the photo from the back of a medieval codex at Hereford. Unless Elaine and Grace have been browsing in the cathedral library at Hereford there is no way they could have seen it before.'

'And yet, they say they know it. So, let's take a moment to think,' said the old priest, quietly.

'Be my guest, I stand ready to be corrected,' said Sam.

'Well,' said Helen, 'what exactly are we looking at?'

Francis leant forward, staring intently at the screen. 'It's a series of eight classical images. Each sits alone, like islands spread around in a circle on a wide sea-blue background and each is linked to the next by a golden vine whose tendrils reach out from the centre. I think they represent various saints. Now who have we got here? Hmmm... Some of them seem a bit obscure; some seem quite familiar. Well, there's St Michael - see, he's armed and slaying a dragon.'

'I thought it was Saint George who slew the dragon,' said Sam.

Francis did not take his eyes off the screen as he replied. 'Yes, you're quite right. Only, if you look closely, you'll see the figure in our picture has wings. That's an angel and it's the archangel Michael, who we call Saint Michael. He leads the host of heaven against the devil. Often he's depicted as slaying a serpent, which represents Lucifer.'

'Sounds like we could do with him on our side right now,' muttered Sam.

Helen nudged him. 'I'm sure he is,' she said.

Francis continued. 'Now, that's an easy one, see, top right of the screen, a woman standing beside the cross? That has to be Mary Magdalene.'

Xavier and Angelo nodded agreement.

'Okay,' said Sam,' accepting Francis' judgement. 'But opposite her you have another woman, who's that then? The Virgin Mary perhaps?'

'I don't think so; it's not the right imagery. See the gold band? That's a crown not a halo. So, it's a queen and she's dressed in white. If that image were found in Scotland and not the Welsh borders, I'd say without any doubt it was Saint Margaret, wife and queen of King Malcolm III. Anyone got another suggestion?'

'Beats me,' said Helen. 'What else have we got?'

'What about that one? The guy with three daggers?' said Grace. 'I know I've seen him before.'

'That is my church,' said Xavier. 'St Bartholomew.'

'Ah yes, agreed Francis. St Bartholomew, I see it. They are not daggers; they are skinning knives. Very nasty way to go, flayed alive, poor man. Horrible.'

'What do you mean by your church?' said Sam.

'My church is dedicated to St Bartholomew, he is our saint,' said Xavier.

'I see, but surely there must be hundreds of churches dedicated to St Bartholomew, he's not yours exclusively.'

Xavier shrugged. 'As you say: hundreds. But he is still our saint.'

'I don't care what you say and you can pull it apart all you like, but I still know this picture and I've never been to Hereford, much less in the cathedral there,' said Grace.

Helen looked away from the TV screen and smiled at Grace. 'We hear you; all we're trying to do is understand the picture. It almost certainly has nothing to do with our problem, but the Templars created it and if it really is from the same period as our own puzzle, then understanding it just might give us an insight into their thought patterns. Perhaps by understanding this picture we will get a steer on how they devised the puzzle that really is our problem. Remember, we think the Hereford mapmaker was related to the Templar up here who created the secret of the daggers and he must have used a map to plan where to hide the daggers. Maybe he even used the Mappa Mundi, who knows?'

'There's a man with an axe, I think he's on skis. What's that one all about?' said Sam.

'Beyond me,' said Francis looking round for help. Helen and Xavier shook their heads and Angelo remained silent. 'Though, that one is familiar. A robin in a tree, a fish beneath, a ring in its mouth. I would guess at St Mungo, but strange, there's no bell. Every representation of Mungo I've seen has a bell; perhaps it's not Mungo after all. And the last couple have me stumped - a book with a sword through it, and a hairy man. I've no idea.'

'Well I guess we've got enough on our plates trying to solve our own puzzle without spending any more time on this. Let's push on now,' said Sam as he flicked his phone screen to advance the pictures, settling on one of the dagger blade patterns. 'Let's have another look at this -'

'I know it, I know it,' said Grace, gripping Helen's arm in excitement. 'Go back Sam, bring the picture up again.'

Sam swiped the picture back on to his phone screen and it reappeared on the TV screen. He looked expectantly at Grace as she looked carefully at the screen, weighing her thoughts carefully. Meanwhile, Helen gently pried Grace's squeezing fingers off her arm.

'It's the church window, almost. Not quite the same, but almost.'

Elaine nodded instant agreement. 'She's right. That's where I've seen it too. Almost the same but in this photo all the plain glass is missing, filled in by the blue. Then our burning bush is replaced with that great vine spreading out to loop round each of the cameos.'

'I think you might be right,' said Sam, trying to recall the stained glass montage he had studied just a few days before.

'She's right, for sure,' said Elaine.

'We must go and see,' said Xavier. 'If this is the same, then the picture Sam took in Hereford Cathedral is linked to the church here.'

• • •

With a groan, Eileen Watkins stirred in her armchair. It offered her a lovely view out through the open French windows and across the gardens to the bottom of her lawn where the Wye ran gently past, glistening in the early evening sun. It should have been perfect, but it wasn't.

Eileen had decided on just a cup of tea and a couple of crackers for her evening meal. The cup sat upended on the carpet where she had dropped it; the crackers lay all broken and crumbed on the floor nearby. Sitting on the sofa was an intruder; he was lounging back and smiling serenely at her, at ease as though this were his own place.

She was in awful pain, didn't want to acknowledge the man's presence, but she could not help but turn her eyes to glance again at the madman. Just like the people searching upstairs, he was dressed from head to toe in a white disposable forensic suit. She glanced away quickly, desperate to avoid any eye contact with the man. Too late, he had spotted her glance.

From upstairs came the sounds of searching. Rough uncaring sounds, smashing ceramics, tearing cloth, breaking furniture. She didn't know what time it was, just knew she had passed out for a while and knew she was on her own. Nobody would miss her tonight. Her children all lived independent lives; they would not expect any contact with her until Sunday.

'Good, I see you're awake again.' Cassiter crossed the room to where Eileen was tied into her armchair. He stood behind her; she felt the fingers of his hand slide through the soft silver grey hair on the crown of her head. She flinched and jerked away and his fingers tracked her movement, maintaining contact, ensuring she understood where control lay.

Eileen had been unconscious for the best part of an hour. Now revived, she shook as his hand slipped onto her shoulder and tracked down her arm. The hand's journey paused, stopped at the elbow. Or she thought it did, below that point was a wall of pain that dominated everything else. Nervously, she glanced down at her hands, immediately shut her eyes in horror. What had once been elegant fingers that had danced across piano keys were now twisted and deformed like broken stumps in a storm-ravaged forest. Eileen moaned quietly.

'Now, tell me again Eileen,' said the voice behind her. 'I don't understand.' The voice fell silent. There was a thump in the room above as a wardrobe crashed over on its side, then the sounds of kicking and the splintering of wood. Every possible hiding place was being explored.

'I told you, I don't have a dagger. It was stolen from us years ago. It's not here. Why are you doing this to me? Please stop. I can't take it anymore.'

'And I can't understand why you would be so careless with such a valuable piece, it's just not plausible.'

'I told you, I told you everything. My husband didn't know it was important. It was an interesting novelty, that's all.'

'And yet the churchwoman and her friend who you met yesterday left you very happy; smiles on their little faces. They would not have been happy if you had told them the dagger was stolen. So what aren't you telling me? Why were they looking so pleased?'

In despair, Eileen searched for some reason, anything that would make the monster go away. 'I don't know. I don't know. How can I tell you what I don't know? Please...'

Cassiter let her arm go and stepped round from behind the chair, moved closer to the French windows. Now he was just a black silhouette.

'What a lovely view you have here, Eileen. My own home looks out over water. Very calming, don't you agree? It certainly helps me think.' He paused for a moment, as the banging sounds from above peaked.

Then, as the sound dropped again, he continued. 'Eileen, I like to think I'm a reasonable man. If you can't tell me where the dagger is, tell me why those two seemed happy that there was no dagger to be had. If I'm content with what you say, fine. If not, well, I'm not always so reasonable.'

'I don't know, I just don't know.' Eileen sobbed. 'They were

disappointed that the dagger was stolen, but not desolate. Not...
maddened. They seemed more than happy with just getting access
to the rubbing. That's all I know.'

'The what?'

'The rubbing, it's a reproduction of the pattern on the blade, like
a picture. They really didn't care about the dagger going. I promise
you.'

'And what is this pattern for?'

'I don't know, but it was what they wanted, not the dagger. I'm
certain of that.'

Cassiter stepped out through the French windows into the still
evening air. Interesting, it was the information on the blade that was
important, not the blade itself; another little snippet that Parsol had
omitted to mention or perhaps he didn't know either. Now, it was
time for action.

He stepped back into the living room. 'Tell me Eileen. One
chance, one chance only or I'm going to be very bad to you. Where
is this rubbing?'

'It's framed, hanging on the wall in the dean's office in the
cathedral. You can't miss it,' Eileen could hold nothing back. Then
she was aware of the presence of a second person beside her, a
young woman - tall and beautiful with long dark hair. For a moment
she felt a surge of relief, she would surely help her. The moment
vanished as the young woman pulled a clear plastic bag over Eileen's
head and tied the handles tight at her throat.

Through the plastic film, Eileen saw the young woman step back
to stand beside the man. She saw them watching the bag inflate and
collapse with her breath, watching her struggling body arch against
its constraints. She knew they heard her little cries, gasps and the
persistent echoey whimpering. Steadily, the inflations slowed, the
bag settled then stopped and Eileen fell silent.

In her dying moment, she saw Cassiter's nodded approval, and
heard his words as she slipped away. 'Get the boys downstairs now.
Burn this place; I don't want anything left standing come morning.
Then we're going to evensong at the cathedral.'

• • •

They all stood in silence, staring up at the great window behind the communion table - then referring back to Sam's phone, then back to the window. Finally, everyone agreed; subject to a few specific differences, it was the same image. Where the photograph had a rich blue background, the church image contained clear, plain glass. Where the church image had a simple burning bush as the centrepiece, the book had a rich golden vine that spread out from the centre, heavy laden with fruit, its tendrils reaching out through the blue to link and bind the other eight images together like some jewelled necklace. For the rest of the imagery, it was as close a likeness as could be hoped for; the same images placed in the same positions within both compositions. To all intents and purposes they were the same.

'So, have I got this right? We recognise St Michael, St Bartholomew and Mary Magdalene. Then, those two might be St Margaret and St Mungo - we're not quite sure. And there are three images we don't recognise at all,' said Sam. His arm pointed up towards the great window selecting images in turn. 'That's one, the hairy guy with two beards. The skiing axe man, and over there, the book with a sword through it. And each cameo occupies the same position in both the glass and photo versions. Everyone agree?'

Sam looked round; it was clear all agreed.

'Well done, Grace, you too, Elaine. I don't think I would ever have noticed this connection,' said Helen.

Sam stepped back a little. 'With your permission, Elaine, I'm going to photograph the glass. On Monday I want to take the problem down to the university's theology people, see if they can shed some light on the three we don't recognise and on the wider issue.'

'Good idea,' said Francis. 'Though, it's a bit embarrassing that between Xavier, Helen, Angelo and myself, we four clerics can't identify them all. I suppose the best we can hope for is that with enough clues we will eventually get a breakthrough. Though I don't understand what the picture was doing in Hereford.'

'I wonder if the Hereford picture was a backup, a failsafe in case things went wrong for the Templars here in Edinburgh where our message was stored,' said Helen.

'Could be, or the window could be derived from the picture. And backup for what? Either way, we've now got several dagger blades engraved with what might be strips of a map or plan that we can't decipher, and on top of that a set of pictures, which we don't understand. It's not getting any easier. This is going to be tricky to resolve,' said Sam.

'To say nothing of the killers resurfacing,' said Helen.

'Well whatever else we need to think about, don't forget we have a night out planned for this evening,' said Francis. His role as the social organiser had long been accepted and his network of contacts always managed to identify the hottest shows. Having a parishioner who worked in the Festival Fringe booking office also helped, ensuring he got priority for tickets. 'We will all need to get ready now. Don't forget I've booked an early table so we can eat in good time for the first show.'

They were determined to make a good night of it. Xavier and Angelo would return to Sardinia in the morning. With all the trouble brewing again and his church's saint's day feast coming up soon, Xavier had decided to return to his parish to consider their problems without distraction and to oversee preparations for his church's festival. Tonight was a chance to put their worries aside, if only for a couple of hours.

Chapter 12

MONDAY 19TH AUGUST

It was already a good while after nine and the rush hour had subsided. Sam's walk into the city centre had taken him past several of the council's street cleaning squads. They were working overtime to clear up the Festival's litter before tourists and performers started to emerge for another round of festivities. Every now and then, he would pass sheepish looking individuals heading home, eyes down and bedraggled, still in last evening's glad rags; the walk of shame.

Pausing on the Mound for a minute, he took in the scene before turning towards New College, the University's school of divinity. Built on the Mound, it both enjoyed the views across the New Town and was part of the imposing vista for those gazing back up to the Old Town.

Exactly on time, Sam tapped on Sandi McLellan's door. She called him in and greeted him warmly. They had never met but each knew of the other's reputation and she was happy to help. Greetings and formalities over, she listened carefully to Sam's puzzle, jotting notes as he spoke. Then she closed the blind to throw her office into shadow and switched on an interactive wall screen. She plugged Sam's USB stick into her computer and tapped in a key sequence. The display screen suddenly projected Sam's photographs of the Hereford codex and the church window, side by side.

Sandi McLellan sat in silence for several minutes while studying the pictures.

'Now then, Sam, this is quite a puzzle you've set me. I agree with what your friends suggested in explanation, as far as they went. Some other things are worthy of comment though.

'Firstly, it's clear both images contain the same set of characters. I can understand why one or two might have been a little hard to identify, but I think I've sorted it for you.'

'That's great. I'm not sure what to make of it all. Any pointers you can give would be gratefully received. And it all seems quite violent, lots of weapons, not like the Church we know.'

'Well, times change, but these messages remain consistent. Your three completely unidentified images first. I can confirm they do all represent saints.'

'Even the image without a person in it?'

'Oh, yes. Look, let's take that one. It's a fairly hefty sword piercing the bible. It's actually quite straightforward. It represents St Boniface, or perhaps we could say the killing of St Boniface. The saint can be in the image too, his absence might have thrown your friends a little. Interestingly he is considered to be an English saint but did all his spiritual work in Europe. Our saint was evangelising to the Franks when he died. You know they were in Belgium, Northern France, parts of Germany. A big tribe, very important for Christianity's early development in Europe.'

'How did he die?' said Sam.

'Good question and that informs the imagery. It happened when he and a group of followers were hosting a conversion meeting. Unfortunately for Boniface, a bunch of robbers turned up instead of the potential converts. The robbers killed him and opened his strong box to take the expected gold. They were very disappointed to find it contained only holy books. So in a fit of anger they stabbed the books, killed them. Hence the imagery.'

'I see; does it have any particular relevance to the Templars?'

'None that I'm aware of. In fact, I have to say, if you had not told me that one of the images came from a medieval book of Templar records and works, I would not have made any connection with the Templars at all.'

'Oh. For none of it?'

'None at all. Now let me address these other two images. It's not really surprising that your friends couldn't identify these. They're not very prominent at all from a modern British perspective. You've got the big pious looking man on skis and carrying a battle-axe, simple when you know, impossible if you don't. That's Saint Olaf. One time king, he helped to establish Christianity in the north. The axe, well that is the land of the Vikings and they were still pretty warlike during his day. Again, no Templar link there either. He'd be based in Norway, as king, Oslo perhaps.

'Now this last one is harder. There are only two clues. He's holding a book, which can indicate thinking or knowledge but there was a lot of that. It's the second clue that really helps, look at the man's face. See the split beard? That combined with the book takes us straight to St Athanasius.' She looked at Sam expectantly.

'Never heard of that one, I'm afraid,' said Sam.

'No, he's bigger in the east though.'

'East?'

'The Eastern Church. He's more popular with the Orthodox churches really. Of course, he was bishop of Alexandria, so that's his part of the world.'

'Could there be a link with the crusades then? At least that's getting us closer to Templar country.'

'Not that I can see, Athanasius lived long before that period. He spent much of his life falling out with Roman emperors.'

'Can you see anything that links the images together?'

Sandi shook her head. 'Sorry, they are clearly all quite early saints but there is no obvious linkage. In fact, we might say they are determinedly distinct. And again, nothing Templarish at all.'

Sam stood, stretched out his hand. 'Sandi, thanks for your time. At least we can understand what each part of the image represents now.'

Sandi avoided Sam's hand, pushing her own palm out in a stop sign. 'Whoa there, mister, not so fast. Sorry I can't find the deeper meaning for you, if there is one, but we haven't considered the chicken and the egg yet.'

'Chicken and egg?' asked Sam.

'Which comes first - the chicken or the egg?' Sandi's arm swept in an arc between the two pictures projected on her wall screen.

'Chicken, egg. Egg, chicken.'

'You think you might have something for me?'

'I can't comment on any Templar links, can't see anything to do with the Templars at all, though you seem to have taken that one for a given, so I won't debate it further.' Sandi turned back to the screen.

'Now, we can both recognise the common content within the two images but here's a puzzle. You've got St Margaret, I do agree with that ID, by the way, Oh, and St Mungo too. Both as Scots as you like. However, if we accept the date as early fourteenth century then it's unlikely that St Margaret would have been included as a key image in an English or Welsh work. So I think her inclusion almost certainly moves the place of conception north, probably to Scotland. So the Hereford codex picture is replicating the original glass imagery.

'Then things get trickier. Why the differences? Look at the beautiful colouring in your codex picture; see the rich blue background, the golden vine, heavy fruited, luxuriant foliage. Contrast that with the austere plain glass and the fiery burning bush isolated in the middle of the glass.'

'Yes, I see they don't seem to sit so well together.'

'And why? I guess that our shared history has got in the way.' She glanced at the table, taking a moment to refer back to her scribbled notes. 'The church that the window is in today has been rebuilt in the past and the glass transferred to it from the earlier manifestation. Something over two hundred years ago you indicated.' She watched for Sam's agreement.

'Yes, and it was rebuilt in pretty much the same spot as far as I understand,' said Sam.

'That would put us in the late eighteenth century. I'm afraid it doesn't quite fit. You're out a hundred years and more.'

'What, how can that be?' asked Sam.

'Scotland during the mid-part of the seventeenth century was in the grip of the covenanter conflict, a war between King Charles on the one hand and the Scottish Presbyterian Church on the other. Charles was all bishops, pomp and circumstance; the Scottish Presbyterians were altogether more austere in their approach to religious worship. I guess we would refer to them in the modern vernacular as being very hard core. I know you know the history of the war so I can leave that.'

'Yes, I know it well enough,' said Sam.

'So you will recognise that any seventeenth century Scottish church with ornate and colourful glass decoration like the codex picture would have been trashed, possibly burnt to the ground.'

'Of course. I've been so close to the problem I couldn't see the obvious.'

'Exactly. The original church glass may well have been the same as your picture from the codex. But it's almost certain somebody removed the glass from display in the original church at some point during the seventeenth century, perhaps even earlier, to protect it from the righteous wrath of the covenanters.'

'And come the rebuild of the church during the eighteenth century, Scotland is a more tolerant society, with the Scottish Enlightenment and so on,' said Sam.

Sandi smiled an agreement. 'And the glass is reinstated. Though the term tolerant is relative. An easing of the national mood did not mean acceptance of all the English frippery, certainly no gloss or pomp and absolutely no rich serpenty fruit laden vines. I think when they restored the glass to its place on display in the new built church some editing was done. All the blue background is replaced with plain clear glass: much more Scottish. The rich golden vine goes and is replaced by a harsher, more austere, burning bush.'

'You know I think that can explain the difference between the images. It certainly makes sense. The starker imagery would be more palatable to the community at that time,' said Sam.

'That's good, I'm glad I've been able to cast a little light on the image for you. Now, going back to your assumption they are both Templar productions, I have to stress again, there is absolutely no evidence in the image itself to support your assumption.'

'The picture from the codex in the chain library at Hereford was a Templar source.'

'I'll take your word for that. But the image itself contains nothing. I don't know what you are searching for but you'll need to look elsewhere for the clue I'm afraid.' Sandi flicked off the wall screen, a signal to Sam that she had other things to do. 'And do feel free to get back to me if you find anything else that you want me to look at. Perhaps you'll find your link elsewhere.'

Sam smiled at her and made for her office door. 'Well, thanks for your time. I really appreciate your help. I'm going straight over to St Bernard's now. In the light of your explanation I want to have a closer look at the glasswork.'

'Sam, wait! Where are you going?'

Sam paused and turned back. 'St Bernard's, where the glass is displayed.'

'Oh, Sam, Sam, Sam.' Sandi shook her finger at him, chiding him. 'Sam, why didn't you say it was from a church called St Bernard's?'

'You know it?' said Sam.

'Not particularly. Just by name. But Sam, that's not the point. If you're looking for a Templar link, that's it.'

'St Bernard's?'

'Yes, of course.' She gave him a little smile of triumph. 'St Bernard was involved in conforming and defining the role of the Knights Templar.' She stopped speaking for a moment and stooped over her keyboard to do a quick computer search.

Sam joined her, keen to see what she was looking for. 'Why wouldn't anyone else have made the link between St Bernard and the Templars?'

'Why would anyone think to? St Bernard is not one of your fashionable saints and, let's face it, the Templars have been out of the loop for a very long time. Only people like me would know to make the link. And only then if prompted to do so.' Sandi paused to review a page. 'Here you are, St Bernard, very big in the twelfth century; pious, Godly and the arch mediator. But most importantly for you, he participated in the Council of Troyes, which establishes the role of the Templars. If you are searching for a Templar connection, you already have it. It's St Bernard.'

She stood and smiled at Sam. His grin in return confirmed she had delivered the goods.

• • •

Flanked by two of his team, Cassiter stepped out of the arrivals zone and into the public reception area. He crossed to the exit, passed by the taxi and bus lanes and made for the public car park. He did not have to wait. Even as he exited Torp Airport's doors, a black 4x4 was manoeuvring through the car park; it halted next to him. Cassiter and his men got into the car and it pulled away, heading directly for Sandefjord.

He had decided to take personal control of business in Norway. His contacts from Oslo were good but now he understood that there was something more to these blades than a rich man's whim, he wanted to oversee this collection personally. Their little informer from inside the bank had confirmed the dagger was still there. Unfortunately, the man was too junior to get access but the information he had supplied was useful.

Today he would survey the situation. Tomorrow they would act.

He thought about Collette again. His French office had been right. Collette had real talent. A good operative and, importantly, a face unknown in Edinburgh. She had slipped into the city unnoticed. Now she could do some work there without any risk of it being traced back to him.

• • •

Collette leant back against the wrought iron rails fixed beside the pavement opposite the entrance to New College. Behind her, and far below, at the foot of the Mound were the imposing National Gallery of Scotland and the rocket shaped monument to Sir Walter Scott, thrusting skyward. Beyond them, the line of Princes Street stretched out in either direction and the distant rooftops of the city dropped away towards the port of Leith and the silver shining waters of the Firth of Forth. Collette was interested in none of it.

She watched the archway entrance into New College and through it the quadrangle, dominated by the glowering statue of John Knox. Suddenly, past the fiery reformer walked Sam, emerging from the archway to look cheerfully at little groups of tourists - a vanguard of the horde that would soon be appearing on the streets. Then he turned and headed briskly away towards the Old Town.

Crossing the road, she hurried under the entrance archway and through the quadrangle. She ignored Knox's frown as she passed his statue, and entered the college's reception area. Collette made no attempt to evade security cameras; her initial reconnaissance had told her there were none. In protecting the façade of the historic building the authorities had given her a free pass to roam.

'Hi there,' she said, flustered, allowing the French in her accent to flourish, hinting at some possible language confusion. 'Look, sorry, I'm late for a meeting. My boss asked me to join him here. His name's Sam Cameron. The meeting must have started now, but I haven't a clue who he had arranged it with. Could you help? Parking was awful.'

The middle-aged man behind the reception desk had noted her stunning figure as she entered. Collette could do no wrong. 'I know; parking can be hell at this time of year. Where did you get parked in the end?'

'Down behind Waverley Station, it's a bit of a climb up the hill.'

'Tell me about it,' he said looking at the meeting list. Then he referred to the visitor book. 'I'm sorry, he's been and gone. The meeting's over.'

The young woman frowned. 'Oh, zut. Sam's going to be annoyed with me. Look, could you at least let me know who he was meeting? I'll be able to send them an email and apologise. That'll placate my boss a bit.'

Nodding, the man jotted down Sandi's name and email address on a notelet, then passed it over the counter.

Collette left, content that her next move would be equally as easy - there were no internal cameras either.

• • •

Sam hung up the phone and looked across the manse kitchen to Helen. She was watching him, realising that bad news had come again.

'Well?' she said.

'That was Charles, the dean from Hereford. Eileen Watkins' home was burnt down. She's dead.'

'Oh, Heaven, no,' Helen felt a burst of sadness sweep over her. 'That's awful; she was such a lovely old lady - so much life. It's tragic, I can't believe it.'

Sam shook his head. 'You don't understand. The fire brigade are investigating; it was no accident. The house burnt down during

Friday evening, when we were all out having fun. She was dead before the fire started. Foul play, I'm afraid.'

'What? Oh, Sam, we triggered this didn't we. That poor old woman, she wouldn't have had a chance against that lot.'

'We don't know for sure yet,' said Sam.

'Oh, we do.'

'There's more. The dean mentioned an odd thing. The framed rubbing on his office wall that we took a photograph of, it's vanished. It just wasn't there when he went to work this morning. He hasn't linked the two events.'

'But we can. They've made her talk and then taken the rubbing. And her life was just so much nothing to be tossed aside. Sam! We've got to stop them. This isn't just criminality, it's pure heartless evil.'

Sam gave Helen a hug, held her for a moment then pulled back. 'The dean said her husband's former church is going to hold a little service tomorrow to allow people to express their grief. The vicar, Jerry, has issued an open invitation to all.'

'I would love to go, but I'm not sure there's enough time for us to travel down for tomorrow and I'm not so sure it's appropriate, knowing what we do about the cause.'

Sam headed for the fridge. Experience told him that Helen would welcome a glass of wine. He didn't bother asking, just poured the rosé.

'I'll send flowers though. It's the least we can do... Thanks,' said Helen, taking the proffered glass of wine. 'I'll send the flowers to Judy; she can put them in the church in time for the service. I don't have the postal address but it's St Michael's, the florist in Hereford will be able to locate it easily enough.'

'What was that you said?'

'Flowers, for the service. You do agree don't you?'

'What? Flowers, oh yes, of course, let's do that. But Helen, what else did you say?'

'I don't know. Let's not start playing guessing games right now Sam. An old woman has just died, and we probably set her up.'

Sam grimaced. 'I know. I feel bad about it too. Sick, in fact. But I think you just broke part of the puzzle.'

'I did? What did I do?'

'You said, *it's St Michael's, the florist in Hereford will be able to locate it easily enough.*'

'So?'

'Look, churches, holy places, they don't need addresses; the names mark them out. Remember the coincidence of Xavier's church's saint, St Boniface, being represented in your glass window and in the picture from the Hereford codex too. Now we find another coincidence with St Michael's in Garway, St Michael features in the window, Garway hosted a dagger. Could the images in the window represent addresses of particular churches?'

Helen thought carefully, took another mouthful of wine. She looked across at Sam. 'It could be. It really could. This might be the break we are looking for. But how can we cross check the idea?' She waved the empty wine glass in the direction of the fridge. Sam headed over to get her a refill.

'We can't cross refer to St Bernard's. There's no image for this church in the pictures,' she said.

'And we don't know for sure where the dunes dagger was destined for nor exactly what the church link was with the museum dagger; that link was broken too long ago. I tell you what though, Helen. It should be possible to find out the name of the church in Norway - the Oslo church where Erling Karlsen's uncle preached. If the saints represent the addresses of the churches, then his dead uncle's church will feature as a saint in our window. I would guess it would almost certainly be St Olaf. What do you think?'

Helen accepted the refilled wine glass. 'Thanks. You know, I think we could just have cracked it, let's check. Oh, no. You get on the web and check the Norwegian church name, I'm going to organise those flowers for Eileen's memorial service.'

It took Sam only minutes to confirm the name of the Oslo church. He gave Helen a thumbs up; it was St Olaf's. She nodded an acknowledgement while completing her telephone flower order, all the while feeling more confident about their address theory - the florist knew exactly where St Michael's church was.

Sam pulled out his mobile phone and made a call; he heard the ring tone break as the call was answered.

'Hello, Sandi speaking.'

'Oh great, I've caught you, it's Sam here.'

'I know. The funny thing is I was meaning to give you a call just now. I've been giving a bit of thought to your little puzzle.'

'Well, that's exactly what I'm calling about. I wanted to sound you out on an idea. We think the individual saints in the illustrations might actually represent specific churches, scattered here and there but linked by the picture.'

'Well, you could only know that if you knew which particular churches the pictures linked with,' said Sandi. 'Otherwise you're faced with a huge elimination problem. Lots of churches are named after any particular saint, and are scattered at random all over the Christian world.'

'I know that, but nonetheless, I think we might have spotted two or three that fitted the bill.'

'I see, Sam, that's very impressive, which ones?'

'Well that's not the problem. If the theory is to stand up, St Bernard needs to feature in the imagery and as you've already established he's not in the frame.'

'Ha, very droll, Sam. But I think you're wrong. What you say fits in quite well with my thoughts, which is why I was about to phone you. You see, and let's run with your idea of a hidden list of churches for a moment; if it were a secret, overtly sticking an image of St Bernard in the middle of the glass would make it all too obvious. However, if you were to hide St Bernard inside the puzzle then only those in the know would even realise the other images represented a message or code to unravel.'

'Yes,' said Sam. 'But where is St Bernard? We can't see him anywhere. I don't see how he features.'

'Oh ye of little faith.' Sandi chuckled to herself. 'Sam, that's why you came to me in the first place, this is my area. Trust me, if you think it's a cluster or gathering of churches, I can show you St Bernard. Have you got the pictures there?'

'Yes, in front of me now,' said Sam sitting himself at the table and pulling two printouts into position in front of him. Helen had finished ordering flowers and joined him at the table. He flicked his handset to speaker mode. 'I've put you on speaker, Sandi. Helen Johnson is with me.'

'Right, nice to speak with you, Helen.'

'You too, Sandi. Go right ahead.'

'Sam was just telling me you suspect that the images represent a cluster of specific churches, each identified by its saint's name, well that would be very exciting. Quite separately, I had been thinking a bit more about St Bernard today. If we accept the premise that he was meant to be concealed in the picture - hidden in plain sight as it were - then the imagery used is actually quite clever.'

'How so?' said Sam.

'Take a look at the codex picture first, which we believe to be a full likeness of the original window. Clearly, this predates the covenanter period, which was when Scottish austerity came to dominance and we think the glass was changed, ditching golden vines and blue seas for a burning bush and plain glass. So, even though I would contend the original imagery was formed in Scotland, I think that today the picture from the Hereford codex better represents the original drafting. The vine is set at the centre, see how its tendrils stretch out reaching to touch each of the other images, wraps round them and then seem to grow further stretching out to link each saint to the next. See, it's not just a radial pattern reaching out from the centre to link with each saint. It's transverse too, creating a perfectly linked network originating from the centre, the hub.

'Yes, we've got that already, but it only works if we can put St Bernard in the image. But he's not in the glass,' said Sam.

'Hmmm, well it's a bit of a leap, needed a bit of digging, but our St Bernard was a man of many parts. Not content with being the spiritual architect of the Templars, I did mention that earlier, he fulfilled a further role for various bishops and even popes. Much of his time was devoted to travelling across the continent reaching out here and there, brokering agreements and drawing disparate groups together. Building a network of related parties. If you wanted to hide St Bernard in your tableau but still show his role to those in the know, I suggest that the vine or *network* would capture that role just about perfectly.

'It reaches out to other places, links up, binds together; trusted with the secrets of others, brokering settlements - yes, the vine's your man. Add in the gold colouring and heavy-laden fruits, which some might read as luxuriant and wealthy, while others might read as smart and highly valued. I'd go for the latter myself by the way.'

She stopped and listened into the silence.

'That is interesting,' said Helen. 'I can follow your reasoning. Can see how that all comes together really well, certainly fits our concept perfectly. But Sandi, what about the burning bush, how does that fit in?'

'Yes this is where the image changes. Remember, I would guess that the original glasswork was removed completely and hidden during or even a bit before the Covenanter period. Otherwise I suspect that it would have been destroyed as idolatrous or popish or some such. Whoever reinstated it, and you're indicating that happened when the church was rebuilt during the eighteenth century, would have had to temper the imagery. Even then, the original would have been too rich an image to be tolerated. I think the bare minimum was included. Hence, the blue glass goes, the golden vine vanishes.

'So, a burning bush in place of the golden vine. The connotations don't align perfectly, but if somebody was trying to recreate a message, using less contentious imagery, then the burning bush was a good idea at a time when colourful thoughts were liable to suppression. Old Testament fire and brimstone, that suited the austere approach of the time, probably still does in fact. Then you pay your money and you take your choice. God speaking to Moses from within the burning bush has been interpreted in several ways. But one option that might fit your story is the idea that Moses, the leader of the chosen people, is being sent out from there to free the people, or perhaps to gather them in. What do you think?'

Sam and Helen eyed each other silently. There was potential in Sandi's line of thinking, a great deal of potential, but they didn't want to drag her into the mix.

'Sandi, I think that's really interesting, something for us to work on,' said Sam. 'Thank you for your time. We really appreciate it.'

'No problem, Sam. Thanks for bringing it to me. It was fun to think about something a bit different. If it really is a code and you need a bit more expert help, then you know where to find me.'

'Thanks from me too,' said Helen. 'You put me to shame; perhaps I should have paid a bit more attention at theology college.'

'No problem, and don't feel bad. Some of this stuff is pretty esoteric. It's not your everyday material.'

'Thanks, but Sandi, just to be on the safe side, be a bit careful. There are people around who seem very interested in our puzzle. And they're not so nice,' said Sam.

'Oh, don't worry about me, I can look after myself,' said Sandi as she hung up.

Helen gave Sam a look that morphed into a smile. 'Well, is this progress?'

'It is. Well actually, perhaps not so much progress, more a second puzzle.'

'What do you mean?'

'Well, first, we believe the daggers represent a map or message. We don't know of what and can only put it together once we've gathered them all in. Agreed?'

'Agreed.'

'Second, we now think the church window, which is also repeated in the codex from Hereford, represents a list of churches.' Sam paused and watched for her agreement.

Helen nodded.

'But we don't know where the churches are. For instance, across Europe how many Mary Magdalene churches do you think there are? Hundreds, perhaps thousands. I don't know. So, to find the missing daggers we have to find the correct churches and we don't have the slightest idea where to look for the churches concerned. It's still a needle in a haystack. Though, granted, maybe now we know which haystacks to search. I can't help feeling we're still missing something else; we're not seeing the whole picture. I'm going to need to sleep on it. In the meantime I think I'll give Xavier a call and keep him posted - Francis and Elaine too. Everyone needs to be up to speed and this is a new perspective.'

'Okay, you do that. I said I would phone home and see how everyone's doing there,' said Helen.

• • •

Lying on the floor of the cleaning store was a woman. Her face quite tranquil, only a slight speck of blood showed on the front of her tabard to signal where the slimmest of knives had slipped under her ribcage and pierced her heart. At that moment, she had felt nothing but surprise as Collette pressed the steel into her body; she would feel nothing ever again.

Now dressed with a similar coloured tabard, Collette pushed the cleaner's trolley along a corridor and parked it next to a lift entrance. Taking a brush and duster, she set off to search for Sandi McLellan's room. Moving steadily along a wood panelled corridor, she allowed the brush to sweep across the black and white flooring. Suddenly she stopped, furious: tucked up high in a corner was a security camera. That has to be dealt with she thought.

At that moment, there was a bustle behind her as a little crowd of visitors made their way into the broad black and white tiled corridor and on towards the performance space; The Church of Scotland's Assembly Hall, which linked directly to New College, was a Festival venue, hosting evening events. The cleaner did not register in the consciousness of the passing crowd and she was effectively invisible as she retreated out of the corridor.

A little while later, Collette smiled to herself. In spite of the inconvenience of the camera, this was no big challenge. By keeping the building open into the evening, the management might just as well have handed her the alarm codes. She paused outside a door marked Sandi McClellan. This should not take too long; her computer records for the day would quickly reveal whatever she was working on with Sam Cameron.

The door was locked and she used the cleaner's passkey. Once in, she powered up the computer and broke the code to search the day's activity. There was a new folder named Sam Cameron, which she copied. Then she searched the office carefully - cupboard by cupboard, drawer by drawer, everything, everywhere. She unearthed printouts of the computer images, saw they had notes jotted here and there across them, they all went into her pocket.

Search over, she rolled her trolley out into the corridor, locked the office and took the lift down, headed back for the cleaning store to deposit the trolley beside its owner and then jam the door locked. No one would find the cleaner until next day at the earliest. By which time she would be long gone.

She had one final task to do before leaving; the CCTV camera recording from the black and white corridor had to be deleted.

Having picked up a floor plan on her travels, she knew now

where she needed to go. Moving quietly through the building, she reached a balcony from where she could look down on to the reception. Behind the reception desk sat her target, a man. Then she saw a second man standing beside the desk. From the men's direction of gaze and the mix of quiet voices reaching her she could tell there was at least one other standing out of her line of sight.

There must be extra staff on duty tonight for the Festival. She was good but she did not think she could take out the three men without risking an alarm being raised. Anyway, right now, festival goers were buzzing to and fro in the quad outside the reception windows - there was no privacy for her to work in. For now, she just could not access the recording. Thinking a curse, she eased back from the balcony and retraced her steps, using the cleaner's swipe card to let herself out of another exit at the rear of the building.

She would try to get to the recording through the university's computer network - but this building seemed such a security backwater, she just hoped that it wasn't an isolated recording device. If it was, she might have an access problem.

Chapter 13

TUESDAY 17ᵀᴴ AUGUST

The early morning air was crisp and salty clean, the tide was out - it was Oskar's favourite time for running. The stretch of recently exposed sand in front of his home was just about perfect for his fitness regime; much better than the rocky run he had to make inland on those mornings when high tides came early in the day.

He'd studied hard, worked hard; reckoned he deserved the rewards his efforts had brought him. He was a happy man running in what seemed a deserted world - though not completely empty. He knew that at this moment Ida, his wife, would be in the kitchen of the house that stood in splendid isolation at the head of the inlet. She would have just put the coffee on, may even now be watching him from the window before going to get their little Magnus up and ready for the day.

In just a few minutes, Oskar would be showered and eating breakfast; ready to share the start of the day with his perfect family in their perfect home. Ida had inherited the house and land around the inlet. That was their good fortune. But they could afford to live there because of his hard work and her willingness to pitch in with whatever was needed.

Heading for home, Oskar ran past their private jetty that stretched out over the now exposed sand. At the jetty's head was his little leisure boat, still just afloat, tugging gently on its moorings, catching the last pull of the ebbing tide.

He kicked off his training shoes in the back porch and stepped into the kitchen, there pausing to drink from the glass of fresh orange juice Ida had left on the table for him. He put the empty glass down, placed his mobile phone beside it. Then he headed on towards the shower. As he stepped into the shower, he thought Magnus was being particularly quiet this morning; then the silence disappeared under a rush of water.

A few minutes later Oskar entered the kitchen, tying his tie and calling out for his son - nothing, just silence. He wondered what was keeping Ida. She and Magnus were always in the kitchen by the time he'd showered. The food was laid on the table and coffee ready. He poured himself a mug, took a sip and wandered along the corridor to his son's room. Still silence. As he approached the room a little tingle of concern ran down his back, there was no reason to worry but it didn't seem right.

The room was empty. Oskar turned to check the living room, nothing, still silence. Now he was worried, it was inexplicable. Where had his family gone? He called out, no reply. He shouted again and again, running from room to room. Silent emptiness; worry turned to anxiety and then to fear. Where were they? Back in the kitchen he looked again at the table, it was laid and the coffee hot. His wife and child must be here; must have been here only moments before. Then he noticed his phone was not where he had put it, and something unusual caught his attention on the table. It was a note. Had that been there when he stopped for orange juice? He didn't think so.

Snatching up the note, he scanned it quickly, didn't recognise the handwriting and didn't understand the message. His brow furrowed as he tried to make sense of it; he followed the written instruction, hurrying to the kitchen window and looking out and down across the beach to the jetty. He gasped in fear and anger. There were people on the jetty and with them, Ida and Magnus. Pulling his shoes on, he sprinted for the beach.

Standing at the start of the jetty were two men, big and mean looking. A few steps further along the jetty was a nondescript man, Oskar scarcely registered them; it was what he saw at the jetty's head that consumed him. Ida was kneeling, her hands tied. A man's hand had a tight grip on his wife's collar, holding it firm and preventing her from rising to her feet. The other hand held the black threat of a pistol that pressed against his wife's skull.

He could see his wife was shaking her head, looking up, mouthing words towards another man who towered over them all. Oskar knew his wife was pleading, begging. The towering man was huge, a troll; in one hand he held little Magnus up high while watching Oskar's approach.

As Oskar neared the jetty, he screamed in anger and redoubled his speed. The two big men braced themselves and broke his charge. As he struggled valiantly to get past them, the nondescript man raised his hand. The troll at the jetty's head immediately thrust an arm out to the side, suspending the frightened toddler over the clear cold sea that lapped gently perhaps five metres below. Magnus' frightened screams reached him, high pitched over his wife's now equally audible cries.

Realising that he was helpless, Oskar stopped struggling and, with his arms held pinned to his sides, glared defiantly at the nondescript man who was now walking along the jetty towards him.

'Oskar, thank you for joining me and at the run too. That's good, I like to see enthusiastic people,' said Cassiter.

It registered with Oskar that the man was speaking English; he glared at Cassiter but managed to compose himself enough to reply in English. 'What the hell's going on here? You can't do this. Who are you?'

Cassiter smiled at him. 'Now, now, stop struggling and I'm sure things will work out well.'

'My boy, Magnus!' shouted Oskar, jerking his head, gesturing beyond Cassiter towards the end of the jetty. 'Stop this,' he struggled again but to no avail.

Cassiter did not turn his attention away from Oskar, but simply dropped his arm. At once, the troll swung the toddler back over the jetty and tucked him under a giant arm.

'Now, shall we talk?' said Cassiter.

Oskar nodded, resigned, he stopped struggling and tried to catch his wife's attention; she only had eyes for the crying toddler.

'What is this about? Are you mad? There's money in the house if that's what you want. Don't hurt the boy,' said Oskar.

'Oskar, Oskar, Oskar. You misunderstand me; we're not trying to rob you. I just need a little help from you that's all. You do what I want and this will all end happily.'

'What help?' said Oskar, confused.

'You have something in your bank vault. Something that's very important to me.'

'What can be this important?' said Oskar. 'Anyway I can't just take things from the vault, it's not that simple. There are procedures to be followed.'

'You're the manager, Oskar. You implement the procedures. You can override them if required. Now stop arguing or I will get impatient.' Cassiter thrust his hand up and the troll swung little Magnus out over the water again. The frightened cries resumed and mixed with the terrified screams of his wife.

'Yes! Yes. Whatever you want. For God's sake, stop. I agree.'

Cassiter dropped his arm and Magnus was swung back in to safety.

'Good, I'm glad we understand one another. Now before I send you to collect what I want, let's look at the sea, shall we?' Cassiter turned to look, pointing to guide Oskar's view. 'I think the tide's about out; it's slack tide now. Not long and it will start to flood. In a little while, I'm going to have my boys tie your wife and son down there beneath the jetty. Look; that spot just there. Nice and dry now but it won't be for long. I think you should have the best part of three hours to get back with what I want. If you make it back in time, I'll let you untie them. Take too long and I'm afraid it's going to get very wet and very deep down there.' Cassiter turned to look at Oskar and smiled coldly. 'I'd hurry if I were in your shoes.'

Cassiter walked past Oskar, headed back towards the house. 'Come on now, you've got work to do. I'll give you your instructions as we walk.'

Cassiter had completed his retrieval instructions by the time they walked round to the drive at the front of the house. There he paused and, stretching out an arm towards Oskar, he handed back the missing phone. 'And don't think about calling the police. We will be monitoring your calls and the bank's too. Any foolishness on your part and we'll immediately do the tide's job for it. You won't have any reason to hurry back then. Do you understand?'

Oskar nodded as a black 4x4 entered the driveway of his home and came to a halt behind his own car; two men were sat in the front seats.

'To be on the safe side we'll give you an escort into town. You go straight to work. And remember it's a long quiet road out here. If you did something silly, we'd see the authorities coming long before they arrived. And you see,' he gripped Oskar's arm and turned him, forced him to look out to sea, 'we don't need the road.' Beyond the inlet, holding its position in the deeper water was a powerful launch. Invisible from the beach level, it explained how Cassiter and his team had been able to appear as if by magic.

'Now off you go and do as you're told. If you do, everything will be fine. But hurry, time is not your friend.'

For a moment, Oskar held his place, stared down at the beach and jetty. The worry in his belly took a further jolt as he saw his wife and son being manoeuvred down on to the sand. His wife was forced to her knees and tied to one of the supporting legs beneath the jetty, close to the water's edge; Magnus was tied across her breast. It was currently dry but he knew it was well beneath high water mark.

'You can't do this,' said Oskar. 'It's inhuman. Mad.'

'No, it's business, my friend,' said Cassiter as he stepped back and waved a hand. His men moved into action at once, hustling Oskar towards his car.

'Drive carefully,' said Cassiter, watching as reality finally surfaced in Oskar's mind and he drove off quickly. The black 4x4 followed.

• • •

The impatient knocking on the manse front door started to repeat its sequence for the third time just as Helen reached it. She opened it and was surprised to see James Curry. Putting on a welcoming smile, she invited him in.

'We weren't expecting to see you here, James,' she said. 'How can I help you?'

With the thinnest of smiles in acknowledgement, James Curry stepped past her and then strode up the hall inspecting as he went.

'I thought I had better come and see how things are proceeding here. We don't want any delays in getting the property on the market once I've got the go ahead from the Church's General Trustees, which I'm confident of getting very soon. How is the clearing out going?'

'What with being away on holiday and one or two problems since I got back, we haven't really got much done yet,' she replied. 'Elaine's made a start in packing up parish archive papers in the basement store and Grace has packed up most of John's clothing, but you know the furniture and everything else belonged to John too.'

'It's all very unfortunate, but the presbytery can't be considered responsible for John Dearly's possessions. He's dead and arrangements must be made. Can't you and Elaine get a skip and dump it or engage one of those house clearance businesses? I want this place cleared as soon as possible. It's no good the pair of you dragging your feet, the inevitable will happen. The manse will be sold as soon as possible. Sadly, the church has to go too.'

Helen could not detect any hint of sadness in his voice.

James Curry opened the kitchen door, strode to the centre where he paused and did a slow pirouette. He cast a critical eye over the upgrading work that the parish elders had organised in her absence and then he sighed. 'I suppose it's an improvement on before, certainly fresher. Could the parish have done the job for a little less money though? I wonder?' James Curry pulled open two or three cupboard doors, swung them shut again. Pulled open a drawer to test its runners. 'Hmmm,' he walked over to the window while tutting to himself.

'We think it's a good job,' said Helen.

'I'm sure you do, my dear. Now, what about the garden? I hope Elaine has somebody engaged to keep it tidy. We don't want prospective buyers put off by a jungle outside.'

'It's in perfect shape.'

'Today, yes. I want to be sure Elaine is not going to let things slide and has an arrangement in place. I certainly don't want to have my office staff's attention diverted into making horticultural arrangements once we've closed the parish down.'

'I'm sure Elaine will have spoken to the gardener and passed on payment arrangements to your office.'

'Well let's hope so. Now we have the presbytery ready to follow a course of action, I want every arrangement in place so we can act as soon as the General Trustees approve the sale request. I want the manse emptied now. The church too. I'm sure neighbouring parishes would welcome the chance to harvest anything of use from it before we put it on the market. I've sent Elaine an email asking her to organise a viewing of the movables. Nothing must obstruct our progress.'

Curry turned from the window and smiled directly at Helen. 'And you must be busy packing up your own flat at Causewayside too. We would appreciate it if you could be out as soon as possible, there's a ready market for such properties and it would be good if we were able to catch the traditional market upswing in September. That will be alright for you, I'm sure.'

Curry walked out of the kitchen and made for the study. He called over his shoulder as he went. 'Don't let me hold you back, I'm going to do a little walk around, inspect the property. I've asked estate agents to call round and do a pre-sale assessment this afternoon and I don't want any nasty surprises. Oh, they will be wanting to visit your flat too. My office told them to liaise with Elaine over access but since you're here, perhaps you could give them a key when they call?'

Helen scowled in the direction of the now vanished James Curry. She turned to gaze out of the kitchen window. Suddenly she understood why Elaine had been expressing so much concern. Curry really was steamrolling the process, there was no negotiation, no consideration, he was pressing ahead with his plan to wipe St Bernard's away completely, with no thought for those concerned. She could sense it was personal and nothing was going to stop him.

• • •

Oskar parked his car in the allocated parking spot behind the bank. Saw the black 4x4 pulling to a halt a little further down the road. It was illegally parked but he did not think the occupants were worried about that.

He hurried to the bank's front doors where his deputy, the

second key holder, was waiting. Together they opened the bank and disarmed the alarm systems. Oskar forced himself to behave normally. He couldn't be seen to be breaching the regular procedures, could do nothing more until the time locks on the main safe released for the day. He sat in his office and pretended to study some documents; thought over events again and again. Could the authorities help? Should he call them in? No, he knew it was hopeless.

One of his staff brought him in a coffee; he thanked the lad and forced himself to engage in a little chat about nothing in particular. Then, alone again, he watched the clock tick away and formed his plan. He called his deputy in and announced he needed to make a visit to one of the other banks in town, a meeting to discuss how they could enhance their participation within the local community - he'd be back before lunch. But first, he had received an all manager email from headquarters, instructing all branches to carry out a snap inventory of the safe custody holdings.

The deputy accepted his reason for leaving the premises without question, but grumbled about the checks. 'Again? We only did a full inventory check three weeks ago. You'd think head office would understand we have other things to do. They keep pushing for efficiencies and savings and then keep throwing these extras into the workload. I'd let them know next time you're up there if I were you.'

Oskar nodded acknowledgement and then shrugged in resignation. 'I know, but what can you do?'

He made himself wait a few minutes after the time lock had disengaged before stepping into the bank's back office where a member of staff handed him a printout of the safe custody holdings. He nodded thanks. His deputy accompanied him through to the vault while still grumbling about the extra work.

'Look, I'll do it myself; I know you have a load on at present. It won't take me too long, and then I'll get away to my meeting,' said Oskar, as he pulled open the heavy steel door.

The deputy looked a bit doubtful for a moment. 'Shouldn't we do this together?'

'Yes, but as you said we only did it three weeks ago and you've got a lot on. Leave it to me, okay?' Oskar started inspecting the inventory without waiting for an answer. After a moment's hesitation, the deputy nodded, turned and left his boss to get on with it.

As he worked, Oskar moved slowly around, manoeuvred his body into a position that formed the smallest of blind spots, just managed to obscure the camera's view. In the unlikely event that any employee was watching him, they would not see what he was doing. He cracked opened the dagger's container, made sure it was inside. With relief, he slipped it out of the container and into his briefcase. The next twenty minutes were hell as he made himself work through the printed list of holdings. Ticking things off, one by one. Eventually he was done. He closed the vault, handed the clipboard over to one of the staff and left the bank, keeping tight hold of his briefcase as he headed for his car.

Driving through Sandefjord, Oskar made himself keep to the speed limit. The one thing he did not need was to attract attention. He noticed the black 4x4 was still behind him. He cursed them under his breath and headed south and west, taking the road that would eventually reach along the long narrow tongue of land that led home to his family.

Once he got out in the countryside, he dared to pick up speed. The road was narrow now but that didn't matter. Pretty houses and well-maintained barns were dotted amongst little fields whose sturdy tree lined fringes were fully greened in the Nordic summer. Here and there were blocks of grey rock thrusting out of the ground, some isolated, some combining together to create barriers around which the road wound. As the road worked south, he got more frequent glimpses of the sea and they told him the tide had turned, it was on the flood. He pushed the engine harder, would he make it in time?

Oskar hadn't noticed when, but at some point the black 4x4 had disappeared. He didn't care. All that mattered was he made it home in time.

Tyres screeched as his car halted outside the house. Jumping out of the car, he sprinted round the side of the house and carried on running for the beach and the jetty. He scanned the scene ahead of him. The big launch had come in with the tide and was now moored at the jetty head. Below the jetty and closer to shore, he could just make out his wife; the water was above her breast, his son's head at her shoulder.

Even now, waves were washing over Magnus' face. He could see Ida straining against her constraints trying desperately to keep their son's face above water. And he could see her despair as she failed and realised finally that she was powerless to save her son - powerless to save herself.

'Stop, stop, set them free,' shouted Oskar as he ran on to the jetty. Two burley men barred his way; he struggled, to no avail.

Cassiter stepped forward as he watched Oskar fighting against the men. 'Oskar, be calm now. Have you done what I asked? Have you brought it? Quickly now, time is against you.'

Oskar forced himself to stillness. 'In my briefcase, here, take it. But hurry, please, my family are drowning.'

'Let me see,' said Cassiter, taking the briefcase and looking inside. He looked up and smiled dryly towards Oskar. 'Well done, that wasn't so hard was it? Though I thought you might have been a bit quicker than you were.'

Oskar struggled free of the two men as Cassiter signed he should be released. He ran out along the jetty, peering over the side as he went. His son's head was beneath the water now, his wife's disappearing under the waves as they washed over her, then reappearing, wet and desperate.

'Let them go, you promised. Please, I have done as you asked, free them,' shouted Oskar.

'No, no, Oskar,' said Cassiter, walking steadily behind him. 'I said you could free them, don't you recall?'

'What? How?' Oskar's voice was rising in panic. 'I did what you asked. Help me free them. In God's name, help!'

Cassiter stood still and smiled. Did you think to bring a knife? I'm sure cutting their bonds would be the quickest way.'

With a cry of exasperation, Oskar leapt into the water beside his wife and struggled to pull her head up. He could tell his Magnus was already gone. Momentary relief came for Ida in a little trough between waves, she looked into his eyes - he could see fear and questions, and most of all grief for Magnus. He ducked under the water, tried to free her; squinting through the clear stinging saltwater, he frantically searched for the knots. Then stopped, knew there was no hope. She was cable tied; he could never undo them. He felt his wife shudder, her chest heave, heard the desperate gurgle reach him from beneath the water; knew it was all over for her. A rage filled him; that man would pay now.

Oskar pressed his feet against the bottom and pushed up for the surface. Revenge: that was all that mattered. He didn't surface. For a moment he puzzled, wondered what was happening. Then he registered the downward pressure of something gently pressing between his shoulder blades, holding him beneath the water, pushing him down, pinning him against the sandy bottom. He struggled, tried to twist, failed. A firmly held boat hook trapped him as the breath in his lungs flowed out in a cry of rage and despair.

He struggled but in the end couldn't resist the need to breathe, and by agonising degrees, cold salty water forced itself into his lungs. He was drowning. Fingers clenching, releasing, arms reaching out and back in a futile attempt to free himself. His neck arched, instinctively struggling to raise his head towards the surface, and he saw his Ida; just a metre away, her hair wafting in slow motion with the water's flow, he saw Magnus. He saw death. Oskar shuddered, sucking more water into his lungs, suddenly the struggle eased, he couldn't force the water out, didn't care - and he was gone.

Oskar never saw the man and his colleagues step on to their launch. He never saw their faces as the launch powered away, all content with a job well done. He never saw the horror on the faces of local fishermen who came down to fish his beach that afternoon.

Chapter 14

WEDNESDAY 21ˢᵀ AUGUST

Helen stepped out of the solicitor's office, satisfied she had done all that she could. Time and tide wait for no woman, and several increasingly anxious telephone messages from Franz Brenner in Switzerland had propelled her to visit the solicitors who represented his bank in Edinburgh.

The nature of its coming meant she could muster no personal interest in her new gotten wealth, but Franz had insisted there were things she needed to know about her inheritance and now really was the time. MacFarlane, Crearer and Cromarty was a long established partnership. She did not know too much about Scottish solicitors but she had found easy confidence in David Cromarty and the firm.

Everything about the partnership spoke of permanence. The address in Charlotte Square, she knew that was as prestigious as it comes. The shining brass plate, long ago rubbed almost smooth by a hundred years and more of polishing. The reception, spacious and populated by an array of comfortable yet well-worn leather chairs, the coffee table sporting a broad selection of the day's newspapers. Partners and staff passing through, confident, unhurried, purposeful.

While waiting in the plush reception she had caught a snatch of the telephone conversation between the receptionist and Mr

Cromarty's secretary. She was quite certain they had referred to young Mr Cromarty. And having now met the man, she guessed David Cromarty was sixty if he was a day. How old was old Mr Cromarty?

It had been a useful meeting, far more informative than she could ever have imagined. She read and signed the various papers David had prepared for her, and then it became clear that the range of her financial powers exceeded even her wildest imaginings.

He slid a brace of plain, unremarkable bankcards across the table to her. 'These cards came direct from Franz Brenner and the bank in Switzerland. You must sign them in my presence, now. And I must caution you to be careful with these, they are very high value.'

'Oh, what do you mean?' said Helen.

David gave a smile. 'Helen, with my card I book a nice hotel room. With your card, you book the whole floor. I book a flight, you charter the plane, no questions asked. So do be careful how you use them.'

She had been just a little startled when David broke off to take a phone call; and again when he flicked his handset to loudspeaker, telling her he had Franz Brenner on the line: a quick conference call.

She left the meeting confident that while she and her friends faced real danger ahead, she was bolstered by good people who would support her. She knew she could count on them and had left David and Franz to come up with a solution to her housing problems. She had also promised, at last, to visit Switzerland; she would book flights today and let Franz know when she was to travel.

Though she would never admit it, she had been avoiding visiting Franz Brenner in Switzerland. Probably because it would cement the transition from John Dearly to herself and, deep down, she desperately wished things had gone differently, and that her predecessor had somehow survived.

• • •

DCI Wallace looked around the reception area, another killing, another mystery. This was a strange one. Killings of migrant workers were very rare. The few such crimes he had been involved with tended to be focused within tightly knit groups. In his experience, the motivation was often simple and frequently it involved money. The dead woman's purse was still in her locker, only metres from where she had died. Theft was not the motive.

It was a puzzle. He had read the initial report his detectives had submitted the previous day. Something had niggled at him so now he'd decided to take this one on himself. According to various witnesses, the cleaner had been seen busy with her cleaning trolley at the same time as she lay dead in the basement. And now this. He drummed his fingers on the visitor log for the day of the killing. Sam Cameron had visited. He would need to visit him and that nice American girl, again. They seemed in the thick of it once more.

'Tell me again,' he said to the man sitting behind the reception desk.

'As the book says, Mr Cameron came in around 09.30. He had an appointment with Sandi McLellan, went to the meeting, he left about 10.30 and never came back. Oh, and his assistant came late. Got here just after he'd left, about 10.35, I would guess. She missed the meeting so I gave her Sandi's email details so she could send an apology.'

'What was her name? I don't see an entry for 10.35. She's not in the visitor book,' DCI Wallace fixed the man with an accusing stare.

'No, she wouldn't be. She only came into reception. People only need to sign in if they are going beyond this point.'

DCI Wallace tapped the visitor book and growled. He looked at DS Brogan. 'Get this bagged. Do we have any CCTV?'

'Nothing for the cleaner's stores.'

'Damn, it's a mystery how the cleaner could be dead on the floor and cleaning elsewhere at the same time.' He looked expectantly at the man behind the desk.

'There's one camera, it might have something,' said the man.

'Can we see it?' said Wallace.

'I can make you a copy from here.'

'Good, I'll pick it up from you in a little while,' said DS Brogan.

'So we've virtually no pictures. This is not going to be easy.'

'And there were scores of people in the building that evening for a Festival performance. Some of the visitors had pre-purchased tickets; some paid cash. It will be hard to trace everybody. Only thing out of the ordinary that night was one of the lecturers has complained her office had been disturbed.'

'A theft? Do you think it's linked?' said DCI Wallace.

'She's not actually sure anything was stolen, perhaps she was mistaken.'

'Well we'd better go up and speak to her, be on the safe side. What's her name?'

'Sandi McLellan.'

'What? Wait.' DCI Wallace turned and looked at the receptionist. 'The book says that's who Sam Cameron visited, am I right?'

The man nodded.

'Come on Brogan, let's go and speak to this Sandi McLellan. Then I want to call on our friends at the church.'

• • •

Helen stood over the manse's kitchen table, palms flat on the top, thumbs hooked under its edge. She leant further forward, pressing her weight on to her arms, locked elbows holding her steady as her head slowly turned from side to side, surveying the documents and pictures spread before her. Francis and Elaine sat at either end of the table; they too looked carefully at the spread.

From his place opposite Helen, Sam tried to shape their knowledge into something meaningful. 'I have tried to unpick this muddle from every possible angle and I just don't make any progress. We started with one puzzle - what do the inscriptions on the daggers mean? I don't know, but we don't have all the daggers yet so perhaps it will become clearer with future finds.'

Sam paused, looked for agreement, both Helen and Elaine nodded.

'Then we have a whole new puzzle - what do the glazed images mean? We made a start on working that out. The pictures represent saints and each saint represents a church. But where are the churches? The ones we have located have been by chance. But there are thousands of possible candidate churches scattered across Europe. It will be a huge task to track the right ones down and even if we eventually approach the right churches we will never know - they will be hiding their part in this too, that's if the knowledge has even survived.'

The group had all listened intently to his introduction hoping for enlightenment. None had come. In particular, Francis was struggling to incorporate all the strands of recent finds with his original understanding. 'Sam, I must be getting old and slow but please take me through this again, I'm not getting a handle on it at all.'

'Okay, try this. Xavier told us before the summer that the patterns on the dagger blades form a message or map of some sort. We can't decipher it at present; to do so requires those daggers we don't yet have.'

Francis nodded acknowledgement. 'I've got that bit. And that we believe the villains started out with one dagger of their own, which means one of them must be a task bearer; like Xavier and John Dearly before he was killed. And heaven knows how we could hope to get that dagger from them.'

'Right,' said Sam. 'But we know more than that now and I think we are approaching this from the wrong angle.'

'How so?' said Helen.

Sam paused to collect his thoughts for a moment. 'So, we know from Xavier that there were nine daggers in total, one stayed here at St Bernard's, the key dagger. The others were distributed in secret by Henri de Bello. Each one kept safe, hidden by trusted knights, the task bearers. Clearly, that bit worked well since here we are today still trying to unpick his secret.

'Each task bearer should have been established in a church in a particular place, waiting to be recalled. Their task passed on from priest to priest over the years. Xavier is a task bearer and he knew the name of Henri de Bello as the originator - now we've even found a gravestone for him, so I'm taking that as validation of the story. And John Dearly was the task bearer here at the hub, which involved some added responsibility or secrets. When John died, he passed his responsibility to Helen but couldn't brief her. So she has all the responsibility but none of the knowledge.'

Sam reached across the table and picked up a copy of the Hereford codex picture, held it up. 'Let's assume the daggers provide the ultimate answer, then we've been trying to solve a riddle by combining parts of an answer, without ever knowing what the riddle was we are trying to solve.'

Elaine's face was as inscrutable as ever, she was staring at her hands, and Francis' face was pained as he struggled to understand what Sam was saying. Helen remained resting her weight on her locked arms but tilted her head to catch Sam's eye.

'Surely we know the question, Sam. It's, where is the Templars' hoard hidden?' said Helen.

Francis' face relaxed a little, recognising his own understanding in Helen's words.

'Yes, you're right as far as you go,' said Sam. Francis smiled in relief and Elaine's head nodded very slightly. They all understood.

'But you only go so far,' said Sam.

Francis groaned and slapped his head. 'Save us all, Sam. Please join the dots before my head explodes.'

Sam grinned at him. 'I think we are looking at a multi-layered puzzle, an onion if you will. And we have started from the inside, it's no wonder we can't see what's going on or solve it, we've bypassed much of the riddle. I think the daggers are the last stage, and we stumbled on them by chance.

'Helen, you remember telling me that John Dearly had told you how important the glass was? I think he knew it was a message that identified the churches where the daggers were being held.'

'So John Dearly had all the answers then?' said Helen.

'I don't think so. Remember, again, what Xavier told us before the summer. He believed the keeper of John's dagger had the responsibility and role of calling all of the daggers back together when the time was right, but he also said the Templars' idea was that no man knew the whole story. So John couldn't have known everything.'

Elaine looked up. 'That's right and remember Xavier's story about his and John's predecessors meeting by chance? That would not have been a chance meeting if one man had known where the other church was.'

'Exactly,' said Sam. 'I think there are three stages to the puzzle. Initially, we have been tackling the daggers, but that's the final stage - building the map or plan to the treasure. It can't be pulled together without first sorting the two earlier stages. One of those was the names of the churches where the daggers were to be kept. That's what John Dearly knew and guarded here, in the glass picture. You know, I think that was the second stage in the puzzle.'

'And what would the first be?' said Helen.

'Well that's it, you see. In the end, it's the same question circling back time and again. *Where are the daggers?*' Sam raised a hand and began finger listing the items as he spoke. 'Stage one, where are the daggers, that is the place - town, country, whatever. Stage two, where are the daggers in that place - the church names, we know those now. And of course, stage three, gather in the daggers from those locations and combine them to assemble the message engraved on the dagger blades.'

Hand still up and with the three fingers raised, he looked around. 'Well? Any thoughts?'

Francis still looked confused as Sam let his hand drop.

After a moment's contemplation Helen spoke. 'So, three layers to your puzzle onion. The first tells where the daggers went, of that we have no idea at all. The second where the daggers stay in those places, their addresses if you like, we have a pretty good handle on that now through the church window. The third is what the daggers tell us, the map. To find the daggers and solve the problem we have to find specific churches and we don't have the slightest inkling how to do that because we don't know what the first layer of the puzzle is.'

'Precisely,' said Sam.

'So we're still stuck,' said Helen.

'Yes, but look on the bright side, at least we've moved on, now we're stuck in a different spot. And I think it's clear that whoever else is in the hunt is in the dark too. Like us, they are in the middle of the puzzle, perhaps not even knowing there is an outer layer that will direct them to where they need to go to find the daggers.'

'And you think that because?' said Helen.

'Because, if they knew where to look, they would have wrapped this up, and us too, long ago. They are just as disadvantaged as we are, stuck in the middle of the puzzle. Well no, actually at least we know the names of the churches and that there is another set of clues to find. I guess that puts us ahead -'

'And maybe that's why we're still alive. It might be they can't solve the problem and are hoping we can,' said Helen.

'You could be right,' said Sam.

'Sam, run the churches past me again. I want to be sure I have a good handle on them,' said Francis.

'Well, it's straight forward, provided we all agree to accept that between Sandi McLellan and you guys there is enough religious knowledge to back up the identifications.' Sam saw heads nodding agreement.

'So, here we go. We have St Bernard's, at the centre, it's the spreading vine or burning bush; reaching out to link the other saints together, its dagger has a number list engraved on the blade. That should determine in what order the other blades should be aligned to create a map from the blade engravings. We have St Bartholomew's, Xavier's church and his dagger was numbered seven. Then there is St Michael's in Garway; that was dagger number eight.' Sam looked knowingly at Helen. 'Then you tracked down St Olaf's in Norway for dagger number five. Four churches, four glass images, four daggers. That works pretty well,' he watched for Helen's acknowledgement.

'Then we get into a bit of a grey area. We have two Scottish saints, St Mungo and St Margaret, and it would certainly make sense if they represented two Scottish churches that we have yet to trace. If we take our steer from the records of the family that donated their dagger to the National Museum of Scotland, we know that the museum dagger was originally based in the northeast of the country, out towards Elgin. I've made time to check through church records. There is no church in the immediate area that fits the bill.' He could see faces around the table dropping.

'Hold on, remember we have already found the dagger, number four - we don't need to find the church. But for interest's sake, I did a bit more digging and established that long, long ago there was a St Mungo's church in the area. I would guess that was our link. As for the dunes dagger, number three, I'm guessing it should be housed within a church called St Margaret's. But think about it, if the dagger was lost on the Fife coast, perhaps on its original journey to establish the church, Orkney maybe, who knows where, it would never have reached its intended destination. There would never have been a church formed to house it or for us to find today.'

'That still leaves three daggers unaccounted for,' said Francis.

'Yes, dagger numbers one, two and six are still missing. Let's assume for the moment that the daggers all reached their intended destinations. From the glass window, we have three as yet unallocated saints' names; these should represent three churches each of which contains a dagger.'

'Sounds easy when you say it quickly,' said Elaine.

'And let's not forget one of these three is the source of all the killings. If we get to the wrong one we could be in big trouble,' said Helen.

'Okay, let's look at the names. St Boniface, seems he's big in northern Europe, Germany and such like. St Athanasius, he's stronger in the south and east. Then we have Mary Magdalene - well she seems pretty ubiquitous: could be anywhere.'

'And that takes us back to the first layer of the riddle - where are these places?' said Francis.

'Yes it does. And I still don't have a clue. Not sure where we go from here. Until we can identify what town or district each of the three churches is in, knowing their names is next to useless. They will take forever to find.'

'And that's still assuming the churches were founded as planned and that they still survive. We know of two that didn't make it, there's no saying that all three of these did either,' said Elaine.

'I know, but let's try to be positive,' said Sam.

'So your suggestion is that rather than trying to unpick the message on the blades we should concentrate on finding the blades' original destinations, and then the local churches through those three unallocated saints' names,' said Helen.

'Right, and the information is here just waiting for us to find it, I'm certain. I know we searched the place once before but I think we need to go over everything again. Bear in mind how the glass window carried a hidden message in plain sight; remember how the parish dagger was hidden in plain sight too. This time let's keep an open mind.'

'We should work quickly. James Curry is determined to have the properties empty and in the hands of the estate agents as soon as he can. Once that happens we won't have easy access to the manse or the church,' said Elaine.

• • •

The manse was quiet now. The others had gone and Helen sat alone in the study. In front of her, the desk was heaped with piles of papers, records and notes. She had skimmed through them during a previous search but now she carefully scrutinised each page before placing it in one of the storage boxes at her feet. Two filled boxes sat on the floor behind her, several more sat empty, waiting their turn to be filled. This was going to be a long task, necessary though if they were to find any hidden message. Also important, the manse's contents needed to be packed and ready to move in case her fledgling plans to deal with James Curry's selling of the property fell through.

The phone rang and Helen broke off from the search to answer it, pleased to have a break. 'Helen speaking.'

'Helen, it's Franz here, Franz Brenner. Thank God I've caught you.'

'Franz, what a surprise, why are you calling? I'm visiting you soon. Is there some problem with the arrangements?'

'Helen, you must come, our meeting remains fixed. I look forward to your visit, but that is not why I am calling you now.'

'Oh. What's new?' she said.

'There has been an...' his voice trailed off for a moment, as though a carefully rehearsed speech was being revised during its delivery. 'I'm afraid, there has been an incident.'

'Go on,' said Helen. 'What sort of incident?'

'The worst, in so many ways.'

The call had not lasted long. News of the loss of the Norwegian dagger was disturbing but ultimately not a disaster; she had given Sam a photographic record of the blade's engraving. Franz had been very concerned at the breach of banking security; she had reassured him she understood some things were beyond even his control. However, news of the death of Oskar and his family was shocking for her and, she could tell, for Franz too. Oskar had been so kind and helpful.

Helen shivered as the image of the man flitted through her mind. She saw him again, shepherding her into his office, surrendering his chair and fussing around to ensure coffee and cakes were served. She steeled herself. Yet more innocents had been dragged beneath the millstone of this evil. It had to be stopped.

Franz told her the police's initial theory attributed it to a domestic breakdown, murder and suicide by a highflier who cracked under the strain. She knew otherwise and hated that the poor man's reputation was being questioned. Franz had parted with an assurance that he intended to alert the police to the loss of their asset and the altogether more sinister possibilities they should consider around Oskar's death.

As Helen hung up the call, the front door bell rang. She really did not want to speak to anyone but it persisted and eventually she answered the door.

DCI Wallace stood alone; he nodded to her as she opened the door and then he stepped forward, scarcely giving her a chance to invite him in.

'Do you have a few minutes please?' He kept walking into the hall as he spoke.

'Come in, why don't you?' said Helen, still holding the front door while looking back into the hall.

'Thanks, where are we? In here?' he pointed at the open study door and walked in.

'Go ahead, don't mind me,' said Helen, following behind. She was puzzled by the policeman's behaviour; it was not like him to be so pushy. But she was not ready for a confrontation, still processing the information that Franz had just given her. She took her seat behind the desk and waved her hand towards an empty visitor chair. 'You may as well have a seat while you're here.' She did not offer any refreshments.

'Thanks,' said Wallace. He sat, pulling the chair close to the desk. 'Now we have to speak.'

'Well, you've got me, detective. What's bothering you? Oh and where's Detective Sergeant Brogan? I don't think I've ever seen you without him.' Her attempt at light chat fell flat.

'I deliberately left him behind. Wanted to speak with you off the record.'

Helen smiled at him, trying to hide the tension that had gripped her following Franz's news. She did not think the detective was fooled.

'Helen, I've been visiting New College, do you know it? Up on the Mound.'

'Of course, I am with the Church of Scotland. What took you up there?' She was on safe ground so far but was unsure of where the detective was leading the conversation.

'You haven't seen the news then?' he asked, almost casually.

'No, the past twenty-four hours have been pretty hectic,' she said, sweeping her arm around to encompass the piles of papers and packing boxes.

'I see, and what's going on here? Are you moving out?'

Helen sighed. 'Not through choice. The presbytery is restructuring the Church's footprint in the city; well I think that's how he described it. But it amounts to shutting us down.'

'And who is *he*?'

'James Curry. He's the presbytery clerk and St Bernard's is in his sights.'

'I wouldn't have thought a clerk could influence the Church's work.'

'Don't be fooled by the job title. That man has a very big stick. When he decides to wave it everyone runs for cover.'

Wallace could understand if the Church needed to rationalise it would make sense to lose St Bernard's. After all, it did seem to have become a magnet for violence and killing - not the best type of publicity. He made a mental note to have Brogan speak to Curry, just in case there were any other influencing factors.

'When were you last at New College?' he said.

'Oh, I don't know. Probably not since the last General Assembly, back in May. I certainly attended a meeting then.'

'I see, and tell me, what about your friend Sam Cameron? Does he ever visit there?'

Helen knew that something was wrong. Something must have happened at New College. 'Yes,' she said more cautiously, 'he was there earlier in the week.'

'That's what I thought. Problem for me is, shortly after his visit somebody was killed there.'

'What? Who? Where? At New College?' Helen leant forward. 'What happened?'

Wallace noted both her sudden change of attitude from apparent despondency to livewire and the look of open shock on her face.

He knew in his bones this latest murder was linked to the church and university killings of earlier in the year, and somehow back to the manse too. He could also tell the news was a complete surprise to her. Whatever her involvement, it was not murder.

He pressed Helen, tried to coax something, anything from her. She had composed herself again and he was being met by a stonewall of concerned unknowing. After a little while, he became frustrated.

'Look, I've handed in my resignation, I'm retiring. In a few weeks, I'll be finished. And right now, I'm ignoring every rule in the budget book. I've been told not to engage with this case but I've detailed members of my team to watch our original suspect because we know he's our man. I've got his people watched and his office too. I'm doing it because I know there is something going down. Something bad and I know you and your friends are caught up in it. By the time my bosses see the work sheets, I'll be on pension and there's nothing they can do about the overspend. But when I've gone, your protection will stop dead. So we need to sort this double quick.' DCI Wallace stood and paced to the window. He rested a hand on the frame and leaned close to the glass, peered out.

'Now I've got another murder on my books. For me, there is too much coincidence. The Church, the university, a dead body and your friend passing through.' He turned, looked back at Helen still sitting at her desk. 'I know there's something going on. Know you and Sam aren't killers, but you are involved. Please, for your sakes and the families of those who have been killed, let me help you.'

Helen stared hard at the detective. She desperately wanted to tell him but knew knowledge was the danger. The man didn't deserve to be put at risk. If she told him everything he would end up on the *to die list* too. What could she do? After a long moment, she stretched out her arm, waving DCI Wallace back to his seat. He complied.

'This is an impossible situation, detective. I don't know what to tell you.'

'Try the truth.'

Helen shrugged. 'The truth? If only it were that simple.'

'In the end, it is.'

'Did she suffer?'

'What do you mean?'

'At New College, did she suffer?'

'Tell me, Helen, if you haven't heard the news, how did you know it was a woman that had been killed?'

'I… I assumed, that's all. Thought you meant it was Sandi McLellan, the lady Sam visited.'

'Why would I have meant that?'

Helen was sick of games. Just minutes before, she had learnt that a lovely young man and his family had been slaughtered. Now she was being pressed by a good man who would simply make himself another victim. 'Oh stop it detective. If I tell you anything, you will become a target too. Was Sandi killed?'

'No. It was a cleaner,' he said.

Helen felt a moment of relief, the killing was not connected; it vanished in just a moment as DCI Wallace continued. 'Though Sandi McLellan has reported that her workroom was rifled that evening. Some notes and papers stolen.'

Helen leant forward. 'You must protect her. She will be a target for certain.'

Wallace could sense the conviction in Helen's voice; it was clear she was not playing a game. Whatever the threat, she believed it was real. Wallace believed it too.

Helen decided to take the plunge. She had to if it could get Sandi McLellan some protection. Too many innocents had died already. 'You said your visit today is off the record. Do you really mean that?'

He nodded.

Helen pulled open the desk's top drawer and pulled out a book. She put it on the table in front of her. It was a bible. Resting her hand on it, she looked straight into Wallace's eyes. 'I swear what I will tell you now is true. I swear that if you raise it outside this room I will deny every word. If anyone ever discovers that you know, you will be in danger and I fear your family will be too - there are no boundaries. I'm telling you only so you can protect Sandi McLellan before they get to her, and they will try, I'm sure. Now you swear to keep it secret.' She slid the bible across the desk.

Wallace hesitated. 'I can't do that. I would be hamstringing myself at work. You know I can't. I'm an officer of the law.'

Unflinching, Helen looked at him. 'Then I can't tell you anything, I'm afraid. Nothing at all. You'll have to leave now.' She stood.

Wallace looked up at Helen; she saw he was torn.

'I don't understand what you meant about my family,' he said.

Helen told him the story of a Norwegian banker and his young family, dead without ever knowing the reason why - killed simply because he had unwittingly had contact with something, without ever knowing its significance.

Wallace stopped her. Made a call, it only took a couple of minutes to get confirmation of the deaths.

Then he knew she was not making up a threat. It was real.

Putting his phone away, he reached a decision. He needed to know. He placed his hand on the bible and joined eye contact with Helen. 'If I am to help, even a little bit, I need to know. But I need to keep my family safe too; nobody will ever know what you tell me. Unless you incriminate yourself. If you're a killer, no oath will stop me bringing you to justice.'

Helen smiled at him. 'I wouldn't expect anything less of you. Don't worry; there are no killers in this room. But I will have to tell Sam that you know. We are hand in glove on this.'

Finally, with a deep breath, DCI Wallace accepted Helen's terms and she pressed her hand on top of his. He repeated her words, parroting the oath she dictated and she listened intently. Then, content, she sat back in her chair. Wallace leant back too. She could see in his expression that a sense of anticipation was pulsing through him.

They talked for a long time. She told him a lot of what had happened. The history, the links with the Templar hoard. The theories they had formed about the killings and who was responsible. Highlighted the things they didn't know. And very deliberately missed some key bits - she avoided mentioning the tunnel, and withheld the information about their presence when the two men had been shot dead earlier in the year. She accepted that her presence at the killings and subsequently keeping quiet about it was withholding information from a murder investigation on a scale that even a retiring policeman couldn't sit on.

DCI Wallace had remained silent as she talked, just nodding. Finally, story over, she looked into his eyes, searching for a response.

'Well, I believe you. But only because I've seen this whole mess unfold over the past months and because I know that none of our own theories even begins to fit and I can see that what you have told me does - incredible but it fits. I also know that if I walk into the station with this story I'll be picking up my pension a good bit earlier than I expected.'

Helen nodded an acknowledgement. Wallace could not see it but he had lifted a weight off her shoulders. A maverick minister, yes, but honest and law-abiding she certainly strived to be. Having told the policeman, she felt better inside, more like herself.

She was suddenly very matter of fact. 'I told you because you insisted. I warned you it would put you in danger. Again, if it is known that you know, I am certain they will not hesitate to get to you, directly or even via your family, so you must be careful. Most importantly, I told you so Sandi McLellan can have some protection. She's another innocent being pulled into this circle of hell.'

'I'll get one of my people on her right away. There's something else I can do; something you don't need to be involved in, leave that to me. But Helen, there's a couple of things I don't understand. If they are so ruthless, why are you and your little group of friends still standing? And how on earth is this going to be brought to a conclusion? My influence ends soon. Once I'm retired, they will be able to move about unchecked.'

Helen stood and stretched out an arm, guiding Wallace towards the study door and out into the hall. 'They seem very happy to take out people on the margins, to contain the spread of the knowledge probably. I think the reason we are still alive is because we don't know all the answers and nor do they. Like us, they are groping around in the shadows. I am sure they are hoping we find those answers, which we can't do when dead. But when we find them we will become disposable and dead very quickly.

'As for bringing it to a conclusion, well Sam is the great hope. He's very clever you know. With a little help from his friends too, of course. I don't know if we can sort this before you retire, I pray so. Your protective screen offers us a little relief. And as I explained earlier, if we can get the whole story together and blow it wide to the public, there will be nothing left to kill for. That will end it.'

'I hope you're right. And I hope Sam gets a move on, my clock's ticking down.' DCI Wallace paused at the front step. 'I'll do what I can for Sandi McLellan, leave it with me.'

Helen thought she could see just the beginnings of a tear in the policeman's eye.

'You're very brave,' he said. 'I admire you. All of you. I never thought I'd say it, but much more of this and I'll be heading back to church myself. And I haven't been voluntarily since my youngest was christened.'

'So, DCI Wallace, do it, you just might feel better. I'm adding you to my redemption list right now, you and Sam Cameron too. And in the meantime, you take care.' She leant over and hugged the older man, kissed his cheek.

Wallace was startled by the gesture but nodded acknowledgement as he stepped back. He paused for a moment, and then delved inside his jacket, pulled out a photograph that had been printed off from New College's CCTV records. He handed it to Helen. 'Do you know her?'

Helen looked at the picture and shook her head. 'I've never seen her before. She's very pretty, beautiful even. Has she been dragged into this too?'

'She wasn't dragged into this; this one jumped in, jumped right into the middle. She was cleaning New College while the cleaner lay dead in her store. Just about the time Sandi McLellan's room was being ransacked. Make of that what you will.'

'Oh,' said Helen, looking more carefully at the picture. 'Well, I've certainly never seen her; this is a face nobody would forget in a hurry. She's a stunner.'

'More deadly than the male, though. Keep the picture; let Sam see it. If he recognises her or either of you see her, get in touch with me right away.'

'I will. I'll show it to the others too. We don't want her coming around unrecognised.'

Wallace growled a quiet agreement and turned to leave.

Helen waved him off. 'Keep in touch now,' she called after him, and then he was gone.

Chapter 15

THURSDAY 22ND AUGUST

This was one of Sam's favourite times of the year on campus, a time of calm. Many of his colleagues were away on holiday, attending conferences, researching abroad or simply working from home. The undergraduates were all away for summer and only a few postgrads dotted about developing their own specialist projects or working on paid tasks for the university. This was the time Sam always found useful for thinking and planning. So far this summer none of it had related to his teaching. He knew he would need to spend some time preparing for the students' return, but not yet. There were more pressing things to consider.

Last evening he'd worried for a while that Helen's revelations to DCI Wallace would bring a late night visit and arrest warrants all round. There had been no knock at the door, no police this morning either. If the detective had chosen to dig in a particular direction, he could easily have dragged both Helen and himself into the mess. That he had not done so spoke highly of Helen's ability to judge a man.

Sam was glad now that he had bitten his tongue, held in the protests he had wanted to fire at her when she had told him of her conversation with Wallace. Seems she had been right.

He was browsing through his emails when the phone rang. He

answered it at once.

'Sam, Sandi McLellan here.'

'Sandi, nice to hear from you again, how can I help?'

'Well you can start by telling me why there's a detective hovering round. It's nothing to do with the murder of our cleaner the other day. He says it's something to do with some church investigations. Now he's a fixture down in reception and has told me not to leave the building without him. The only church investigation I know of is this business of yours. What have you got me into?'

'Ah,' said Sam. It seemed Helen's revelations to DCI Wallace had produced some immediate results. If it protected Sandi then anything Helen had revealed had been worthwhile. Wallace was clearly a man who could separate right from rules, thank God. 'Listen, Sandi, I know it will seem a bit intimidating -'

'Not intimidating, Sam. Imposition. An imposition. I want to know what's going on. What have you dragged me into?'

'Listen, we're the good guys here. I'm sorry you have become involved, that was never the intention.'

'So what was your intention? For goodness sake! I'm now of interest to the police. Me!'

'Sandi, don't do anything precipitous. Why don't we meet for lunch and I'll tell you what I can.'

The call ended with Sandi grudgingly accepting the lunch date. Sam took a few moments to think about what and how he would explain the situation. Then he returned to his email. One stood out as unexpected. It was from Davy, the student who had been attacked in his home up in Oban at the start of the summer. Sam wondered what he wanted in the middle of the summer holidays.

Hi Sam,

Hope the summer is going better for you and Helen now. Julie and I are doing great. Barty the dog is too! He's eating sausages again. I've found something interesting, re what happened before summer break. Can we meet sometime in the next two days? Julie and I are in Edinburgh for the Festival.
Davy.

Sam read it again, thought it through. What had Davy been up to now? The message couldn't be ignored; they would need to meet.

All and any information was welcome but, after the previous round of troubles, he had specifically cautioned Davy and his girlfriend Julie not to dig any further. Surely, he had learnt his lesson by now? This was not a subject to be meddling with. He fired off an acknowledgement and suggested a coffee meeting in his office next afternoon, and then moved on to review the rest of his messages.

Before he had finished a reply came back from Davy confirming the arrangement. Sam noted the speed of reply. This must be something that was weighing on Davy's mind. He wondered for a moment what it could be then turned his thoughts back to his lunch meeting with Sandi. He had a lot of grovelling to do.

• • •

DCI Wallace looked calmly into the camera lens, expressionless, waiting. It was hard to maintain eye contact with a camera, disconcerting, but he was determined not to flinch. For a very long moment, nothing happened, but finally, in response to his persistent finger pressing on the buzzer, the lift doors in front of him opened - prompted by an unseen instruction from whoever sat at the other end of the camera feed. He let his finger release the pressure from the buzzer. Smiled briefly at the camera and stepped into the lift. Round one to him.

A minute later, he stepped out of the lift into the now familiar penthouse office suite. His team had spent days searching it earlier in the summer. This had been the centre of activity; if he wanted to deliver a message this was the place. He looked directly at the sour faced receptionist. She stared back as unwelcoming as he had expected.

'Is he in?' said Wallace.

'Is who in? And anyway, I understood you weren't meant to come here without a prior arrangement.'

'You know who I want, the boss, and I'll go where I choose in my city, thanks.'

'He's not here.'

Wallace looked about. 'It's very quiet here today, where is everyone?' He knew from his team's covert observations that most of the staff they had previously linked with this office were gone.

'It's none of your business, but as it happens much of the work has transferred abroad. Your heavy-handed and unjustified approach spoilt things here.'

'You haven't begun to see heavy-handed yet. Now, I asked where he is.'

'My instructions are to direct any police enquiries to our solicitor. I know you have the contact details, but here, this should help you.' She reached across the reception desk to offer him a business card. 'Why not phone now? Use the office phone, and tell him you're here. That will save me a call.'

Wallace did not bother taking the proffered card; instead, he walked down the hall and opened an office door, stepped inside. It was empty. No papers, no work in progress. He could make out computers on desks, all covered by thin clear plastic dustsheets. This office really was closed down or mothballed at the very least. Just the reception was active, place holding.

He was aware of sour face beside him, could feel her glare. 'You have to go now or I'll call the police,' she said.

Laughing at the irony of the situation, he backed out of the office, closing the door behind him. He headed back to the reception and sour face matched him step for step. She opened the lift door for him, and stared unflinching, defiant. The she-wolf guarding her den.

Wallace didn't enter the lift. Instead, he delved inside his jacket pocket and pulled out a slim sheaf of photographs. 'Well, I'd heard things were going a bit quiet here. But I actually wanted to speak with you. You see, I've been a bit naughty. Yes, I was told to back off from you and your friends, but you know what? I didn't. And I've found out one or two extra things now that I know will enable me to reopen the investigation - if I'm minded to.

'Your boss was very clever getting the original case closed off while I was away. He must have some very important friends. But I'm back now and, unlike the juniors in my team, I can't be bullied by any political management. Now, you and your boss know who I'm worried about, I have a protective watch on them all at present, but that shouldn't be necessary anymore. Tell him, anything happens to any of them and I will be pulling him in and he won't walk away a second time. Do you understand?'

'You can't come in here making false allegations and threats. I'm calling the solicitor now. Get out before I have you arrested for harassment.' She picked up the telephone handset from her desk and started to call. Wallace stretched across and killed the call at the base station.

'I haven't finished yet. You should listen carefully. Oh, here you might want to look at these.' He handed her the photographs. She took them and looked at the first in the stack.

'That first one is taken from the security camera inside New College on the evening of the recent murder. It's the only face we can't place.'

'So, what's that to do with us? She's never been here. I've never seen her before.'

'I've had my photographer on the case. Yesterday he followed someone to a coffee shop. See the next picture, two people meeting for a friendly coffee. Two girls having a chat. Oh look, one's passing an envelope to the other. Who can it be? You know, I'm pretty sure it's our friend from New College, but here's what's really interesting, do you recognise who she's passing the envelope to? I do. A very memorable face don't you think? It's you. And yet you've just told me you have never seen her. What was in the envelope?'

'You can't spy on me like this, there must be laws. Anyway, you were told to leave us alone.'

'I know, but it's like I said before, I've been naughty. Now here's the thing, take a look at the next picture. See if you recognise anyone there.'

Sour face glanced down at the picture and then looked up, for the first time Wallace thought he saw a flicker of emotion. 'It's him, isn't it? And look who's walking right beside him. It's your friend from the coffee shop, my friend from New College, the killer lady. And I have to say, I don't like the look of those heavies walking behind them. Is it an escort, a little team? See the big man, right at the back? You know him. I do too. We had him in with the rest of your workmates; earlier in the summer, remember? I wonder what's happening here.'

'Where did you get this?' demanded sour face. 'It's a forgery. You won't get away with it. I've had enough of you.' She thrust the pictures back into Wallace's hand, was still defiant but now Wallace detected a note of worry.

'It's no forgery. It's from Hereford Cathedral, their security footage. Fortunately for me, their CCTV system is not online, not so lucky for your boss; I know how good your team is with online systems. But you've missed this one and it puts your boss next to the lady we want to speak to in connection with the killing at New College. And it links them both to a robbery in the cathedral that took place immediately after this image was recorded. Oh, and it's only a short step from there to the killing of an old lady. She suffered horribly, poor woman, but you know what's very interesting? It left her with some what I might call trademark wounds.'

Wallace forced himself to smile at sour face as he gently placed the photos on the reception desk. He stepped into the lift and spoke before pressing the descend button.

'Tell him. Show him the pictures. The originals are in a safe place, along with the linking information. This is a one-off offer. I'm retiring soon; my priorities have changed. He stays out of Edinburgh now, stays out of Scotland and leaves my people untouched and I'll let this settle quietly. I'm sure there will be plenty of other officers hunting him elsewhere and eventually they'll pull together a package without me.' The lift doors started to close and he thrust out a hand to keep them open.

'Oh, and make sure he understands I have the evidence safe. If anything untoward were to happen to me or mine, the pictures and all the linking evidence would hit a hundred news outlets within a day. You speak with your boss quickly. I want an understanding by tomorrow morning or I'll be gunning for him, for you and your murderous lady friend.' He pulled his hand back from the lift doors and they slid shut. Pressing the descend button, he took a deep breath. Round two to him.

Chapter 16

FRIDAY 23RD AUGUST

Sam was standing behind the desk in his office, his back to the window. He leaned one elbow against the window frame while regarding the student who sat on the other side of his desk. Davy had come to the campus, as promised, and after the briefest of greetings he had excitedly blurted out his discovery. Sam didn't know whether to be annoyed at the young man's dabbling or delighted at his findings.

'Davy, you of all people should know the risks involved. You should have kept well away from this.'

'I know, I know. You and Helen both stressed that at the end of last term. But once those guys had been lifted by the police, I reckoned it would be safe enough. Especially after we heard the guy who attacked me was one of those who were killed.'

'Tell me again about what you unearthed. In fact, my computer's logged on, show me.'

With a little shrug, Davy stood and walked round the desk, sat in front of the screen and started searching for a website.

'Well, you'd better be warned. It seems the police case has unravelled a bit. I'm not sure why, just know you have to continue to be as careful as ever,' said Sam, while watching how Davy confidently worked the keyboard. He clearly knew exactly what he was searching for.

'I get the reasons for worry. But I've followed the instructions Helen gave us before. I haven't told anyone, except Julie of course. Nothing's written down or emailed, it's all up here.' He quickly tapped the side of his head with the index finger of his right hand, then jabbed it down to prod the return key. 'And here online, of course.'

'So, tell me how you found it,' said Sam.

'I've been stuck indoors these past few weeks, recovering after the attack. Between my mother and Julie fussing round, I haven't been getting the chance to go out and about much. So I had a look at the modules coming up for next year, thought I'd see if I could do any prep. Get a head start. I quite liked the look of the digital research course, right up my street.'

Sam nodded. It had been apparent throughout the last year that Davy was keen on applying technology and using the high tech gadgets - perhaps more than getting his hands dirty in the trenches. But it takes all sorts and Davy was a good student.

'So, I'd read some stuff about all the artwork and historical artefacts that the Nazis had looted during WWII. How some of it had been returned. But for a lot, the original owners couldn't be traced. It's sad and interesting at the same time. Fascinating really, who does own all that stuff? Then the really tricky bit, if you wanted to trace something that your family owned, or even another museum once owned - how would you even know where to look?'

Davy half turned his head to look briefly at Sam then turned back to the screen. 'There are official websites now, created to display artefacts that are suspected war loot. It's a lot easier for people to work through some databases than to spend months, years even, going round museums and trying to get into physical archives. Doing that circuit is hard for the individuals who are searching; physically facilitating endless visits is just about impossible for the institutions - hence the websites.'

'Yes, I'm aware of them. I haven't really looked though.'

'Well some of them are a bit clunky, the data displays well enough, but searching is still quite hard work as the presentation is not always logical. It can be a bit frustrating. Ah, here we are. What do you think?' Davy leant back and let Sam get a good look at the screen.

'Obviously, for us, you search medieval weapons, and then daggers come up pretty well top of the list, Knights Templar too. I refined the search a few times and suddenly there it was.'

Sam leant in over Davy's shoulder. Any misgivings about Davy's renewed involvement vanished in an instant. On screen was the image of a dagger, grainy, but a dagger he knew very well. It was one of the set.

Sam put a hand on Davy's shoulder, squeezed a little. 'Tell nobody about this, okay? You've done well, really well, but there are still some things it's best nobody knows you know. Understand?'

Davy nodded.

'Good, let's make sure Julie understands the risks as well.'

'Oh, she's okay. She was the one that insisted I come in person and not use emails to tell you about it.'

'Can you jot down those website details for me, Davy? I will need to go and verify your find. The picture resolution's not high enough to see all the detail. To be certain and to get any useable information I actually need to see the dagger.'

Sam reclaimed his seat at the computer and reviewed the find carefully. Then he phoned the museum. He was fluent in German but Bernhard Richter, the German archivist, insisted on practising his English skills, which were good. Happily, this proved to be one of those moments when working for a renowned university paid dividends - he could have sight of the dagger by arrangement.

As Sam spoke down the phone line, he also worked the airport schedules on his computer. He made an arrangement to visit Frankfurt on Monday. The German seemed a little surprised at the speed of Sam's visit but took it in his stride. Sam thanked him, ended the call and wrapped up his work. He walked out of the building with Davy and there they parted company.

• • •

Cassiter sat stony faced staring at the screen. He could see an equally expressionless face staring back at him. Sour face had just delivered DCI Wallace's message. Cassiter was not happy. He was particularly unhappy that he found himself linked to pictures with Collette at

Hereford Cathedral. Only circumstantial, but nonetheless he was in the pictures. This detective was proving to be far too independent for his own good but Cassiter had a lot to deal with right now.

Fight all your battles, he told himself, but only one at a time and in an order to best suit the project. There was no doubt the detective would have to go. But Wallace had indicated his main concern was he wanted Cassiter and his team to leave Edinburgh, and to leave his wards unharmed. Getting out of Edinburgh was on the agenda and most of his team were already away. Surrendering ground was fine. He would retake it once the other issues had been dealt with, and they were already well in hand. When the moment came, he'd return and he'd start by cutting away the churchwomen's protective shield, Wallace. Then he would work down the list and enjoy every moment. Particularly that American minister from the church, she had a lot of suffering to face. But for now, it could wait.

'Okay, here's what to do. Tell Collette to reverse out of Edinburgh. She is to harm nobody, just slip out quietly today. I want you to book her on a flight right now. The boys have picked up some interesting footage in Sardinia and I have a job for her there. She's to contact me as soon as she's out of the UK.' He paused for a moment, watching the screen as sour face bowed her head to write a note on her pad. Finished, she looked up again.

'The team have spotted Sam Cameron's booked on a flight to Frankfurt. I will have somebody in Germany positioned to find out why he's going there.

'I want you to contact Wallace, arrange to meet with him. You know the drill, control the timing and venue, just in case he tries to organise some electronic monitoring, speak to him somewhere that can't be bugged. Let him know you have spoken to me. Tell him our interests now lie elsewhere. Only you will remain on station to oversee a wind-down over the coming months. Tell him his every wish is met.'

Cassiter watched the sour faced woman nod in silent understanding. His mind was already ordering how events should play. 'I'll have somebody dispatched from this end to take the original CCTV images from Hereford Cathedral and from the local police down there. When the time comes to be active in Edinburgh again, which will be sooner than you might think, we will have to remove the images from Wallace too.'

He tapped the printouts on the desk beside his screen. 'Clearly Wallace is using the pictures as a bargaining chip. To do that he has kept them out of the police system; we can use that. These pictures of you and Collette doing the transfer, taken by a police photographer, your job is to dig around discreetly, find out who the photographer is, where they live. One day we will want to retrieve the originals of those pictures, wherever they are being hidden. And you are to build up a folio on Wallace. Before we strike back, I want to know any weak points he has - wife, children, the usual. And where he might hide his pictures too. Keep in touch,' and with that, he leant forward and broke the link.

Cassiter went for a stroll, made for the Seine. He always found the flow of a river conducive to clear thinking and this was a moment of importance. The move of his headquarters had been easy enough. Almost everything was digital, the team were more than happy to spend some time in France, and the office he maintained in the Rue de l'Université was as well-equipped as Edinburgh. Joining up with the French section was straightforward - they all interchanged often enough on assignments to know one another well anyway.

As soon as he knew what Cameron's purpose was in rushing to Frankfurt, he would contact Parsol. The evidence was amassing, but it made no sense to him: the Norwegian dagger, the picture from Hereford Cathedral, the dagger he had ordered snatched from that churchwoman's father in the States. All things he knew Parsol wanted, all seemingly unintelligible. Then there was the information Collette had gathered on the church's glass window to add into the mix. After much thought, he decided it would make sense to give it all to Parsol. That was what he was contracted to do, and then his next moves could be determined by how Parsol interpreted the information. In the meantime, he had another lead to follow up and it was almost time for his team to act on it. He'd wait for Collette's call.

• • •

Helen raised her glass to Sam. 'I hope you are going to give him good marks next year, he's got talent has our Davy.'

'Yes, he has. But once again, he's put himself in danger. Still, I have to say I would never have found it.'

'Nobody would. It's so obscure, but it's there. How will you handle it?'

'There's no problem getting to see it, that's arranged already. I intend to verify it and get a high-resolution picture. The website doesn't give much detail in terms of provenance, but I understand from Herr Richter that there are some records offline. If I can get access to them, we may well be able to work out not just where this dagger came from, but which saint or church's name it represents.'

'We've got three left to identify: St Athanasius, St Boniface and Mary Magdalene. Any informed guesses?' said Helen.

'Let's wait and see what the records show. If it were local to Germany then we might think about St Boniface. Sandi McLellan said St B was big in parts of Germany, Belgium and France. But the Nazis looted from across Europe, so without further information it's impossible to say.'

'Okay, I'm going to try and sort something out about James Curry as well.'

'Yes, that's important; if we lose access to the old tunnel we may never solve this. Good luck with him, he seems a real -'

'Yes, he is,' said Helen. 'But with a bit of luck I might just be able to throw a spanner in his works. I'm not saying anything until I know for sure. I don't want to build people's hopes up until I know.'

Chapter 17

SATURDAY 24ᵀᴴ AUGUST

It was past mid-afternoon when the doors of St Bartholomew's swung open and Xavier emerged. He stopped on the top step and looked down at the crowd filling the narrow street below, and they greeted the appearance of their priest with a great cheer. The air was thick with cigarette smoke mixed with the smell of garlic and wine, and the sweat of happy jostling humans; it all warmed together in the still air to form the smell that, for Xavier, was forever St Bartholomew's Day. His day, his church's day.

Xavier smiled, raised his hand to the crowd, made the sign of the cross and blessed them all. The cheers rang out again, bouncing to and fro between the buildings that lined both sides of the old cobbled thoroughfare. The volume soared, the sound hemmed in between the plastered walls; some whitewashed, some faded yellow ochre, occasional creams. Quickly the noise rose above the crowd, and past first and second floor balconies where elderly ladies revelled in the spectacle and recalled days past when they had marched with the procession. Up the sound continued, funnelling out of the street's shadows to spill over the terracotta-tiled roofs from where it dissipated into the sunlit sky.

The space on the step behind him was quickly occupied by several priests from neighbouring parishes, come to lend support on the big day. Angelo, never far from Xavier's side, stood closest.

Xavier saw the district band mustered in the street a few paces to his left. Everything was as it should be. As the blessing ended, the bandleader signalled and the music struck up in a greeting for him. Then as the band began a slow march past, heading down towards the harbour, he led the clergy down the few broad steps from the church to the street below, pacing himself to arrive a moment after the band had passed. To his left the street ran a hundred paces up to the town square. The procession would end there in about half an hour. He turned right, heading down the hill, following the music.

The priests were followed from the church by four sturdy looking men, each supporting a corner of a litter on which perched a statue of St Bartholomew. Behind them, a crowd of parishioners streamed out of the church to join the procession. Those that lined the little street cheered and clapped. Xavier knew they too would join the end of the procession, which grew as it went. Camera flashes identified the tourists in the crowd and extended arms signed the presence of smartphone users intent on recording life as it happened.

Ahead, at the foot of the street, he could see the sea; still and glistening blue. He knew that the fishermen's boats would be moored along the little quayside, cleaned and tided especially for the moment. The fishermen and their families would clap and cheer as he passed, then, in their turn, join the end of the procession. Eventually, once the procession had wound its route through the little town, it would have gathered in all the families. Then on the final approach into the square, he would find the way lined with the farming families from the homes scattered into the high hills beyond the town. By the time the band led Xavier and the effigy of St Bartholomew into the square all the families of his parish would be represented.

And so it was. The procession came to a halt in the square, directly outside the municipal hall. The band continued to play as people settled on to the benches that lined the trestle tables arranged around three sides of the square. Already seated were the old ladies, whisked from their balconies directly to the square as soon as the procession had passed them by. Xavier climbed the steps of the municipal hall; he welcomed Angelo's supporting hand as he went. Waiting at the top was the mayor, half Xavier's age and brimming with confidence and pride. He welcomed Xavier with a warm handshake and a kiss then deferentially stepped back, allowing Xavier the limelight. For the second time that afternoon, Xavier looked down on his flock.

He watched the crowd; saw toddlers hurrying to clamber up beside grandmothers, saw parents, mostly laughing, as they separated little groups of children and herded them to their places - knowing they wouldn't stay put for long. Meanwhile, the statue of St Bartholomew had worked its wobbly way up the steps and been settled on a table beside him. From here, the saint would watch over the parishioners during the festivities. The band stopped playing and the crowd fell silent. Xavier saw all the faces tilted up expectantly towards him, the younger ones hoping his speech wouldn't last too long.

They were not disappointed. Xavier's voice was as strong as ever, it filled the little square, bounced back off the walls. Everyone heard as he thanked St Bartholomew for the parish's continuing success and commended by name into God's safe keeping all those the parish had lost through the year. Then he called for prosperity in the coming year and finally he blessed the feast.

The band, never silent for long, struck up and, to another round of cheers, Xavier slowly stepped back down to the square. As he took his place at table, the doors of the two local bars and the restaurant burst open to further cheers. Smells swirled out from the doorways to tease the crowd: fresh baked breads, pastas, sweet fragranced lamb dishes and, from the restaurant, roasting pig. Xavier laughed and waved the waiting staff out, encouraging speed. He watched the waiters streaming back and forth across the space in the middle of the square, left clear for the dancing that he knew would accompany the singing and gaiety into the small hours. The waiters fanned out, delivering their loaded trays of food to the seated parishioners. Others carried water, bottles of wine, and fizzy drinks for the children. The feast had begun.

• • •

As night fell on the sound of distant festivities, three visitors wandered up from the calm of the empty quayside where they had left their car. The middle visitor was a beautiful young woman; to either side of her, big men. Collette glanced over her shoulder back towards the car where a fourth visitor had stayed behind the wheel. She saw the headlights flash as the fourth man acknowledged her look.

She turned her attention back to the street ahead. A couple of streetlights had failed outside the church and everything in the vicinity was in darkness. Beyond the church, she could see the lights in the square glowing warmly and hear the music and shrieks of fun continuing unabated as the population partied. Perfect, she thought, pointing her companions up the steps towards the church doors. They hurried up and while she and one of the men glanced to left and right, the second man produced a short crowbar and jemmied the door. They were in within moments and Collette pushed the door tight shut behind them. They stood still in the darkness, listening - silence. Without going any further into the church, each pulled forensic suits from their shoulder bags and donned them.

Collette produced a little torch and switched it on, careful to keep the beam low to the floor. The architecture, designed for cool comfort, had few windows, and those that were there were small and set high. As long as she did not shine the beam upwards there was little chance of it being spotted from outside. 'Come on,' she said, leading the men directly up the centre aisle.

Halfway up she paused and directed one man away to the side. She watched as he hurried between the pews. Reaching the side wall, he climbed on to a pew and stretched up to retrieve a little covert camera from a wall-light mounting. He gripped it and ripped hard; pulling it out along with the power feed he had previously hooked into the light fitting. Pocketing it, he returned to the aisle, joining Collette. She noted his nod of success and pointed him away to gather in the rest of his bugs from around the building. She led the other man on up the aisle.

Reaching the altar, she brushed past it and stopped at the reredos beyond, allowing her torch to roam across its façade. The decorative screen was impressive. It was sculpted from marble, which shimmered in the beam of her torchlight. It featured a dazzling array of religious images. Ornately worked saints and angels were picked out as the beam moved; each figure was gold leafed and seemed to move and glisten, snatching its moment in the beam before surrendering the spotlight to the next and fading back into the dark.

'That's the one,' said Collette, suddenly swinging the beam back to one of the figures. It was St Bartholomew. She didn't know who it was, didn't care; knew only that it was the one the old priest had used. Their cameras had been in place for a week. It had begun to seem a pointless task, nothing had happened, no revelations, it had made pretty boring viewing. Likewise, the cameras in the priest's home had offered nothing, completely uninspiring. But then, ninety percent of their job was waiting and inaction.

Because of the disruption to the team in Edinburgh, it had taken a while for them to link the priests' visits to Edinburgh with a series of flights by a private plane to and from Cagliari Airport earlier in the summer. Once the connection was made, it had been a simple process to trace the priests back to their home, after which the surveillance had begun.

Yesterday things had changed, the priests had behaved oddly and Cassiter had immediately ordered action. In her mind, she reviewed the images again. Together with the younger priest who always seemed to be nearby, Xavier had locked himself in the church. They had paused reverentially at the altar before proceeding beyond it to the reredos. They had stood where she stood now. The old one had messed about with the odd little figure, the one with the knives. She remembered laughing to herself when she first watched the pictures; that would be her saint if she cared about such things. She didn't.

He had done something clever with his hands, they had not been able to work out exactly what, and the upshot was the little figure had slid forward to reveal a compartment, a drawer from which he had removed a silver dagger. Exactly what Cassiter was looking for. And now here they were.

She reached out, felt the figure, tried to twist, pull and push, and got no response. This had been anticipated and with time at a premium, she immediately signalled her companion forward.

The man stepped up with the crowbar he'd used earlier on the front doors. He worked it behind the figure and pressed, trying to lever the compartment open. Applying more and more pressure against the figure had no effect. He stopped and dipping inside his shoulder bag pulled out a chisel and short handled mason's hammer.

Collette saw his questioning glance and nodded in response. 'Do it quickly.'

He looked back at the sculptured figure, set his chisel against it and hammered hard. It took several blows before St Bartholomew fell with a crash to the ground. He kicked it aside and looked carefully where the beam of Collette's torch shone on the damaged marble. The figure had sheared off and there appeared to be no opening behind.

'Smash it. Break it up until you get through. Spare nothing,' said Collette as she glanced round to acknowledge the arrival of the other man. He had completed his gathering. 'Hard now, hurry,' she urged the hammerer on.

The church filled with the sound of splintering stone as, bit by bit, the chisel dug through the marble. Then the man began beating the reredos directly with the hammer. For a little while, there seemed to be no response, then, suddenly, marble started to break up under the repeated blows. He had broken through. Putting aside the hammer, he wedged his short crowbar inside the broken front of what appeared to be a drawer compartment and started to lever against it. Slowly at first and then in a sudden rush, the drawer slid out.

Collette stepped forward and pushed the man aside. She reached in and lifted the dagger, shining the torch on it. 'So this is what all the fuss is about. I hope you're worth it, little knife.' Then she signalled the team to leave. They reached the front door and were about to strip off their forensic suits when they heard a noise. The door was opening.

Lined behind the door they could not see who was opening it but could hear worried mutterings and invocations of the saints. A young, square-shouldered man appeared. Stepping cautiously out from the opened door into the church, he was followed by a much older man. She knew who they were; had seen the two priests often enough in video. The sound of feet running away up the street told of an alarm about to be raised. She pulled a knife from her jacket and silently stepped behind the old priest. Springing an arm round his neck, she brought her other arm round to press the knife against his chest.

The young priest spun round and took a half step towards them to effect a rescue. He never reached her, first hesitating when he saw the knife pressed against Xavier's body and then confronted by Collette's two accomplices. The first of her men went down under a furious blow, as un-Christian as you like. The second slipped in under Angelo's guard and grappled with him. In the temporary stalemate as they wrestled for supremacy, the first man got up and swung his shoulder bag hard at Angelo's head. The full weight of a mason's hammer caught Angelo behind the ear and the young priest dropped instantly.

Collette shifted her focus to the old priest and leant her head in close to his. 'Good bye old man,' she whispered and slipped her dagger's point beneath his ribs, pressed hard, felt the momentary resistance in his jacket, then felt it fade as the blade sliced through the cloth. It paused again, catching in the metal of the heavy chain that kept Xavier's gold signet ring close against his skin. Surprised at the resistance, she pressed again and finally the blade slid into his flesh. She heard his gasp of distress as he dropped onto the cool marble tiles.

She could make out a distant noise building in the street outside. 'Let's go, quickly,' she ordered. They stepped out and, still in their white forensic suits, hurried down to the car that was now waiting at the foot of the church steps. They were pulling safely away as she saw the first of the parishioners approaching from the square.

Chapter 18

MONDAY 26TH AUGUST

Sam was sitting in a Frankfurt museum workshop. Bernhard Richter had just laid a dagger on the table in front of him. 'There it is, my friend,' said Bernhard. His confidently sounded English words were slightly clipped though entirely clear. 'I hope it is what you expected to see.'

Sam looked over the table to Bernhard and stretched out his hands a little. 'May I?' he asked.

'Of course. You must be my guest. But here, take these.' Bernhard handed him a pair of white gloves. 'I brought a big sized pair for you. I'm sure they will fit.'

Sam pulled on the gloves and examined the dagger carefully. He noted the Roman numeral six. There was absolutely no doubt, it was part of the set. 'Oh yes, this is what I was looking for. No doubt at all.'

'That's good, but tell me, why are you so interested?'

'We found a similar one during a dig in Scotland earlier in the summer. I think we might have parts of a set. Can't say much more than that I'm afraid. There are a lot of gaps in my knowledge. But tell me what you know of your dagger.'

Bernhard opened the slim folder that he had brought into the room with him. 'Not much,' he said while scanning the document it contained. 'The museum received it during the war. It appears it was received from the authorities, the Nazis; sadly that was a very common thing.' He turned over the page and continued to scan the document.

'Any indication of where it came from or who owned it?'

'Yes, this record is very simple and quite clear. But a little surprising, I think. It was taken from a small place near Mainz. That's not so far from here.' Tapping his finger on the document, Bernhard looked across at Sam.

'The Christian church and the Nazis is a bit of a mixed bag, I think you say? Some supported Hitler at first, some stayed quiet and some preached against him and the intolerance he promoted. Quite a few of the dissenting pastors were sent away to the camps.'

'Concentration camps?' said Sam.

Bernhard gave a crisp little nod in assent, and then continued. 'It seems the owner of this dagger was particularly fierce in his criticism of the Nazis. They didn't like that sort of thing. One day the Gestapo must have decided enough was enough and just took him...' He paused for a long moment and then read on a little further. 'Yes, that's right, took him and his assistant pastor too. Both were interrogated and then sent away. His possessions were examined by the state, and as was the practice then, anything of historical or artistic value was taken, some of it then distributed to designated museums. That's how this dagger would have reached us.' Bernhard shifted uncomfortably. 'Of course, we don't want to keep things taken like that. It is not ours, but then who does it belong to?'

'I don't know. Maybe you'll never find out now. But who was he? What do we know?'

'Ah yes. So, our pastor, his name was Schmidt, Andre Schmidt, a bachelor. No family noted, so it's difficult to make links now.'

'His church?' said Sam, casually.

'Hmmm, let me see...' Bernhard referred back to the file. 'Yes, here we have it, it was his address. The church's name was St Boniface. Oh, this is a sad end. It seems the church was burnt down and deliberately left in ruins. It doesn't actually say, but it seems likely that the Gestapo burnt the church too.'

Inside Sam was torn. Buried amidst all the evidence of the

darkest of human deeds, they had found another dagger. They needed it, but there was nothing to celebrate here. St Boniface, another saint represented in the church window, and another linked dagger. This must absolutely confirm the assumption that the saints were the church names. 'Tragic,' said Sam. 'Horrible times.'

'Just so,' said Bernhard.

Sam produced his camera. 'May I photograph the blade? It would help in fixing a definite link.'

'I'm sorry, that's not allowed. There are very strict rules. I'm sure you will understand.' Bernhard could see that Sam was unhappy. 'Do not worry, I anticipated your need. It is permissible for you to have a copy of our official photographs.' He pulled out hard copies from the file and slid them across the table. 'I printed these for you earlier.'

Sam quickly reviewed the pictures and was delighted with the outcome. He acknowledged it was a great help and promised to keep Bernhard in the loop. After a short chat, he thanked Bernhard and left. Keen to be alone to think over the news, keen too to catch an earlier flight back to Edinburgh, if he could.

• • •

Helen opened the door to her Causewayside flat and stood waiting while her visitor wheezed up the stairs to join her. She had allowed Francis into the stairwell in response to an incessant sounding of the buzzer. Sam was not due back from Frankfurt until later in the day; in the meantime, she had taken some time to start packing her possessions. James Curry was determined to see her out of the flat. She had no intention of begging for extra time.

Peering over the bannister, Helen saw the old priest's head bobbing up and down in time with his paces up the steps. As he neared the top, Francis spotted her and gave a little wave of greeting - too out of breath to speak.

'Francis, I wasn't expecting you. Come in, you'd better have a seat before you fall over. You've taken those stairs far too quickly.' She shepherded him into the lounge and pointed him towards a comfortable sofa.

Gratefully, he sat, took several deep breaths and began to

compose himself.

She could see the worry in his eyes. 'So what's the big rush? You're the last person I expected to see this afternoon.'

'Your phone…' gasped Francis, '… I've been trying to call you. You didn't answer.'

Helen nodded. 'Oh yes, I've got it charging in the bedroom. I'm sorry Francis, I didn't hear it.'

Francis gave a little snort, acknowledging her statement and dismissing it now as inconsequential. 'Come sit here with me,' he said, patting the seat beside him. 'Come quick.'

Picking up the anxiety in his voice Helen sat beside him. 'What's wrong, Francis? What's up?'

Francis reached out and gripped her hand, squeezed it. 'It's not on the news here yet so you won't have heard it, but I've just been speaking with a priest in Rome, finalising details of my visit there. You know I've workshops to attend there next week.'

'Oh yes, Francis. You've mentioned it more than once! What's up?'

'It's the story of the week in Italy, two priests attacked in their church on a Saturday night. Helen, they've got to Xavier and Angelo. They got them in the church.'

Helen's heart sank. 'What do you mean, got them?'

Francis gave a low moan. 'In Xavier's church, it happened while the whole congregation was attending the St Bartholomew's Day festivities. It seems robbers had broken into the church under cover of darkness. For some reason Xavier and Angelo had returned to the church. They must have disturbed the robbers. There was a fight, Xavier was stabbed and Angelo clubbed down.'

'Oh Lord, no! How are they? Do we know?'

'I'm afraid my information is not up to date, but my contact said it was touch and go for Xavier; he's in hospital in Cagliari. Angelo too, poor boy, he's alive but hasn't recovered consciousness. I understand it could have been worse, but not much. Apparently, Xavier's gold chain and ring deflected the blade; otherwise, it would have reached his heart. Thankfully, a young deacon managed to raise the alarm and the robbers had to leave sharp before a lynch mob caught them. Otherwise, if it was the ones we're facing, I suspect they would have made a point of finishing Xavier and

Angelo off before leaving.'

'If?' said Helen. 'There's no if about it. You and I both know that.' She pulled her hand out from Francis' grip and rested it on his shoulder, squeezed gently. 'Come on now Francis. What did your contact say? Did he give a prognosis?'

Francis shook his head. 'No, everyone is fearing the worst though. I don't know what we should do.'

'I wish I could go out there,' said Helen. 'Perhaps I can but I am booked on a flight to Switzerland and can't put Franz Brenner off any longer. I might be able to fly over to Sardinia in a few days. I'll need to check and make some bookings.'

'Yes, I know Xavier has no family, not sure about Angelo. It would be good to go.'

'Well why don't you? You're not due in Rome for a while yet and your parish here is geared up for your absence already.'

'It would be good…' Francis sounded enthusiastic then trailed off.

Helen realised what the problem was. 'Look, I know a parish priest doesn't have money to spare. And from what everyone has told me, Sardinia is about as expensive as it gets. Let me pay, I'll book flights and accommodation, a hire car.'

Francis started to object.

She raised her hand, a single finger pointing up, silencing him. 'I've got the trust fund, remember. If this isn't a good use for the money, I don't know what is. No arguments, I'm going to book for you now. In fact, I'm going to book for you and Elaine. She will want to go. You phone her, let her know and then phone your contact in Rome, get all the details you can. You travel tomorrow.'

The worry remained on Francis' face but she could sense the relief in the old priest's demeanour as a plan formed. 'I'm going online right now; you get on the phone to Elaine.'

'What about Grace? She loves Xavier,' said Francis. 'I don't think she could bear being left here alone.'

Helen thought for a moment. She knew he was right. Cost was no object and, anyway, neither Francis nor Elaine was in the best of health right now. Grace would make an excellent escort if nothing else. 'Great idea. Let them know and I'll book for all of you. And I'll book your onward flight to Rome while I'm at it.'

Francis nodded appreciatively and rummaged enthusiastically in his pocket for his phone while Helen headed for the computer.

• • •

Bernhard Richter could not believe his luck. For a man like him, it was a once in a lifetime experience. Truly, he was a Good Samaritan rewarded. That evening, as he left work, he had paused in the street to save a young woman. He'd bravely chased off the attacker who had knocked her over while attempting to snatch her bag.

Once he helped her to her feet, she had been so grateful, insisted on buying him a drink. One thing had led to another and here he was in her bed. She was such fun, talkative and fascinated by his working day. Most of the women he knew weren't interested in his work. But this one, she hung on his every word. Once he'd run out of anecdotes about his life and job, she'd even listened politely when he had told her about his visitor from Scotland. In fact, she'd wondered what the treasure he was so interested in looked like. Since she was interested, he promised to let her see a copy of the pictures when they met again the next evening.

Chapter 19

TUESDAY 27ᵀᴴ AUGUST

Grace stood motionless, leaning back against the kitchen worktop. The morning light flooded through the window behind her to fill the manse kitchen. The bright sunlight was in Helen's eyes, preventing her from gauging Grace's mood accurately but she guessed from her stance that there was a problem.

'Grace, I'll need you to look out for Francis and your mum. I know Sam will be with you for a day or so but he's going to have to focus on the wider problem. You're really the only fully fit one amongst the rest of you.' Helen crossed the room to the window. 'I want you to take this too.' She handed Grace an envelope containing a wad of Euros. The hire car is paid for; it's to be picked up at the airport, the accommodation is covered too. Use this for meals and as a reserve in case something goes wrong. It should ensure that anything else you all might need is covered.'

Grace took the envelope, glanced inside. 'I don't think we'll need this much,' she said.

'Who knows what you'll need. Better safe than sorry. And Grace, if there's anything left when you're finished; buy your mother something nice. She's had a rotten time these past few months.'

'Thanks, Helen. This means a lot to me. And mum too. Xavier has always been around; he's part of the furniture of our lives.'

Grace reached out and hugged Helen.

'I know. Give the old boy a hug from me when you see him. Sam made a phone call to the hospital earlier, getting an update - thank God for multilingual boyfriends. Xavier's in a bad way, a lot of pain, lost a lot of blood; he's been sedated and is only half-conscious most of the time. He'll be pleased to see you all. Remember and tell him I'll be coming too, as soon as I can.'

'I will, don't worry about that. What about Angelo?'

Helen hesitated. 'He's still not recovered consciousness. They are more worried about him than Xavier now.'

Grace scowled. 'How's this all going to end? What's next?'

'I don't know but do be careful, though I'm sure the attackers will have left by now. Sam spoke with the deacon who recently joined Xavier's parish. It seems the robbers didn't take anything obvious from the church. But the reredos had been smashed to reveal what he thinks looks like a secret compartment. It's empty.'

Grace looked still more worried. 'Do you think that's where Xavier hid his dagger? Have they got away with it?'

'At a guess, I'd say yes, wouldn't you?' Helen gently pulled Grace away from the window so she could finally see her face properly. 'Sam is driving round to pick up your mum and Francis. Then he's coming to collect us. He'll be here in a few minutes. Now, there's a flight to catch, what's the big mystery that needed me to meet you here?'

Grace pointed towards the kitchen table; something was on it, covered by a tea towel. 'Last night I decided to give that a polish before we go to Xavier's. So I went down to the tunnel to get it. They really made a mess of John's cross didn't they?'

'Yes, I'm sorry. I know you treasured it for the memories you shared with him.'

'Well yes, I did. But that's not it. I know it's just the smashed up base but it feels funny.'

'Funny?'

'Yeah, kind of squashy.'

'That's odd. I'll have a look.' As Helen started towards the table the sound of a car horn tooting in the drive reached them.

'That'll be Sam,' said Grace.

'Right, come on. Quick, let's put the base away in the tunnel again for now and get on our way; we'll look at it properly once everyone gets back.'

• • •

Cassiter climbed the now familiar steps. The guards, the bag carrier, his escort, nothing had changed. Except, this time his arrival was marked by Parsol's appearance at the head of the steps. He was smiling, hand outstretched. Cassiter took the hand and then, after the warmest of greetings, the two men walked into the chateau.

Cassiter's bag was carried up to his bedroom while Parsol guided him straight into the opulent study. It was in this room where he had first been let into Parsol's inner circle. But he was mindful he had not been let too far in. Taking his seat, Cassiter declined wine, settling for sparkling water and a sharp mind.

Parsol went to his wall safe and discreetly executed an elaborate sequence to unlock and open it; codes, locks, alarms and finally a thumb scan combined to release the door. He swung it open and withdrew a small wooden case that he placed on the desk and then carefully opened it. The inside was lined with plush blue velvet padding; there were slots to hold things.

Cassiter's jaundiced eye assessed it as a cutlery canteen. True, a special canteen, but canteen nonetheless. It had been made to hold a set of knives or daggers and he could see several, housed snuggly in their designated slots. He could see several gaps too.

Parsol stared almost reverentially at the box. He allowed his hand to glide across it and then looked up at Cassiter. 'Well?' he asked, straightening up, expectant.

'My teams have been busy since we last met.'

'So I understand. I had been a little concerned over what direction you would choose to take. But now, so much, so quickly. May I see?'

Cassiter had spent some time weighing up how much he should tell Parsol. Finally, he decided the information was of no use without Parsol's insight. While he was quite aware that Parsol had not told him everything, he decided his best advantage was to run with Parsol's expectations.

He reached inside his briefcase and pulled out a clear plastic packet. The label read Sandefjord. The dagger inside was accompanied by a neatly printed sheet of paper, providing a detailed account of its gathering and a list of the five Norwegian lives disposed of in the process - the lives didn't matter, just incidental account items to be charged and settled.

Parsol picked up the package, held it up and beamed. 'Excellent. Very good, and Sandefjord. Who would have thought it?' He carefully opened the package and pulled out the dagger, allowed his hand to slide across the silver, tracing part of the pattern and then looked back at Cassiter. 'You said you had retrieved more. What else have you got?'

'This is very special,' said Cassiter, pulling out another clear plastic package. It too contained a dagger and printed sheet with the retrieval details. 'I only received it this morning. My team took it during the weekend. Took it from somebody you and I know only too well.'

'Oh?' said Parsol as he put down the Norwegian dagger and reached for the new packet. 'How so?'

'It belonged to the two priests who wrecked our plans in Edinburgh.'

'Ah ha. The Latins. This explains their involvement. I have wondered a great deal about exactly what their connection to Edinburgh was.' He paused for a moment, looking thoughtful. 'Of course if they are formally connected to Edinburgh then that indicates there is a network against us. It is not just a scattering of ill-informed church people.

'But this is the best of news. I hope the priests suffered, your people weren't too easy on them. It's not good practice to let our opponents survive. Especially those two. They did so much harm to our plans.'

'The younger one had his head broken and the old one's belly was opened. Unfortunately, my team had to evacuate early when the alarm was raised. So they didn't finish things as I would have liked. My information is that both priests are in intensive care in Cagliari. I have somebody on location to tie up loose ends.'

'Good, very good. Cassiter, you have excelled yourself. Every expectation is met, such progress could only have been dreamt of.'

Sensing his opportunity Cassiter pushed at Parsol. 'Perhaps I would have done more, faster, had I known the full story. It's difficult working with only half the facts.'

The smile vanished from Parsol's face. He carefully placed the Sardinian dagger on the table and turned to look out of the study window. He stood silent and motionless for several minutes. Cassiter sat still watching, waiting.

'My friend... I can call you that now, I think,' said Parsol, still staring intently out of the window. 'I have been cautious not to tell you everything because while we know knowledge is power, knowledge can also be very dangerous. For me and for you. You know I have always trusted you. If you now agree to join us formally, I will introduce you to my friends and tell you what else remains to be told.'

Parsol turned from the window and fixed Cassiter with a steely gaze. 'You must understand, once you are in, you can never leave. For all your team's special skills, they could never resist the weight of our organisation.' He smiled a cold telling smile. 'Like you, we view the rules as obstacles for others to contend with. Not something that constrains us. Think about it carefully. On the outside, you are useful to us, but always outside. Come in and you are part of us, always. You are staying tonight. In the morning, you can let me know your decision. If you agree to join us, I will tell you all you need to know over lunch with some very important people who are gathering here tomorrow.'

Cassiter held Parsol's gaze. 'Until the morning then,' he said.

'Good. Now I believe there is more for me to see.'

Cassiter pulled out a third plastic package. He handed it over, the contents less inspiring, a little picture snatched from the dean's office at Hereford Cathedral.

Parsol took it. Looked carefully and smiled again. 'It has a set of blade markings. The dagger?'

'Lost long ago, we were fortunate to track this down.'

'Fortunate, nothing. You are a magician my friend. The pattern is everything. The blade is lost yet still you produce the pattern.'

Cassiter accepted the compliment, did not attempt false modesty. He reached inside his briefcase again and pulled out the parish dagger. It was the great prize that Parsol needed. He slid it across the desk. 'This is the one you wanted most, I think.'

Parsol leant forward and quickly pulled the dagger from its wrapper. With a cry of triumph, he held it up to the sunlit window and studied it carefully. 'This is the one. This is the key. Perfect. Perfect!'

'Well it makes little sense to me,' said Cassiter. 'But I'm sure you know what it means.'

Parsol nodded. Looking at the number sequence, he stroked the blade and, wanting to be alone with the new discoveries, started to draw the meeting to a close.

'I'll have something else for you tomorrow,' said Cassiter, 'pictures from Germany. But in the meantime, I've got these too.' He pulled out the packet of notes and pictures taken from New College. 'I'm not sure what the relevance is but the church people seemed very excited by it all.'

Parsol glanced at the packet, absently nodded an acknowledgement and promised to review it later. The meeting ended. Cassiter could tell that Parsol only had eyes for the parish dagger.

• • •

Sam steered the hire car into the hotel car park and came to a halt. It had been a long journey. A planned change of planes at Heathrow had been accompanied by a long and unplanned delay. A French air traffic controllers strike had once again clogged up the skies over Europe. It was nearly evening when the flight had finally landed at Cagliari and they had all agreed to head straight for the hotel. Everyone wanted to clean up and get something to eat before going on to the hospital.

Chapter 20

WEDNESDAY 28ᵀᴴ AUGUST

Zurich. Helen picked her case off the carousel and made her way from arrivals into the airport concourse. She scanned the cluster of drivers holding up name cards, spotted her name and approached the holder. He was impeccably turned out in a crisp chauffeur's uniform and immediately welcomed Helen with a warm smile while reaching for her case.

A first visit for Helen, she thought about asking the driver for some information but he was clearly focused on getting the big Mercedes through the traffic with the minimum of delay. Instead, she settled back and watched the scene unfold as the car rushed into the city. Suddenly, they were crossing a bridge. To her left hand was a broad expanse of water.

'This is the Quaibrücke' said the driver. 'See on the right, that's the Limmat River feeding into our lake, the Zürichsee.' The driver nodded his head towards the broad waters. 'You maybe call it Lake Zurich.'

As Helen took in the scene, the car left the bridge behind and turned right, muscling through the traffic and into the financial district. 'If you get lost don't worry. Remember the bridge; the bank and your hotel are only four hundred metres away. Here, up ahead, see.'

A couple of minutes later he was nudging the car to a halt halfway along a short street lined on both sides by old terraced buildings. Each was fronted with the same ornate dressed stone, similar windows, similar doors. Here and there, symmetry was broken where a café had rolled out its pavement canopy, but for the most part it was elegant anonymity.

The chauffeur jumped out and opened Helen's door for her. She stepped out and he shut the door behind her before guiding her towards a doorway.

It took Helen a moment to realise she was at the bank. The discreet polished wooden doors were swung in and hooked open to allow free access to a pair of glazed inner doors, through which she could see a plush reception. Standing inside the glass doors were two men, wearing uniforms identical to the chauffeur's. One stepped forward and opened the door for Helen. They were younger than her chauffeur, but she noticed them nod discreetly to him as he followed her in. The slightest flash of holster strap and the telltale bulge in their jackets told her these were security guards, not just doormen.

A lady behind the reception desk beamed a smile at her as she approached. 'Miss Johnson. How nice of you to visit us. I hope you had a good flight.'

Helen nodded and smiled.

'Herr Brenner is expecting you. Please, let me take you up to him.' She stood, came from behind the desk and guided Helen towards a lift. Its doors slid open silently as they approached. 'Simon will take your bag directly to the hotel for you. It's just round the corner.'

Franz Brenner had appeared exactly as he had done on their first meeting earlier in the summer; perfectly turned out and impeccably polite. He was well aware of the horrors that had taken place in Norway but his normal calm air prevailed and exactly mirrored the atmosphere of his bank. This was like no bank Helen had ever been in - no cash machines, no tellers, she hadn't seen any other customers.

They had spent an hour talking, going over various papers and signing documents; finally Franz had sent Helen away with a folder of papers to study and promises of dinner that evening in his home.

Simon would collect her. In the meantime, his staff would process the documents that would formally consolidate her position as the trust account holder. Thereafter, she could access the safe deposit box that was stored in the bank's vault.

• • •

There were perhaps thirty people ranged around the table. All men, all impeccably turned out and every one exuding an air of self-confidence; it sat very close to arrogance - businessmen, diplomats, politicians. The range of accents told him this was a multinational group but everyone spoke English during the meal.

Parsol sat at the head of the long table; Cassiter to his right hand. From his position at the dining table, Cassiter carefully reviewed the elegant room and its occupants. Parsol had stood at the start of the meal, called the group to order and introduced Cassiter to the guests. It seemed they all knew who he was and about the progress he had made. His formal induction had followed. It had started with a simple oath - secrecy and loyalty unto death. Cassiter was not overly concerned with oaths, and loyalty was not high on his list of priorities either, though he did approve of secrecy.

Today, he was intrigued to understand more about Parsol's group and its strengths. Perhaps more pressing, he was aware of the damage and losses his own group had suffered over the summer. Many more manpower losses and his group might start to lose critical mass. Certainly, joining with Parsol offered the chance to offset that loss.

Earlier in the day, Parsol had briefed him on the organisation. It was not a masonic lodge, almost but not quite. Cassiter interpreted the description as an international spider's web of rich and powerful men, self-serving, self-preserving. At its head was Parsol, the hereditary master. Many of the others around the table had inherited their places and wealth from fathers or grandfathers. A few others had come from nowhere, excelled in their line of work and, having demonstrated a suitable disposition, been invited to join. Cassiter fell into that category.

Cassiter lived a life invisible to the wider world but his desire to be known amongst his peers as the best in his field had found him accepting the invitation to join. He would remain free to go about his own business, but would be ready to help members without question when called on and could call on such help himself. On first inspection, Parsol and his friends had goals that interested him: yes to self-preservation, yes to joint development and yes to mutual protection and support: yes to all of them. But additionally, they had a collective goal - to retrieve the wealth, and most importantly, the lost religious treasures of the group's founder, Parsol's ancestor. It appeared this was not just a group of wealthy men interested in more wealth, which Cassiter could appreciate. There seemed to be some additional aspect - some religious element that was harder for him to get a handle on. He would sit on his scepticism for the time being.

It was a big step to become part of a group but the opportunities, the scale and the motivations attracted him. For someone who had never belonged anywhere, it almost felt like a homecoming.

As the meal ended, a man at the foot of the table stood, he gave a further welcoming speech to Cassiter and exhorted everyone to redouble their efforts to finish the task. He thanked Cassiter and acknowledged it was due to his efforts that the goal was within their grasp at last. A round of polite clapping ran round the table and glasses were raised in Cassiter's direction. As the noise faded, it dawned on Cassiter who the speaker was. Tall and square shouldered with an impressive quiff of hair and the lightest of French accents - it could only be Parsol's son, Eugene Parsol, Junior.

• • •

In response to a message from the hotel reception desk, Helen slipped her phone into her pocket, left her hotel suite and made for the lift. Simon was waiting in reception to take her to Franz Brenner's home for dinner.

She was feeling a little easier in herself now. The folders Franz had given her had made fascinating reading. More importantly, a message from Sam indicated that there had been no further deterioration in the priests' condition today. They were not out of the woods but at least there was no more bad news.

Chapter 21

THURSDAY 29ᵀᴴ AUGUST

Helen stepped towards the bank's glass inner entrance door. It was pulled open by the same guard who had opened it the previous day. Beyond him hovered the other guard while the receptionists beamed welcoming smiles from behind their desk. Just as she stepped in, the lift doors opened and Franz Brenner emerged. He greeted her warmly, accepted back the paperwork she had brought with her from her hotel and passed it to one of the receptionists before guiding Helen into the lift.

He didn't select the top floor button that would have carried them up to his office. This time, the lift travelled down into the deepest basement. Franz smiled at her. 'My wife thoroughly enjoyed your company last night, Helen. Sara wonders if you would like to return one day as our houseguest. Perhaps allow us to show you something of our country.'

'That would be great, Franz, thank you. You have a lovely house and what little I've seen of Switzerland seems so beautiful. It would be great to spend some time here.'

'Excellent, that's agreed then. Sara will be delighted. We can make a plan in due course. And of course, the invitation includes your friend Sam. He sounds a splendid fellow. I... no, we both look forward to meeting him when you visit.'

'That's a deal then. I know Sam would love it here too.'

The lift came to a halt and the doors slid open to reveal a broad and empty corridor. At the end were clear glass doors set in a glass wall. Beyond she could see three men, all smartly dressed like the men on reception - more guards.

Her approach was being monitored through the thick glass. Armoured she guessed. Franz stopped at the glass doors and waited patiently as the men watched respectfully from beyond the barrier. 'Why won't they open the door?' said Helen.

'They can't, I'm afraid,' said Franz. He turned and pointed back towards the lift. Helen turned too, wondering what the delay was. 'The staff can't open the doors; they remain auto-locked until the lift has returned to reception level. Just a little security measure to ensure the guards can never be rushed unexpectedly while the strong room doors are open.'

'Is that ever likely to happen?'

'No, we have made other provision to prevent it. However, in private banking, you assume the worst and plan accordingly. That ensures things don't happen. Likely or not.'

They both watched the lift indicator light marking the lift's progress up through the building until it reached reception level.

Franz turned back towards the glass doors, which were immediately opened for him. As they entered, the guards gave respectful greetings and one opened a side door, holding it, allowing Helen and Franz to enter, then closed the door after them.

Franz sat Helen in a seat beside a broad table, a solid piece of polished hardwood; it filled the middle of an otherwise empty room. The walls' wood panelling sported a grain that was repeated in the table - all cut from one tree. She glanced at the arm of her seat, touched it; suspected it was of the same ilk. He gestured towards a closed hatch set in the far wall. 'I will go and organise your box. When the hatch opens, you will find it inside. Please, take all the time you need. When you're finished lock the box and place it back inside the hatch. Then just leave the room. You will be escorted back to the lift. Please come up to my office and we can have coffee before Simon runs you back to the airport.' He pressed the buzzer on the wall beside the door. The door opened and, with a polite nod, Franz was gone, pulling the door shut behind him.

Helen sat and waited. From the white ceiling, a pair of strip lights flooded the room with a crisp white light and a white marbled floor shimmered reflections of the strip lights above. Not a place to come with a hangover, thought Helen. She smiled to herself: something to keep in mind for future visits.

A minute after Franz left, Helen sensed a movement. The hatch cover was silently slipping down and out of sight to reveal a plain metal box. It was around 150 centimetres long, 50 centimetres deep and 50 centimetres high. She sat still, looking at the box, considering what might be inside that was so important. Finally, she stood and crossed to the hatch and carefully tested the weight of the box. It was heavy, very heavy; she could scarcely lift it. How much of that weight was the metal casing and how much was the contents, she could not tell.

In any event, it was too heavy for her. She crossed to the door and pressed the buzzer to summon help. A guard hurried into the room and lifted the box over to the table, then left, closing the door behind him.

Helen gently laid her hands on the box. 'Well, John Dearly, what have you left for me here? I hope it's going to help unwind this mess we're in,' she let her eyes close for a moment. 'God rest you.'

Pulling out her key ring, she selected the one she had recently taken from John's key ring in Edinburgh. It was the only key of his they could not find a use for in church or manse. Then she had spotted a tiny engraving on the shank and inspection through a magnifying glass had revealed the crest of Franz Brenner's bank. She slipped the key into the lock and turned it.

Taking a deep breath, she lifted the lid. It hinged up and back. Helen let her breath out slowly. There were several packages inside the box, each wrapped in cloth: velvet she thought, reaching out and stroking the old and perfectly smooth material. She could feel hard things beneath.

Looking at the array, for a moment it felt like a birthday. Which to open first? Her eyes focused on the largest package. Long and slim, her heart sank a little; she could guess what it was. Reaching in, she lifted the package and placed it on the table, then unwrapped the velvet cover to reveal what she had guessed, a sword. Perfectly preserved in the controlled environment, she could tell this was the real thing. A Templar sword, and not just any Templar sword; her long past predecessor's sword. He had been the first in a long line. A line that led through the ages from a preceptory at Temple all the way to her standing here today.

She looked more closely at the weapon. The pommel carried the unmistakable Templar cross, the wire wrapping round the grip was still taut as though fitted only yesterday, waiting for the owner to lift and wield it in battle. Then the cross guard, still bearing the scar where it had once blocked a sliding sword stroke. And finally, she gently slid the scabbard away to reveal the blade. Carefully, her hand stroked its length. It was shining under a fine film of oil that some hand had applied. John Dearly? Archie Buchan perhaps? She would never know now. Perhaps she should refresh it one day. She would speak with Sam about that. He would want to see this anyway.

Midway down the blade, Helen's hand stopped. She looked more closely at the blade's edge and shivered. Repeated sharpening and polishing of the blade could not hide the telltale nicks and scratches in the metal. This was a blade that had seem a lot of combat, had tasted blood many times. She let the sword rest on the table, stepped back a little to review it. Had things always been like this? Had death always stalked the task like a shadow? Will it ever end? She slid the blade back into its scabbard and put the sword to one side.

Turning her attention back to the box, she continued her review of the contents. An ancient leather bound ledger, its pages thick and stiff with age. Were the pages even made of paper? Again that was something Sam would consider. The earliest entries were in Latin. Other than some dates, she couldn't make them out at all. Then, if anything the writing became even more impenetrable - she wondered if this was Lowland Scots - more work for Sam. The chronology of entries indicated it was a record of something. She guessed this was a type of journal.

As the record developed, the scratching quill was replaced by copperplate script, that in turn gave way to the more fluid style of modern writing and these later entries became progressively more legible for her. She saw the final entries had been by John Dearly. The most recent, a simple nothing to report entry dated three years before his death. She traced his messages back through time. Over the years, he had left several other similar messages while his first entry acknowledged a handover from Archie Buchan. Before that, a series of similar entries by Archie, the last of which declared the handing on of the task to John.

She concluded that the handover itself was an oral procedure. There seemed to be nothing in the legible entries that cast any light on their current problems. Perhaps the earlier entries contained something, they seemed far more extensive, but that might just be an older writing style and more formal language. She could not tell. Sam would need to cast his linguist's eye over the ledger. She toyed with the thought of writing an entry of her own but decided against it and put the ledger aside.

Next, she went to lift out a little wooden chest, it was deceptively heavy, she opted to leave it inside the safe deposit box and just open it in situ. She was staggered to see a neat row of slender gold bars. Each was the length of her middle finger and just a little thicker. She lifted one bar out and saw another layer below; she instinctively knew there would be further rows beneath that. Lifting the bar up to the light she marvelled for a minute and then replaced it, understanding now why the box had seemed so impossibly heavy. Hugely valuable, all this on top of her trust fund. She had no idea of its full value - a lot.

She unwrapped a small box; it contained half a dozen ancient gold coins, each different and each in mint condition. She did not recognise them but assumed they would have had some special significance for whoever established the cache. Beneath the coins were four gold medallions, all equally meaningless to her. Again, she expected Sam would be better able to recognise their meaning, if any, when time allowed.

A wooden box next - around the size of a jewellery box that a woman might keep on her dressing table. Highly polished, all sides worked by an intricate marquetry pattern. She studied it carefully, thinking it odd since the pattern of repeating imagery was more typical of Islamic art. It seemed out of place amongst the Templar relics and there seemed no way of opening it. Stumped, Helen put it aside. Sam was going to be busy.

She turned her attention to another package that rested at the bottom of the box. Again, it felt heavy as she lifted it out and placed it on the table. Unwinding the velvet wrapper, she stopped, puzzled.

The artefact seemed to be of little obvious application. It was a thick sheet of almost clear glass, square shaped and set within a gold frame. The glass was undecorated, quite plain, with a single strand of gold thread embedded inside it; the strand traced a random pattern like a child's crayon scribble across the glass. The gold thread presented no hint as to its meaning or purpose, yet the effort involved in creating the piece, in embedding the gold, would have been significant. It must have a purpose but she just could not begin to imagine what.

Then Helen looked more closely at what she had at first taken to be an imperfection in the glass; suddenly the hairs on the back of her neck rose and she gave an involuntary shiver of recognition. Lifting the glass plate for a closer look, she fished inside the collar of her top and pulled out the signet ring on its heavy gold chain. Putting the glass and ring close together, she studied them carefully.

There was no doubt in her mind, embedded in the glass, perhaps three quarters of the distance along the length of the gold thread was a tiny ruby. It was identical to the one set in her signet ring. It could not be a coincidence, but what did it mean? Of all the treasures, this was the only one that seemed to have a direct link of any sort to her and their current situation. What did it signify?

She turned the glass over, carefully considered both faces. Then focused on the gold frame, it was set tight to the glass' edge, all around. The gold framing encroached over the glass' surface forming an even lip of gold, just like a picture frame - a uniform four centimetres in width all around the glass. Set within three sides of the gold edging were slender strips of blue stone, she guessed lapis lazuli; the blue stone was positioned close to the outer edges of the frame, as distant from the glass as possible. The fourth side was plain.

She set the gold frame carefully on the table with the plain gold surface of the fourth side furthest away from her. The steady electric light picked out markings she had missed on first inspection, very lightly made, but clear. On the right hand side of the frame, positioned so close to the lapis it was hardly visible was a tiny cross, a Templar cross.

On the side nearest to her she realised the lapis was not straight edged, instead it arced inwards towards the glass and then out again.

Near the apex of the arc was a faint ridging line marked into the gold frame: an etched zigzag across the gold, from lapis to glass, almost imperceptible, possibly even a casting flaw.

Turning the glass over, she looked at the frame beneath. The gold was plain with no marks or signs. But like the rest, it had been finished to the highest standard. Along two opposing sides of the base were a series of nine or ten evenly spaced crenulations - forming little feet to support the underside of the gold frame, each crenulation identical and perhaps a centimetre deep. She put the plate back on the table, stooping to peer more carefully, and was impressed to see that each crenulation rested perfectly on the tabletop. The crenulations formed a host of little feet to keep the glass tray level and each foot rested perfectly flat.

Taking her smartphone from her pocket, Helen took photos of the object from several different angles. The ruby told her this was significant today and Sam would need to review it as soon as possible. As she packed each item back into the bank box, she took more pictures so Sam could have a better feel for the contents. When there was an opportunity, he would need to come and spend some time here to understand exactly what they had.

Finally, with a slightly wistful glance inside the box she closed the lid and locked the strongbox. She pressed the buzzer to summon the guard who moved her box back into the hatch and left. She wondered what to do next, but no action was required. The weight of the box triggered a sequence and the hatch's sliding front panel rose to seal off the strongbox from the room. Helen headed for the door, for a brief meeting with Franz and then the airport. She needed to get back to Edinburgh as soon as possible.

• • •

Sam steered the hire car into one of the empty parking bays and eased to a halt. He turned to Elaine who sat in the seat beside him. 'All set?' he said.

Francis and Grace were already getting out of the rear passenger doors.

'Come on, Mum,' said Grace, stepping forward to open the front passenger door. She leant an arm down to help her mother out.

They had spent the previous day in the hospital visiting Xavier and Angelo, and the environment was becoming quite familiar. It was clear that neither priest was going anywhere in a hurry.

Angelo was still being maintained in an induced coma while his head injuries and brain swelling subsided. Though he had seemed quite unaware of his visitors, they would all spend some time with him again today, hoping that his subconscious might recognise their presence.

Xavier remained very weak. He drifted in and out of consciousness and could scarcely lift his hand off the bed. But at least when he was awake, his eyes had followed the visitors, flitting from one to the other as each spoke. At the moment, it was easier to be confident in the older priest's recovery.

Before they returned to their hotel the previous evening, Sam had held a long conversation with the doctors. They were quietly hopeful that, given time, both priests might make it.

Now, in the sunshine, the hospital seemed a less ominous place. Yes, it was still the same mass of concrete and glass that typified modern hospitals almost everywhere, but it was warm and sun kissed and the smells of the sea and the mountains combined to diminish the city's diesel fumes to just the faintest of background hints. All four visitors were returning to the wards in a more positive frame of mind.

They entered the hospital and took the lift up to the floor where Xavier and Angelo were accommodated. Angelo was in the intensive care unit at the north end of the corridor, his condition constantly monitored by a team of ICU staff. Towards the south end of the long corridor was a nurses' station, well placed to service a short row of individual private rooms that ran beyond the station to the end of the corridor. Xavier was in the most distant room.

The group stepped out of the lift and Sam instinctively glanced left and right, reviewing the environment before they split up. The broad corridor was full of bustle and busy staff dressed for the part, darting here and there. He noted a man in weathered grey and brown clothes propped against the wall immediately outside ICU. Turning to look in the other direction, he could see two more men in similar attire sitting quietly on a bench just beyond the nurses' station.

Out of place within the environment, the men did not bother the staff and the staff were careful not to look too closely at them. Sam smiled: similarly clad men had occupied the same positions during their visit the previous day. Xavier's parishioners were leaving nothing to chance now.

Elaine and Francis headed towards ICU and Angelo; Sam and Grace made for Xavier's private room. Pausing at the nurses' station, Sam asked how Xavier was doing and listened attentively to the nurse's reply while Grace focused on Xavier's parishioner guards.

Sam saw Grace give one guard a discreet wave and smile - saw the warm response, yet noted with approval that the young guard made no attempt to move from his place beside his older companion. Sam had also seen the young man before, somewhere; he gave the lad a friendly nod of recognition. The young man nodded back at him.

Sam placed the face - he was one of the guards Xavier has sent to Edinburgh, to guard Helen and the manse earlier in the year, when things had first gone so very wrong. Grace would have met him then.

As Sam continued to speak at the nurses' station, another nurse walked past, greeting the people at the station with a polite 'Buongiorno,' which Sam and the station nurses responded to. Grace received a friendly smile and she smiled back. The guards' appreciative eyes followed the stunningly attractive nurse's progress along the corridor.

She entered Xavier's room, closed the door and slid shut the little vanity curtain, preserving Xavier's modesty as she did whatever was required.

The nurse let her hand fall from the closed curtain and turned to survey the little room. Nice and airy, the tinted window combined with a window blind to let in some light while deflecting the heat of the sun.

She looked at the bed and smiled to herself. Xavier was dozing, still weak and unable to move. Stirring, he opened his eyes to greet his visitor and she saw the little spark in his eyes. His eyes flicked to the door, saw the window curtain was closed. They were alone.

'I see you are bearing up well,' said Collette. Her Italian accent very formal, she was clearly not local. She knew Xavier knew. Stepping confidently across the room to his bedside she pulled a syringe out of her uniform pocket, held it up, jabbing it into a little drug bottle held in her other hand. She drew the dose down into the syringe and put the empty drug bottle back into her pocket.

Xavier shook his head and mumbled an objection, his fingers repeatedly clenched and opened in frustration as the nurse leant over him. She stroked his cheeks gently with the back of her hand. 'You recognise me, don't you?'

Xavier nodded. He tried to turn away as she leant forward but her right hand gripped tight to his jaw holding it fast as she closed in. She kissed his lips hard. Eventually she pulled back a fraction, allowing her tongue to trace a wet path up his cheek and slowly lick across his now closed eyelids.

'I've always wanted to kiss a priest,' she whispered, 'wondered what you tasted like. Now I know.' She pulled back just a little further. Her left hand set the full syringe down on the bed and she moved to force his eyelids open so she could look in his eyes. 'Are you defiled now priest? Feel humiliated before your God?' She smiled a sweetly sick smile then released his eyelids. Xavier's eyes glared at her. She straightened up and retrieved the syringe.

Collette pushed the syringe needle into the meds port of the hanging drip bottle that fed fluid into Xavier's arm; she emptied the syringe into the fluid and withdrew the needle. Then she turned back to the bed and looked into Xavier's eyes. 'You were lucky in the church old man. I couldn't press the knife deep enough into you. But now it's done properly. You have time to say a few prayers but no one will save you. I'm going to visit your young assistant now. He's in a coma you know, I'm afraid he will never wake up. He's going to get some of what I've given you.'

She carefully slipped the now empty syringe into her pocket, leant forward again, and whispered. 'You're my first priest, you know? And now it's just as your British friends would say, you wait all day for a bus and two come at once! Sleep tight now.' She closed in on Xavier's face and once again worked her tongue extravagantly across his cheek, ending with a determined kiss. She straightened, looked back into the sad, furious eyes of the old priest, smiled contentedly and turned away.

Collette opened the door just a fraction and discreetly squirted a little tube of superglue against the door latch, then twisted the nozzle and allowed more glue to smear across the strike plate fixed on the doorframe. Leaving the vanity curtain closed, she stepped into the corridor and closed the door behind her.

Grace was standing closer to the young guard now, filling the space in the middle of the corridor. She stepped back to let the nurse pass, glancing at her again as she noticed both the guards were unable to resist giving the woman appreciative looks. She felt a twinge of irritation that the young guard could be swayed so easily, but that feeling passed as she acknowledged within herself that, even without makeup, the nurse was a quite stunning beauty - tall, shapely, long dark hair, full lips and dark eyes, a complete driving hazard.

'Grazie,' said the nurse with a little smile, acknowledging Grace had made space for her to pass. Then she was beyond them, then passing Sam who was still discussing Xavier's condition at the nurses' station.

Grace shook her head in faux exasperation as she watched the guards swivel their heads to trace the nurse's passage. Then she stopped as a sudden panic gripped her and she rushed to the nurses' station.

'Sam, Sam,' she hissed, gripping his arm and pulling him round to face her.

'What's up?' said Sam with an enquiring smile.

'It's her, the nurse. It's her, from the photo you showed me, the one from the CCTV at New College.'

Sam glanced over his shoulder to look at the form of the retreating nurse. 'Are you sure? It seems unlikely.'

'I know it's her, now I see her in the flesh, there's no mistake. She's the one for sure. Sam, come on, she's just come out of Xavier's room.'

Grace looked into Sam's eyes and could see he recognised the implications. He stepped away from Grace and into the middle of the corridor, waved to the guards and shouted a warning while pointing towards the nurse as she continued to move steadily away down the corridor.

Hearing the commotion behind her the nurse sped up without

looking back. The two guards were suddenly up and running, shouting to their colleague at the far end of the corridor. Instantly the wiry little man converted from slouch to sprint athlete. He ran towards the nurse, she was caught in a pincer movement.

'Come on,' said Sam as he headed for Xavier's room. 'They can deal with her. We're needed over here.' He ran towards Xavier's room.

For a moment, Grace stood transfixed. She could see that the guard from the far end of the corridor was going to catch the nurse before she reached the stairwell. Saw the nurse fumble in her pocket, saw the blur of something black rising in her hand. Saw the flash, heard the crack of a pistol and gasped as the wiry guard dropped to the floor. Nurses and doctors scattered amidst a round of shrieks and screams.

Unable to pull her attention away from the clash, Grace saw the guard's momentum carry him along the marble floor towards the nurse. She saw him roll sideways while producing his own pistol. As he raised it, the nurse fired again. The guard flinched, slumped slightly; a sheet of blood suddenly covered half his head.

'Grace! Come on I need you,' shouted Sam as he approached Xavier's room.

The guard was clearly a hard man. A grazed head was not going to put him out of action. Grace could see the pain on his face as he fired once. The nurse recoiled as the round bit into her right shoulder. Right arm useless, her pistol fell to the ground; as she reached the stairwell and headed into the stair the guard fired again. With a cry, she fell, prone - only her long legs visible, jutting out into the corridor, her torso hidden from view in the stair.

Grace watched the wounded guard stand, saw him step across to the stairway. He wiped blood from his eyes and raised his pistol, aimed into the stairway, fired twice. Grace flinched, she didn't see the bullets hit but knew the nurse was dead. She bit her tongue hard to avoid adding her screams to those that already filled the corridor.

Suddenly, the corridor was silent. Frightened staff realised what they had witnessed. The dress and demeanour of the countryman who had just fired the killing shots registered in twenty minds at once. All the staff looked away, everyone determined not to see the man; determined not to be able to recognise him. No one wanted to be drawn into a feud that might bring a similar hell down on them and theirs.

The wounded guard stepped back and stooped to pick up his broad cap that had fallen in the rush. He theatrically dusted it against his leg and placed it on his head, which was still running with blood. Then he stepped across to the lift beside the stairwell and pressed the call button. Grace saw his nod towards the other two guards who had not had the chance to participate. Then he was gone, carried down and away by the lift.

Grace was called back to the present by Sam's urgent call.

'Over here! The door's locked or jammed - we have to get in!' Sam rattled the door, pressing his shoulder against it. Nothing moved it. He stepped back and kicked hard on the door. 'Come on, more muscle needed here,' he called, kicking again.

The two guards rushed past Grace and threw their weight against the door, bursting it open. They stepped back and allowed Sam in.

As the guards retreated away towards the lift, the young man paused beside Grace. 'We have to go. Remember, you do not know us.'

Grace nodded and he was gone.

'Grace, I need you!'

She hurried into Xavier's room just as Sam reached the bed. She heard unintelligible mutterings, saw Xavier's eyes rolling hard towards his hand and up towards the drip, back and forth, back and forth.

'What did she do to you?' said Sam. Looking quickly for wounds and finding none.

'He's trying to tell you something,' said Grace.

'Yes, but what?'

'Has he been drugged?'

'Hard to tell, he was drugged already.' Sam looked closely at Xavier who continued to roll his eyes back and forth.

'What is it?' Sam was desperate, knew something was amiss and couldn't work out what. Then, in a moment of clarity, Xavier's eye signals made sense - the eyes repeatedly glancing from drip bag to wrist and back.

Instantly, Sam leant across the bed and gripped the plastic tube linking the drip to the cannula fixed in Xavier's hand. Sam kinked the tube, stopping the flow from the drip. He saw Xavier nod and relax, knew he had guessed right, but had he done it in time?

At that moment, nurses and doctors appeared in the doorway. Sam released a stream of urgent Italian explanation that triggered an instant response. The tube was disconnected. Hands guided Grace out of the room; the drip bag was whisked away for analysis. Xavier was surrounded by caring souls who knew him or of him. He was a respected priest and was in good hands.

Sam joined Grace in the corridor as Francis and Elaine appeared hurrying from the direction of the ICU, their worried faces anxious to understand what was happening.

Grace felt Sam's arm slide round her shoulder. 'Come on, Grace. You take the others, go down to the cafeteria, sit quiet there until I join you. Be strong, I'm sure Xavier's going to be fine. He's in good hands.' She pressed in closer to him as they walked.

'It's never ending, Sam. What's going to happen?'

'Don't worry right now. It will end. We're going to end it. I'm going to wait here and speak with the police. They will want to speak with you too. When they do, just say you saw nothing, okay. That's what everyone else in this corridor will say. I'll be with you, don't worry. In the meantime, you get Elaine and Francis up to speed. Can you do all that?' Sam waited for a nodded response then Grace found herself being propelled into her mother's arms as Sam hurried back to Xavier's room.

Chapter 22

FRIDAY 30ᵀᴴ AUGUST

With one hand, Helen held the mobile phone against her ear, with the other she opened the manse's front door and beckoned Sam inside. She could hear the rumble of a black cab's diesel engine receding into the distance and broke off from the call for just a moment to kiss Sam's cheek. 'It's Grace on the phone,' she said, 'she's sending you her love.'

Sam returned the kiss to Helen. 'And mine back to her,' he said moving into the hallway.

Helen closed the front door and ended the phone call as she followed Sam towards the kitchen.

'She says everything is as you left it, better in fact. Xavier's going to make it. You stopped the drip before much of the drug had got into his system. It was some sort of sedative or anaesthetic. Word is, if it had all got into him there would have been no way back. Thank God, you were there. Tomorrow the doctors are planning to bring Angelo out of his induced coma. That's great news too.'

'Brilliant news, let's hope for the best.'

'Sam, let's pray for the best.'

'Yes, okay. But, you know, it was Grace who spotted the woman. It was down to her we were able to react so quickly. Though it was all pretty horrific for her.'

'Yes, so it seems. She's bearing up well, isn't she?'

'Hmmm, I think she's done really well. When I left the hotel for the airport, she seemed to have taken charge, though a couple more of Xavier's parishioners had turned up there and were keeping an eye on things.' He held the kitchen door open for Helen, letting her go ahead of him and kissed her again as she passed. 'I don't know what Xavier's set up is over there, but it all seems a bit cloak and dagger, like he's the friend of the local godfather.'

Helen gave a laugh as she filled the kettle. 'Perhaps he is the godfather! Coffee?'

'Yes please, just what I need. I'm exhausted; I didn't get a moment's sleep during the journey back. You're joking about Xavier, but I'm wondering, maybe he is the big man there. There must have been a score of doctors and nurses in that corridor and not one of them saw a thing. Still, I'm not complaining. It seems to have worked in our favour in the end.'

'I know, Grace was just telling me. She said the police have posted proper guards over Xavier and Angelo. They'll be safe now.'

'That's good, though Xavier's boys pretty well eliminated the threat. They literally don't take any prisoners. That's a message that should hit the mark. Xavier will be safe now.'

'Thank God. Oh, you'll never guess - it seems Grace is quite the celebrity. After you left for the airport Xavier's new deacon arrived at their hotel. There may have been no witnesses in the corridor but everyone who needs to know knows. Now Xavier is out of danger they are laying on a party for Grace and Elaine on Saturday. They plan to stay on over the weekend, make sure Xavier and Angelo have surfaced properly; should be back in Edinburgh on Tuesday, provided nobody takes a turn for the worse at the hospital.'

Helen placed mugs of coffee on the table and sat herself on Sam's knee. They hugged in silence. She felt the pressure of his hand rubbing gently across her back and turned her face to press her lips against his neck.

• • •

Cassiter and Parsol sat regarding one another. The death of operatives was an industrial hazard, though Cassiter invested so much in developing each of his people that such losses were always a heavy cost - even on those occasions when he chose to sacrifice one, which he had not in this case. The news and the manner of Collette's death had been unexpected. Once again, those Latin priests had surprised them and that was not good.

Cassiter let his eye drop to the array of daggers on the table. No matter, they had the Sardinian dagger. The execution of the priests was to have been a punishment for compromising the previous operation in Edinburgh. They could die another day. The real question was what had Helen Johnson been doing in Switzerland? For the time being his activity in Edinburgh was constrained by that damned policeman Wallace, but he would be retired soon. Then restrictions would start to ease. In the meantime, he had his people monitoring, searching from afar, for whatever information they could find.

• • •

Sam had spent an hour sitting at the manse's kitchen table while looking at the photographs Helen had brought back from Switzerland. Professional interest made each picture a magnet for his thoughts and he really wanted to see all the artefacts up close, to touch and turn, consider and conclude. For now, he had to make do with the pictures.

In general, he agreed with Helen: only the gold framed glass seemed to have any direct linkage to their current predicament. Its little ruby did seem a perfect match for the one in Helen's ring. The tiny Templar cross emblem on the gold framed glass was identical to the ones engraved on the dagger blades too. Looking again at the picture, he let his finger trace the strand of gold, following its winding route across the glass face.

'These photos are useful but I really need to see the original artefact. Talk me through the pictures again.'

Helen leant across and, as Sam listened attentively, she carefully pointed out each facet of the gold framed glass as she described what she had seen. Then sat quietly, allowing Sam to weigh up her description.

'What about the edges of the frame, these little crenulations? Are they really the base? Feet for it to stand on or might they point up instead? So leaving the glass to rest on the surface,' said Sam.

'Well, it stood pretty well perfectly on the crenulations, just like little feet. So I think the crenulations are just that - feet. And look,' she pointed to another photo that showed the other side of the frame. At the edge of the picture, she tapped the blue. 'See the strips of lapis lazuli? They're set into the gold frame so they're only visible when the frame is placed with the crenulations down. What would be the use in setting beautiful blue stone into the gold frame and then hiding it?'

'Point taken. So we agree; it's the blue decoration facing up, crenulations down. But what's its purpose?' He looked up to make eye contact with Helen. 'Just as confusing as your daggers I'm afraid. Why couldn't those Templars ever do anything without a puzzle?'

'I don't know, Sam. I guess it was important to them; and don't forget those Templars end up with me and now I've co-opted you. So they're our Templars and it's our puzzle now.'

'Yes, and solve it we will. Before those rampaging madmen can do any more damage. The problem is nothing seems to make sense. None of the daggers fit together, though we believe they should merge to form some sort of map or message if combined correctly, and we don't have all the daggers. So I have no idea what the message is.'

Helen nodded sympathetically. 'I thought we had a breakthrough with the glass pictures in the church. There's no doubt you've linked the names of the churches we know hold daggers with the saints in the pictures. Logically we should be able to narrow down the number of churches we need to consider, focusing just on those churches that share names with our unallocated saints. But even then, there could be thousands of churches dedicated to Mary Magdalene alone. Never mind any other churches and chapels dedicated to her that may have grown up and then vanished into dust during the past seven hundred years. The places we are looking for might not even exist anymore.'

'Yes Mary Magdalene is a real problem; I haven't even begun to come up with a solution to tracing that church. But at least St Athanasius may not be quite so hard. I've had Davy working on that problem for the past few days. He wouldn't let things drop so I thought I might as well make use of his skills - already had a phone call from him this morning.'

'So what's he found?'

'Well, thankfully St Athanasius is not quite as popular as Mary but nonetheless, he's still big in the Eastern Church. Davy's last count was several hundred possible churches scattered here and there, from Christian communities in Egypt right round the Med to Greece, up around the Black Sea and on into central Europe. Even some dotted about the UK. He'll be able to narrow the list down further still by applying various criteria; things like the age of the church and does its location feature on the Mappa Mundi. So, not so many churches to consider but scattered wide, with accessibility and language barriers just the first of the obstacles to overcome.'

'If only we could find a way to narrow the search down more.'

'There will be a way. I don't know how yet, but we will find it, just needs a bit more thought. The real problem is we have no scope for error. One church should represent a trusted task holder, if it survived. But the other is where we think the trouble is coming from. We will have to be careful not to approach the wrong one or we will walk into the lion's den.'

'How do you propose to avoid that?'

'I don't know yet. We need to do the narrowing down first. Without a breakthrough on that front, we've got a long way to go before we have to worry about where the bad guys are based. To be able to find the churches that hold the last two daggers we need something more, something tangible. Something we haven't got yet.'

'Okay, you're the brains trust; I'll have to leave it with you, no point in me breaking your train of thought just now. I think I'll go down to the tunnel and bring up the base of the cross. Just before you all set off for Sardinia, Grace said something odd had happened to it. I'm not sure what she meant but I'd better look.'

Sam nodded absently as his mind returned to the puzzle at hand and he was only vaguely aware of Helen leaving the kitchen.

• • •

An almost inaudible click signalled the opening of the doorway into the tunnel beneath the manse. Helen stepped into the tunnel. She glanced about and spotted where Grace had placed the communion set box for safekeeping.

She stooped and picked out the broken base. Looking at its familiar shape, she took a moment to reflect how for so long she and so many others had failed to see it for what it really was.

Helen tried to remember exactly what Grace had said was wrong; she had been a bit vague. With both hands, she held the base out at arm's length and looked carefully. It seemed exactly as she had last seen it. Rotating the base through 360 degrees, she saw nothing that marked out any obvious change and wished she could recall what Grace had actually said.

Slipping her hands from the base onto the stock, she turned it upside down and looked underneath, nothing. Then, just as she was deciding that Grace had imagined a change, her fingers sensed some give in the metal.

Helen shifted her grip and brought it closer to get a better look at the stock. Nothing. Had she imagined it? She gripped the stock more tightly as she turned it round. And there it was again, very slight, just as Grace had described, spongy. She looked and squeezed at the same time and her heart leapt. She squeezed again and felt the slight compression, saw a tiny sliver of metal move - sliding, silver over silver. It wasn't a solid cast tube as they had all assumed. This was a coil of metal, wrapped tight, its end flap sealed against itself, and the metal then polished and worked until the join had become invisible. Once again, it was quite exquisite workmanship.

Helen did not know what it signified, but knew it was something to share with Sam at once. She stepped back into the stair, paused to close the doorway into the tunnel and hurried up into the manse.

• • •

'Sam,' said Helen, as she entered the manse kitchen. 'Sam, I've got something for you to look at, what do you think?'

She placed the base on the table in front of him, rested her hands on the edge of the table and gently leant her weight on to them, her shoulders raised a little and, for just a moment, she seemed to loom over Sam.

He registered the tone of her voice and the earnest stare. 'It's the base of the cross; we've studied it several times,' he said.

'Yes, but it's changed.'

'Oh, how?' Sam reached out and took the cross.

'It's like Grace said, the stem is spongy. In fact, I've looked, it's actually springy, it's a coil.'

'Really? That's an unusual construction method. I hadn't noticed it before.'

'No, me neither. I'm guessing that the coil and the leading edge were somehow sealed down tight. All the bashing at my father's church must have broken or weakened the sealed edge. Once Grace started giving it a good polish, the seal has given up the ghost and opened a little. Squeeze the stock, you'll feel it give.'

Sam did as she suggested and immediately felt the slight movement under his hand. Pulling the base closer to him, he studied it carefully. He ran his finger up and down the stock, held it up to the light and squinted along its length. Then began flicking a finger across what he suddenly knew could only be the leading edge of a scroll. He let his finger brush gently from side to side as though he were testing the sharpness of a blade - felt the slightest of resistance, there was definitely something.

'This is very interesting,' he said.

Sam pulled his phone from his pocket and took a photograph of the stock. He looked carefully at the picture and expanded it, zooming in.

Helen had circled the kitchen table and was now standing behind him, looking at the picture. 'What do you think?'

'I think this is very odd.' He stood and leant over the stock to take a second picture. This time he took a cross-section of the tube-like stock.

He reviewed the picture, expanded it as much as possible and then almost shouted. 'Yes. Look at this. Unbelievable.' He twisted the camera to give Helen a better view. 'Your Templars just keep on giving!'

He could see Helen looking at the image. There was no doubt that the stock was actually a tightly rolled sheet of metal. With his finger, he highlighted the faint spiral that now showed running through the cross section of the stock, marking the edge of a metal sheet tightly rolled against itself.

'What does it mean Sam?'

'I'm not sure yet. But I do know it means something. You see, rolling a sheet of silver so tightly and sealing it so carefully that nobody could see the join would be hard for silversmiths today, and hugely demanding at the time when this was made. There is no construction advantage to this method over a simple cast - it would take far longer and demand more skill for no obvious benefit, so it must have been done for a reason. I don't know yet, but I'd like to take this into the university and have a closer look. What do you say? May I?'

'Of course, I'll come too. How do you unravel it?'

'We don't. It would wreck the metalwork and perhaps damage any message on the inside. We use a CT scan.'

'Really? I thought that was for medical analysis.'

'It is, but it does the same job for us, imaging the insides.'

• • •

Sitting in Sam's office, Helen had watched his face change from optimism to dejection as this latest in a series of phone calls to the medical department played out. The one-sided conversation made it clear that while doing a CT scan on their roll of silver was technically feasible, it was just not possible right now. She had already known it was feasible; Sam had told her of several instances where the technique had been successfully used before. The problem seemed to be access. The scanner was fully booked for medical scans for the next few weeks.

Sam's hand slipped across the handset and Helen watched as his eyes linked with hers. He was clearly frustrated.

'Last chance saloon,' he said, quietly. 'Could we pay as commercial clients?'

'Whatever it takes, just make a deal.' She had a fortune at her disposal, when money was needed, she was happy to use it.

Sam's phone conversation proceeded rapidly to a conclusion. Paying top commercial rates made them a priority and, provided the right operator could be encouraged to attend as overtime work, the

CT scan could be done that night without interrupting the daytime medical bookings. Sam made an offer to be passed on to the scanner operator, a bonus that would be hard to resist. And the call ended with a provisional arrangement for 10.00 pm that evening.

'Looking good so far,' said Sam. He turned his attention back to his phone and started scanning through the numbers. 'Ah, this is it.'

'What?'

'The CT scan team are very experienced, but on bodies. My friend Jay, from the computing department, is a bit of a wiz on imaging. He's worked with my department before. I'd like him to come in and advise on the work, and we'll need him afterwards to help interpret the data, convert it quickly into a useable form for us.'

'Great, let's get him in. Will he be available?'

'Provided he's in the country he'll come in. He's a decent guy; problem is he's quite greedy. I'll need to make it worth his while. He won't see this as part of his university duties.'

'If you think he's the man then get him.'

Jay was more than happy with Sam's offer and once it had been confirmed that the hospital's senior scanner operator was prepared to work into the night for the bonus Sam had offered, the job was on.

Chapter 23

SATURDAY 31ST AUGUST

Morning found Sam sitting at the kitchen table in his flat. Once again, he was flicking between the pictures Helen had brought back from Switzerland, and, in particular, trying to make sense of the gold framed glass. He knew it was related to their problem but, frustratingly, just like almost everything else, it raised more questions than answers. And why all the crenulations? If you wanted to make feet to stand it on, four little legs in the corners would have done perfectly well. It didn't need twenty odd legs. Or just a solid metal rim to rest on would have done. The maker seemed to have made its construction as complex as possible for no apparent reason. Except, of course, thought Sam, with these Templars there was always a reason. We just can't find it.

He glanced at his phone - it remained silent. Jay had insisted on being left to work on the scan data alone. Working out what was inside a tight roll of metal was complex. He had promised to call Sam as soon as he had pulled it all together.

Helen was away finishing packing at her flat. He would help her bring her things round to his place once she was ready. There wasn't that much left to do and she hoped to be finished over the weekend.

Sam's thoughts turned again to the glass, and to the gold thread that traced an intricate path across it. Then the ruby, set at a point along the thread. It seemed random, but couldn't be. What did it mean? His thought train was interrupted by the ringtone on his phone. It was Jay. Sam grabbed the phone.

'Sam? Jay here. How are things? Manage to get any sleep yet?'

'No sleep, Jay. Been waiting for your call. What's the news? Find anything?'

'Oh yes. I've found stuff. You were spot on with the idea about a message.'

'What have you found?' Sam's voice was as calm as ever. Inside he was thrilling. Could this be the breakthrough?

'Well, it means nothing to me but I live in the digital world. Mostly looks like a bunch of engraved images.'

'Any text?'

'Yes, a few lines near the start, looks like Latin. But I'm bushed, the sooner I get into my bed the better - I've been up for way over 24 hours now. Tomorrow I'll have another look, but call me first, let me know what I'm looking at, that might help me to focus on particular parts of the data.' Jay stopped speaking. The sound of his voice on the line was replaced by a series of decisive taps as he sent an email. 'There, I've sent you an attachment with the details; I hope it's what you want. But I'm away now, let's speak tomorrow.' The line went dead as Jay headed for home and bed.

Sam did not get the opportunity to object. He'd told Jay not to use email, but it was too late now. They'd all just have to hope it was not being monitored by any third parties.

· · ·

In a cool office set above the Rue de l'Université, a technician opened a file attachment and looked at it with puzzlement. He had been monitoring the university's network, watching for any emails and connections to Sam Cameron. There had been very little activity and now there was this, some text he didn't recognise and a meaningless image. It meant nothing to him. He quickly typed a covering message and forwarded the mail to Cassiter - presumably, it would make sense to the boss.

· · ·

Sam stared at his laptop. Jay had done a good job - meticulous work and absolute attention to detail. He had aligned each strip of scan with the next to create a single, simple to view, seamless image that represented exactly what the original engraver would have seen seven hundred years ago, just at the moment before rolling the silver into a scroll.

After a few minutes' study, he decided the screen was too small. He switched his work into the living room where he could display the image through his ultra-high definition TV. He gave a little laugh to himself - this might be the first time he would actually see a real benefit from it.

Sitting back, he looked carefully at the whole scroll, displayed larger than life and in all its glory. Quietly, he assessed the image. Then, after much silent thought, he stood and moved closer to the screen, staring intently.

Bits of the iconography he recognised; most of it was meaningless, yet strangely familiar for all that.

At the top was the Templar cross; clear confirmation they were on the right track. Beneath it and to one side was the Templar seal, two knights riding a single horse. Perhaps, thought Sam, it was an indication that this scroll carried the full weight of the Templar hierarchy: serious stuff. Alongside the seal was a peculiar spiral design. He knew it, not sure where from.

Then some text. He scanned it and moved on, a Latin prayer. If it carried any deeper significance, it would be for Helen and Francis to fathom.

Beneath the Latin text was engraved a band of simple repeating vine pattern. It separated the imagery and text at the head of the scroll from the body and then spread down both edges of the scroll and across the bottom, creating a distinctive frame that enclosed the main message on the scroll.

Sam recognised the vine leaf as identical to that in the Hereford codex picture. They were on the money.

Engraved within the frame were a range of separate images, clear but somehow distorted, like the tiny toy houses and castles a child might have. Each image was distinct from the next and yet each one was too small to include all the lifelike features that might be expected. Perhaps with just a little door or a single window or a tower - some engraved with a battlement or a flag. Some were just distinct shapes but without any internal features added.

Then he saw the bigger pattern; nine elements, one in the centre, eight scattered round it. It was the church window again. At the centre must be St Bernard's; though the little image used had no obvious link - was it a little tower of sorts? Perhaps, but tenuous. The other images meant nothing. Frustratingly familiar, but nothing.

Just as Sam was getting ready to admit he could not make any further links there was a sound from the hallway, a key unlocking his front door. 'Hi Sam, I'm back. Are you home?' It was Helen.

'In here, we've got the scan back from Jay, come and see.'

Helen came in and looked at the screen; she sat beside Sam, kissed him briefly and turned back to the TV. 'That's a really clear picture, what have we got?'

'Well not much I'm afraid. The top part's clear enough - the cross and the seal, not so sure about that spiral though. That inscription is a Latin prayer. Then there's that vine-like border, we know that design already. But so far, the main imagery has me stumped. There are nine images: one central, the others placed around it. I was thinking each engraved image on the scroll might be positioned to correspond with an image in the church glass - establishing links between them, forming pairs. What do you think?'

'It's possible, but let's face it, Sam, you'll know better than me.'

'Hmmm, sometimes we need fresh eyes to see what's in front of us. One thing I'm struggling with is this; we have a hugely elaborate concealment of the scroll, made by the very best of craftsmen. At the top we have exquisite engraving, the cross and seal, the spiral design, then the intricate border pattern, yet look at these images in the main body of the scroll, hopelessly out of proportion, incomplete buildings or whatever they are.'

'I see what you mean,' said Helen. 'But I guess as everything else has been so carefully done it's not an accident. They must have wanted to do that.'

'Yes but why? Look how carefully they have done the vine leaf borders, look at the cross and seal above. Look at the spiral pattern, and I have no idea what that represents either, by the way.'

Helen looked again at the screen. 'I see what you mean, but surely that's not a spiral, Sam. It's a maze isn't it? I've seen it before too. You showed it to me.'

'I did?' Sam looked back at the screen.

'Yes, in those guidebooks and leaflets you showed me when we stayed in the hotel.'

'You're absolutely right. I did, in Hereford. It's not a spiral, it's a maze.' He stood up while speaking and leant sideways to kiss her in the passing. 'Helen Johnson, you are a genius.'

'I am?' she said while getting to her feet. 'Why's that?'

'Because you have just told me where I have seen these images before - all of them. Now I know why they are so distorted.' Sam left the room, rummaged in a hall cupboard and returned with a plastic tube. 'Remember this?'

'Oh yes, that's your copy of the map from Hereford, isn't it?'

'Yes, the Mappa Mundi. I think we might have cracked this.'

'How's that?,' said Helen warming quickly to Sam's enthusiasm.

'Well, remember the first link we found, our Henri de Bello and Lincoln? Then we found the de Bello name has a family link to the mapmaker who created the Mappa Mundi? Back in the 1300s that map was state of the art. If you were going to plan something back then what better map to use? And made by a trusted family member too.'

'I'm with you so far.'

'The task bearers' destinations were planned and plotted on something. Imagine if this map was used.'

'I can accept that but how does it move us forward. We still don't know where the other daggers are hidden.'

'I think we do. Look,' said Sam while unrolling the map and holding it up.

Helen came to stand beside him. 'What have you got?'

Sam waggled the top of the scroll and Helen took it from him, freeing one of his hands to point. His finger traced across the map. 'See, that's Jerusalem right in the middle.' He tapped his finger on the spot. 'And look here, it's the maze you recognised. It represents the labyrinth on Crete, of course. It's a classical icon that any self-respecting medieval mapmaker would include, if only to show their education and culture. Now it gets trickier. Remember, its presentation is all back to front for us today. East is at the top, not north. So Europe and Britain are offset - north is to the left and west to the bottom. See, there's Britain, down here on the bottom left edge of the world. And look closely, that little turret thing is Edinburgh, Scotland.'

'Right,' said Helen cautiously, keeping up but not knowing where Sam was going with the map theme.

Sam stepped across to the TV screen and pointed to the image in the centre of the scroll. 'And that is the same image right there. Edinburgh's Mappa Mundi icon, bang in the middle of our Templar scroll and surrounded by other icons that I bet represent the places where the other daggers were sent. I'm going to check right now.'

Helen moved to join Sam at the screen. 'Is this it? Have we done it?'

'I think,' said Sam. 'And I think it was you that made the breakthrough by recognising the maze.'

'Well, I didn't actually recognise it.'

Sam ignored her self-deprecation as his mind raced on making links where a few minutes before none had been.

He tapped the map. 'Look, there's Hereford, see the little icon?' and then pointed at an image on the TV screen. 'And there it is - Hereford on the scroll.'

He stepped back and looked at the screen again. 'Once again, I think we have struggled from the outset because we have been coming at it from the wrong end. Trying to identify the daggers. They are the last step in the chain and easy to find once you sort the first two steps. And that is remarkably easy if you know the steps, as your predecessors would have done right from the beginning.'

'How's that?'

'Well, imagine you are the Templar knight who was first appointed here by Henri de Bello, all those years ago. You know the daggers are hidden around the Christian world, they are important; today, we're thinking they might be a message or parts of a map. But you don't know where the daggers are; don't need to know until they are to be recalled. You just know how to find them when the time comes - that's your job. The big job that everything else rests on -'

'And how do I know where they are without knowing where they are? In fact, stop for a moment Sam. I feel the need for a glass of the pink stuff. What about you?'

'Oh, nothing for me.' He followed her into the kitchen and continued his explanation while drawing a cork and pouring her a glass of rosé. He paused for a moment and then grabbed himself a bottle of beer after all.

'The only thing each of your predecessors needed to know, as the minister entrusted with the task, is where the map icons were - sealed within a scroll inside your church's cross - not what icons were actually on the scroll. Only when the time comes for recalling the daggers would you break the seal on the shaft, unwrap it and there you are; then you get the knowledge. It will tell you what towns or places are being used to hide the daggers.'

Helen lowered the glass from her lips. 'I follow all of that. But it still doesn't tell what circumstances would demand a recall of the daggers, when my predecessors should open the scroll.'

'I've thought about that. I don't think we can ever know for sure. The Templars seem to have compartmentalised each piece of knowledge. Maybe there's more information in that ledger you discovered in Switzerland, I'll really need to look at it. But whatever the starting trigger was, it doesn't matter now, we've read the scroll anyway.'

Sam took a mouthful of beer, grimaced theatrically and then beckoned her to follow him back into the living room. He unrolled the map again, held it up for Helen to see. 'Every place is drawn on the Mappa Mundi with a simple icon to represent it. But look closely, every icon is different. The mapmaker could never have visited most of these places. They are representations based on flimsy descriptions, hearsay and guess work. But they are all unique images, so if you have the Mappa Mundi or one of its copies, and there were known to have been other copies made at that time, you could find any place of significance across the known world, based on the map icon representing it.

'Of course, the only real problem your predecessor would have faced is accessing the Mappa Mundi itself, but seven hundred years ago that might not have been such a problem. It's quite probable there would have been a copy hidden somewhere in the parish, it might even still be here. But we've seen no sign of it, I suspect that was lost a long time ago.'

Helen took another drink of the wine. 'But that wouldn't really matter because the master map is safe all the time in Hereford Cathedral.'

'Exactly - a backup.'

'Sam I can see how you find the place now, but you haven't explained how you find the associated dagger.'

Sam sat beside her. 'You don't need to search for it at all.' He waved a hand towards the screen. 'If I'm right, and we will check soon enough, each icon on the scroll occupies the same relative position as a saint's image in your church glass. So, first you know what town or district to go to, that's identified by the icon in the scroll. Then, from the corresponding image of the saints in the glass, you know what church to go to in that place. Once there, you don't need to search. You have the ring to identify yourself, as will the task bearer at that place.' Sam gave a little shrug. 'Presumably there is some instruction to them to hand over the daggers to you or for them to bring them to Edinburgh. Who knows?'

'Xavier will,' Helen raised her glass towards Sam.

'Right, though I don't think the doctors will let us ask him about that right now,' he raised his beer bottle and they clinked glass, 'but we're making progress at last,' he said.

'We are. What now?'

'We are going to have to cross-refer each glass image of a saint with each map icon. Then research to confirm there is a church of the right name in that place. I think we can get Davy to help with the research. First of all, I need to speak with the experts in Hereford; the landmass and town locations on the Mappa Mundi are distorted so I want to check what some of those images represent on today's maps. Make sure we're on the right track to pinpoint the right places.'

'Yes, but let's not forget there is a killer lurking in one of the two places we have still to find. Even when we know where they are we will have to be very careful,' said Helen.

'We are going to have to keep this quiet. If the killers get even the slightest idea that we have solved the problem they will come for it and we become completely expendable. I don't think even DCI Wallace could stop them once we move into the end game. I don't think we should even tell the others until we see them face to face. There have been so many leaks.'

'There have, but we are still here and making progress. Let's just keep it going and, like you said when it all blew up first of all, if we can solve it and place the whole thing in the public domain there will be no secrets, nothing to kill for. That's how we will end this. So, Mr Cameron, to work - let's find the facts.'

Chapter 24

MONDAY 2ND SEPTEMBER

'I'm going to the manse now,' said Helen. 'I promised Elaine I would help with organising it in her absence.'

'Well, I suppose it needs to be done. But I thought you had a scheme to outwit James Curry, didn't you?'

'I did, I do. But apparently, nothing's guaranteed in this world and, right or wrong, he's determined that St Bernard's is to close. There is no point in antagonising him just for the sake of it.'

'I don't know. It might be good to put his blood pressure up a bit.'

'Not unless we're sure to be on the winning side. Otherwise, he would just make life harder for everyone concerned. Anyway, what are you up to today?'

'Well, I've taken the church names and locations we know for certain and double checked that the corresponding icons on the scroll actually represent those same places on the Mappa Mundi - all perfect matches. They were quite easy to confirm. I knew the present day locations so knew roughly where to look for the icons on the Mappa Mundi. The problems start with the two icons we've not yet matched up to definite locations. There are hundreds, perhaps thousands, of icons on the Mappa Mundi and they all start to merge together in the end. Trying to match up our unidentified scroll icons with the Mappa Mundi is like searching for needles in a haystack. I've hit a bit of a brick wall with them. It doesn't help that my print of the Mappa Mundi is only half-size. I really need to use the original map.'

'You're going back to Hereford?'

'No, not just now anyway, I've copied the icons I can't identify and am going to send them down to Hereford Cathedral to get Simon Owens' opinion. Hopefully he can confirm exactly which places those unidentified scroll icons represent on a modern map. From that, I can use the church's window to identify the names of the churches we are interested in at those locations and hey presto, Davy does some research and we know where the remaining two daggers are, or were.'

'Good luck then. It sounds very simple, though nothing else has been so far. Just be careful not to do anything that might alert anyone else.'

'No problem. And don't let James Curry upset you. Will we meet for lunch?'

'I don't know. There's quite a lot to do. Why not come over to the manse when you're finished and we can see how things are getting along.'

They kissed briefly before Helen turned and made for the door.

• • •

'It means nothing to me,' said Cassiter. He leant back in his chair while maintaining eye contact with Parsol who was staring back at him via the computer screen link.

'I have nothing either. It must mean something, but what? Are you sure you can't have one of your people press them in Edinburgh?'

'Absolutely. A senior policeman has thrown a protective screen around them. And he has somehow acquired pictures that link me with Collette, Collette and my PA, and hence me with killings in Britain. He has his own agenda so the pictures haven't made it to the investigation files yet and I have no intention of precipitating that.'

'I understand your caution, but we can't allow others to dictate our actions for long,' said Parsol.

'No, but in the meantime I'm keeping out of Edinburgh just as he has demanded. The fool retires shortly and then his power will simply melt away. I have people digging in the background and his little family will provide the perfect tool to extract the pictures from him. Then he will pay a price for crossing me... Us.'

'Good, retribution is always justified, a sound policy and a good example to set for others to see. When the time comes, make sure he understands why he has to die. For now, the question must be what does this picture mean?'

'Yes. And where did it come from? That would help our understanding. For now, we can wait. We will know if they leave Edinburgh and if we catch them far enough away from that meddling policeman's jurisdiction, we can ask them about the picture. They'll be keen enough to tell us once I get started.'

Shortly afterwards, Cassiter brought the video conference to an end. Then he reviewed some reports from his people; elsewhere, all seemed calm. He decided to take a stroll, perhaps go as far as the Seine again, and stop for a nice coffee somewhere. Call into a gallery for an hour or two. Things were going to get very busy, very soon. Perhaps this would be a good moment to take a little quiet time - before the storm.

• • •

A large brown and black removals van was backed into the manse's driveway. Men were bustling to and fro. First, they took the boxes of clothes that Grace had spent so much time packing, then the boxes of books and papers from the basement storage. Thereafter, room by room, they had taken all the furniture. John Dearly's life was being steadily packed away. At the start, Helen had taken up position in the hall, overseeing the work. As the work gathered pace, she realised her contribution was just slowing the workmen down. They knew what they were doing and so she retired to the kitchen, sat at the table with a coffee and left supervision to the foreman.

About midmorning, she heard a cheery voice in the hall and her mood began to sink.

'Very good. You're making excellent progress. I'm very

impressed.' James Curry's voice purred with pleasure. 'Is the lady of the house in?'

Helen watched as a beaming James Curry entered. He paced into the room, crossed to the window, looked out into the garden. She saw him admire it for a moment before turning to speak to her.

'Such a pity the Church is going to have to lose these lovely properties. But we must consolidate and I'm afraid it has to be.' His smile contradicted the emotions his words spoke.

Helen gave just the slightest of nods, acknowledging he was speaking.

'We have to look ahead, I know a few of the parishioners are upset, but they'll settle down once they get used to attending the neighbouring churches.'

'All of the parishioners are upset. It may be you can justify it on your spreadsheets but the church exists in its communities, not in ledgers. You've crashed a perfectly sound parish.'

'I don't want to get drawn into another argument. The arrangements are going ahead so there's no point in fighting it all over again. In fact we've had a rather good offer, exceptional in fact; it's quite focused our minds.'

'Oh?' said Helen.

'I'm not at liberty to say but they want the contracts completed in quite a rush, so it's for the best that you are moving John Dearly's things out now. Where are they going by the way? Auction or a charity shop perhaps? I understand he had no close family.'

'Storage for a while, and then we'll see what's to be done once the dust has settled.'

'Oh well, very good, though I can't help feeling that you are all making extra work for yourselves. Surely the easiest thing would be to just dispose of it all?'

Helen glared at him while forcing herself to remain silent and seated.

James Curry gave a shrug. 'Whatever you think best, as long as you ensure the property is cleared. But I think you have a set of keys for me - your own flat. I assume you've emptied it by now. If you have the keys on you, I'll take them now, the sooner the better.'

Helen opened her bag and pulled out the keys for her church flat. She placed them on the table and James Curry hurried across to pocket them.

'Very good, that's one thing less for you to worry about. If you could drop the manse keys into the presbytery office that would be a big help. Now what about the church?'

Helen looked at him for a moment. 'Elaine has been dealing with that. As you already know, neighbouring parishes have taken various things from the church and the church hall. There are still all the big things to move - the pews and so on. And most of the fittings in the church hall remain. But shouldn't there be some deconsecrating ceremony or something?'

'We don't do that in the Church of Scotland. There will be just a little service of thanksgiving - quite short, quite simple.' James Curry was starting to sound irritated by Helen's questioning. 'It's all in hand as per procedure. Just, it's going to be a bit tight, time wise. It needs to be held before change of ownership takes place. I don't know who made the offer, but their solicitors are really quite insistent that we move quickly or not at all. So it may well be we have to hold the service of thanksgiving on the morning of sale.'

Curry puffed his chest out and stalked across the room. 'Let me tell you, it's taken quite an effort to get the General Trustees to allow the sale. I've been petitioning them to sanction a quick sale for some time; they're always determined to ensure the Church gets full value. But once this offer was received, there was no longer a problem; they all saw things my way. It's essential to proceed now. I have stressed that our purchaser might walk away if there are any delays and we'd lose the sale completely.' As he spoke, James Curry headed for the kitchen door. 'So keep up the good work and chop, chop - let's do nothing to upset our buyer.'

Alone again in the kitchen, Helen sat quietly for several minutes, letting her irritation subside. The man was impossible.

A light knock on the door and the foreman led his team in to clear the kitchen table and chairs. The appliances were being left. A final flurry of effort and the removals team was finished. Helen was alone in an empty building.

For a little while she wandered through the rooms, remembering what had happened - the good and the bad. Then it was time.

Helen set the alarm and pulled the front door shut before locking it securely. For a moment, as she pulled the key from the lock she felt a sense of guilt. Was she closing the door on all the warmth and kindness she had found in the manse, abandoning John Dearly's memory? She hoped not and shivered in the sunlight, as though somebody had stepped over her grave.

Looking up into the blue sky, she watched a pair of small clouds unmoving in the still lunchtime air; she smiled. She had done her best. Sometimes things were beyond influence, sometimes not. Time would tell and she had faith that John Dearly and Archie Buchan would know she had done everything she could to preserve their story.

The sound of a car horn caught her attention. Blocking the entrance to the manse's driveway was Sam's car. From the driver's seat, he smiled and waved in her direction. She could see him mouthing a question. *Lunch?*

Stooping to pick up the carrier bag of oddments she had gathered at Elaine's request, she walked down to join him in the car.

'How did you get on?' said Sam, as he slowly drove the car away from the manse. He paused it at the junction with the main road and then took a right and headed towards the city centre. As they approached St Bernard's church, he slowed again, let his hand slide off the wheel and gently squeezed her thigh for a moment.

'Want to stop here for a while?' He glanced towards Helen, saw her head shake; he drove on.

'James Curry drives me absolutely mad.'

'So you've said before, but this whole thing is getting pretty close to the line now. If developers get their hands on the properties it will only be a matter of time before they stumble on the tunnel and who knows what. That would be tragic because I don't believe for a moment we've seen the last of the secrets down there.'

'I know, but I've done what I can. It's in God's hands now. We'll just have to let it play out. Hope for the best. The manse is cleared now, ready for the new owner. We left the carpets and curtains, and the kitchen appliances. Everything else has gone in the lorry. Elaine's job is to plan and organise clearing the church and hall. Turns out, James Curry has found some architectural salvage company; they are going to take a lot of the big stuff, pews and so on. That will leave Elaine to worry about the religious materials.'

'Right. Perhaps we should try and make time to have a trawl

through the tunnel later in the week, before it changes hands. Who knows what your Templars have stashed in it. Thursday or Friday maybe?'

'I'm up for that, but I really ought to visit Xavier first. We can do it once I get back. I'm sure we can find a quiet half day then.'

'I think we should try to get it done as soon as possible. If the sale goes through as quickly as Curry told you, the buildings may well be sold before we get another chance.'

'Still, there's nothing more we can do to influence things,' said Helen.

'What are you up to Helen Johnson? You're being too calm about this. Too calm by half. And what have you done already to influence things?'

Helen let her hand rest gently on Sam's upper arm as he drove along. 'Like I say, I've done what I can. I'm praying for a good outcome. Right now, a sympathetic owner is about the best we can hope for; let's see what happens. Now, let's get something to eat. Where are we going?'

'The Gallery of Modern Art.'

A ten-minute drive took them through the heart of the Old Town, down The Mound and into the New Town where they passed quickly through the symmetrically laid out Georgian city streets and on beyond the Dean Bridge. A few minutes later, Sam swung the car into an impressive driveway that ran between broad green lawns and directly ahead stood the gallery.

'Why here?' said Helen.

'Just fancied a change of scene. There's off street parking and the food's good too.'

They left the car and strolled round to the front entrance.

'Let's go down to the café first,' said Sam. 'We can have a look round afterwards if you like.'

'Sounds good to me,' said Helen as they crossed the entrance hall and headed downstairs to the café.

They worked their way round the self-serve counters and both got the same order: soft drink, carrot and coriander soup with crusty bread, and impressively large cheese scones and butter to follow. They chose to sit outside and slipped through the glass doors that led on to a walled patio. Selecting a quiet table, they put their trays down and sat.

'So, enough of my stresses and woes, any news?' said Helen.

She noticed he looked around to ensure nobody was within hearing distance. Sensing the caution in his manner she leant forward, both to promote their privacy and because she was eager to hear his news.

'I called Grace, she and Elaine are returning tomorrow. Xavier and Angelo are in better shape now; both are going to make it. Xavier wants to know why you haven't been out to visit. I said you would phone Grace this evening to make arrangements for collecting them from the airport when they get back.'

'No problem, I'll call. I need to keep Elaine up to speed on what James Curry is doing anyway. And I'll get them to pass a message to Xavier for me.' She felt guilty that she was the only one who had not been over to visit. 'I hope to get out there in the next day or two. It would only be a flying visit. You might want to come with me?'

Sam shook his head. 'Sorry, more news means I really want to go elsewhere as soon as possible.'

Oh, what's happened? What have you found?'

'Hereford Cathedral has been very helpful, as usual. They have given us a steer on what the two unknown Mappa Mundi icons represent.'

'And?' asked Helen, leaning in closer. 'Where are they?'

'One is near the French Mediterranean coast. They were not quite sure exactly where, it might not even be a town. We have to accept that some of this stuff is subject to modern interpretation; everything is viewed through seven-hundred years of change. To be frank, I thought the image looked like a row of seashells but the experts suggest it might represent hills or mountains - the space between towns rather than a particular town. It's to the west of Marseilles for sure.'

'That's not much help. In fact it's pretty vague.'

'Yes and no. The other shape they have identified as Kefalonia. Easy, when you know the scribble on the icon is actually the name. And of course, Kefalonia is in the east, where one of our saints is more popular.'

'St Athanasius.'

'Exactly, our old two beards. Which means we know the church in the south of France is or should be dedicated to Mary Magdalene.'

'Well I suppose that narrows it down a bit.'

'A good deal in fact. I've got Davy on the case. He's found a church in Kefalonia dedicated to beardy. I think that must be one of the targets.'

'And in France?'

'He's compiling a list of possible churches just now - country churches in the hills of the Languedoc. It won't be too big a list and I bet by the time he's applied a seven hundred year age condition to the list it will be pretty small. But Helen, think about what else we know. The unidentified men who were killed here earlier in the summer, they wore French labelled clothes. You were pretty sure the old man who escaped had a continental accent and Elaine reckoned it might have been French. I'd say that the odds are our villain comes from the French connection.'

As she took a sip of her drink, Helen considered what Sam had said. She had to agree with him. 'Okay, I buy into what you're saying. So how should we approach this?'

'I want to go to Kefalonia right away.'

'On your own? Don't you think I should come?'

'Probably. But I just intend to nose about a little. Not break cover. Remember, after all these years there might not be anything to find anyway.'

'I think I should be there too, Sam.'

Sam's head nodded. 'I agree, but you need to get Elaine sorted out here and you must go to visit Xavier. Why don't you do what needs to be done here, for the church; then visit Xavier, and finally join me in Kefalonia if I haven't already returned to Edinburgh? By Friday we can be happily searching the tunnel together, what do you say?'

As usual, Sam's argument carried logic and was a practical solution to the competing pressures they faced. Helen smiled and lent across the table to kiss his cheek. 'You're right, let's do it your way. We'll go home now and get tickets and hotels booked. But don't be getting in any scrapes without me. I need you.'

• • •

Cassiter glanced again at the screen. Why had Sam Cameron just bought a ticket to Kefalonia? What was he up to in such a hurry? It needed to be investigated. A sudden dash half way across the continent could not be ignored. And the Johnson girl - she was going to Sardinia. He could guess why she was going there, no problem with that one.

He thought for a little while, spun in his chair to look out of his office window. All he could see was the building on the opposite side of the street. For all the beauty of Paris, his office had an uninspiring outlook. He missed the view from his Edinburgh office, the panorama that he could lose himself in while weighing issues, or just allow his mind to sink absently into the scene. He was away from it now because of all this business but mostly because of these church people who repeatedly obstructed his moves. He had lost good team members because of them. A bill had to be settled and they would all pay. The sooner they were swept away the sooner he could start restoring his life.

He needed to get people to Kefalonia but he was becoming short-handed. It would take him a couple of days to get teams in place. Suddenly he spun back to the computer, leant forward and started typing. After a minute he stopped, scanned what he had written, made a couple of minor adjustments and sent the email. This was the opportunity to put to the test Parsol's claims of having people everywhere and his group's concept of mutual support. If the man could put a team on Kefalonia by tomorrow, he would be a worthy partner. Skills were important but Cassiter had to concede, sometimes scale was just as valuable.

He walked from his private office out to the reception, looked at the middle-aged Frenchwoman sitting at the desk; he saw her glance up at him and smile a professional greeting.

'I'm going now. Be sure to forward any information that comes in my absence. There must be no delays.'

Chapter 25

TUESDAY 3RD SEPTEMBER

Sam hunched the rucksack higher onto his shoulder. He had left it half-empty to ensure it could accompany him into the cabin as hand baggage. He really was travelling light.

Helen slipped her arm through his as they approached the airport's automatic glass entrance doors. 'You be careful, Sam. I know we agree the French location is probably where the trouble stems from but this is still unknown territory.'

'Don't worry. I have no intention of stirring up trouble. In, out and away. I'll probably be back before you finish visiting Xavier and Angelo.'

'I hope so. Look, I'll go and get us coffees while you check in, okay?'

'Fine,' he said and Helen watched him head off towards the check-in desks. He paused briefly to look at the departures board then continued on.

In the café, Helen chose a quiet table where she sat and waited for Sam. She passed the few minutes idly watching a group of young men standing in the all-day travel bar. Tourists catching a late summer break. The empty glasses arrayed around them indicated they had been in the bar for a while. One or two were becoming a little boisterous. She wondered if they would all get on the flight.

Sam eased himself into the seat beside her; he followed her gaze, saw the young men and grinned. 'Oh to be nineteen again,' he said.

Helen smiled a noncommittal smile, she was not so sure. 'Is there anything I can do while you're away? Anything we should be looking out for?'

'No, I think you have your hands full as it is. Though, you should have a word with DCI Wallace, just a general update, nothing heavy. I know he finishes soon, but the man has gone out on a limb for us.'

'You're right; I'll give him a call this morning. It's the least he deserves.'

'Yes, he certainly seems to understand the real meaning of duty. That's a rarity these days. Once I get back, we'll check out the tunnel, use the church entrance. I think we should arrange to go to Switzerland together as well - I really need to look more closely at that glass plate or tray or whatever it is. The ruby clearly shows it is linked to the signet rings and hence to the daggers. We have to work out how. What does it mean or do? I'm certain it is central to the puzzle.'

'Okay, Franz Brenner has invited us to stay, I'll get in touch with him, but let's plan it once we're both back from our travels, and after we've been down and searched the tunnel.' She pointed up at a flight information board. 'Your flight's been called. We'd better make a move or you won't get through security in time.'

• • •

There was definitely something to be said for direct tourist charter flights, limited legroom or not. If he ever came back to Kefalonia, that's how he'd travel. A fourteen-hour journey, including two flight changes and one very long delay at Athens had filled his day - so much for scheduled travel he thought. Then he laughed to himself - no, if he ever came back, he'd try to get access to Xavier's private plane; now that was how to travel.

Having booked into the neat low-rise hotel that sat proudly facing on to a square in the middle of Argostoli, he had taken a quick shower to freshen up and then headed straight back out. A quiet buzz filled the air as tourists flitted between shops and restaurants or just wandered about, enjoying the warm evening air. He could hear bouzouki music drifting out from one of the restaurants. The sound was accompanied by the smells of roasting meats that blended with the sweet scent of the island air and the slightest tang of the sea drifting up from the harbour. He found himself irresistibly drawn towards the restaurant.

Eating over, Sam finished his cool beer and then, tourist map in hand, he wandered out into the evening. The square was a little busier now as more tourists came out for food and fun. He worked his way round the square and took the street leading down to the harbour.

The lights from the shops and cafes that lined the street shone like beacons, each competing with the next to catch the attention of passing tourists. Low canopy trees were spaced at regular intervals along the pavements, casting shadows to disrupt the light show. They would offer shade for pedestrians during the day. Sam wondered if they were the source of some of the sweet evening scent that was stronger here than in the square. Beyond, where the street sloped down to the harbour, Sam could see glimpses of sea, reflecting the harbour lights. He glanced again at his map and hurried on.

About two thirds of the way down the street, just a stone's throw from the harbour, he stopped. Puzzled, he looked again at the street map, looked at the note Davy had given him, and finally he backed up the street a little. This was not right. He checked the street name and the building numbers and then headed back down the street towards the harbour. Reaching his previous stopping point, he paused again. This was still not right.

Where the church of St Athanasius should have stood there was nothing. No signs, no rubble even, just a wire fence enclosing an empty, overgrown building plot. Sam looked about for something, anything that would give him a steer, finding no inspiration he walked down to the harbour. From there he turned and quickly traced the other routes leading up from the sea. None contained the church he wanted. It simply wasn't there. This was not how it was meant to be.

He continued to walk, spreading his search wider and wider, as he methodically checked each street in the vicinity of the harbour.

He drew a blank, no sign of St Athanasius' anywhere. Tiredness was catching up with him as he decided to call it a night and head back to the hotel. The problem would have to wait until he had a chance to sleep.

Chapter 26

WEDNESDAY 4ᵀᴴ SEPTEMBER

Morning came and Sam woke with the same problem he had gone to bed with. Where was the church? It could not have vanished. Had Davy got his facts wrong?

He crossed to the window, swung open the blinds and looked down into the square. It was deserted now save for a street sweeper clearing away the tourists' droppings, and a waitress wiping tables in anticipation of another busy day.

An hour later and Sam had readied himself. His breakfast over, he presented himself at the hotel reception. In response to his questions about the church of St Athanasius, the teenage girl behind the desk shook her head, unknowing. Her English was quite good, which relieved Sam - for all his language skills, Greek was not a strength. He asked where he might make some formal enquiries. She shrugged and called for her grandfather, the hotelier, who emerged from a back office to stand next to her.

'Sir, how can I help you?' said the manager in good, albeit heavily accented, English. 'Please, you should call me Haris.'

'St Athanasius' church, it's on the street map but I can't find it. Can you explain? Maybe point me in the right direction.'

Haris tutted and hurried round the counter to take the map from Sam. He looked at it carefully, slapped the back of his hand on the map and tutted again as he returned it to Sam.

'It's no good. Old map, very old.'

'Can you sell me a new one?' said Sam.

'No sir, you don't understand. New paper, old map.'

'No, I don't understand,' said Sam.

'Very sad, many years ago, when I was just a baby the whole town was wrecked by an earthquake, devastated.' His hands went up and described a circle to encompass the hotel building. 'My family lost everything - hotel, furniture, car, all gone, everything. The family got out in time, me too, of course.' He suddenly laughed. 'Not so bad now, my family had good standing in the town, my grandfather was able to rebuild from scratch and now I own the finest hotel in town. Yes?'

Sam nodded a polite agreement while trying to take in the information. 'So this was all destroyed. The church too?'

'Yes everything came down in this part, very bad. But I don't know about the church, it has never been there in my memory. But, what do I know? I was a baby then.'

'So it was never rebuilt after the earthquake. But why is it still on the map?'

The manager waved his hand dismissively at the map. 'Like I say, new paper, old map. Nobody has bothered changing the print yet. This is our island; we all know the church isn't there just now, even though the map shows it. Who would bother changing it? I read there is a new map coming out this year, maybe the church is gone from that one - maybe not. Maybe one day they'll rebuild it, who knows?'

Sam was fighting to find some sense in what the hotel manager was saying. The church had been gone for over half a century. How on earth would he find what he wanted? Perhaps it had all been lost in the earthquake. Was this the end?

Haris could see Sam's disappointment. He turned and shouted into the back office. The stream of Greek words were quite meaningless to Sam.

An equally unintelligible response came right back from the office, an older voice, female. The manager grunted acknowledgement and turned back to Sam. 'She knows something, just a minute, she's coming.'

A few moments later, a much older lady appeared at the doorway and shuffled out, her stick clicking on the marbled floor. The manager hustled Sam over to a group of comfortable occasional chairs opposite the reception desk. 'Here, you sit with mama, I will bring you coffees. Talk. She will know more.'

The old lady fixed Sam with glinting eyes; they seemed much younger than her stooping body. 'You're British,' she said. Her genteel English, fit for a garden party, contrasted starkly with the clatter of Greek that had poured from the office moments before.

'Yes,' said Sam, 'Scottish too.'

The old lady smiled. 'We like the Scottish, we like the British too. Your navy were the first to help when it all came down. Saved many lives. How can I help you?'

'I was looking for the church of St Athanasius. It's on the map but doesn't exist. Can you tell me anything about it?'

Mama sat quiet for a long moment before answering. 'The church. Yes, I knew it well. It was my church back then.' She waved a hand towards her son who was approaching with a tray of coffee. 'Haris was christened there. Though you'd never think it, he never goes to church now. Hey, what example is that to set my great-granddaughter?' She smiled towards the girl at the reception desk. 'What hope has she got if that lazy son of mind won't set a good example? I ask you.'

Sam nodded thanks towards Haris as he put coffee cups on the table beside them.

Haris gestured gently towards the old lady. 'Don't set her off about going to church or she'll be moaning at me all day,' he said and bent to give his mother an affectionate kiss. Sam could see the old lady was delighted, though she feigned annoyance and shooed her son away.

'Nobody has mentioned St Athanasius' to me for a long time. What is your interest? I'm surprised a tourist would even know of its existence.'

'It is still on the map,' said Sam, waving his map.

'Oh, you can't go by that, Greek tourist maps! It was full of errors fifty years ago and it's just been reproduced in fancy wrapping.'

'But the church was there once?'

'Oh yes, it was there. But it's gone now. Poor Father Andreas, such a good man.'

'Father Andreas? Was he the priest? Did he die in the earthquake?'

The old lady looked at Sam, tears forming in her eyes. 'Back then Father Andreas was such fun. He was my priest but we were also friends. He was my age and from here. I had known him all my life, so we had plenty in common.' Her voice was tinged with the deep sadness of age looking back at what might have been.

'I'm sorry, I didn't mean to upset you,' said Sam. 'It's just I was keen to trace the priest. Certainly didn't mean to drag up painful memories.'

The old lady was nodding, but only half-acknowledging Sam's words. She had slipped back to her prime, remembering fun and friendships all broken suddenly and forever in a torrent of falling buildings.

'I'll leave you now,' said Sam, making to stand.

She raised a hand to stop him. 'Don't go. Tell me more. Perhaps I can help.'

'Is Father Andreas still alive? Can you tell me where to find him?'

'Well I'm not sure how to answer you; it's some time since I have spoken to him. But he didn't die in the earthquake. He was badly hurt, rushed headlong into a building to save others. He was very brave and got some people out of a house, just round the corner, off the square. A mother and her children, two boys and a girl. When he went back in for the husband there was an aftershock. They never got the husband out but they did find Father Andreas in time, he made it, but his body was broken. It was awful.'

'So he is alive. Can you give me his address?'

'As I said, it was a long time ago. Leave it with me; I will see what can be done, if anything.'

'Of course, but I'm not here for long, just another day. Will you be able to organise anything in that time?'

The old lady smiled at him. She waved a hand out towards the square. 'You go out, relax, visit the harbour. Enjoy yourself and for lunch eat in the open-air café directly across the square from here - Dimitris'. Take your time, enjoy. I can recommend the food, I hear our guests talk of it from time to time. If I can make an arrangement for you Dimitris will let you know after lunch.'

'Dimitris? Is he reliable?'

The old lady gave a hollow laugh. 'Reliable? Why would he not be? And why would a tourist worry about such a thing?'

Sam gave a resigned shrug. 'Lunch then, at Dimitris'. But how will I know who Dimitris is and how will he know me?'

'Stop worrying young Briton. I told you, I like the British. You helped us. It was the British sailors who pulled Father Andreas from the rubble. There are no tricks, we are just private people, we like the shade, not the glare of the sun. As for Dimitris, his father ran a restaurant right there, across the square. He's one of the little boys Father Andreas pulled from the rubble. Though, of course, he's as old as my own son is now. Now go.' She waved him away with a parting smile and leant her head back into the seat's headrest, closing her eyes. The interview was over.

Sam stepped out into the warm sunlight and felt the heat envelop him. The cool of the morning was already gone. This was going to be a scorcher. He wandered across the square to reconnoitre Dimitris' restaurant and then headed down the street towards the harbour. He'd some time to fill.

A car nosed its way round the square, keeping Sam in view. The occupants were two men in smart but casual dress. The car registration confirmed what their dress said - visitors from the mainland. The men watched Sam carefully. As he left the square, the passenger jumped out of the car and followed him at a discreet distance. The driver drove the car calmly on, made for the harbour side where he would link up with his partner again.

It didn't take Sam long to rumble his tail. It was a few years since he had put aside his security training but during the past two or three months it had come back in a rush, and once again, the skills were serving him well. His tail did not know he had been rumbled, nor did the driver. Sam did not know who they were. In the mad world he found himself in, his tails could be anybody: the police, security, perhaps the usual madmen or even friends of Father Andreas. He didn't even try to guess, time would tell. In the meantime, he'd just wander around a little, take in the sights and keep them busy.

Eventually, Sam settled down beneath a parasol outside a little roadside café. He enjoyed the shade it afforded him as he drank a cold drink. He scanned his phone messages and texts, nothing urgent. Then he sent Helen a text message - reporting in. All the while, he kept an eye on his watchers; they were now clearly feeling uncomfortable in their sun-baked car. Sam gave a little smile to himself. Time for lunch he decided; he stood, put some cash on the table to cover the drink bill and then darted up the street, heading back towards the square and Dimitris' restaurant. He had shaken his tail off almost before they had realised he was on the move.

Sam had finished his lunch and sat alone wondering if the old lady had failed to make a link for him. He filled his time by idly watching the cook at work in the open fronted café. The vertical rotisserie turned endlessly, its dripping meat juices trickling down as great slices of meat were carved away to fill kebab orders. The cook pierced a variety of meats and vegetables with fierce skewers, filling the metal rods till they could take no more. Then, knowing the customers' eyes were on him, he wielded the loaded skewers, expertly, theatrically, like some medieval swordsman, lifting and swirling and effortlessly slotting each one in turn into a grid beneath the grill where they were held tight in the heat. A little while later he would return and, with a further flourish, pull out the kebabs, turn the skewers and slot them back in beneath the heat.

Most of the other diners had now left the open-air tables of the square. A few tables had been reoccupied by other tourists seeking a late bite to eat or a cool afternoon drink. Sam had spotted his tail of the morning return to the square. He was unconcerned. In such a small place, they were bound to track him down again, especially as he was not hiding. There was nothing he could do about them, so he chose not to worry.

Just as Sam was about to give up on any contact, the short plump man who had spent the whole lunchtime buzzing around the front of the restaurant, directing the waiters and shaking hands with passing locals, came towards him. White shirted, sleeves turned up to the elbow, black trousers. His gait was almost sailor-like as he deftly rolled amongst the crowd of tables and chairs, never quite touching any. He exuded the confidence of command, this must be his restaurant, and so this must be Dimitris, thought Sam.

Dimitris paused to laugh and chat with two middle-aged ladies, tourists who were happy to take a few moments of his time. Leaving them with a little plate to which their bill was fixed, he continued his meander between the tables. Sam watched him approach. The man appeared just a friendly restaurateur. Finally, he reached Sam.

'Your bill, sir. You liked the food, I hope?' said Dimitris.

Sam nodded an acknowledgement, and glanced at the bill. He pulled some Euros from his pocket to settle up. 'Are you Dimitris?'

'I am, sir. And I have a message for you. Look over there, in the corner of the square. See the Peugeot 205? It's waiting for you. Go now, it won't wait for long.'

Sam did not bother looking. He had noted the worn and dusty old Peugeot arrive a minute or two before. Its young driver had been staring at Dimitris from the moment he had pulled on the handbrake - willing the restaurateur into some action.

It was immediately clear to Sam that the Peugeot driver was an amateur - a local? By extension, he was not linked with the two men sitting in the other car, currently parked on the far side of the square. They were tailing him and while Sam did not rate their skills too highly, they were certainly persistent.

'Thanks,' said Sam. He didn't wait to pass the time of day with Dimitris, just stood and walked quickly off in the direction of the waiting Peugeot.

As Sam reached the car, he noted the change in engine revs as the young man behind the wheel played nervously with the accelerator. He got into the front passenger seat and smiled at the driver before buckling his seatbelt. 'Shall we go?'

The driver smiled in response but did not reply. Sam assumed he did not speak English, then he registered that the driver wore the black of a priest's robe. As the Peugeot pulled into the traffic, Sam noted that the car carrying his tails was drawing away from the kerb. He reached out his hand to adjust the passenger door's mirror; he could monitor his tail easily enough. The young priest either didn't notice or didn't care that the mirror was moved; he was focused only on getting Sam to his destination, wherever that was.

The Peugeot had left town in minutes. Its old engine struggled against the incline as the car continued along the road and up into the mountainous interior of the island. As they wound round hairpin bends, Sam would notice the following car, maintaining a discreet distance; it would pop into sight then vanish again as the Peugeot took the next bend. With each passing kilometre, the landscape became more remote, more isolated. He got regular glimpses of the sea shining blue in the distance below. Nearer to hand, they occasionally passed little clusters of mostly whitewashed houses, hunched barns and stores, a little chapel, and always the bleached white bedrock breaking through the vivid greens of scrub and trees that nowhere quite managed to maintain a complete blanket of cover.

Eventually, the car turned off the road and on to what seemed an impossibly narrow and steep track that climbed up to a ridge running parallel to the road they had just left. The engine laboured valiantly as the car strove towards the top, but finally, with what Sam imagined might have been a groan of relief, the car rolled over the crest and cruised the short distance down into the little mountain valley below.

At first, it seemed the car was carrying him into an empty place. Then he noticed a building, old and weathered but strong. Almost hidden in the landscape, it was built of the same stone as the hills that surrounded it. As they continued down the slope, he started to get a feel for the building's shape and scale. It was built around an enclosed courtyard. Almost like a fort, two storeys he guessed, three at most. He could not make out any windows in the outside walls, just a shadowy gap where large double gates were swung inwards to reveal a deep archway leading into the courtyard beyond.

As the Peugeot drove under the archway, Sam glanced into the wing mirror, no sign of the following car. Had they given it the slip at the turning off the main road, or was it just holding back? The Peugeot drove straight across the courtyard and parked directly in front of the main entrance. A pattern of black iron studs reinforced its wooden double doors. Each door was fitted with a heavy ring handle of black iron. They hung hot in the sun.

Stepping out of the car, Sam glanced about. Even the inner walls of the courtyard contained no ground floor windows at all. Security conscious, he thought. But there were windows at first floor level, placed evenly round all four sides of the courtyard. And the main part of the building in front of him included a further row of yet higher windows, a second floor.

At the midpoint in the courtyard wall to his left was another set of identical wooden doors. Directly above, a little tower emerged from the roof; he could see a black bell hung within. It must be a chapel.

The young priest got out of the car and beckoned Sam to follow him up the steps and into the building. Sam noted he had left the car keys in the ignition, obviously not too worried about security and access today. After allowing the priest a couple of paces' space, he followed, noting the cement ramp that had been built to one side of the steps - access for a trolley or perhaps a wheelchair. It was a relief to enter the cool shade of the hall and he pressed the door closed behind him, keeping the heat out.

Long shadowy corridors ran away to left and right but the young priest beckoned again and walked straight ahead, leading Sam towards the back of the building to reach the stairway up, passing what Sam reckoned was a particularly modern passenger lift. As they climbed the stair, natural light from the windows above provided better illumination. He began to notice the heavy wooden panelling and the regularly spaced display of religious icons.

Having reached the first floor, he was led a little way along a corridor and into a long room whose windows looked out over the courtyard. Sam stepped inside and the door shut behind him. He was alone in a reception room: calm, unthreatening. Here, close to the door were a scattering of reception chairs and occasional tables, old but not well worn. Clearly, this place did not receive many visitors.

A little further along stood a broad table surrounded by high backed wooden chairs. A boardroom table or a dining table? At the far end of the room was a desk and the entire wall behind it was occupied by a bookcase, full of what were mostly very old books. Sam found himself drawn toward the books. Perhaps he could get a feel for the place from its reading material. Just as he reached them, the sound of a door opening stopped him and he turned towards the sound. It was a panelled door, set in the room's long wall at the corner adjacent to the bookcase. He had not noticed it during his initial scan of the room, then he realised why; it was panelled in exactly the same wood as the walls.

An old priest entered through the opened doorway, his electric wheelchair rolling almost silently across the wooden floorboards. He looked up and smiled, stretching out a hand.

'Welcome, Mr Cameron.'

Sam took the priest's hand and shook. Looking the old man in the eye, he could sense an unflinching determination in the man. 'Thank you. And I'm assuming you are Father Andreas.'

'I am. Please, won't you take a seat? Let's talk.' Father Andreas pointed back along the room towards the occasional chairs and then motored towards them. Sam followed.

Father Andreas paused near the window, pointing Sam towards a seat with a view out across the courtyard. Without hesitation, Sam sat and briefly glanced outside. There the stillness of the afternoon was dictated by the burning sun. Anything that lived was sheltering, waiting for the cool of evening to seep in with the shadows - there was a while to wait. He turned his attention back into the room, where Father Andreas had now manoeuvred his wheelchair closer.

'Perhaps I can offer you some refreshment, Mr Cameron? A cool drink, perhaps?'

Sam was happy to accept and, as if by magic, a middle-aged priest appeared carrying a tray with glasses and a jug of iced water. He placed it on the table between Sam and Father Andreas, then poured iced water into the glasses and left without a word.

Father Andreas lent forward, lifted his glass and drank. He smiled at Sam. 'Please drink the water, Mr Cameron. It has lemon juice added, the fruit picked fresh from our orchard this morning.'

Sam took a sip, enjoyed the refreshing taste. He complemented Father Andreas on it and then placed the glass back on the table. 'Please, call me Sam and thank you for seeing me. Though it's all a bit mysterious. You could have just passed on the address and I would have come by taxi.'

Father Andreas nodded acknowledgement of Sam's comment and took a sip of water himself. Then he gave a wry smile. 'We live a quiet life here, out of the way; not secret, just very quiet. We find it easier to bring guests when we want them. I think open invitations might set a precedent that could prove unwelcome one day, don't you?' Father Andreas' voice was gentle yet still conveyed a sense of unwavering firmness.

'And yet here I am. You were happy enough to see me. I wonder what criteria I met,' said Sam.

Father Andreas chuckled to himself. 'We have no criteria, but you are certainly interesting. You come from Edinburgh, seeking St Athanasius' church, yet you are not a priest; I understand you are a university lecturer. I wonder what might have triggered your interest in such a thing.'

'You know who I am and where I'm from. You've certainly done some homework.'

'Yes, we have. And having seen press reports over the past months it seems your name has appeared more than once. What should I make of that? Have you stories to tell?'

Sam fixed Father Andreas with a steady gaze. 'Not quite sure where you're going with that question.'

'Come now, Sam. We live in a backwater. We are not backward. Why are you looking for us? And why did you organise a tail? Oh yes, Father Christos spotted your friends and their car from the moment they started to follow back in the square. Who are your friends? Why do you feel the need to have an escort?'

Sam was impressed. Clearly, his driver had been alert after all - though he had misread the signs. 'They're no friends of mine. Only came across them myself today.'

'It seems they are interested in you. I wonder why. So many people, so many interests. You say they are not your friends so why would they be waiting in their car just over the ridge? They are dedicated; it must be very uncomfortable in the afternoon heat.'

'No good asking me. Why not ask them? I'd be more than happy to learn what they're about.'

Father Andreas gave a little shrug and glanced briefly out of the window towards the ridge. He raised his hand and pointed gently towards the window, then let it fall into his lap again. Instantly, beyond the door there was the faint sound of footsteps hurrying along the corridor, then receding to silence as they descended the stair.

'Perhaps we will,' said Father Andreas. 'But why do you want to speak with me?' What brings a university lecturer more than 2000 kilometres with little more than an overnight bag? That's not holiday travel is it?'

'Well, I always like to mix a bit of business with pleasure,' said Sam.

Suddenly his attention was caught by sounds from outside the window; car doors slammed, the Peugeot engine coughed into life then roared under the pressure of a hard pressed accelerator pedal. The car appeared rushing across the courtyard, two priests on board. He guessed they were going to challenge the men parked in their car. He had not recognised either of the priests and wondered how many people were in the building. For all its outward quiet and stillness, it seemed a busy place.

The car disappeared from view as it passed under the courtyard's entrance arch. A few moments later, it reappeared, following the dusty track up the slope. Then as it reached the top, it crossed the ridge and dropped out of sight. Sam guessed it was heading directly towards the car that had trailed him here earlier. He felt a pang of anxiety. How would it play out? He hoped the priests did not get into trouble but it was beyond his influence. Father Andreas clearly ran things his way.

'I am not a fool, Sam. Have you a sign for me? Have you brought a message? Or do you have another motive? Are those men trailing you or serving you?' The softness had gone from Father Andreas' voice. This was clearly no game. He had a secret and was not simply going to give it up.

'I have nothing for you. No message. But I do have a friend who might like to speak with you.'

'Oh? Tell me of your friend then. Why might I want to speak with him? And why has he not come himself?'

Sam was about to answer when more sounds forced their way through the glass of the window. The Peugeot was racing back down the slope towards the archway. The engine was revving, horn sounding and a second car was following. A man was leaning out of the front passenger window of the following car, pointing towards the Peugeot. Neither Sam nor Father Andreas needed to wonder what was happening. A series of little flashes from the man's hand made clear it held a gun and he was firing at the priests.

The Peugeot raced under the arch and into the courtyard, followed by the other car. Sam and Father Andreas moved closer to the window. In horror, they looked down towards the Peugeot; it had come to a halt directly below their window, in front of the steps leading up to the front doors. The priests got out and made for the steps as the pursuing car roared under the archway and into the courtyard. The driver did not brake, gunning the car hard across the open space as the passenger continued to fire towards the priests.

'What are they doing? Are they madmen?' Sam pressed up against the glass to get a closer view. 'Come on, I must help your priests!'

'No, we must act quickly to get you away, come with me,' said Father Andreas.

Sam looked back towards Father Andreas. 'No, I must go and help your people; you take cover where you will.'

'That is not necessary, come with me.'

Action seen in the corner of his eye called Sam's attention back to the courtyard and he felt a slight tightness in his stomach, that flash of tension that always came to him in the moment before action. The rearmost of the two priests had not quite made the steps when he was hit in the leg by a bullet. With a cry, he collapsed grasping at his leg.

The leading priest turned back in response to the cry for help, he stepped down from the steps and was about to bend to lift the wounded priest when he was shot in the chest. He stood transfixed, swaying gently in the burning sun. A dead man standing, the bullet had nicked the edge of his Aorta artery. The black of his vestments masked what little blood seeped out of his wound; inside, his lifeblood was pumping into his chest cavity and with each heartbeat, he weakened. The pursuing car rolled right over the downed priest, a tyre crushing his ribcage in the passing and he was dead before the rear wheels reached him.

The standing priest saw the car crush his friend, saw it racing on towards him, but he was beyond pain as the car smashed into his legs to throw him up high in the air like a rag doll. The car hit the bottom step and stalled. As the priest's body landed on the bonnet, the attackers hurried out and rushed up the steps and into the building. In that instant, the silence returned to the courtyard, but there was no peace now.

Sam found himself hurrying along the first floor corridor behind Father Andreas whose wheelchair seemed to have developed quite a turn of speed. 'Where are we going?' said Sam.

'Stick with me, it will be alright. I have a safe place. The others will deal with the intruders.'

'I don't think so. I should go and help.'

'You should stay with me. Come on.'

Sam followed. He noticed the middle-aged priest who had earlier brought them water was standing beyond the stairwell, at the far end of the corridor; he held something in his hand. Sam was not sure what it was.

'Up ahead is our place of safety, we just need to get past the stairwell,' called Father Andreas. 'Keep going. Nearly there.' The middle-aged priest was beckoning them on, urging speed.

Just as they approached the stairwell, the two men from the car reached the top of the stairs. They immediately turned their attention and pistols towards Sam and Father Andreas.

'Stop,' shouted the first man, his gun pointing directly at Father Andreas' chest.

'No moving or you are both dead,' shouted the second man, his gun trained on Sam.

Sam was still, he'd been in similar positions during his service days. He knew from the repeated peaking in the men's voices that they were strung taut. Any false move would trigger a shooting spree and he and Father Andreas would be on the receiving end. 'Stay still, Father Andreas, just sit tight,' said Sam.

'Good. Do as I say,' said the first man, his voice steadying as he registered that his prisoners were acquiescing. His finger eased slightly on the trigger. 'Now where is it?'

'Where is what?' said Father Andreas.

Sam noted the calm voice; the old priest was not being phased by the experience one bit.

'Don't get smart, you know what we want. Now hand it over.'

'Okay,' said Father Andreas. 'But I keep what you want in the chapel. We will need to go there.' He waved a hand, pointing beyond the stair towards the lift. 'I'll need to go down in that.'

'We'll all go together,' said the first man. Then he suddenly staggered a pace towards Sam and Father Andreas; he coughed, it turned to a frightened little gasp and he looked down at his chest. A steel bolt had punched through his back and was sticking proudly out through his chest, dripping red. He dropped his pistol, carefully moved his hands to touch the bolt and looked up and over to the second man, puzzlement writ across his face.

In that instant, Sam knew what the middle-aged priest at the far end of the corridor had been holding: a crossbow. Conditioning, the product of long past training sessions, kicked in and Sam sprang into action. Brushing past the dying man, he lunged for the second man who was still trying to register what had happened.

Sam was on him before the man could refocus. They grappled; Sam grabbed the man's pistol hand in an effort to ensure he could not aim again. It fired two, three times up and into the ceiling as the struggle continued. Sam was strong but the man was heavy and as they twisted at the top of the stair, Sam went down, his foot slipping in the pool of blood spreading from the skewered assailant's body.

Sam was in trouble. On his back and upside down, feet still on the first floor landing but his head three steps lower on the staircase. All his efforts were focused on keeping control of his opponent's pistol hand but Sam had cracked his head as he fell and the blood now streaming from his head wound was obstructing his already blurring vision as his mind started to spin. He was beginning to fade, knew he had only moments before he lost consciousness and the fight, but he had nothing more to give.

He saw his opponent's big face loom closer, saw his dirty toothed smile. Even as he wilted, he smelt the bad breath, was furious with himself and was aware that the pistol hand was slowly turning, the muzzle coming to bear on him; he was losing consciousness, losing strength, losing the battle. He should have been able to take this man. As he blacked out, he saw a flash but heard no roar of a pistol's discharge. He couldn't understand. Then his assailant's head seemed to roll away to one side, leaving his body behind, along with a spurting, jetting, fountain of red. The body immediately eased and relaxed on top of Sam.

In place of his assailant's head, Sam could now see a long shimmering streak, a shining sword, and above that, peering down on him was the face of an angel. No, thought Sam, as he finally slipped into unconsciousness, the face of Father Christos.

Chapter 27

THURSDAY 5ᵀᴴ SEPTEMBER

Cassiter was not pleased. Yes, Parsol's team had located Sam Cameron on Kefalonia and there was no doubt the operation had gone well, initially. From there it had gone rapidly downhill. Parsol's men had reported following Cameron here and there, all very straight forward. A car journey into the countryside was reported. There then followed a vague message about his visiting some church or monastery, somewhere out of sight in the hills, set back from the road. No directions, no locations: what sort of training did these men get? Then a final message: they were being approached; they had been spotted, and were going on the offensive. Then there was nothing; complete silence since yesterday.

He listened to the messages again. Each listening just confirmed his view that it was always best to rely on his own people. Yes, he had made a link up with Parsol, but he still had more confidence in his own staff. He had already sent out several messages this morning. By tomorrow, he would have some of his own team members to hand, recalled from their various stations. He needed his people here and they were coming. Then he would go to Kefalonia himself to find out exactly what was going on.

• • •

Helen sat in the airport café, her cup of coffee gone cold in front of her. For what seemed the hundredth time she checked her messages. Nothing, Sam had been out of the loop for a full day.

His last text had mentioned a possible meeting, then nothing. She had phoned his hotel in Kefalonia; they seemed not to know where he was. Sam had not been in touch with Elaine or Grace either; he had simply dropped off the radar.

It had been good to visit Xavier and Angelo; both were on the road to recovery and each receiving the most attentive protection from the police. The old priest had been glad to see her and even from his sickbed seemed to worry over her like a protective uncle. Much as she hated a fuss, she had been delighted to take up his offer, made as soon as she explained Sam had gone missing in Kefalonia.

Xavier always seemed to come up trumps and, this time, even while in his sickbed, he had really pulled a rabbit out of the hat. She was sitting in the private lounge at Cagliari Airport. Xavier's private plane was sitting on the runway ready to take her to Kefalonia, but only on condition that she allowed a couple of his parishioners to accompany her. An insurance, he had said. After introductions, the men had gone to collect travel bags. As soon as they returned, they would all board and the flight would take off.

The men were quiet, respectful but friendly towards her, and she knew they were as loyal and hard as the land that bred them. Perfect if you needed protection - and she was beginning to suspect she might.

She noticed an alcove set back from the main lounge; there she found a little prayer space and bowed her head, praying for a speedy journey. But most of all she prayed for Sam. Prayed and prayed again.

● ● ●

In Edinburgh, others were also turning to prayer - out of faith and also out of desperation. Elaine had finished transferring the last of the files from the church office's filing cabinets into packing boxes. She had more boxes ready to be filled with the church's hymnbooks and the pew bibles. Suddenly this was all very real.

She left the office and walked through the vestry; it was as she always liked it, thoroughly clean and tidy, but sadly, now very bare. She hurried on, pushing aside memories of what had happened here, and entered the nave, pulling the vestry door shut behind her.

In the quiet of the church, she selected a pew at the front, sat, bowed her head and prayed quietly, sliding into a period of quiet contemplation. She was worried for her friends, her daughter and herself. Amongst all that concern, she found she was worrying for the building too. She and John Dearly had invested so many years in it and it was to go, swept aside just like that. Elaine was unhappy, Helen had promised to do what she could, but what could she do? And in any case, events were taking Helen elsewhere just when she was needed most in Edinburgh. Their time was almost up. She prayed again for some salvation and then slowly straightened her head before standing, ready to face the next hurdle.

She did not have to wait. James Curry stood inside the front entrance to the church. He walked up the aisle towards her.

'Elaine, good to see you. I'm sure you've been busy,' said Curry. 'How are things proceeding? All done?'

Elaine glanced around for a moment. 'We're keeping to your schedule, so I'm sure that will please you. But what about the service of thanksgiving for the church, we should have one.'

'Yes, I have agreed to that. One or two procedural problems to iron out but we certainly don't want to make a big thing of it, bearing in mind all the grizzly goings on here. A quiet exit is what's required, don't you agree?'

Elaine did not bother answering.

'Now we will certainly want to hold it as soon as possible, but minimum fuss. The transaction is going ahead fast; we've had a very good offer in for the parish property.' He gave a cold little smile. 'One our Italian-American friends might describe as an offer we can't refuse. As an elder you'll have sight of the offer soon enough but let me tell you, off the record, the presbytery has really landed on its feet here. We have been offered double the independently assessed market value provided we expedite the sale. A remarkable sum, clearly we must move to clinch the deal. It's a once in a lifetime opportunity that has to be grabbed with both hands.'

Elaine's heart sank at the news. There was no way back.

'You see, my dear, it only goes to prove the decisions we reached under my guidance were for the best. I have had to push and pull at one or two committees to enable the sale without exposure to the market, but it's so clear we would never receive such an offer on the open market that the General Trustees had to recognise it makes sense to proceed at once.

'I'm going to leave you to sort out the details of a thanksgiving service. It will have to be next week; I think organising it will be a fitting last act by the parish elders. The question is who would you like to lead the service? Feel free to think of me, I'd be only too happy to oblige.' He looked at Elaine expectantly.

'I haven't given it a moment's thought,' she said. 'I will sound out the other elders; we are having a meeting this evening. I'll see what they think.'

'Good. I'll leave it with you then. I'm sure you'll pull it all together. Though, and of course I have no say in the matter, it might be politic to avoid involving Helen Johnson. After all, she is something of a newcomer - no real history within the parish. And she has a nasty habit of rubbing people up the wrong way. Well, I know the presbytery can rely on you to do the right thing, my dear. I leave it entirely in your hands now. Must dash.'

Elaine did not walk down the aisle with him. She stood and glared at his back. Yes, she thought, leave it in my hands but rest assured, Helen will be there.

Tears welled up in the corner of her eyes and spilled out to roll down her cheeks. Alone in the church she loved, Elaine made no attempt to stop them. She sat down in a pew and bent forward seemingly in prayer. But this was grief. It was her place, she had married her husband here; her daughter had been christened here. It was here she had said a last goodbye to her husband. Her life revolved around the church and that man was just throwing it all away.

• • •

Helen stepped out of the hire car. She thanked the Sardinian who held it open for her and then made straight for the hotel reception.

He followed her in while the second guard drove round to park the car in the hotel's tiny rear car park.

After booking all three of them into adjacent rooms, she asked for access to Sam's. The teenage girl on reception couldn't help but promised to arrange for her grandfather, the owner, to speak to her as soon as he got back. Helen left for her own room to freshen up. The flight had been smooth and far less stressful than the normal flying experience. She laughed to herself; she'd need to keep in with Xavier. This was the way to travel, for sure.

A little while later, cleaned up and relaxed, she was scanning her messages in the hope that Sam might have resurfaced when there was a light knock on her door. She called out at once. 'Door's unlocked. Come on in.'

She had expected to see one of the Sardinian men making a periodic check on her. With Sam having gone missing, they clearly did not intend to have to report to Xavier that she had been lost too. Instead, it was an old lady; she walked slowly into the room, her stick tapping out a steady pace across the marbled floor tiles. Behind her came the teenage girl who had served them at reception earlier. She carried a tray, laid with teapot, cups and saucers, sugar bowl and milk jug. The old lady waved the girl towards a table where she placed the tray and then left the room after directing a little smile towards Helen.

Helen watched the old lady select a chair and sit, settling herself comfortably before glancing up to make eye contact.

'Now, Miss Johnson, Helen. May I call you Helen?' The old lady looked down at the tray in front of her. 'Shall I pour?'

For a moment Helen stood, transfixed, who was this old lady? Clearly, she did not present any sort of physical threat. But what was the reason for her just barging into the room? Pulling herself into the moment, she stepped across the room, close to where the old lady sat. 'I'm sorry, but who are you? Why are you in my room?'

'Do sit down, Helen. I can't speak with you towering over me; I'll get a crick in my neck.' The old lady's voice was gentle, educated, disarming.

Helen sat, mostly because she realised it was the only way the woman sitting in front of her was going to explain herself and a little because she actually saw something to like in the old lady, for all her brass neck.

'Who are you?'

'Just call me mama, everyone here does.' The old lady finished pouring the tea and put down the pot. 'Would you like milk or sugar?'

'Just milk please. But who are you?'

'I own the hotel. Well, my son Haris thinks he does but, believe me, it's mine until my time's up,' she gave a sharp little laugh, 'and I'm not going anywhere yet!'

'I see.'

'You have a friend you were asking after, a guest here.'

'Yes, Sam. Sam Cameron. He seems to have vanished; I'm very worried about him. Do you have any news?'

'We'll see what can be found out. I have put out some feelers. I'm sure it will be fine. Don't worry; I'm certain he will turn up. We don't like to lose guests,' the old lady fixed Helen with surprisingly bright eyes. 'Meantime tell me about yourself and Sam, how do you know one another?'

'I'm sorry; I haven't got time to chat. I need to find Sam.'

'Now, now, I told you I have made enquiries for you. I am sure we will find him soon enough. Now have some tea and let's chat.'

Accepting the inevitable, Helen picked up her cup. Almost before she realised it she was deep in conversation with the old lady, who proved a real charmer and seemed keen to know all about her and Sam.

Finally, after twenty minutes or so of conversation, she told Helen of her own talk with Sam, about his search for the church of Saint Athanasius and of Father Andreas. Then the old lady stood and made her excuses.

Mama could see her story had given Helen hope but she determinedly swept aside the younger woman's renewed flood of questions. 'Don't go far, I'll see what news there is of Sam and keep you informed,' she said and left Helen alone in the room.

• • •

It was mid-evening when Helen got news. She was sat in the square, letting her fingers drum lightly on the bill for the evening meal she had just finished with her two Sardinian companions. They were all sipping coffees when she spotted a man making his way towards her from the hotel.

The Sardinians bristled at his uninvited approach but Helen laid hands on their forearms and they settled down. 'Yes?' she said. 'Have you news?'

'My name is Haris.' He eyed her two companions a little nervously. 'Mama says you should go in the car.' He pointed across the square towards a battered old Peugeot 205.

'Where will it take me?'

Haris shrugged, irritated at having been reduced to a messenger boy. 'Mama says go; we go. Mama says jump; we jump. Who knows? Always this, always that, always secrets.' He stepped a little closer, bending a little, and added in a rueful tone. 'But I tell you, she's always right.' Then he turned and left, waving his arm in the direction of the car.

Looking more closely at the car Helen could see the driver was a young man. She stood, walked to the restaurant counter, settled the bill and crossed to the car. The Sardinians followed, close, like shadows pinned to her heels.

Bending down she spoke to the driver through the open passenger window. 'You want to take me somewhere?'

Father Christos turned his face to look at her more closely. She could see his eyes conducting an appraisal, could not read the conclusions. He nodded. 'Yes,' he said. 'But only you.'

Helen knew the Sardinians would not allow her to travel alone. 'They're with me,' she said.

Father Christos shrugged. 'Then you must stay. Sorry, only you can come.'

Helen thought for a moment before trying another tack. 'Do you know Sam Cameron? We are his friends.'

As her eyes adjusted to the light and shadow within the car she realised the man was dressed as a priest. 'You're a priest,' she said.

'That is so. Are you coming?'

'What's your name?'

'Father Christos.'

One of the Sardinians rested a hand on Helen's forearm, drawing her attention to three neat little holes spread across the rear of the car - bullet holes. She looked at the man and nodded an acknowledgement before resuming her conversation with Father Christos.

'Looks like you've been busy. Seen much action recently, Father Christos?'

Father Christos gave a shrug.

'Is shrugging all the men in this part of the world can do?'

Father Christos shrugged again and then smiled at her.

She smiled back. 'Mama says I'm to come with you and I'm happy to. But my friends won't let me go alone. I just need to find Sam, that's all. Mama trusts me, I trust her. So I'll trust you, but you have to trust me too. My friends come, that's final.'

There was a long pause as Father Christos weighed up the options. He shrugged again then nodded agreement in Helen's direction. 'We should go now.'

Without waiting for any further discussion, Helen pulled the front passenger door open while waving the two Sardinians into the back seats. She got in and fastened her belt.

'Where are we going?'

Father Christos drove off in silence. Helen tried once or twice to engage in conversation but finally gave up. They quickly left the lights of town behind. Driving through the darkness, lit only by the car's headlights, it became pointless trying to keep a handle on their location.

From high in the hills, they could look down into the blackness to see the light patterns of little villages and farmsteads glowing in the distance. Suddenly the car took a hard turn off the road; they were in complete darkness, climbing yet higher. Then, crossing a little ridge, they started to drop down the other side and Helen could make out the shadow of a building ahead of them. The car drove under an archway and into a darkly shadowed courtyard, a couple of faint lights showed through the slats of shuttered windows. Wherever they were, they had arrived.

Leaving the car, Helen and the Sardinians followed Father Christos into a dimly lit entrance hall, up a flight of stairs and along a corridor. He guided them into a long room. Standing to one side Father Christos pointed towards the occasional chairs, 'Your friends can sit here, and you may join Father Andreas at the desk.' His hand swept to the other end of the room and Helen suddenly noticed a man sitting low behind a heavy wooden desk.

Father Andreas beckoned for her to join him.

Helen looked at the Sardinians, waved in the direction of the chairs and left them and Father Christos behind as she walked alone across the room to the desk.

Father Andreas stretched out a hand to greet her. 'Forgive me for not rising; I'm afraid that is a little beyond me now.'

Helen circled the desk to shake the old man's hand, while taking in the wheelchair and the strength in the man's quiet voice.

'Sit now,' said Father Andreas, pointing her to a chair beside the desk. 'Sit and let's talk.'

Helen was not in the mood for small talk. 'I understand you have news of my friend Sam Cameron. It would be good to hear it and maybe get back to town.'

'Yes, of course. But sit first, please. We have things that need to be discussed.'

'The only thing I want to discuss is Sam. Where is he?'

Father Andreas looked at Helen for a long moment; saw she was strong and concluded she was not going to give any ground. 'Okay,' he said. 'You shall see him, but he cannot speak with you.'

'Where is he? What have you done with him?'

'We have done nothing; your friend was injured saving my life, for which we are all very grateful. I'm afraid he has been unconscious for some time. But we think he will be fine.' As he finished speaking, Father Andreas raised his hand, giving the slightest of waves - the door beside the bookcase opened silently. A middle-aged priest stood beside it.

Helen leapt up. 'What? Where is he? Why am I here and not with him at the hospital?'

'I'm afraid we had to keep him here. I didn't think it was safe to go beyond these walls.'

Helen glanced towards the opened door. She pointed. 'That way?'

Father Andreas nodded, the middle-aged priest disappeared into the hallway and Helen chased after him. A commotion of Sardinians, priests and a wheelchair hurried behind her - it registered only slightly as she focused on what lay ahead.

271

She followed the priest upstairs and into a room lit only by light from the corridor. Inside, lying asleep on the bed was Sam. A darkened line across the side of his head marked the site of a nasty gash. It had been cleaned and stapled. She knelt beside the bed and gently touched the wound.

'What have you done to him?' she said. 'Why isn't he in hospital?'

The room darkened further as the chasing men caught up. 'Give me some light here,' ordered Helen and the men backed out of the room. Father Christos reached a hand round the doorframe, flicked on a wall switch and electric light filled the room just as Father Andreas arrived via the lift.

'There's no need to worry; he's in good hands,' said Father Andreas.

'Good hands? Good hands is a hospital, not this back of beyond place. Why hasn't he been treated properly?'

'We've done the best we could; Father Manos was a military doctor before he received the call. Sam has been given the best of attention.'

Father Manos, the middle-aged priest who had led the rush upstairs, inclined his head very slightly.

'He's been unconscious; he should have a head scan,' said Helen.

'Well, yes, but we were attacked here yesterday. I could not be sure there were not others watching who might attack again even in the hospital,' said Father Andreas.

Helen checked the flood of reprimands that were on her tongue, as she thought for a moment of the attack on Xavier in hospital in Cagliari. Perhaps Father Andreas was right. She looked again at Sam, his wound had been treated well and he seemed comfortable. 'Okay, until morning anyway. I'm going to stay here with him until then. Once it's daylight we can sort something out.' Helen was not asking and nobody was arguing with her.

'I agree,' said Father Andreas. 'You may stay here with Sam. Father Christos will organise refreshments for you all and show your, urh, your colleagues to some sleeping quarters.'

Then Helen was alone with Sam. She spoke to him through the stillness of the night, telling him off, telling him of her feelings, saying the things she would never dream of mentioning to him under ordinary circumstances. She kept talking until at some point before the dawn she fell asleep on the bed.

Chapter 28

FRIDAY 6ᵀᴴ SEPTEMBER

Helen woke late in the morning. Days of worry had caught up with her on the warm bed beside Sam. She sat up quickly and checked him. He was breathing, she gave a sigh of relief and then a gasp of joy; Sam's eyes were blinking. He was awake.

She kissed him and, under the circumstances, he gave what passed for a reasonable response. Helen began checking him. Could he feel this? Could he feel that? What could he see? What could he hear?

'Helen, stop it. Stop worrying or I'm going back under, that's a promise,' said Sam.

'Well, we need to know you're functioning properly. It's not as though you've been in hospital. You've had a head injury. And I thought we had agreed you'd keep a low profile - fact finding, avoid any risks. In, out and away, you said.'

'Just five minutes more. Then I'll be fine,' he muttered as his eyes closed. Helen let him sleep. Feeling happier in herself, she headed off along the corridor in search of a bathroom to freshen up. She really wanted a shower but that would have to wait for now.

A little while later, she emerged from the bathroom just as Father Manos was emerging from Sam's room. He nodded to her and smiled. She found herself smiling back. The priest beckoned to her and headed along the corridor towards the stair. Helen followed, glancing in on a sleeping Sam as she passed his room.

'Nice job with the wound staples,' she said to Father Manos' back. 'Your work?'

The priest raised a hand in acknowledgement.

Entering the long room, she found herself directed towards the broad table where a place had been set for her. As soon as she sat, a much older priest appeared. He was wheeling a trolley with a canteen of coffee on it, some croissants, butter and a selection of fruit. The old man lifted the breakfast on to the table, and gave her a little smile in acknowledgement of her thanks. Another non-talker, she thought. Then she ate.

Once finished, she stood to look out of the window, anxious to get a feel for their location. It took just an instant to confirm they were remote, very remote. The courtyard below was still. Beyond the building, the land rose up to a ridge. Its slope covered in determinedly green scrub and punctuated by occasional pines and little stands of slim pointy cypress trees. The grass, turning gold and dry was less resilient in resisting the late summer sun that bore down on everything - nothing moved. Just a worn single-track lane led away up the slope - not much passing trade here she thought.

A creaking floorboard had her turn as Father Andreas rolled across the room in his chair.

'I see you're up. Good, good. And I'm told Sam is awake. Success all round.' He glanced at the table as he rolled past it. 'You've eaten. So things are looking better. Yes?'

'Yes, it's good news about Sam. Though I still don't understand what happened here or why. Perhaps you're gonna tell me now?'

'Sit, sit,' said Father Andreas. Waving Helen towards the cluster of easy chairs, he wheeled across to join her. 'Yes, we should talk. There are some things I don't understand either, things that I would really like you to explain.'

'Shoot,' said Helen. 'You first. What do you want to know? Then I'll want some answers too.'

Father Andreas bowed his head slightly in acknowledgement. 'Your friend Sam came to our island as thousands of tourists do every year. But he didn't come as a tourist, though he did ask about a church. Not churches, you understand; some tourists like churches. No, he asked about a church, my church, one that has not existed for a long, long, time: not since I was a young priest, a lifetime ago. Do you know, I'm over ninety now. Most of my friends from then are gone. Mama you met, we grew up together. There aren't many others left.

'Even the locals don't think about the St Athanasius church any more. The church is history. So naturally, I was interested when I heard Sam was asking questions.' He paused and fixed Helen with a quizzical look. 'And he is from Edinburgh, Scotland.'

'Uh huh,' said Helen. 'Is that any reason for him to have his head broken?'

'That was not us,' protested Father Andreas, throwing his hands up in horror. 'No, no, I was, how would you say? Interested; yes, interested to speak with Sam.'

'Well, that was some heavy chatting.'

'No, I told you, trouble followed him here. Oh, don't worry now; we dealt with it. But I had thought he was somebody. Somebody I hoped to meet… No, somebody I prayed to meet before my time. But it was not him.'

'How do you know he's not who you wanted?' said Helen.

Father Andreas gave a drawn smile. 'Oh, I would know. He is a lecturer. I am looking, hoping for a priest.'

'A priest? Why's that?'

'It doesn't matter. I think that moment has gone now. It was not to be…' His voice trailed off into a moment's silence. Then bringing himself back to the present he carried on with his questioning. 'But you are his friend. An American, I think. Can you explain what brought the trouble to our door?'

'Maybe, I'm not sure what happened. Sam can tell us now he's awake. He has an eye for things. But now my question. Tell me, if you were priest of St Athanasius' in town, why are you up here?'

The old man sighed. The sparkle and power that she had seen the night before were gone. He suddenly looked washed out, shrunken. His vitality was visibly ebbing away as though his moment had passed him by and he was ready for an end.

'After the earthquake my body was broken, I needed time to recuperate. So many innocents were killed.' Suddenly, there were tears in his eyes. 'I did what I could but how could you save everyone? It was not possible. St Athanasius' church had always maintained this place, part of our heritage. A retreat, a sanctuary, for priests and for lay people who needed time and quiet. We moved everything up here after the church was destroyed and I have been happy to stay ever since.'

Helen leant forward, reached her hand out and squeezed his forearm. Deep inside, she knew she had found her man. A poor, brave, man who had fought a long struggle against adversity. She could tell he was near the end. His body clock had simply wound down.

His eyes looked up to hers. A sad smile played across his lips. Kneeling beside him, she put her arms round the old man and hugged, kissed his cheek, and then pulled back a little, looked him in the eyes. 'You have been waiting for a priest. A priest from Edinburgh?'

He nodded. 'All my life.' His eyes dropped to his lap. 'Waiting in vain. Perhaps one day he will come for Christos. But not for me now, the moment is gone. When Sam Cameron turned up it lit a fire in me, for a moment I was fifty years younger, I thought the time had come.' He was talking to himself now, happy to be close to somebody, anybody, but almost unaware of who.

'Come on Andreas, don't give up, there's always time, another chance.'

He gave a smile; the tears had stopped now and he looked at her again. 'No, it's over.'

'Andreas, you need a priest, a priest from Edinburgh. A particular priest? Maybe one who carries a ring?'

Father Andreas nodded, head down, forlorn. 'Yes, a special ring.' Slowly his head pulled up, he looked at Helen again. 'And how do you know this?'

Helen leant forward and kissed him again, on both cheeks, pulled back and, gently squeezing the old man's arms, she almost whispered to him. 'Not all the clergy are men today.'

He looked puzzled, trying to grasp what she said and what lay behind it. 'Yes, I know that.' He looked at her, trying to find something in her words.

'Father Andreas, I am a minister of the church.'

He nodded acknowledgement, without really understanding.

'Father Andreas, I am a minister from Edinburgh. I sent Sam to find you.'

The old man looked at her, hearing but not quite understanding. Helen fished under the collar of her polo shirt and pulled out a gold chain. She could see his face change the instant the chain began to emerge. He understood. By the time the ring was fully in sight, his eyes were filled with tears for the second time that morning.

Hands shaking, the old man reached out and touched the ring. He leant forward looking carefully, in almost euphoric disbelief. Craning his neck, he kissed it reverentially. Almost absently, Helen noticed he was checking the ring, touching it, letting his finger run over the surface, searching, feeling, finding.

The old man leant back, looked Helen in the eye again and smiled. Now the contented smile of a life fulfilled. Then forcing himself to take control of his emotions he sat up straight in his chair.

'Now,' said Helen, gently, 'your turn, I think.'

Father Andreas needed no further prompting; defying the years, his gnarled hands moved quickly to produce a gold chain and signet ring from under his shirt collar.

Helen reached out and touched his ring. 'Welcome home, my friend.' She didn't know what had prompted the words but could see they meant something to Father Andreas.

She had not heard the door opening behind her nor heard the feet crossing the wooden floor, but was suddenly aware of another person close by. She looked up to see Father Christos hovering a couple of paces off. Clearly, he wanted to support Father Andreas but was unsure of what to do. She waved him in and stepped back, allowing the old man's hands to gently slide off her own. Christos stood close to the chair and Father Andreas grasped his hand. Helen realised it was no longer despair but new found jubilation that was now fuelling the old man's responses. As she stepped away towards the door, she heard the old man gasp words towards the young priest.

'They are come. Christos, they are come!'

She left the room, suddenly keen to check on Sam, eager to share the news.

When she reached Sam's room, she found him awake again, sitting on the edge of the bed, half dressed.

'Should you be up?' she said.

'I'm fine, just need some fresh air.' He pulled on the shirt that had been washed and ironed whilst he slept. 'But what are you doing here? You're meant to be visiting Xavier in Sardinia.'

'I was, until you got yourself into trouble. Somebody had to come and sort you out.' She knelt down to help with his shoes.

'How did you find me?'

'Oh, we have our ways,' she said with a laugh. 'I'll tell you later. Right now, I need your help. Sam, we've found it. The St Athanasius dagger, it's here.'

Sam nodded. 'I'd guessed as much, have you seen it?'

'No, but we will. The old priest, Father Andreas, he's really cut up. I think, at first he thought you were the one. Then he realised it wasn't you so thought you were a bad guy, until you stepped in to save his life.' She gently stroked the staples that traced the wound across Sam's head.

'And what about you?' said Sam.

'Oh, we're good. Father Andreas and I have an understanding. But I'm pretty worried about him. He's had a lot of stress for someone his age.' She took Sam's arm and started to help him up. 'Come on, let's go down and see how he is now.'

'I can manage,' said Sam, shaking her arm off. 'I'm not an invalid.'

A moment later, she felt the grip of his hand on her arm and she smiled to herself as they set off together.

Having taken the lift down a floor, they entered the long room. Father Andreas was composed again and sitting at the head of the big table, Christos sat at his right hand.

'Come, sit with us,' said Father Andreas. 'Here, beside me.'

As they sat down at the table, another priest entered the room, bringing food for Sam and iced water for them all.

Father Andreas explained that he was dying; was quite matter of fact about it. A man in his nineties was dying anyway, it was just about timing. If he lived even a few more months he would be lucky, and then Christos would take his place. But today, when Sam finished eating, Helen could see the dagger, take a photograph, whatever she wanted.

'Tell me, Andreas,' she said, 'I saw you touching my signet ring.

What were you feeling for?'

The old man smiled, produced his ring and held it out for her. 'See, my ring is set with a ruby as is yours. Identical.'

Helen nodded acknowledgement, pulling out her own ring. The ruby was dark red in the shaded room, almost black.

'But look, in mine the ruby is set a little to the side. Yours is set in the middle. I believe each of the other ruby rings is offset to a different point on the dial. Together they form a virtual circle around your ruby.'

'Just as the icons in the glass of your church window are arranged around the symbol at the centre,' said Sam.

'Only the bearer of the ring whose ruby is centred can recall the task. You have the ring,' said Father Andreas, 'you have control.'

Father Andreas had seemed puzzled by Helen's plan to place everything in the public domain; but he deferred to her. Such a decision must come from the centre.

'What about the dead bodies, how will you handle them?' said Sam.

'We have a little cemetery for our dead friends, they already rest with God. As for the attackers, well, up here is a wild country. High valleys that nobody ever visits, crags nobody ever climbs. Secret places, unknown, a body can easily vanish here and never be found.'

There was a moment's silence as Helen and Sam digested the information.

'Tell me, Andreas, why didn't you rebuild your church after the earthquake?' said Helen.

The old priest was quiet for a moment, looked wistfully at Christos. 'Perhaps I should have. But we had this place too, have always had this place, and by the grace of God it survived the earthquake. And there was so much to do then, everywhere. So many people needed help. Oh, many of the big buildings were restored and eventually assistance got to lots of others. But it was never enough - the little back streets, isolated farmer's buildings... Everywhere there were problems. It did not seem right to rebuild the church at once.

'There were so many in need. Gradually, I spent most of our resources helping the people rebuild their lives - what other choice could I have made? The poorest people needed so much help. Now we don't have the money to rebuild the church. In fact, we struggle to keep this place going. We get plenty of food and help from farmers and people round about, but I'm afraid I have left Father Christos with a financial burden that might not be carried for so long.'

Helen sympathised. 'What can we do to help?'

'Nothing. We stand as we have always done. God will support our church, somehow. I just thank Him that the task is completed in my time. Now come, you are here on a mission. I have something you need to see and I should not delay.' He rolled off in the direction of the bookcase.

• • •

Cassiter was satisfied. Followed by four of his own team members he stepped on to the flight from Paris to Athens. He had other members still travelling back from around the world to join him, but he was happy that those already with him would be more than capable of dealing with this issue.

First, he would find out what had happened to Parsol's men, and then he would find out what Cameron was doing on the island. Cameron needed watching. He now seemed a far more unpredictable adversary than expected.

Cassiter had reviewed Cameron's track record again. As before, the academic stuff had been clear enough. His military record showed the normal things, some active service, and a handful of diplomatic postings, which was hardly surprising as an Intelligence Corps officer with his language skills. Generally, he seemed a good and clever officer but nothing so outstanding. An unremarkable, almost routine career course - three years' service and then he had plunged back into academe.

Then something had twitched at the corner of his mind. He had read the report through again, his sense of disquiet accentuated. He started flipping back and forth between screens. Yes, there it was - or rather, there it wasn't. There were occasional time gaps between his postings, small but measurable holes in his record. A few days here, a few weeks there but they quickly added up. What had Cameron been up to during those gaps? There should have been no gaps in a service record. There was more to this man than met the eye. And yet, it seemed from Cameron's own letter of resignation that he had quit the army, unhappy with the service. It didn't make sense, didn't add up.

Still, the easy way to deal with such a problem was to eliminate it. And the easy way was often the best way.

Chapter 29

SATURDAY 7ᵀᴴ SEPTEMBER

Sam was sitting at the kitchen table in his flat. He'd managed a few hours' sleep once they got back but he was wishing it had been more. Thanks to Xavier's plane, the journey home from Kefalonia had been much better than the torturous outward leg, but it had been broken by a stop at Cagliari to drop off Helen's Sardinian protectors. And this morning, at Helen's insistence, he had been for a check-up at A&E. Helen had driven, he suspected to make sure he went. After five hours he was back home.

Seemingly content that he was all in one piece, she had gone off to speak with people about the parish, which seemed to be going rapidly down the plughole - with James Curry gleefully holding the plug aloft.

In the quiet isolation of home, he could at last push his tiredness aside and focus on the issue at hand. In front of him were a series of printed pictures. He had cut away their backgrounds to leave the shape of daggers. Eight of them. He then set to one side the picture of the parish dagger with its list of Roman numerals engraved on the blade. He believed it simply listed the numerical order that the other daggers should be laid in.

He organised each of the remaining seven picture shapes in the order determined by the parish dagger's numerical list. But he was stumped. Couldn't see any logical pattern on the waving and swirling lines engraved on each blade - yet this had to be how they were assembled.

His thoughts turned again to the one blade that was missing, the French dagger, and he wondered if that was the key. It was the one that they knew must be in the hands of the bad guys. He was not sure if they would ever be able to get it. Looking at the number list engraved on the blade of the parish dagger, it was clear that the missing French blade's number was two. It was the top one in the number sequence. Once the blades were all aligned, it would make up one edge of the greater pattern. That meant it was either crucial or peripheral; he needed more information to make that decision. And the information, like everything else to do with this problem, was hidden. Dragging things out into the open was like pulling teeth.

After a while spent working through possibilities, he put the problem to one side, tried a change of tack. The one icon on the silver scroll he had not resolved was the maze. It was a reproduction of the Mappa Mundi labyrinth symbol that in turn represented Crete. Did it mean Crete was involved or simply that there was a maze or puzzle to solve? He laughed to himself: there were certainly plenty of those.

The one thing he had ruled out was that the labyrinth icon meant the labyrinth at King Minos' palace in Crete. That had lain buried for thousands of years until archaeologists uncovered it last century. The Templars could not have known it was there, so couldn't have used it. The maze symbol meant something else.

Still stumped, he picked up his printouts of Helen's Swiss photographs. Another problem to consider, but a change was as good as a rest.

Flicking through the photographs he tried to form meanings or links but without any luck. He worked back through the stack of pictures again, coming to a halt at the image of the gold framed glass. He still suspected this was significant, somehow. The gold thread wandering its apparently random way across the glass did not make any sense. Why was a ruby set in the glass? That at least made a link to the signet rings, and by association the daggers, but what it was he did not know.

Twisting the photograph round, he wondered again which way

up the item should sit. He tried to visualise it, flat surface down, the crenulations facing up to the sky like the battlements of some miniature castle. Or should the crenulations face down forming an array of little feet for the artefact to stand on?

The phone rang; he answered it. 'Sam speaking.'

'Hi Sam, I'm working on a bit with Elaine, trying to get the parish paperwork signed off. There is so much to do and James Curry has not allowed her nearly enough time. He's being as unreasonable as ever.'

'I see. Anything I can do to help?'

'No, but let's not bother cooking. I'll bring something in when I come. What do you fancy? Fish and chips, a kebab maybe? You choose.'

'Let's go for fish and chips, I don't think the local kebabs could compare to the one I had in Dimitris' restaurant.'

'Great, I'll bring some in with me. See you then. Love you, bye.' She was gone before Sam could respond or even think about how her call had ended. He smiled. It didn't sound so bad. In fact, it didn't sound so bad at all.

He crossed the kitchen to make himself a coffee, let his mind drift for a moment and found it settled on the wonderful kebabs Dimitris' served. They would be going there again and next time without all the threats and mystery. He'd make sure Helen tried the kebabs.

Abruptly his mind stopped idling and ploughed straight into fifth gear. His hand abandoned the kettle, coffee forgotten as thoughts and ideas and images fell into place - no, he thought, *slotted* into place. He visualised the cook at Dimitris', the kebabs being wielded theatrically through the air en route to the grill. He pictured that single flowing motion, how it always ended with a flourish as the cook so deftly slotted each kebab into its place in the grid beneath the flaming grill.

Sam looked at Helen's picture of the glass plate; he looked closely at the crenulations. Could they be a grid, a grid to hold the daggers? Yes, he thought, yes they just might. He studied the crenulations; they were not cut at right angles to the gold frame. Each crenulation was actually cut at an acute angle, forming almost wedge shaped slots, slots that would trap and hold the daggers in place - fixed beneath the glass. He tried to gauge the breadth of gap between each crenulation, reckoning it would be just about perfect to slot a dagger in. And provided the daggers were slotted into the frame alternately, one from the right, one from the left, the daggers' quillons would not jam against each other, perfect. He counted, a sense of pleasure rising in him. If these were functional slots, not decoration, then there was exactly the right number to hold eight daggers.

Sam punched the air in delight. He knew how the daggers were combined and used. Not why, but that would come. He sent Helen a text:

Don't make any plans 4 tomorrow. U need 2 go 2 Switzerland.

Now, thought Sam, we already know the order they are to go in, so why slot all the daggers into the frame? He looked again at the picture. Helen had got it exactly right: crenulations down. There would be no use having it the other way up, the glass would be obscured by the daggers. At least with the daggers beneath the glass they and their engraved patterns could be seen, as could the blue lapis lazuli edging, the gold thread, and the ruby - everything could be seen at once. If they couldn't all be seen what was their purpose? Sam was certain that every element Henri de Bello had included had a purpose.

He thought hard about where it got them. Once again, he laid the pictures of the daggers out in order on the table. It didn't help. In a rudimentary attempt to model the gold framed plate, he went to a cupboard and lifted down a glass trifle dish - rectangular with deep sides. He'd never used it. His mother had given it to him at some point in the forlorn hope that, by association, it would get him creative in the kitchen; at last, today it was coming into its own.

He rearranged the pictures of the daggers, laying them in the prescribed numerical order, but now with each blade placed to lie point from left to right or right to left alternately, as they would be if slotted in the crenulations beneath the gold framed glass. Then he carefully placed the glass dish over the pictures and looked down through the glass at the swirling lines. They now seemed to sit together more comfortably to his eye. Referring back to Helen's photograph he realised something was still missing, the ruby and the gold thread. In his mind's eye he tried to superimpose them onto the glass dish, it brought no additional insight. He walked round the table, slid his makeshift assemblage across to let the light from the window strike directly on it.

And then he saw it, clear as day. Neatly arranged beneath the glass were the engraved dagger images, all brought together and ordered as they should be - an assembly of lines. Now, superimpose a gold thread, let it represent a route amongst the lines, and there right in the middle lies the ruby. The ruby, our X marks the spot. It is a labyrinth. It's a labyrinth map with a gold thread that marks the route through the labyrinth to the ruby.

Sam sat for a long time while thinking through the idea. It worked, well it worked better than any other idea they had come up with and all the parts fitted together well. Except, where was the labyrinth?

Hearing a key in the door, Sam hurried into the hall. He greeted Helen, kissed her and led her into the kitchen while talking slowly and methodically. Helen didn't get the chance to ask why she was going to Switzerland or to talk about her day, and in any event, within seconds she was only interested in hearing Sam's thoughts. The fish and chips cooled in their wrappers as she gazed at the pictures of the daggers and the pattern they made when laid together in the correct way and viewed through the base of the glass dish. Then she followed Sam's direction as she imagined the twisted cable tie he had placed on the glass was the thread of gold, tracing a route amongst the engraved lines of the daggers. And the orange pip he'd placed at its side, a ruby at the end of the rainbow.

The patterns on the daggers were not a map. Rather, he thought they were sections of a plan, a plan of a maze or labyrinth, and the superimposed gold thread the route through it, guiding the user directly to the orange pip - the ruby.

'And the ruby is?' said Helen.

Sam raised his view from the glass dish to meet her eyes. 'Who knows? Whatever it is, it's worth enough for people to be killed over.'

'What do we do now?'

'Well that cable tie just illustrates the point. It's the gold thread in your Swiss glass that will prove or break the theory.'

'What we need to do is put the parts together, and that means we need the glass from Switzerland.'

'No problem, I'll go ASAP. Xavier's plane is still at the airport. I can go in the morning. But Sam, where is the labyrinth? It must relate to a place in the real world otherwise it's meaningless. We need to know.'

He flashed her a confident grin. 'I have been thinking about that. Each element of the puzzle when viewed in isolation has seemed cryptic. Mostly we've been banging our heads against a brick wall.'

Helen nodded. 'Just a moment Sam,' she said while heading for Sam's fridge where she pulled out a half-empty bottle of rosé. Glancing back at him, she pointed towards the beers resting inside on a chill shelf. Sam shook his head and she shrugged, closed the fridge and picked a wine glass up from the draining board before re-joining him at the table.

She sat and Sam took the bottle from her hand to fill the glass. He watched her drink a little, saw her cheeks draw in as she savoured the flavour.

'Ah, that's good. What a day! The hospital with you, then I've been coping with James Curry's mischief and finally I come home to this.'

She stretched her hand out, resting it on his. 'Do you really think we are getting close? Tell me more.'

'Close but not there yet.'

'Well?'

'Remember, I thought our problem has been that we approached this from the wrong end - we started with the daggers first, but they are the final round of clues. They could never have any meaning in isolation.

'The scroll told us to what places the daggers were sent. The church's window named the churches in those places. The signet ring confirms the legitimacy of the individuals, the task bearers who protect the daggers. The daggers, once combined create a plan of a labyrinth and your glass plate with its gold thread is the route through the labyrinth. And finally, X marks the spot.'

'The ruby.'

'Exactly.'

'So all we're missing is the location of the labyrinth? Oh, and the final dagger,' the enthusiasm in Helen's voice faded a little, 'which we think is in the hands of our enemy.'

'I think I have some answers in those respects too.'

Helen put her glass down and rested her elbows on the table. Placing her chin in her cupped hands, she fixed Sam with an intense stare. 'Well?'

'For all its cryptic mystery, when you follow the leads in the correct order, it's a relatively simple process, and certainly would have been for any of your predecessors in the parish, each of whom would have known about the hidden scroll and the symbolism in the window. They were the custodians of the parish dagger with its index list of numbers and of the gold edged glass plate. Your predecessors were the trusted ones. They didn't have the knowledge, but they had the tools to find the knowledge when it was needed. They knew how to put it together.'

'Yes, I've got all that.'

'Okay, but think, if you are in the know and just follow steps one, two and three, in the right order, you can't go wrong. It's virtually impenetrable for outsiders but easy for the informed user since the apparently cryptic is always actually quite literal. So I think the sign of the labyrinth, just like the other signs, means exactly what it shows us. It means a labyrinth and it means on the island of Crete.'

'But you said the maze on Crete was only excavated last century and it had been buried since antiquity. The Templars could not have known it was there.'

'Right. But the island has always been associated with the labyrinth of the Minotaur. I think the Templars must have had knowledge of another maze, not the palace maze of King Minos. I think there is another maze on Crete and we need to find it. While you go to Switzerland to retrieve the gold framed glass, I'm going to Crete. We need to move fast before anyone gets the same idea.'

'Okay,' said Helen. 'I'll go with your interpretation, but what about the missing dagger, the French dagger?'

'The number sequence on the parish dagger starts with a two. That's the missing blade, the French dagger. Logically it should be slotted in first, there at the top end of the plate, against the plain side of the frame farthest away from the lapis lazuli. I think that blue colour represents the coast and see how the gold thread runs from the blue through the glass to the ruby and on to reach the other end of the frame - the plain gold side, where the number two dagger should slot in. If I'm right, there are two approaches to the ruby, the treasure, one from the sea, and one from inland. If so, we don't need the final dagger. If we approach from the seaward side, we have all the parts we need.'

'Wow. That would be brilliant. But why would there be two routes?'

'I guess because there are, I'm not sure. Remember it's a secret. Perhaps it was an insurance, in case a part of the labyrinth collapsed - an alternative access route. We'll never know for sure.'

'I'll go to Switzerland tomorrow; get in position to collect the gold framed glass as soon as the bank opens on Monday morning. I guess I've done everything I can for now to support Elaine here.'

'Yes, but what exactly have you been up to? You've been very secretive. Is there any hope of staving off the developers or whoever it is?'

'Not secretive, Sam. Discreet! It would be wrong of me to give Elaine and the others any false hope. Yes, I spoke with David Cromarty to see if there were any legal angles to exploit or ways of blocking the closure of St Bernard's, but that wouldn't work. So I've done what I can - don't want to say anything that might mess things up. So let's just wait and see how it plays out. Fingers crossed!'

'Yes, if that's all we've got, its fingers crossed then. Though I thought you were more the praying type!' Sam looked at Helen. She smiled back at him with her particularly innocent smile that could open closed doors and stop passing taxis. It told him nothing. 'Hmm,' he said.

'Much as I want to help the parish, right now I need to focus on this problem. What will you do? Come with me to Switzerland?'

'No, I think I should head directly to Crete, start having a look around. I've already booked myself a flight for tomorrow. I think we're ahead of the pack right now, let's keep it that way. I'm going to phone father Andreas just now and ask if he will send one of his people to Crete, to act as a translator for me.'

'Good idea. But where will you start your search? It's a big island.'

Sam held up her photograph of the gold framed glass. 'Assuming you have it oriented correctly, and I think you have, the lapis lazuli blue is positioned on three sides and I think the lapis represents water, the sea. See the little Templar cross on this side, beside the right hand strip of lapis. I'm taking that cross as marking the top of the frame. The projection of the Mappa Mundi put east at the top. I'm assuming, if they do share the same origin, they'll using the same projection. He twisted the photograph to put the edge with the cross at the top. Now, see, lapis at the top, east. Lapis on the right side, south. And lapis on the bottom side, west. That would mean the left side of the frame is north, where the plain gold is.

'So, viewed in the round, I'm guessing it represents a headland, on the south coast of the island, bounded by the sea on three sides with land to the north side. I'm going to work on narrowing it down further right now.'

Chapter 30

MONDAY 9TH SEPTEMBER

The morning sun was hot, the air still. Cassiter was quite motionless; he stood on a carpet of tinder dry grass amidst a stand of slender cypress trees that screened him from any searching eyes. Behind him, green scrub bushes climbed up to a ridge. In front, less than twenty metres beyond the trees, was an archway leading into a courtyard. He could see several bullet holes in the arch. The raw edges told him these were recent additions to the patina - very recent.

Two of Parsol's men were missing, assumed dead, and based on the location of their final phone transmissions they probably died near here. Cassiter did not care about the deaths, Parsol's men were disposable, but it was useful to know, useful to avoid underestimating an opponent. He and his little group had been joined by four more of Parsol's men. These had already been detailed to circle round to the far side of the building. Their only job, to ensure nobody on the inside could escape from the rear.

Once Cassiter had received the signal that Parsol's men were in place, he moved. Unhurried, he walked the few paces to the archway, a man from his own team walking to either side of him. He looked through the archway and could see a broad courtyard; on the far side were the main entrance doors to the building.

They walked under the arch and continued at a steady pace towards the main entrance. The group had almost crossed the courtyard when a big black SUV broke the crest of the hill behind them. It kicked up a cloud of dust as it powered down the little track and came to a halt under the arch, blocking the exit. Robertson and another man got out and walked to the front of the SUV where they stopped to survey the courtyard.

Cassiter had reached the steps leading up to the front doors before any occupants realised there was a problem. He glanced to his left where the chapel bell had started ringing out an alarm. Turning back towards the archway, he stretched out an arm, pointing towards the chapel. Instantly, one of the men standing at the SUV sprinted towards the sound.

As Cassiter and his wingmen entered the front doors, the distant sound of a door breaking reached them. It was quickly followed by the reports of three gunshots and the bell fell silent.

Standing in the central stairwell, Cassiter sent his two men along the shadowy corridors to left and right. They swiftly and methodically checked each of the windowless ground floor rooms, mostly storage. Having found no one, they rejoined him at the stair. With a wave of his neat little pistol, he directed his men up.

On reaching the first floor his lead man gasped and fell backwards, dropping his handgun to desperately claw at his throat. His shirt soaked with blood as he wheezed and gasped in distress and fear. A crossbow bolt had punched through his windpipe and travelled on to lodge in the wooden panelled wall beyond.

Quickly stepping over the body, Cassiter left him for dead. Ahead he could see the cause of the wounding. A middle-aged priest was urgently engaged in reloading a crossbow. Bringing his pistol to bear Cassiter fired off two rounds. The priest screamed as a shot tore through his thigh muscle and then he was hit in the lower abdomen; he fell.

Having carefully checked the corridor to left and right Cassiter stepped across the landing to where Father Manos lay curled up in pain, hands pressed to his belly.

Cassiter kicked the ancient crossbow away and then, looking down, he admired his handy work. One shot in the leg, ensuring the target went nowhere in a hurry. One shot in the lower abdomen, ensuring a long painful death, with plenty of scope to inflict further punishment should the man not oblige during interrogation. Cassiter smiled to himself. He still had it.

He knelt down behind Father Manos, his knees against the small of the priest's back. Then, slipping a hand beneath the wounded man's shirt, he forced his probing fingers between the priest's wounded belly and protective hand. Cassiter straightened his middle finger and pressed it into the bullet hole. He heard the screams, the sound multiplying as echoes reverberated back and forth along the corridor. He felt the priest's back straighten then arch as the man tried to roll away from the penetrating finger, Cassiter's knees locked him in place. After a few moments of probing, Cassiter pulled his finger out and the priest curled into a foetal ball, protecting the wound.

'Can you hear me priest? How many people are in the building?' He waited for an answer. None came, just a steady groaning. Cassiter's hand slid into the curve of the priest's belly, forced its way back beneath the wounded man's protective hands - hands that were now too weakened by shock and pain to resist him. Quickly, Cassiter's middle finger forced itself back into the wound - pressing the edges, wriggling, working deeper into the hole. Again, the screams echoed up and down the corridor, washing over Cassiter like a refreshing shower.

He watched deadpan as the man's pain continued pulsing with every wriggle of his penetrating finger. He allowed himself some moments to drink in the suffering.

'How many of you are in the building, priest?'

'Four,' said Father Manos, teeth gritted against the pain. 'Four. Stop. Stop. Please stop.'

To a deep groan from the priest, Cassiter allowed his finger to slide out of the wound. Cassiter was interested to note the priest's eyes were half-open, watching Cassiter's pistol rise, but making no attempt to avoid what was coming.

The shot punched a hole in the priest's skull. Death was instant, and welcome.

Cassiter wiped his hands clean on the dead priest's clothing.

The surviving wingman suddenly redirected his attention down the stairs where he had sensed someone's approach. Then he relaxed, lowering his pistol as he recognised his colleague who had just dealt with the chapel's bell ringer. They exchanged nods of acknowledgement and joined Cassiter in the corridor.

'How many in the chapel?' said Cassiter.

'Just one, he's been dealt with,' said the newly arrived.

Cassiter nodded approval. 'Then there are two more alive in the building. I don't want them dead until they have given me the information I need. Wounding's fine.'

The team worked along the corridor, checking rooms, moving on. It took only a couple of minutes of careful searching for them to reach the long reception room that fronted the building. Cassiter stepped into the room, which at first glance appeared empty. As he took in the full length of the room, he saw a movement behind the desk at the far end and brought his pistol to bear on the target. Looking along the barrel, he thought for a moment the old man was trying to hide, then he realised he was sitting in a wheel chair. Keeping the pistol trained on the target, he paced steadily towards the desk.

'Where is everyone, old man?' said Cassiter.

'I am alone and, more to the point, who are you to burst into my home?' said Father Andreas.

Cassiter smiled at the old man. 'Your home? Is this your place?'

'It is God's place and you have no right to be here. You are not welcome.'

'That's okay. I'm quite used to not being welcome. So, I think you are in charge here. Where are your people?'

'I will not speak with you.'

'Then I will break you, old man.' Cassiter rounded the desk to stand beside Father Andreas. Having checked the old man was unarmed, Cassiter laid his pistol down on the desk. He gripped the wheelchair's joystick and manoeuvred the priest out from behind the desk, giving himself more room to work in. Without a moment's hesitation, he took the old man's left hand in his and forced the middle finger back a little. He paused, looked into his victim's eyes and smiled thinly. 'Are you sure you have nothing to say?'

Cassiter felt a little thrill; now, he thought, now. He applied more force to the finger, eye contact was broken as Father Andreas suddenly arched in his chair, pulling his hand away but there was no escape. His finger snapped, first at the middle joint, then, as Cassiter forced the stub back yet further, the sinews of the knuckle joint itself ripped and parted.

Father Andreas howled in distress, Cassiter took the broken hand and raised it by the wrist; he inspected his handy work. Satisfied, he selected the index finger and began to work it gently back and forwards.

'Priest, you have something I want. Give it to me now.'

Cassiter's men had crowded in to watch the show. The taller of the two had seen it more than once before but always enjoyed the spectacle. The shorter, a newer recruit, had only heard stories of Cassiter's technique. He was determined to take it all in.

'Priest, tell me where you have hidden your dagger. I know you have one. I want it.'

'There is nothing for you here in God's house.'

Cassiter looked at his men. He smiled at them. 'These priests, they always seem to put up a good resistance. But he will break.' Cassiter let his own fingers release Father Andreas' index finger and return to the broken middle finger. He gave the grossly distorted digit a gentle twist and then pressed, compressing the breaks.

Cassiter wondered how far the screaming sounds would carry and looked out of the window towards Robertson while he snapped another finger.

The priest's renewed screams filled the room and carried through the glass of the closed windows, it travelled on across the courtyard to Robertson who still stood beside the SUV. An old hand, Robertson knew exactly what was happening and grinned while glancing up at the window. Experience had taught him that whoever was suffering, they would break soon enough. Cassiter spotted the head movement; it was clear Robertson could hear. The old man had a good pair of lungs on him.

Turning his attention back into the room, he instructed his men to continue the search of the building and find the priest who remained unaccounted for. But just as he started to focus on the old priest's thumb, his plan began to unravel.

He was not quite clear about what exactly happened, it played out so quickly in the corner of his eye, but now Cassiter found himself in a spot of bother.

His two men had followed the search instruction, choosing to leave by the little door close to the bookcase. The shorter of the two men pulled open the door leading into the corridor then stopped. As he swung the door in, it had been followed by a swinging broadsword. Cassiter's man swayed. The blade chopped in a sideways arc, brushing against his shoulder and sweeping on, slicing into the neck. The head hit the ground while the body still stood, rocking gently, and squirting blood against the ceiling. It toppled down as the priest pushed past.

The tall guard had his pistol in hand and fired off a shot, wounding the priest's left arm just before the thrusting sword split his belly open. The sword pulled out from the wound, drawing the tall guard's innards with it. One hand gripping at his belly, the tall man slipped to his knees, roaring in pain and fright. The finger of his pistol hand squeezed against the trigger in a despairing effort to control something, anything, as he moved towards death. Bullets sprayed around. Shattered windows showered glass into the courtyard below.

Cassiter took it all in and realised he was suddenly in a difficult position. The priest, with his blood stained sword was stood between him and the desk where he had placed his pistol before commencing the interrogation. Without it, he was vulnerable to what looked like an impressive 36 inches of very efficient traditional killing technology.

He acted. Stepping behind the wheelchair, he bent down, pressing his head close to Father Andreas and wrapped one hand round the old man's throat; some leverage to exert control over the environment. He reached his other hand out to the arm of the chair and gripped the driver's control joystick. Pulling it back, he got the wheelchair reversing slowly away from the desk and shuffled backwards in pace with its retreat.

The bloodied priest advanced, sword pointing at Cassiter. Now the initial onslaught was passed, the priest was unsure how to proceed. He was worried for Father Andreas, and Cassiter smelt the growing fear, the anxiety; he could exploit that.

Cassiter tightened his grip round Father Andreas' neck. 'Back off or the old priest dies.'

The point of the priest's sword wavered a little as he looked from

Cassiter to Father Andreas and back. His assault had been launched as a forlorn bid to save his leader. He had not thought the details through, certainly not considered the possibility of a hostage standoff. Now he was out of his depth.

Cassiter could sense the confusion. It was something he could work on, but carefully, very carefully. The priest had demonstrated remarkable ability with the sword. Cassiter could not think where or why the man would have developed such a skill, but the ability was there and right now the odds were all in the priest's favour but he was not experienced enough in real combat to understand that and press home his advantage.

Step for step, the bloodied priest tracked Cassiter's retreat across the room. Cassiter could read the priest's confusion, the wavering blade, a free hand repeatedly raised to sweep perspiration away from his forehead. The man was right out of his depth.

Cassiter stopped his retreat and saw the wounded priest stop his advance. Cassiter smiled dryly, now he was in control. 'I think we can sort this out don't you?' he said.

The priest did not reply to him. Instead, he directed a short stream of Greek towards Father Andreas. The angst was clear in his voice, though Cassiter did not understand a word.

'He does not speak English,' said Father Andreas, managing to force his words out in spite of the arm locked around his neck.

'Well tell him I will not kill you provided he backs away and, of course, you must give me what I want.'

'I do not know what you want.'

'You do. The same thing that Cameron and the American girl wanted. The dagger. Last chance,' said Cassiter, suddenly tightening his grip around Father Andreas' neck. The old priest grimaced in pain and the younger priest thrust the sword blade forward a few inches in response, then pulled it back, at a lost how to proceed.

Cassiter smiled again. Then he whispered into his captive's ear. 'You will die old man. That's certain. I've dealt with others like you, so I know you won't mind that, but look at the boy there. He could live. I can let that happen if you give me what I want.'

Father Andreas hissed his words through the pain in his neck. 'Ease my neck so I can speak with him. He needs some guidance if this is to end well.'

Cassiter nodded and very slightly eased the pressure on the old priest's throat.

Father Andreas took a moment to gasp in a couple of breaths; then he looked intently at his acolyte and spoke quietly and calmly in Greek. Cassiter read the measured pace and intonation in the old priest's voice, he saw the confusion in the young priest's expression, saw the doubt as his eyes flicked back and forth. Cassiter was satisfied. The old priest was following his advice; this would soon be over.

But Father Andreas was not. 'Listen carefully to me, my son. This man will kill me; no matter what you do I will die. I want you to save yourself. That is what our God would want today. You should live. When I say, I want you to raise that sword, the sword that came here at the very beginning. Came in the hands of my, our, predecessor. Raise the sword and cut through me to kill the monster. One great stroke and it is done. Father Christos and the others will support you when they return. Listen carefully. This is not a request, this is an order, you must do it, save yourself and make sure Father Christos and the others know what happened. Will you do that for me?'

'Well priest, have you persuaded him? If he backs away I'll release your neck.'

'I hope I have persuaded him, we will see in a moment,' said Father Andreas.

Then he spoke in Greek again. 'God bless you my son. Do it now. You know the American has what she needs. End the story. Alpha and Omega, the beginning and the end. I have done my duty, now it ends - do yours. You and Christos must build a new story. Strike! Strike now!' his voice rose to a shout, urging the blade into its killing arc.

Too late, Cassiter realised he had been duped. The blade was moving. He had seen it in action, knew that the old priest's body would provide no protection for him. They were both going to die. He could hear it hissing through the air. His last thought was fury; there was not even time to break the old priest's neck before the blade would start its butchery.

An explosion of noise filled the room. For just a moment, Cassiter wondered if this was what death sounded like. Then he realised he was alive. In a single instant, the sword blade lost its momentum, twisting and dropping, hitting its flat edge against the old priest's arm before clattering to the wooden floorboards.

Cassiter looked across the room; the priest was on his knees, hands frantically reaching behind him, clawing to find the bullet holes that had just appeared in his back. A red smear was spreading over his fingers. Confusion was writ across the priest's face, but now mixed with horror at the realisation that he was dying and had not done his leader's bidding. Standing in the doorway behind him was Robertson. Pistol in hand, he was scanning the room for further dangers.

Cassiter straightened up, nodded to his man and then patted the old priest on the head, allowing his hand to linger, playing with his thin silver hair. 'Should have taken my advice old man,' he said, as Father Andreas shook his head to dislodge the hand.

The wounded priest was gasping, mouthing silent words. Cassiter stepped closer to him, raised his boot and kicked him hard. Instantly, the victim collapsed from his knees to the ground. Stooping, Cassiter picked up the sword and hefted it in his hand; the weighted counterbalance of the pommel was perfect. Moving the blade was almost effortless; he swung it back and forth two or three times. Then he looked down at the despairing priest who lay wounded on the floor.

'This blade could have done me some damage,' said Cassiter, glancing back towards Father Andreas. 'I think you must have told him, yes?'

'Spare him; he is young, just following my orders.'

'No, I can't do that.' Cassiter prodded the wounded priest with the toe of his boot. 'And now, this is down to you old man.'

Cassiter raised the blade above his head and watched Father Andreas avert his gaze. He saw the young priest raise his hands in futile defence. Then he swung the blade down hard to the sound of the young priest's scream of fear.

The sword swept through the outstretched arms, severing one completely as the irresistible cutting arc continued its journey on into his flesh, resting only after it had sliced open chest and belly.

For a moment or two Cassiter admired the efficiency of the blade, then threw it down and left the man to bleed out while he retrieved his pistol from the desk.

'Good timing,' he said to Robertson. Then he waved his pistol towards the dying priest. 'That was the last of them. Now let's do what we came for. Oh, and call the others back from behind the building. They will be more useful here now.' Cassiter looked appreciatively at his man who showed no sign of concern at the bodies strewn across the room. That was what he looked for in his people, unflinching.

'Now old man, let's get it over with. Give me the dagger.'

'Never,' said Father Andreas defiantly. 'Never. Butcher!'

Cassiter took the wheelchair's joystick and steered the chair across to the room's centre window. He directed Father Andres' attention outside into the enclosed space of the broad courtyard.

'Look, see how quiet it is? When will the rest of your people return? Later this afternoon, perhaps? It won't be so quiet then. The rest of your little band; your little choir boys, tired from a day of service, anxious for their evening meal and eager to share the events of the day. How will that play out I wonder.'

Father Andreas closed his eyes tightly, as though it might bar the car access to the courtyard.

'Will we wait for them to come back? What events will we share with them, old man? And look, here are more of my people coming.' Cassiter slipped his fingers down over Father Andreas' forehead and pulled the old man's eyelids up, forcing his eyes open, compelling him to look out into the courtyard where the men who had been posted on the hillside behind were entering through the arch.

'Give me what I want or you can watch from this window as the rest of your people die one at a time and very slowly. You're dead already old man. But you can save your people. They are nothing to me, provided I have what I want.'

Father Andreas sagged further into his chair. Sighed, nodded, and pointed towards his bookcase. 'And the others will live?'

'Provided we can be away now, so our paths don't cross. Delay and I make no promises.' Cassiter stepped back, allowing the old priest to drive his chair across the room.

He watched as Father Andreas struggled to work some secret lever at the bookcase. With only his right hand functioning, it took a little while, but he managed and suddenly a small section of bookcase swung out and to one side. Behind was a safe. Father Andreas quickly keyed in the code and then turned to Cassiter. 'The key is in my trouser pocket,' he raised his twisted and broken hand. 'This won't work.'

Cassiter retrieved the key and quickly unlocked the safe. Pulling open the safe door, he reached in and withdrew a dagger. He reviewed the artefact. It took only the most cursory of glances to confirm this was what he had come for. It was just like the others but with a Roman numeral one engraved on the blade. He stroked it gently and nodded in satisfaction before glancing round the room. He had lost three people here today. A very high price. He could not afford many days like this but it was a price worth paying on this occasion.

Gripping the dagger handle, he looked at Robertson. 'We're done here. Let's go.' He walked for the door without even a glance towards the broken old man. 'And finish him,' he said, almost as though it were an afterthought.

As he reached the doorway, a single shot rang out behind him. He did not bother looking back. It was done.

• • •

Helen stepped out of the limousine and made straight into the airport terminal. A different driver today; Simon was walking beside her. When Franz Brenner had heard she intended to take the gold framed glass from the safe deposit, he had insisted that Simon travel with her, at least until she linked up with Sam. Simon was trusted and knew how to handle himself. After all, it was a dangerous world. She knew it, was happy to accept the offer and was now hurrying for the private departures gate. She was getting quite used to the benefits of private travel.

Next stop, Crete, she thought, where Sam was waiting to test his theory about a labyrinth map. She hoped he was right and could track it down. For now, they were ahead of their enemy, but no matter how many steps she and Sam took, their pursuers always seemed to be close behind.

• • •

Sam stood on the beach with his back to the sea. He looked up the course of the ravine he had just spent the past half an hour working his way down. He could see Nick standing at the top of the cliffs. The young man that Father Andreas had sent from Kefalonia as a translator was not dressed for rock climbing so Sam had left him at the top, he'd get him kitted out properly this evening.

Right now, it was the ravine that interested Sam. It offered the only landward access to the beach where it cut down through the rugged cliffs. Without a boat, there was no other access point and the rough terrain and steep incline of the ravine was not exactly tourist friendly. This was a lonely spot.

He glanced down at the map in his left hand, then looked at Helen's photograph of the gold framed glass in his right, and then back up at the cliffs. This was the best candidate; no, he told himself, it was the only candidate.

He had spent the past day rushing along the Cretan coast and this had to be it - unless he had read the whole process incorrectly.

He knew medieval map projections could not be trusted; hence, the topography was normally open to question. Only very localised line of sight mapping could bear any relation to the reality on the ground. He was certain that the gold frame was very precise; he trusted that, like every other part of the puzzle, whoever created this section had paid the same attention to detail as had been accorded everything else.

Always with the proviso that his interpretation was correct, then he knew there really was a labyrinth where something was hidden. It was on Crete because the scroll said it was - it had been accurate in every other respect. The unanswered question remained, where on Crete? And here he was, on the coast. The Templars would have wanted to be able to slip ashore and leave unnoticed, that was certain.

Once again, he followed the logic. The cross, engraved into the golden frame, would mark the top - in medieval times, the top was east - and that side was trimmed with a perfect inlay of lapis lazuli to mark the sea or coast - so, water to the east. The side opposite, west, had lapis too, and the right hand side that joined them, representing south, was also lapis blue. To the left the remaining side, north, was plain gold - landward. That configuration meant the labyrinth must be situated at a promontory on the south side of the island. His attention had been taken, on what he had determined was the south side, by the way the otherwise straight edged lapis inlays were laid into the gold to form a concave shape. Nothing was sloppy about the construction, it was all meant. But meant what? It had taken a while but finally he settled on the concave representing a bay.

There had been half a dozen candidate promontories scattered along the coast. He had visited them one by one and quickly ruled out all the others: too open an aspect; ancient fishing villages nearby; too accessible; disappointing bay; and finally, rocks off shore that barred access from the sea.

He turned, looked at the sea, turned again to look back to the cliffs. Here was a rectangular promontory - three sides bounded by the sea, and northwards lay the land. It was rough and isolated terrain, no signs of the area ever having been populated. Finally, here at the south side of the promontory was a sheltered bay, almost inaccessible by land and certainly only visible from the sea. It had all the features of the line of sight mapping so perfectly represented in the gold framed glass by some ancient craftsman and mapmaker. Here at last was everything they needed.

He looked carefully at the photograph again, touched where the gold frame came between the arc of lapis and the glass. His finger rubbed the photograph where the otherwise perfectly smooth gold frame seemed to present an anomaly. He didn't buy it as an imperfection in the craftsmanship now. He squinted at what appeared the slightest of ridging running through the gold; starting from the blue of the lapis defined bay, it ran through the gold frame edging, which now clearly represented the cliffs bounding the bay, to finally reaching the edge of the glass - from where the gold thread started its winding journey. Instinctively, he knew it was no anomaly; knew the ridging marked the ravine he had clambered down to reach the beach.

Somewhere, up in the ravine was an entrance to the labyrinth. He was sure of it. Now he needed Helen and the gold framed glass itself to put his theory to the test.

He began the climb back up the ravine. Beyond that lay a

kilometre's hike to the little road where he had parked his car. Helen would be landing quite soon. He'd better get to the airport to collect her and the package from Switzerland - it would provide the answer to all their questions, he hoped.

Chapter 31

TUESDAY 10ᵀᴴ SEPTEMBER - AM

Helen glanced towards Sam; she could see his full attention was focused on the road ahead. Out here was a lonely place, far from the tourist hotspots. They had left the main road a while back and driven across a plateau dotted with villages and homesteads, places where locals eked a living out of the uncompromising land. Now, high in the mountains that bounded this part of the island's coast he had to be vigilant. A moment's lapse or a simple slip and they would plunge down into one of the anonymous ravines that the narrow road traced on its route to the sea.

Helen turned in her seat and looked into the rear. Simon looked back at her. The previous evening he had declined the chance to join her on a trip to buy suitable clothing and footwear. Now she could see why; Simon was clearly a man who planned for every eventuality. From his walking boots through the tough but lightweight trousers and top, and on to the wide brimmed hat, he was dressed for the occasion. Every occasion, she thought, noting the slight bulge beneath his lightweight cotton jacket. He may have abandoned the suit but the tools of his trade were always with him.

Next to Simon was Nick, the young Greek Orthodox priest sent by Father Andreas. Together with Helen, Nick had been kitted out for the hike last evening. Then a late night phone call from Father

Christos had left him devastated, quite inconsolable. But morning had brought with it a determination to fulfil Father Andreas' wish, no matter what. Helen smiled encouragement to him. Nick tried to smile back but it was clear his heart and mind were far away.

She wondered if it would have been better had they left him at the hotel. But her attention was pulled back to the direction of travel as Sam spoke.

'Nearly there. See the little layby ahead, that's our spot.'

In the distance, she could see the blue of the sea where it occasionally showed between dry, scrub covered ridges.

They got out and Sam hefted a heavy rucksack onto his shoulders and made sure everyone was carrying plenty of drinking water. Then he pointed them towards the ridge that rose away in front of them before dropping off unseen to the coast. 'Let's go. Watch your step. It's quite deceptive. Even where the ground looks solid, there are plenty of loose stones. It's a fair hike up to the ridge; then it slopes gently down for a bit towards the coast, that's easier walking. But after that, we've a tricky climb down through a ravine to the beach. We'll need to go right down to the beach and then work our way back.'

As they walked steadily up, each rocky feature merged unremarkably with the next. When they finally reached the ridge, they were all relieved to start heading downwards. The going underfoot didn't alter but with gravity on their side, it got a little easier. Then, almost imperceptibly, there was a change. A dried out streambed formed ahead of them. Initially it was hard to spot amongst the rough rocks, scrub bushes and stunted olive trees that dotted the landscape - but it was there; slowly it grew in size, opening a narrow cut into the rocky surface. Then the cut steadily widened and steepened, cutting a sharp V channel into the rock; it became a ravine, formed by the action of many thousands of winter rains.

To reach the beach they had to scramble down the ravine, its rocky slopes sprinkled with more of the dry looking bushes and stunted trees. Quickly, the ravine broadened and deepened, opening a gash in the cliffs as the streambed dropped sharply away. Taking real care, they continued their descent, following the streambed's course down through the ravine. Suddenly it turned hard right and there, way below them, they could see a little bay, its sandy beach empty and still beside a vivid blue sea.

Helen was glad of the boots and trousers she had bought the night before. The climb down was hard. Bumps and slips and thorns made it treacherous. She knew it would have been an impossible struggle without the new kit.

Finally, reaching the bottom, she let out a whoop and sat down on the clean sand, took a drink and glanced around. Sam and Simon seemed unfazed by the journey, albeit both were wet with sweat. Nick sat on the sand beside her; the look of despondency had faded. He was quietly taking handfuls of sand and slowly releasing them, watching as they trickled back on to the beach.

'You're looking a bit better now, Nick,' she said.

For the first time she saw him smile properly. 'Yes, this is a bit like the land at home - it's not nearly so green here though… Things are not good for me today. But this brings me a little closer to where I ought to be.'

Sam stepped over and rested a hand on the young priest's shoulder.

Helen smiled encouragement. 'We appreciate you coming. I know it's difficult for you, for all your friends too. You want to be there and we'll get you back as soon as we can. But remember, this is what Father Andreas had devoted his life to. Being here, you are serving his wishes, perhaps more than you can ever understand.'

She scanned the sea. A few fishing boats sat against the horizon, one or two yachts caught the gentle breeze to work their way down the coast, while well off shore a couple of jet skis buzzed around a luxury cruiser. Other than themselves, the beach was deserted.

'Well, Sam. Take us through it. Then I guess we had better make a start. This puzzle won't solve itself,' said Helen.

Sam opened his rucksack and pulled out a bundle of protective bubble wrap. From within he produced the gold framed glass. He stood with his back to the sea and aligned the frame so he held the east and west sides in his hands, the blue lapis decoration showing around his thumbs.

The plain gold side of the frame, the north side, was furthest from him and aligned with the cliffs. Closest to him was the south side, its lapis decoration vivid against the gold of the frame; unlike the perfectly straight edges of the east and west lapis inlays, this one was different. Here it described a distinct concave shape arcing gently in towards the edge of the glass then out again.

At once, the artefact presented a message one hundred times clearer than the photograph he had relied on the previous day. The blue of the lapis exactly matched the curve of the bay. Now he knew he was right, could suddenly feel his pulse beating against the gold in his hands.

For two or three minutes, Sam stood in silence. He squinted up at the headland, down to the beach, and turned slowly to gaze around the bay. Then he let his hands run across the gold framed glass, twisted it this way and that, lifted it up to eye level and then reoriented it in his hands, considering how the real thing added to Helen's original photograph that he had relied on the previous day. Now, at last, he had a handle on things. With an audible sigh, he closed his eyes and let his mind still for a moment. When he opened them again, he found three spectators waiting, expectantly.

'Look,' said Sam. 'I think the gold framed glass is a representation of this headland. The land juts out square, bounded on three sides by sea, the three sides of lapis set in our frame. The fourth side is the headland's landward boundary near where we parked.

'Now look there, right in front of you; see, it's the only headland I have found on this side of the island with a little bay just in the right place as represented by this arc of lapis set in the southern side of our gold framed glass.'

'Okay, I can see your idea, I can see the proportions are about right,' said Helen.

'About right? It's perfect. Look here,' he touched the lapis inlay then swept his hand round the bay, 'the curve of the lapis exactly captures the arc of the bay.'

'I'll give you that, Sam, but what does this all mean?' Helen pointed her finger at the glass beneath which Sam had fixed the scale pictures of seven of the eight patterned daggers. Then she pointed up to the ravine they had just scrambled down. 'That's not a labyrinth; it's a cliff face. Nobody is going to start buzzing about that. They'd break a leg or fall to their death in a minute.'

Sam gave a little grin of triumph. 'You're right. Well, partly right. That surface is far too dangerous, but that doesn't matter if the labyrinth is below ground. Very much like the old myth, a series of tunnels.'

Helen took the glass from Sam and aligned it herself. Nodded, squinted through the glass and looked at Sam. 'Okay... and?'

'Look. The gold thread set in the glass weaves a route from roughly south to north, yes? On its way, it touches the ruby. Marking the point where we think whatever is hidden lies. And look at the pictures of the blades I've fixed beneath the glass. All combined, their patterns provide a plan of the labyrinth - and see how the gold thread overlay provides a route to follow. Those little gaps between each blade don't matter now. Just count turnings as we pass them and only turn when the gold thread turns.'

Helen was following Sam's explanation exactly. But he had not covered every point. 'What about the missing dagger?' she said.

'No problem, we've been lucky, see, its slot beneath the glass is the most northerly in the set. It's on the far side of the ruby. I'm sure, as we suggested before, it does mark an alternative entrance from the landward side.'

'So we don't need it?'

'I don't think so. Maybe we've got a break at last.'

Simon had been listening in silence, watching. He didn't know the background at all but he could see a simple flaw. 'Excuse me, it's your baby, I'm just along to provide support in a crisis, but I don't understand.' He paused for a moment waiting for an invitation to proceed.

Sam tilted his head slightly. 'Go on, what's up?' he said.

'Well if it's a tunnel, where is the entrance? It must be hidden or somebody would have found it sometime.'

'Good point,' said Sam. He turned his attention back to Helen who was waiting for an answer to Simon's question. 'Look here, at the southern edge of the frame. You can't really see much, but there is what appears to be a flaw in the metalwork. See, here in the edging lip of gold, between the blue lapis and the glass - between the sea and the cliffs. When I first saw it in the photograph, I had attributed it to a lighting quirk in the bank, or a shaky photographer's hand, who knows?' He glanced towards Helen, she responded with a glare of mock indignation. 'But then I began to think it might actually be there in the gold, meant as a signpost, why not? Everything else has a purpose. Now, just run your finger over the metal and feel; it's real.'

Helen let her finger run gently over the gold of the frame. There was a very slight yet quite discernible ridging in the metal. 'Perhaps in the past somebody dropped it or dented it somehow.'

'Possibly,' said Sam, 'but now look carefully, see how the ridging is V shaped, describing the shape of a funnel or if you hold it up and compare it to that ravine we've just climbed down -'

'It's a plan of the ravine. The entrance to the labyrinth!' Helen finished his sentence.

'Yes, and see, look up there where the ravine narrows and suddenly turns away to the left, out of sight?' Sam pointed and they all looked.

'Yes,' said Helen, 'we see.'

'Well, look again at the marking on the gold frame, at the corresponding point just there; see the marking bends to the left too. This is no metalwork flaw. And do you see the lightest of marks offset to the left of the main mark? I think that's where we'll find the entrance, to the left-hand side, just at the bend in the ravine.'

'We didn't see any tunnels on the way down,' said Simon.

'No, but we didn't look on the way down and of course, as you said before, it's going to be hidden.'

'There's only one way to find out. Let's go see,' said Helen.

'Okay, but let's be very careful. Believe me, if you think coming down was tough, you haven't seen anything yet. I discovered yesterday that going up is twice as hard,' said Sam as he swung his rucksack on to his back and quickly took the lead.

Simon hung back a little, allowing Helen and then Nick to follow in Sam's steps before he brought up the rear. Though by far the oldest of the party, Simon was a fit man with more than his share of strength, and a life based mainly in Switzerland had given him plenty of experience in working the mountains: mostly for sport, but very occasionally his employers at the bank would find little off-piste tasks - retrievals, recoveries and such private things. Sometimes these demands would carry him into the high mountains. For him, today's little scrabble was nothing more than a cakewalk.

While Helen kept step for step with Sam as he climbed up into the ravine, she frequently cast worried glances back towards Nick; she could tell that he was not a climbing man. They paused frequently to ensure the group did not split up. During one such pause, as she and Sam shared a drink of water, she admired the perfect sea. In the ravine, they were sheltered from the gentle breeze but it had carried the yachts farther away, they were almost on the horizon.

Only the luxury cruiser was still in the vicinity. Its two jet skis were tied up alongside now and she could just make out some people at the back of the cruiser. They seemed to be messing about with a RIB that was bobbing around the stern. 'Oh to be a millionaire,' she said wistfully.

Sam had been following her gaze, he laughed. 'Well if anyone can afford that lifestyle it's you.'

Helen joined in the laughter. She could still not quite come to terms with her inheritance and had certainly not considered spending it on herself.

Just as they resumed their climb, she glanced up at Sam; saw he was looking again at the luxury cruiser - wistful or worried, from below she could not quite read the expression. Then it was past and he set off again, leading the ascent.

Finally, they reached the point where the ravine narrowed and turned away to the left. Sam called a halt at the turn. Here the ravine's sides were close, and squat trees were well established in the gaps between the rocks. Protected from the wind and burning sun many of them had managed to stretch branches out across the divide to form a shaded arch under which the climbers rested.

After a few moments, while Simon sat with Nick, Sam began to search. Helen scrabbled to join him.

'The mark was on the left-hand side, wasn't it?' she said.

'Yes, so let's concentrate our search around here, on the left side of the ravine. Though I'm not sure what we're looking for.'

'No, let's hope we know it when we see it. What do you think? A big slab or something?'

'Maybe, let's just cast about and see.'

Sam and Helen spread out a little and climbed a couple of metres up the side of the ravine but it quickly steepened, barring any easy progress.

Simon's voice rose from his resting place. 'Look for a ledge with a flat surface; better still, one with a raised lip. That would form an inclined surface, something that scree could rest in. Can you see anything like that?'

'I can see a ledge. Just above us, can't tell from here if there is any scree lying on it though. Why does that matter?' said Sam.

'This is a steep slope, it would be hard to move a slab big enough to cover an entrance and if you did manage it the thing would stand out like a sore thumb. A nice inclined ledge, set well above the flood level during the winter rains can hold scree forever, pretty well. The perfect cover in this environment. Who's ever going to start climbing the sides of a ravine to move scree off a ledge they can't even see?'

'Good suggestion,' said Sam, impressed. 'I'm going to climb up this next little bit and see what's there.'

He gripped a gap in the rock and hauled himself up. 'It's definitely a ledge, and it's really quite broad and deep,' he called out, providing the team with a commentary on his progress. 'The ledge slopes back from the edge... Yes, it's definitely inclined away from the edge, that'll prevent any scree from falling off.' He stopped talking as he concentrated on pulling himself up over the edge and on to the ledge.

'Bingo! Scree, the ledge is covered in it, a thick layer. And you know, Simon, it would look perfectly natural if you hadn't suggested it might be otherwise.'

Helen started to climb. 'You wait there Sam Cameron, do not start moving stones until I'm there. Or else!'

Helen heard Sam's voice coming from above. 'Don't worry; I wouldn't dare start without you.'

The ledge was around five metres from end to end and under two metres wide. It had an incline, dropping from the lip towards the wall of the ravine, creating a trough in which the scree was held. It was impossible to guess how deep the trough was, only digging would tell. Helen watched Sam pull small tools from his rucksack: a collapsible shovel and a trowel. She found herself laughing as he started carefully removing the surface scree with his trowel.

'Sam, only an archaeologist would have that kit in his bag on the off chance.'

'No, there's no off chance about it, if you're looking for old and lost things they are invariably underground. On the surface, they wouldn't have stayed lost. Anyway, as I said, if we are to make progress, we will be facing a tunnel. Check the bag, we're kitted out for that too.'

Helen glanced in the bag. Beside the bubble-wrapped glass was a packed lunch, bottles of water, a cluster of head torches and a rope. Yet more things lay beneath, obscured by the rope. That's our Sam, she thought as she put the bag down, always ahead of the game.

Simon pulled himself up on to the ledge and seemed to purr in approval at what he saw. 'Man, if you want to cover a hole this is how to do it. You could sit over it for your lunch and never know. I think you may have found what you're looking for.'

Sam grinned. 'Let's hope so.'

'Yes, let's. But we'll never know if we follow your approach,' said Simon. 'Forget the archaeology; you can come back another day for the signs. You guys need to get answers before whoever is dogging your steps turns up. They sure as hell aren't going to stand on ceremony. And from what I'm hearing, they'll just do away with anyone in their way. I'm guessing that includes us.' He picked up the collapsible shovel, extended it and made to dig away the scree.

Helen looked at Sam. 'He's right you know; we probably don't have time to excavate this properly.'

Sam stopped trowelling, turned his head up towards the sky and screwed his eyes shut, holding the pose for a long moment.

Helen saw his eyes open, could see him nodding gently. It went against his every instinct but he recognised Simon was right. Without another word, they started clearing the scree as fast as possible.

A little while later, Helen reached her hand down to help Nick up the final step and he made it on to the ledge just as the last of the scree was being cleared.

All four stood and looked down at the ledge. At its deepest, the trough they had excavated was over twenty centimetres deep. It had been a mammoth task to complete in such a short period of time, but nobody was complaining. At their feet, set hard against the wall of the ravine was a level section of ledge perhaps a metre long by a half metre wide. It was quite uniform and a very slightly different shade to the surroundings; to Sam's trained eye, it was clearly not natural. Though even when exposed, as it now was, the uninitiated might well have missed it.

'I think it's an entrance,' said Sam, 'but an entrance to what? And look at the work that's gone into it. Something underneath is supporting it, but I'd guess they have sealed this up with mortar and covered it in a fine mosaic of rock from the ravine walls, like a camouflage.'

'Well, let's break it open,' said Simon, raising his shovel.

'No wait,' said Sam, he produced his mobile phone to take pictures. 'Once this is broken it will be lost forever.'

Simon lowered his shovel and waited. He raised it again as Sam put his phone away.

'Wait,' said Helen. 'My turn, please. Whatever else we think or expect from this place it was made and sealed by men of God. From what I understand, men who mostly went on to die to preserve its secret. I want to say a prayer for them and all those who have suffered through this, whatever it is.'

Simon rested his spade again and gave a little nod, lowering his head. Sam found himself rising to his feet; together with Nick, he bowed his head as Helen said a short prayer for all those who had suffered over the years for whatever lay within. Then in a silent minute, they thought about those they knew who had died, hoping this would be an end to it.

'Right,' said Helen. 'Get to it; let's see what it's all been for. Nothing can be worth the suffering, but let's hope there is something.'

Simon wielded the shovel, bringing it down hard on to the mosaic patch. Time and again, it crashed down, nothing.

'This stuff is hard as the stone it sits in,' said Simon in frustration.

'Wait, I've got an idea,' said Sam. He rummaged in his rucksack and produced a little steel pry bar. Holding it close to the edge of the mosaic, he pointed towards a large rock that sat at the far end of the ledge. 'Get that and use it as a hammer to hit this. We'll drive it in; make a narrow hole then work it wider.'

After just a few blows, Sam could feel the bar begin to penetrate. A few more and they could see progress and then, suddenly, they were through the surface layer and chipping into a solid slab of mortar. Sam shifted the angle of the bar so each successive blow of their rock hammer forced it under more of the exposed mortar. The mosaic started to come away in bits, then great chunks. Helen knelt to sweep away the debris as Simon continued to beat down on the bar.

They eventually cleared the mosaic and its mortar base to reveal a further layer of stone slabs beneath. Neatly arrayed, tight fitting, six of them; they had formed a foundation below the mosaic. This was the product of a master craftsman's work.

Sam tried to work the pry bar under one of the stone slabs but after a few moments he stopped; the gap was just too narrow, each of the stones sat flush one to the next. He examined the edges where the stones fitted neatly into the bedrock. Finally, he found what he was looking for. At one end, there was a little notch, cut into the bedrock.

He worked away with his fingers, clearing out sand that a long dead hand had compacted into the notch. Finally, he got it cleared, revealing a slot, just wide enough to take a chisel, or a pry bar. He slotted the bar into the notch and glanced around the group. 'Well, this is it, the moment of truth.'

Helen touched her hand against his shoulder. 'Go for it, Sam.'

Sam pressed on the bar, trying to lever the slab of rock up. Nothing happened. He pressed again. 'It's solid,' he gasped between presses.

Simon knelt beside him. They leant their combined weights on the little bar and after a moment felt the slightest of give.

'It's coming,' said Simon, redoubling his effort, 'it's coming now.'

The slab shifted a fraction. Then with a grating noise, it was prised up and a little apart from its neighbour. Helen forced the trowel into the gap allowing Sam and Simon to ease back on the pry bar and then Nick scrabbled with the shovel to lever the stone further up. It was quickly clear that the stones had been cut with perfect precision. Each was little more than half an inch thick - very heavy, but manageable. The remaining slabs offered little resistance and were quickly stacked to one side.

Everyone paused, still and silent, momentarily awestruck by the realisation that Sam's interpretation of the signs had become real -

there, sunk into the ledge was a tunnel mouth, a place not passed by a soul in seven hundred years.

Sam fitted his head torch in place, switched it on and then Simon and Nick took tight hold of his waistband as he slid headfirst into the hole.

Looking down into the gap between Sam's body and the edge of the tunnel's mouth, Helen could just make out the torch beam as it flicked to and fro. 'What do you see?' she called down.

His slightly distorted response came up to them from the cave mouth. 'It's a shallow natural cave that the Templars concealed. It slides away at about a forty-five degree angle for about a metre and then it drops down into a tunnel, which looks manmade. It's all dry, looks safe enough. Pull me up now.'

At once, Simon and Nick heaved on Sam's waistband and extracted him. Sitting on the ledge Sam looked at Helen. 'This has to be it. No doubt, we've found the entrance. But it might be dangerous, are you sure you want to go in?'

'Just try stopping me, mister,' said Helen.

Sam grinned. 'That's what I thought. Look, let's take a break and eat our lunch here. Then we can see what history has set aside for us.' Sam could not quite hide the excitement in his voice but he wanted a little time to reconcile what was going to happen next. This was an archaeologist's dream, his Howard Carter moment, and he was about to consciously blunder in without any thought for the evidence that might be lost in the process.

'Okay, that sounds like a plan,' said Helen.

'But we should not wait too long,' said Simon. 'I know we are ahead right now but the guys you are up against, they move pretty quickly.'

Sam agreed as he handed out rolls, tomatoes and slices of cheese. They all ate, suddenly discovering they were very hungry.

'I don't understand how the Templars would have had time to dig a tunnel through this cliff face if they were just slipping in here and away without being noticed. They would have had to be here for ages. How did they manage it?' said Helen.

'Well, I'm not sure they did,' said Sam.

Helen looked at him quizzically. 'Yes they did; you've just been headfirst down their tunnel.'

'Not quite. There are several places around this island that were mined way back into antiquity. One or two have been proposed as the real source of the Minotaur's labyrinth myth. These cliffs may have been mined out long before the Templars arrived, perhaps a thousand years earlier, more even. What we've just dug through was a natural opening; maybe ancient miners just broke through from the other side and moved on. The Templars were known for their inquisitive approach. It may even be that some of their order found this place long before they used it - we'll never know. But they certainly found it somehow.'

'So they didn't need to dig the tunnels at all?'

'Probably not. We'll see when we get in, but I would think the heavy work was done long before their time. I think they could have easily slipped in and out unseen. And if they had to leave a few people inside to work the stone for a little while, and come back for them later, that would be straightforward enough.'

Once they had finished eating Sam issued each of them with a head torch and spare batteries. 'Everyone ready?' The question was met by a round of nods. 'Great, everyone be careful. Remember, there's no backup team; we're on our own. I'm going to lead and Simon's done a bit of caving, so he'll bring up the rear. You two, stick close and watch your footing, don't take any risks, and watch your heads too.' Helen watched Sam's eyes as his gaze shifted from Nick to her. She smiled at him and from across the ledge mouthed the slightest of kisses; he reciprocated. It was time to go.

Then, as she watched Sam, a surprised look crossed her face. 'Heaven's sake, Sam. What's that for? What else have you got in that rucksack?' she said, as Sam produced a rope and a spool of fishing line.

'Well, there's a big lantern torch and a first aid kit and I'm afraid that's about it now,' he said. Freeing one end of the fishing line, he fastened it to the base of a stunted and gnarled old tree that clung on beside the ledge; he handed the spool to Simon.

'Oh, I see,' said Helen. 'Theseus and Ariadne's thread. You're actually taking a leaf out of the Minotaur story. Very smart.'

'Well, I am an archaeologist. That's what history and legends are for; to learn from,' said Sam as he secured the short rope to the tree and tested the weight with a pull.

'All right,' said Helen with a laugh. 'I said you were smart, don't get smug.'

'Right, everyone, the fishing line is your backup. If we get separated just follow it and it'll lead you back here. Now, let's go.' He sat on the lip, swung his legs into the hole and lowered the short rope into the black. He switched on his head torch and, gripping the rope tightly, slipped off the lip and into the hole. He slid easily down the short forty-five degree incline of the natural cave, controlling the speed of his descent by gripping the rope and allowing it to feed slowly through his fingers. Suddenly he felt his legs dangle free as they entered into the tunnel below and then he dropped with a gentle thud, his feet were on the tunnel floor.

Helen saw the beam of Sam's torch cutting the darkness and immediately followed him, Nick and Simon behind her.

Once everyone was in, Sam swung his rucksack off his back and delved inside; producing the gold framed glass, he handed it to Helen, 'I'm leading, but you're navigating. I'm quite certain there is no sense of scale to this thing, so count the turnings carefully as we pass them, and compare that to the turnings that are shown on the image beneath the glass. We only deviate left or right when the gold thread does.

Helen understood exactly what was expected of her.

• • •

Cassiter pulled himself up on to the ledge. Two of Parsol's men were already there peering down into the black hole. They looked for guidance and Cassiter raised a hand, indicating they should wait. They were closing in at last but it was for Parsol to give the order and, with the assistance of two more of his men, the older man was still making his way up to the ledge.

Joining the men at the mouth of the hole, Cassiter looked down, considered the rope and traced it back to the tree. He tugged on it and was satisfied it was secure. Just as he turned to acknowledge Parsol's arrival, something caught his eye. Bending down, close to the tree trunk he reached out and stroked it. He smiled to himself, hooking his finger under the fishing line, tweaking it gently then letting it go. He stood, greeted Parsol and then waved down towards the fishing line. 'Sometimes life just gets too easy,' he said. 'They've very kindly left us a little trail to follow. We'll be on them in no time.'

Chapter 32

TUESDAY 10TH SEPTEMBER - PM

Helen could see the beam of Sam's head torch flicking from left to right and up and down as he cautiously led the way. Though she did not pay too much attention to the environment they were in, she was aware that the tunnel walls were rough-hewn and the floor even, with the roof proving to be of a good height. She just focused on counting turnings and keeping to the route marked by the golden thread as it wove its way across the glass. It seemed to be working.

She was not sure how long they had been walking but by tracing their progress along the gold thread, she had worked out there were now only two more turnings before they reached the ruby. She had just passed on the information when Nick cried out, stopping them with his anxious exclamation.

Simon closed up on Nick, 'What's up man?' he said. There was a silence as Simon followed the moving beam of Nick's head torch to where it came to rest on the tunnel roof. 'Holy mother of God! What is that?'

It was the first time she had heard Simon use anything other than professional language and it brought her up with a jolt. She strained to see what had caused the concern. Sam joined her and all four torch beams shone on the same spot.

Helen could see the shape fixed to the wall just at roof height, but wasn't quite sure what she was looking at. 'What is it Sam?'

She heard his gentle whistle. 'Not good. Not good at all.'

'Not good.' parroted Simon. 'Not good? It's a death trap, that's what it is.'

She could tell Sam was nodding agreement as the beam of his torch bobbed on the wall before turning back to the object. 'It's an explosive device,' said Sam. 'Not the first thing we'd expect to find here.' He moved closer to get a better look.

'Be careful,' said Helen.

'It's okay, we're all too close anyway; if this goes off we're all done for.'

Nick's torch beam turned from the explosive to Sam, highlighting his face. 'Who put it there?' he said.

Sam raised a hand to shield his eyes from the torch beam. 'Them, not it. See the wiring? It runs here from ahead of us, links to this explosive and continues down that side tunnel. This must be part of a much bigger multiple charge.'

'What's going on Sam? Have they got here ahead of us? Is it a trap?' said Helen.

'No. Well, it may be a trap, but not for us.' He got closer to the explosives, stood on tiptoe and peered intently at the bomb. 'I think these are German. Second World War stuff.'

'What?' said Helen. 'That's ridiculous. What are they doing here?'

'Unfortunately, not so ridiculous. The Germans are known to have used tunnel complexes on the island as ammunition dumps. When they pulled out, the idea was to destroy the dumps. For some reason this was not set off. I suspect we are probably making our way into just such a dump.'

'Is it safe?' said Nick.

Sam gave a laugh. 'If you're going to light a cigar, be careful where you throw the match, that's for sure.'

'Shouldn't we get back, think about a different approach?' said Simon.

'That would be the sensible thing to do. But you know what, I think if we go out now the sensible thing would be never to come back in. You're right to be worried. I'd say calling this place a death trap is just about right. I certainly wouldn't want to let Helen back in.'

'*Let Helen back in?* Sam Cameron, you don't *let* me do anything. We're a team. Look, it's only two more turns to where the ruby sits on the plan. Let's push on; it will only take a few minutes. And I promise not to light a cigar, if that makes you feel any safer.'

Helen heard Simon's throaty laugh. 'Well that's you told, Sam. I guess we're pushing on, regardless.'

Sam looked again at the aged explosives, still held in the torch beams, and shrugged. 'Okay, but everyone be very careful. Old stuff like that can be very unstable and I like to think we've come far enough to warrant a safe passage home. Come on.' He resumed his spot at the head of the column. 'Let's push on if we're going to.'

Two quick turns and they were there. 'This is it,' said Helen. Her voice echoed back, and they realised they had entered into a wider space - a cavern. Here their personal headlamps were just little beams cutting forlornly through the black.

'Hold on,' said Sam. He dug into the bottom of his rucksack and pulled out his torch lantern. 'This'll do the trick,' he said and, placing it on the ground, he flicked it on. The cavern burst into being under the flood of white light.

'That's our Sam,' said Helen. 'Always plans ahead, always gets it right - well, mostly anyway.'

They looked around the space. The roof had risen to over three metres in height. The chamber was around ten metres long and five wide. At the far end, the cavern tapered down into the mouth of a tunnel similar to that from which they had just emerged. The floor, the walls, the roof, all dark shadowy stone and all bone dry. Rough-hewn, but definitely hewn - chisel and pick marks scored every surface, no drill marks, this was a manmade feature and very old.

As the others took in the environment, Helen noted that Sam was busy tracing the German wires that continued their run; pinned to the roof, they ran the length of the chamber and disappeared directly into the tunnel ahead. Sam asked them all to check the cavern for Templar signs while he went on to see if there were any explosives further ahead. Taking the fishing spool from Simon he set off, laying a trail behind him.

After twenty minutes had passed, they were beginning to worry. Then, just as Simon was readying himself to go in pursuit, they spotted a distant headlamp in the tunnel, bobbing towards them.

On a couple of occasions, it paused, shone up, shone down then continued its approach. Finally, Sam emerged from the tunnel, wiping his hands and tucking his pocketknife into the leg pocket of his cargo pants.

'I've been about six hundred metres up the tunnel. There are more charges spread along it and up some of the side chambers. I'm guessing there will be even more that I didn't see.'

'But we haven't seen any stored ammunition,' said Helen.

'No, the store could be anywhere, further ahead, in one of the side tunnels, maybe the munitions were actually taken out and somebody missed these explosives when, if, they even bothered to make it safe. I don't know. I've cut all the ignition cables I could find so, touch wood, there should be no problems. I've done what I can to make it safe but everyone just be very careful.'

Helen looked at the gold framed glass. 'You know, if you think about the explosives, it ties in exactly with your idea that there is another access route. The gold thread continues beyond the ruby. That probably marks the route the Germans would have used.'

'I agree. That seems the most obvious answer. But here we are at the ruby point. Our X marks the spot. So I wonder where it is. What did you all find while I was away?'

'The Germans have obviously been in this chamber. Could they have found the treasure? Has it already gone?' said Helen.

Sam shook his head. 'I don't think so. All the way along, nothing in this business has been obvious to the uninformed. I think whatever our Templars placed here was hidden. They must have recognised there was a slight risk of somebody stumbling upon the chamber and planned accordingly. I'm pretty certain of it. We just need to look carefully.'

They spread out and checked the chamber again. Every inch of the floor, it was all solid bedrock, and nothing could be beneath it. Then they scanned the ceiling for any little access point they had missed. Nothing.

A sense of doubt was beginning to settle in as they started to check the walls. Helen paused to lean on Sam's arm for a moment. They had come so far, too far for it to end in failure. 'It's not looking too good, Sam.'

'No, but let's keep going. If there's one thing we know, it's the

Templars were masters of concealment. I think there must be something; we just need to focus.'

They carried on, scanning the walls. Concentration was difficult as the chiselled and fractured wall seams progressively merged into a bland sameness.

'Let me see the glass again,' said Sam. Taking it from Helen, he studied it closely, then handed it back. 'Look, the ruby isn't exactly on the gold strand, it's set beside it, see, on the right. Let's concentrate on the right hand side of the chamber.'

Nick glanced at Simon. 'Did you hear that?' he said.

'What? Don't start getting jumpy on us.'

'No, I'm serious, I heard a noise.'

'Ha! Sam, your man's scared of the dark.'

'I tell you, I heard something.'

'What?' said Sam.

'I don't know. It came from back up the tunnel.'

'I heard nothing,' said Simon again. 'Come on let's continue the search, we've got work to do. You don't need to be jumpy.'

'I'm not jumpy,' said Nick. 'I heard something.'

Sam moved to stand next to Nick. 'It's okay, Simon's only winding you up,' he said, casting a cautionary glance towards Simon. 'Look, don't worry, I'll go back a bit and check for you, for all of us. I'm sure it's nothing. You just concentrate on the search.'

Sam turned towards the tunnel and froze. Emerging from it were men. Half a dozen at least and most had guns, trained on him.

'No need for you to go and check, Mr Cameron. The young man was correct; there was a noise, and here we are,' said Parsol.

'Who the hell are you?' said Sam. As he raised his arms in a show of surrender, he stared stony faced at the tall, elderly man who had spoken to him, then quickly glanced over his shoulder to ensure the others were following his lead. They were. His attention turned back to the intruders.

The tall man's gaze ranged beyond Sam, scanning the prisoners. Helen shivered as she felt it settle on her. 'Mr Cameron, you can call me Parsol. Don't do anything silly or you will die, immediately. All of you.'

He walked past Sam and approached Helen. 'It is you, isn't it? Yes, it is. Cassiter, do come over. Look, it's the little lady who caused us so much trouble in Edinburgh.'

Cassiter crossed the cavern to join Parsol. He met Helen's gaze with a cold stare, allowed his eyes to scan her body, and then looked back over his shoulder. 'Watch this one. She doesn't look up to much but believe me she packs a punch. Secure her wrists now. In fact, secure all their wrists.'

Two of the armed men holstered their guns and hurried forward. One of them cable tied her wrists in front of her. The other, Robertson, checked for weapons, patted her down, just a bit too thoroughly. She gave him a furious look and he responded with a long leer before re-joining his partner to help secure their three male prisoners. Helen noticed that they had found Simon's pistol.

'Now, who do I speak to?' said Parsol.

His question was met with a stony silence.

'Come, come. We have all covered a lot of ground to get here. Don't be shy at the end because, be assured, I won't let it rest.' Parsol walked across to Nick and Simon. 'I don't think it's either of you.' He allowed his pistol to stroke Simon's cheek. 'Not you. You look like muscle to me; you're just the brawn aren't you?' He turned his attention to Nick, bringing the pistol close to the young man's left eye. Nick instinctively drew back and Parsol pressed the pistol forward again. 'Is it you? No, I know it's not. You are just a waif they have picked up on the journey. Quite disposable.'

Parsol half turned away from Nick, glancing back at Helen and Sam who stood in silent defiance. Then he turned his attention back to the young Greek. 'They won't speak with me. Perhaps this will encourage them.' Without any warning, he fired a round from his pistol into Nick's stomach.

Nick fell to the floor, screaming in shock and pain. Blood spread quickly around him, he was wounded twice from the same shot - first it had passed through his hand then it had drilled into his belly.

Helen and Sam started across the cavern to offer Nick aid but were restrained by Parsol's men.

'You've shot him, you butcher. Why did you do that?' shouted Helen over Nick's screams.

'That was pointless, he didn't present a threat to you,' said Sam, his voice steady as ever.

Leaving Nick to bleed, Parsol turned his attention back to Helen.

'So, young lady, you and I have unfinished business. I think you have plenty to tell me and I know you will.'

'Leave her, it's me you want,' said Sam.

Parsol looked at him. 'Oh yes, you're right; you have something coming your way. But first of all, I think this little lady is the big prize.' He turned back to Helen. 'You have all the answers I'm sure. Now will you speak with me in a civilised way or must I reintroduce you to my good friend Cassiter? I know you're familiar with his, urh, his handy work, yes?'

Helen dropped her eyes to the floor; there was no point in inviting hell. But for all the danger, she had learnt something. Wallace had been right; the man had used a false identity. It didn't matter today but somehow it felt better that she knew the monster's real name - Cassiter. 'Please, let me see to Nick; then I'll help you. I promise.'

Parsol stepped closer to her. 'Oh no need to promise, you'll help me, I know it. Now let's start with this shall we. What have you got here?' He pulled the gold framed glass from her bound hands. Looked at it blankly for a moment then put on his glasses and stepped closer to Sam's electric lantern. 'Now this is interesting,' he said. 'Do come and see Cassiter. What do you make of it? Very ingenious, I think it's a plan of the labyrinth.' He looked at Cassiter. 'I didn't know about this. I wonder what else I don't know.' He glanced meaningfully towards Helen then tilted the glass so Cassiter could see through it.

'Do you see? Images of all those daggers you have so diligently gathered for us. I see now, the patterns on the blades represent the labyrinth, and this gold thread plots the path through and I'll bet the ruby marks exactly where we stand now.'

Parsol looked over at Helen and Sam. 'But look, there's one dagger missing. Let's see what we can do about that, shall we?' He swung his shoulder bag round to the front and delved inside. 'Here we are,' he said, as he pulled the Mary Magdalene dagger out into the torchlight. Parsol examined the crenulations in the frame; he muttered to himself, then aligned the French dagger with the gold frame and slotted the eighth and final dagger into its place. He looked down into the glass at the completed plan then glanced up at Helen.

'You didn't have that one did you? Now look, there's a nice easy route out for those of us who are going to leave.'

Cassiter rested a finger on the glass, stroked over the embedded ruby. 'So where is it? There's no sign of anything here.'

'That, my good friend, is what they are about to tell us.'

'We don't know anything more than you,' said Helen.

'There's nothing here. It's been a wild goose chase,' said Sam.

Parsol laughed. 'I don't think so. There has been an answer at every stage; there will be an answer to this. You just need to provide it for us.' He waved Cassiter towards Helen. 'I think we can dispense with formalities, perhaps you would like to encourage her to speak now?'

Cassiter stepped across to Helen. Sam started forward, forcing his body between them; a blow to his head from Robertson's pistol knocked him down to his knees. Sam swayed, dazed, and blood streamed down his face from his reopened head wound. A violent kick in the chest from Cassiter put him on his back.

Sam instinctively rolled on to his side as another kick came in, aiming for his head but glancing off to connect full with his left shoulder. No more blows came as he struggled for consciousness, trying to maintain focus by forcing himself to stare at the base of the wall, which was now just a few centimetres in front of him.

Helen's eyes met Cassiter's. She did not flinch as she felt his hands search out hers, felt his fingers slide between hers, interlocking. He smiled a cold, cruel smile. Then she could see something in his eyes, not just cold. Now there was a flicker of life; no, it was a flicker of excitement. He wanted to hurt her, needed to.

Parsol moved a little closer to Helen. He put the French dagger and the gold framed glass into his shoulder bag, then raised his hand and ran it through her flowing red hair. For a few moments, he let his fingers twirl and entwine in it. Then he gripped it tight, held her still as he leant in close to her face. 'Cassiter is going to hurt you, you know that. Why not just tell me what I want. You're going to die, all of you; that is a fact. But you don't need to die in pain. My men can make it quick if I say so. Or, of course, they can make it very slow.'

'I don't know what you want. There is nothing to tell you.'

'Dear girl, there's always something to tell. You just have to think very hard.' He let her hair go and stepped back, giving Cassiter a nod to signal he should take over proceedings.

Cassiter was motionless, so close that had he pursed his lips he could almost have kissed her face. She could feel his exhaling breath on her. Its warm moistness repelled her but she would not flinch. Now his hands weren't still and Helen felt a little pressure building on her fingers. She pressed back, a fit and strong young woman but no match for Cassiter. She felt him apply more pressure to match her own, then yet more to dominate her. Her fingers began to twist, little jabs of pain merged into something bigger.

She bit her tongue, pursed her lips, determined not to give ground as her twisted fingers began to buckle. Involuntary tears began to form in her eyes.

'Tell the man what he wants to know, it's only going to get a lot worse for you from here on in,' whispered Cassiter.

'Stop. Stop, I've got the answer for you,' shouted Sam. Helen registered the excitement in his voice, quickly followed by the slightest relaxation of the pressure on her fingers as Cassiter's head turned towards Parsol, seeking guidance.

'Well Mr Cameron. What answer have you got for us? I hope you're not playing any silly games. That would make us very angry,' said Parsol.

'No games, I've got what you want. But let her go first.'

Cassiter backed away from Helen in response to Parsol's nodded instruction.

Sam still lay facing the wall; he turned his head to look up at Parsol.

'Do tell Mr Cameron. One chance only.'

Sam turned his head back to the wall and gritted his teeth, fighting the pain that pulsed from his damaged shoulder as he moved his arms to touch the base of the cavern wall. Seeking to feel confirmation of what his eyes were seeing. 'This is not a wall. It's a door,' he said.

One of the guards beside Simon gave a little laugh. It ended quickly under a withering look from Parsol.

'It looks very much like a wall to me Mr Cameron. I hope you're not being deceitful.'

'No, it's a door. We found the same construction method at the tunnel entrance. The Templars were masters at this sort of thing. It's actually a panel of chipped and splintered stone, assembled to match the way the surrounding wall had been hacked out by the original miners. It's a mosaic, come and see for yourself.'

Parsol and Cassiter bent down to look more closely.

'Well I don't see it,' said Parsol.

Cassiter was looking carefully, letting his hands run across other parts of the wall, then back to the part Sam had indicated. 'He might have something. I'm not sure, but once you look for a difference there seems to be something. Just the feel, the way the light reflects. Come look again. Touch it, feel it,' he said.

Parsol returned and allowed his hand to run across the section of wall, he inspected it more closely. 'So open it, Mr Cameron. Let's see what's beyond.'

Sam struggled to his feet and crossed to Helen. 'We had to use brute force to open the other one. I think it'll be more of a sealed panel than a door. Opening it is a once only job.'

Parsol had Sam and Simon set to, to break the wall. Under the supervision of the guards Sam held his pry bar and Simon beat it with a stone. With a damaged shoulder and their wrists cable tied, it was heavy going and they could not apply enough pressure to break the panel.

'Get out of the way,' ordered Cassiter, producing his pistol. 'Everyone over there,' he waved them back towards the tunnel mouth. As they backed away, he crouched down, aimed at the wall and fired. Amidst the wild and echoing roar of the discharging weapon, shot after shot hit the panel, each bullet punched through the stone mosaic and buried into the ancient mortar behind. His magazine emptied, he loaded his reserve magazine clip and repeated the process. When he'd used up his ammunition, he stood, waving ineffectually at the billows of gun smoke that were misting the scene, and crossed to inspect his work.

'There's a hole,' he shouted. 'You guys get over here and blast this wall with your guns; we'll be in it in no time.'

Three of the guards joined Cassiter and began blasting at the wall. They paused to reload their reserve clips and then resumed the fusillade. By the time their ammunition was spent, there was a hole in the wall big enough for a man to thrust his head through.

Parsol insisted on looking first. As his head disappeared into the hole, a silence fell on the watching group. After a long moment, Parsol pulled back from the hole and waved Cassiter towards it. 'I think we might just have hit the jackpot.' His normally impassive face showed just a hint of triumph.

Sam had manoeuvred himself to Helen's side. As all eyes were on the hole in the wall, he nudged her, glanced down to the leg pocket of his cargo pants; he raised his leg slightly. She followed his eye line and responded. Bending her knees a little she reached her bound hands into the pocket, felt about, delved to the bottom and found a slim little pocket knife - low on Sam's thigh, the pocket had been missed by his searchers. She pulled it out and looked expectantly at Sam, then held the knife tight as he gripped the thick edge of the blade with his fingertips and drew it open.

Sam thrust his wrists out, allowing her to cut him free. He reciprocated.

Simon had sidled alongside them as the guards shuffled closer to the hole in the wall, anxious to get sight of the prize. Parsol and Cassiter had exchanged places again. His muffled voice reached them from within the wall. 'Cassiter, I need this opened up, now.'

Parsol pulled his head out from the hole, saw how anxious his men were to see the sight and waved them forward. 'A quick glance men, then to work.'

He looked at Helen, standing between Sam and Simon, each with their hands secured in front of them. 'Well young lady, it looks as though you came up trumps. I did mention you'd all die, didn't I? That's quite true. Sadly, you've caused me a lot of bother and I'm afraid I can't let you go quietly. And I think Cassiter here has some business to finish with you too.' He looked at Cassiter who gave the slightest of nods.

'Now, your friends can watch with me while Cassiter does what he does best. Then if you're still able, you can watch them have some of the same; before we end it for you all.'

Cassiter stepped in front of Helen, leant forward and breathed in her face again. His hands sought out hers, their fingers interlocked, he smiled happily into her eyes as he applied pressure, started to bend her fingers back. A brief moment of puzzlement flitted across his face as her wrists parted, he didn't understand. Then he felt her knee hammer into his crotch. He squealed, buckled, squatted down and cradled his genitals.

Parsol had been standing, quietly anticipating the punishment the American girl was due. Before he could pull his pistol, Simon was on him. A forearm into the jaw had Parsol reeling back, falling, and Simon helped him down with a hard kick to the ribs. Parsol's pistol fell to the ground and Simon instinctively kicked it beyond his opponent's reach.

The four guards were working at the hole in the wall; Sam had marked out the one who had not emptied his ammunition into the wall. He put him down with a clenched fist hard into the temple. Didn't bother to watch him fall - from the moment he'd connected he knew it was a home run; the man was out of the fight. Sam pushed on; the guards were becoming aware that things were out of hand but the second one went down as Sam used his body's full momentum to propel the guard's head into the wall he had been about to break. Sam wrapped his right arm round the third guard's neck and used it as a pivot to swing round and land a kick on Robertson who grunted in distress as Sam's boot met his midriff. But with the impetus of the initial assault nearly over, and with only one working arm, the odds would quickly start to turn against Sam.

Helen brought her knee up into Cassiter's face, heard the groan as his nose folded, didn't notice the flow of blood on to her trouser leg, but did join her hands and bring them down hard on the back of his head. She looked on with satisfaction as he sprawled on the ground, dazed, groaning and bloodied.

She hurried across to Nick. He was quiet now, hands clasped across the stomach wound. The wound needed attention way beyond what she could offer. Carefully, she looked at his face; it was pallid, waxy - Nick was in a very bad way. He tried to smile; she leant forward and stroked his brow. 'We'll fix this, just hold on.' Then she was up and returning to the fray.

Hurrying back across the chamber, she could see their position was unsustainable. Cassiter was still down but showing signs of revival, as was Parsol. Sam and Simon were struggling with three of the four guards; the fourth was still out cold from Sam's initial assault. Like Sam, she had marked him out as the only guard who had not emptied his gun into the wall panel. She knelt beside the prone man and felt inside his jacket. Finding his pistol, she pulled it out.

Simon was on the ground, only a couple of metres away from her, one guard grappling with his arms; another, standing over him, had managed to land one kick to the ribs and was trying to line up the head kick that would take Simon out of the equation. Beside them on the floor, Sam and Robertson wrestled for supremacy. Sam had taken several heavy blows before Simon had joined him to share the burden but those blows and the damaged ligaments in his shoulder had weakened Sam, enabling the bigger man to work himself into a dominant position.

Robertson's forearm slipped round to the front of Sam's neck. His other arm locked against it. Sam was choking. With his good arm trapped behind him, only his ligament damaged side could resist and to little effect. If Sam didn't suffocate, his neck would snap.

Helen crossed the gap between them in just a moment and used all her strength to bring the pistol's handle down on the giant's head. He seemed startled by the blow but did not release Sam; instead, he tightened his neck lock.

'I'm guessing you don't have what it takes to use that pistol,' said Robertson as he applied a little more torque on Sam's neck. He leered at Helen. 'Him first, then I'm coming for you. Better run while you still can.'

In a single flowing movement, she pressed the muzzle of the pistol against the taught bulging muscle of Robertson's upper arm, and carefully angling the aim away from Sam's neck, she pulled the trigger. The shot filled the chamber with a roar that swept away all the sounds of fighting.

Robertson bellowed in pain. His arm turned blood red and his upper arm bone shattered into fragments as it stopped the bullet. He rolled back, the arm flopped, now just a useless leaking bag of flesh and broken bone. Helen ignored the screaming man. He had guessed wrong.

Sam gasped for air, clutching at his throat. Simon and the other two guards stopped for a moment to assess what the shot meant. As Helen brought the pistol to bear on them, the guards realised at once. They glanced at Robertson and any thoughts of testing

Helen's nerve were dispelled. Raising their arms, they backed away from Simon.

Sam pulled himself to his feet, rubbing his throat; then shifted his hand to rest it on Helen's shoulder. 'Thanks, that was getting a bit hairy.'

'You're welcome,' said Helen and she handed Sam the pistol. 'What now?'

As Simon pushed the two standing guards on to the ground, Sam weighed their options.

He looked down at Robertson, then at the other two sitting beside him; they were making no attempt to help their wounded comrade. The fourth guard had come to and was gingerly sitting up. In the middle of the chamber, Parsol and Cassiter were standing now, both faces loaded with fury.

'We need to get Nick some treatment right away,' said Sam. 'I'm afraid we are going to have to retreat.'

'That means we'll leave this lot with your treasure,' said Simon.

'Well, there's no choice unless we shoot them,' said Sam.

'So shoot them,' said Simon. 'They were going to shoot us.'

'We won't shoot anyone - unless we have to,' said Helen. 'Sam's right, we must put Nick first.'

Simon shrugged towards Sam. 'It's your call. Just sticks in the throat, that's all.'

'Yes, it's my call. We're not stooping to their level. Simon, I want you to help Helen get Nick back along the tunnel. I'll stay here with the gun to give you a head start. Then I'll follow you.' Sam moved closer to Helen and whispered. 'Ten minutes, no more. I can't keep all of these covered for too long before they begin to think it's worth chancing their luck.'

'So let them live,' said Simon, 'but at least let me stay here to cover them, you and Helen get the boy out of here.'

'My shoulder is out of action. I couldn't manage to get Nick through the tunnels.'

Simon looked at Sam for a moment then nodded acceptance of the obvious. 'Fine, let's do it then.'

'You'll need your pistol, Simon. I would bet they have posted guards at the tunnel entrance.'

Simon nodded a curt agreement and retrieved his weapon,

shoved it in its holster. Then, to the slightest of groans from a semi-conscious Nick, Simon lifted him up.

Helen rested her hand on Sam's forearm for a moment; she glanced at the men ranged in front of them and went quickly to help Simon move Nick. 'We can't do anything for him here so I think speed is the answer,' she said and they hurried away down the tunnel.

• • •

Sam reckoned the others had been away for around ten minutes; it was hard to tell for certain. Blood was trickling down his forehead. Though he kept wiping his eyes, his vision was being repeatedly obscured. He knew that his captors knew too, could see glances being exchanged. He felt trouble brewing. 'Stay where you are,' he snapped.

As Sam again wiped the back of his pistol hand over his eyes, shifting the blood away, a rapid movement in the room was followed by instant darkness. Cassiter had thrown himself on to the lantern torch and killed the power and at the same moment, one of the guards went for Parsol's pistol that lay unattended across the floor on the far side of the chamber.

Crouching down at the mouth of the tunnel Sam's gaze cast about through the darkness. He listened acutely for any sound. Nothing, silent, black; now it was a hunting game.

Then he heard a sound, but not from where he had expected; it came from the tunnel behind him, approaching fast. His heart sank; it could only mean Parsol and Cassiter had posted guards at the exit. They must have taken Helen, Simon too. He weighed up his chances, not good - between a rock and a hard place.

Suddenly a distant light flickered behind him, streaking past him into the chamber, silhouetting him in the tunnel mouth. He was a sitting duck. As he threw himself to one side, a pistol flashed and roared in the darkness. He gasped in pain as his damaged shoulder took a bullet and another shot ricocheted off the wall beside his head. Then he was into the dark shadows, crawling away towards the wall. His weapon dropped.

Parsol's voice filled the cavern. 'Here comes the back-up, men.

Let's get the light on and finish Cameron off once and for all. Cassiter, where are you?'

Cassiter switched the lantern torch back on. The room flooded with light again, revealing Sam, propped up against the far wall.

'I'm here. Situation recovered,' said Cassiter.

Parsol stooped to lift the pistol Sam had dropped.

'Yes. But Cassiter, that church girl. It's not enough now that she dies. She must be punished; she has to suffer in every way you can imagine. I want to hear her praying, begging her God for death, long before it comes. Can you oblige?'

'It will be my pleasure,' said Cassiter, as he and the guards got to their feet.

Parsol brought his pistol to bear on Sam. As he refined his aim, a shot rang out from the tunnel. For a moment, Cassiter and the guards assumed Parsol had fired at Sam. But as Parsol suddenly swung his pistol and fired into the tunnel they realised they were under attack. Parsol fired two shots. They heard cries; he had hit somebody, for sure. But shots continued to come out from the tunnel mouth, lots of them.

Immobile, Sam watched as the guard with a loaded weapon started firing into the tunnel. But the return fire was rapid, overwhelming and moving closer. 'Let's go,' shouted Parsol as he headed for the opposite end of the chamber and the sanctuary of its tunnel mouth. Cassiter joined him, together with Robertson and the other guards. As they entered the tunnel, Parsol handed his pistol to one of the guards then shouted at him and the guard with the other loaded gun. 'You two, cover the retreat. Hold them off.'

A few metres into the tunnel the armed guards turned and knelt. Raising their guns, they started to fire back into the cavern at the onrushing men.

Sam blinked, peering through dazed and blood drenched eyes, fighting to remain conscious. Where was Helen? Who were these men entering the cavern? Six, eight, ten and more, they spread out and moved through the cavern while maintaining a steady rate of fire into the tunnel at the far end. One man went down, and another, but still they advanced. Only serious training and discipline produced this sort of behaviour. A scream from the tunnel signalled one of Parsol's men was down and the newly arrived attackers continued their assault, four of them disappearing into the tunnel in hot pursuit. One took up station at the tunnel mouth and the others paused to tend the wounded and secure the scene.

Sam tried to speak to the man who was approaching him, but found his mouth was too dry, he couldn't form the words. So he just looked, wondering if he was to get a bullet or a bandage. The man loomed over him; just as Sam had given up worrying about the answer, the man was pulled aside and in his stead stood Helen.

She knelt beside Sam, checked his wounds. Pulling open a medical kit, she began to patch him up while delivering a normalising stream of chatter. 'You're going to need the hospital, Sam. There's a bullet in your shoulder. Just a flesh wound I think, you'll be fine.'

The sound of sporadic gunfire continued to emerge from the tunnel, but it was more distant now.

As she tended to his reopened head wound, Sam registered another figure in the background. He looked again but his vision was obscured by a wet swab wiping across his forehead and eyes. 'You'll need more stitches there,' said Helen, leaning in to look closely before wiping the wound again. 'You'll be okay though. No long-term harm to your looks.' He felt a light kiss on his cheek, and then a gentle pressure as a pad landed on his injured head. 'Hold that in place for a moment while I sort out the fixing,' she said.

He complied and a couple of minutes later she finished the dressing, rocked back on her heels to take a look at the whole. 'You'll live,' she announced. 'Just be careful who you play with next time. I've warned you about the bad boys before.'

She helped him take a mouthful of water then leant forward and placed a firm kiss on his lips before making a start on dressing his shoulder wound.

'What's going on? Who are all these people, where's Simon and Nick?'

She looked into Sam's eyes and gave him a reassuring smile. 'Everything's all right, I think. Nick's been taken down to the doctor, Simon's gone with him.'

'What doctor?' said Sam.

'The doctor, down on the cruiser. They've got all the kit, I'm sure he'll be fine.'

Sam's head ached. 'I don't understand.'

'Apparently, Francis blabbed to the Pope's boys.'

'He did what? How? When? Come on Helen, get me up to speed.'

'I've told you, Francis sneaked on us in Rome, but it doesn't matter; if he hadn't we'd all be dead by now.' There was a glint in Helen's eye. Whatever was happening, she clearly wasn't worried, didn't feel threatened; he relaxed a little.

• • •

The shadowy figure he had seen previously reappeared behind Helen. This time it didn't vanish. It knelt beside Sam.

'Might I assume you are Sam Cameron, the urh, friend, of the Reverend Helen Johnson?' said the man.

Sam looked at him. 'I am and who's asking?'

'I am Monsignor Acciai, a most humble member of the Papal Curia. Guided here today in the service of God.'

Sam snorted. His time in Italy had been spent mostly in the south but once or twice he had met members of the Papal Curia when they visited his university. He had yet to encounter a humble member.

Sam tried to sit up properly. 'I don't understand. Why are you here, how?'

'Helen is correct in saying your friend Father Francis alerted us to the danger you faced. But let me assure you, he did not, how did you say? Blab? The Vatican authorities have been very concerned over what had happened to our priests in Sardinia recently. When it was realised Francis was their friend and had visited them on his way to Rome, naturally, we wanted his perspective and he was vigorously encouraged to explain. And, well, one thing led to another, and here we are.'

'And thank Heaven you are,' said Helen.

Sam grimaced with pain and struggled to rise. Helen and Monsignor Acciai reached out to help him to his feet just as the earth rocked.

It had started as a dull thud, only a little louder than the sound of the intermittent gunshots that still carried down the tunnel towards them. Then it had doubled and redoubled into a roar that filled their ears to bursting. A plume of smoke jetted out of the tunnel and filled the chamber. The force of the blast knocked all three into a heap and swept dust and debris past them and on into the tunnel beyond.

For what seemed a long time nobody moved. Then, one by one, torches appeared; pinpricks at first, then dull lights, gradually glowing stronger as the cloud of dust started to thin and settle. Italian voices called out to one another, a roll call of sorts.

Heralded by a fit of coughing, Helen fumbled to her knees. 'Sam, are you okay?' Relieved, she felt his hand give a reassuring squeeze to her hip. 'Monsignor, are you unhurt?'

'I am, thank God, and thanks for you both too. But what in the Lord's name just happened?'

Sam coughed. The blast had stunned the others; for him it had swept away the fog that had been clouding his mind. 'The whole place is rigged with explosives. Someone must have triggered the blast. Probably a stray bullet,' he said.

The monsignor's voice cracked a little. 'My goodness. We must retreat. How did we survive? It's a miracle.'

'No miracle,' said Sam. 'We were just lucky. I'd cut the cables to the explosives in this chamber and further back, but that blast was probably not triggered by a regular ignition system. Just a stray shot setting off some of the explosives. Luckily the blast didn't spark a chain reaction or the whole lot would have gone up.'

'Hmmm. Perhaps you are right,' said the monsignor. He broke off to stand up and fire instructions to his men. Through the clearing dust, two armed figures set off cautiously towards the source of the explosion.

Helen stood and then helped Sam up to his feet.

Sam watched as members of the strike force maintained its guard on the tunnel mouth, while others commenced the evacuation of the wounded.

Monsignor Acciai turned to Sam. 'We are here to rescue you in the furtherance of God's work. You will all be evacuated to our vessel. It is safe there. There you will meet my superior. His Eminence is very keen to speak with you all.'

'You have a cardinal on your ship?'

'I do. A very powerful cardinal. Very close to the Holy Father and very close to the Vatican Bank. I will say no more.'

'And the treasure?' said Sam.

'We will ensure it is taken to safety.'

'Which means?'

'Taken to Rome, of course. It is the rightful property of the Catholic Church. The Templars were an organisation of the Church, founded by the Church, and ended by the Church. Therefore, any assets must naturally belong to the Church.'

'Do we have any say in this?' said Sam.

'No. No say, but you do all live safe and free. For many that is enough.'

Helen put a hand on Sam's arm, restraining him. 'Sam, let's not fight. We're all alive and going home. Remember, we never wanted the treasure; we just wanted to end the killings. Let's get down to the cruiser. Francis is there. He'll be desperately worried.'

Sam bit his tongue. It felt like a rip off. But Helen had a point. They didn't need the money and perhaps Monsignor Acciai had a point too. The Templars had been part of the Church of Rome. He nodded a begrudging acquiescence.

By some unspoken agreement, the trio stepped across to the gaping hole in the cavern wall.

'Ladies first, I think,' said Monsignor Acciai, bowing very slightly towards Helen and waving her forward to the hole.

She smiled and did not need a second prompt to look inside. 'Oh… my… God,' she said. 'You are not going to believe it. Just have a look at this.' She stepped back from the hole; smiling and beckoning them on, Monsignor Acciai waved Sam forward.

'Go! Go look! You made it possible,' he said, while beckoning to a couple of his men who had appeared equipped with hammers.

It took only a few minutes for the men to clear the false wall panel away completely. It then took real restraint not to just rush into the chamber. Having been sealed for over seven hundred years, Sam insisted they wait a little while to let the air inside exchange and freshen. Eventually, he gave a nod and they crowded in. Sam and Helen stood close to each other, he felt her hand slide into his, he squeezed gently, felt the same back.

The chamber was around two metres high, two metres wide and

five metres long. Three shelves had been hewn out of the rock, tiered; each one set back a little from the one below. Horseshoe like, the shelves ran round three sides of the compartment. On the shelves were tightly packed rows of small iron bound wooden chests, each somewhat bigger than the size of a modern shoebox, but chunky and solid.

Monsignor Acciai waved Helen forward to open the first chest. She had seen one just like these before, in Switzerland. She lifted the lid from a chest; it took a little pressure, though she was careful not to damage the integrity of the ancient wood. The lid lifted and Helen saw a familiar sight, a row of little gold bars. From their position in the box, she knew there were more layers beneath. There was a collective intake of breath as the gold was revealed. She lifted one out; held it up for the men to see.

Monsignor Acciai reached out and took it, pressed it to his lips and muttered thanks to God. There were tears in his eyes as he looked round. 'My friends, you do not know how important this is. You have saved the Church. The Vatican Bank has had its troubles in recent times, some public, others private, but all in all, we were very short on reserves. And this, praise God, this will save it for a hundred years, no, save it forever. His Eminence will be delighted!'

'I think that's code for, we were broke and now we're not,' whispered Sam into Helen's ear.

'How can we thank you? So much gold, praise the Lord for his generosity.' As he spoke, Monsignor Acciai moved along the chamber, opening lids at random to reveal many more gold bars and other chests full of gold coins. 'What reward can we give you? Any wish, I know it will be met. Now, we must hurry this news to his Eminence.'

Helen stepped forward, putting a friendly arm round Monsignor Acciai. He looked a little startled, unused to such feminine proximity, but he tolerated it. His new-found bonhomie even extended to forward young ladies, and particularly to *this* young lady.

'Monsignor Acciai, there is one thing you can do,' she said.

'Yes, I am sure his eminence will look kindly on any request.'

Helen reached out her hand and patted one of the bullion boxes. 'I reckon I know of a deserving home for one of these.'

'Yes?' said Monsignor Acciai. He had been expecting a reward request, but when it came, it surprised him.

'There's a little church community in Greece. Kefalonia. You've heard of the island?'

Monsignor Acciai nodded.

'Well that's where our young friend Nick comes from. His people were like mine. But their resources have gone helping to save the poor people of their island. Their church needs to be rebuilt; they need a lot of help. They made real sacrifices; some gave their lives to get us here today. Without them, you would never have reached this point. Help them. The man you need to speak with there is Father Christos.'

Monsignor Acciai nodded acknowledgement. 'Leave it with me; consider it done.'

Sam stood up from where he had been crouching down to inspect the sides of the chamber beneath the shelving. 'One thing strikes me as odd.'

'Only one?' said Helen.

'Well, one in particular. It's all coin and bullion. I was sure there were meant to be religious artefacts. Holy texts, icons, statues and regalia, that sort of stuff - I don't know what, but all the things the Templars had collected. You know, from Jerusalem and so forth. I'm sure that's what Xavier and Francis thought; it's what all the myths suggested too.'

Monsignor Acciai listened intently but whatever he intended to say was left unsaid as Sam swayed and leant against the wall to stop himself from falling. Helen moved swiftly to support him as Monsignor Acciai beckoned over two of his men.

'Sam, your wounds may be more serious than we thought. Let's get you to the cruiser at once. Let the doctor take a look before things get any worse. My men will assist you.'

Helen stepped away from Sam to allow the men to support him. And he offered no objections as they moved him into the main chamber and on towards the tunnel. She followed, pausing for a moment to turn back. 'Thank you, Monsignor Acciai. Will we see you down on the boat?'

His head dipped slightly towards Helen - part salute, part agreement. 'I will join you, but later, there is much to do here first.'

Helen smiled an acknowledgement and turned away to catch up

with Sam and his helpers.

Chapter 33

THURSDAY 12ᵀᴴ SEPTEMBER

Helen stood to one side of the communion table looking out across the congregation. Every pew was full. The congregation's numbers were swelled by supporters from the neighbouring parishes, representatives from presbytery and members of the public who just wanted to be there for the occasion. Some to mark the end of a parish, some just to say they had been there. One or two reporters were dotted amongst the congregation but she knew the majority of the media were gathered outside.

She tried hard to concentrate on what James Curry was saying but, after everything that had happened, it was hard. The sound of his voice rolled down from the pulpit to wash over her and fill the nave. In the end, as presbytery clerk, it had fallen to him to speak - though Helen could think of others who held the parish dear and would have been more appropriate choices for this final act.

The service of thanksgiving for the parish, its history and all its former works was nearly over. She looked out across the congregation. Faces she recognised came into focus to deliver supportive smiles before merging back into the mass.

She knew that sitting behind her in the apse were Elaine and the other elders, their seats arranged in a semicircle following the shape of the building. Above them the great black wooden cross, fixed to the eastern wall - higher still, the glass of the Templar window. The elders' duties all done, now this final thanksgiving, a last goodbye, and the church would be closed.

A prayer, a blessing from James Curry and it was all over. He stepped down the aisle, she followed and the elders fell in behind her. Passing each pew, she saw more and more friendly faces; it seemed so unfair that St Bernard's had been railroaded to closure. In front of her, James Curry set a pace that seemed just a little too fast, hurrying them all towards the exit.

Stepping out through the great doors of the church, she thought, for just a moment, perhaps Curry was right. Below her, at the bottom of the steps, the media swirled and rippled like a shoal of piranha. They jostled for position: cameras, flashing lights, shouted questions and sound booms swinging their microphones close in. The media would never forget the brutal killings of the summer past. St Bernard's could never go back to being the quiet, anonymous parish it had once been.

The elders, led by Elaine, clustered stoically around Helen as she stood with Curry on the church steps. They listened politely as he delivered carefully prepared sound bites to the media. All the while, the congregation funnelled out behind them, channelling to either side and down the steps, skirting the media pack; there some of the congregation paused, gathering together to watch, others dispersed into the neighbouring streets.

With Curry's PR words spoken, it was finished. The media turned away, dispersing quickly towards their cars and vans. Still on the top step, Helen and Elaine found themselves facing James Curry. He was elated, no hint of sadness at the ending of St Bernard's. Pointing along the street towards a parked removal van, he beckoned the driver of the van forward. 'There they are,' he said. 'Elaine, would you get the removals team over please. Show them in. We have a midday deadline for handover of the keys. I want those porters at work right away.'

Elaine gave a resigned nod and stepped down to the pavement to wait for the removals van as it edged up the road towards them.

James Curry turned to Helen. 'I don't think we need you now. There's nothing you can do. You may as well just go.' He paused for a moment them stepped a little closer to her. 'You see, my dear, it's all gone now. I told you I'd win. No minister and no parish will stand above me in my own presbytery. Oh, and don't look to the presbytery for a reference. You defied me, backed the wrong side and now you're beaten.' He leant closer still and spoke in a theatrical whisper. 'The pity is this parish was more viable than one or two others. Under other circumstances, it would not have been the one to close. Still, on the bright side, we've got more money than you could ever dream of, twice the market value for a quick sale. Now, I'm afraid you're in the way a little. Perhaps you should just go. Hmmm?' And he turned to monitor Elaine and the removals work.

Helen stepped to one side, allowing space for the porters who were swarming into the church. Everything was to go, the communion table, lectern, elders' chairs and yet more packing cases from the vestry. At the church doors, Elaine was busy filling boxes with the hymnbooks and pew bibles, now retiring after their last service.

Finally, the church was almost bare. The pulpit stood as a lonely sentinel overlooking rows of redundant pews; the apse cleared, just the blackened wooden cross remaining - left at the specific request of the purchaser.

'Yes, yes. Well done. Thank you. Thank you all,' Curry's voice carried down the church steps to Helen. In his haste to have the building clear, Curry seemed to be almost wishing the removals foreman down the steps and away. She had been reluctant to follow Curry's instruction to leave her friends. Now she stood at the foot of the steps, speaking with those other members of the congregation who had also been reluctant to disperse. Pulling the church doors shut, Curry glanced down at his watch for the umpteenth time. 'I think we've made it in time.'

Helen looked up to the top step, watching him as he pointed across the street.

'Look, Elaine, that's the Church solicitor parking now. They're doing a handover of the keys here. A ceremony, Heaven knows why. It all seems a bit theatrical but money talks, as they say. Wait with me. You may as well see the process through. If we need a witness you'll do.'

He glanced down the steps towards the pavement, where Helen was standing. He waved a dismissive hand in her direction. 'Perhaps you could encourage that lot to move on a little? We don't want a crowd getting in the way or making a fuss.'

Just as the Church solicitor arrived at James Curry's side, Elaine followed his instruction, and stepped down to stand beside Helen. Clustered around Helen were Sam, Francis, Grace, all the other elders, and a good number of friends and parishioners. Nobody wanted to follow Curry's instruction. They were determined to see it through to the end.

Helen glanced about; so many good people here to witness the day. Even her mother had made it; she was standing beside Sam's parents who Helen had met for the first time only the previous evening. Father Christos stood with the young deacon from Xavier's parish, she was sure she spotted a couple of familiar Sardinian parishioners hovering in the background too. Quite a crowd - Davy, Julie, and away at the back DCI Wallace and DS Brogan.

Helen watched Curry and the Church solicitor exchange pleasantries, then saw Curry glance in her direction with a disdainful look. The keys to the church were in the Church solicitor's hand now, the keys to the manse and the church hall too.

Curry was muttering in a theatrical whisper. 'Is all this rigmarole really necessary? I'm sure it would have been easier to transfer the keys between your respective offices. That's what would normally happen.'

'Yes, it is,' agreed the Church solicitor, 'but you don't normally get a buyer offering you twice a routine property's value for an off market sale. The Church is making something more than four million extra. So, if your buyers want a key transfer ceremony, you'd better give it to them.'

'Well let's get on with it then. Where are they anyway? As a point of interest, what do we really know about them?'

'Nothing more than I've already told you. They want to keep the manse as a private dwelling and use the church and the church hall for worship and community work - no change of land use or restrictions; just a simple sale and transfer.'

A taxi drew to a halt at the roadside and an older man stepped out; smart, perfectly turned out.

The Church solicitor waved towards him. 'That's their man now.

David Cromarty, decent type. I hope you've got a few words ready.'

David Cromarty returned the friendly wave and stepped up to greet his counterpart who promptly made introductions to James Curry.

'So where's your client?' said Curry. 'I'm keen to shake his hand and conclude this business. The Church is very pleased with the transaction, and we hope he will be happy with the properties.'

David Cromarty released Curry's hand and smiled graciously. 'It's nice of you to say that. But surely, you know my client?'

'Oh, oh, twelve o'clock. Time to complete the transaction, transfer the keys,' said the Church solicitor while checking her watch.

She glanced at David Cromarty, they exchanged nods of agreement and the keys changed hands. 'All yours now, congratulations,' she said.

David Cromarty thanked her, took the keys and shook her hand. Then half turned towards Helen as she joined him on the step.

James Curry started to wave her away. 'Whatever it is, this is neither the time nor the place. We have important Church business. I'm expecting a VIP at any moment. Please, just step away.'

David Cromarty reached out a welcoming arm, taking Helen by the elbow and drawing her up to the top step. 'Helen, there you are. The Church people were just getting a bit worried that you weren't here and I know they are eager to learn of your plans. Do tell.'

As Helen joined them on the top step, David Cromarty handed her the keys with a flourish. She beamed him a smile of thanks then turned to James Curry, who was standing in stunned silence.

'James, I wish I could say it's been a pleasure doing business with you. But at least I can say the outcome is a pleasure.'

'What's going on?' said James Curry, spluttering, his face turning slightly red, the volume of his words rising. 'Is this some kind of joke? I don't think it's funny. Let's get on with the presentation, where's the buyer?' He turned to the Church solicitor who had stepped back slightly and was watching with a bemused expression on her face.

'There's no joke. I can assure you,' said David Cromarty as he waved a hand to embrace the whole property. 'Helen is the representative of the trust that has bought the property. Helen do you want to say anything?'

'I just want to thank James for giving us the opportunity to ensure good work continues to be done at St Bernard's. We're going to maintain all the community activities in the church hall and keep the name of course. And I'm sure he'll be delighted to know that Elaine has agreed to take on the role of director of the St Bernard's Community Trust, which will be based in the church buildings.'

Helen saw the wrath in James Curry's stare as she shook the Church solicitor's hand to thank her. He was about to slip away in disgusted disbelief when Helen's friends, who had remained at the foot of the steps, finally surrendered to impulse and rushed up, cheering and bursting open champagne bottles as they came. Grace took delight in ensuring her opening bottle burst over Curry's suit and Francis just managed to restrain her before she splashed more of the contents over the man.

In a melee of excitement Curry disappeared, the Church solicitor took a half glass of champagne before excusing herself, and then the party moved inside the church.

As the doors opened to cheers and the popping of more champagne corks, David Cromarty pulled Helen to one side. 'Helen, I'm so pleased it's worked out for you as you hoped.'

'Thank you,' she said. 'But you and your firm made it all possible. Without your acting on my behalf, it wouldn't have happened. The look on James Curry's face was priceless.'

'He certainly didn't seem very happy. But you have what you want?'

'Oh yes, I do.' She leant in and kissed David on his cheek.

Sam joined them. 'We'll have to throw a proper celebration. I'm sure Helen will want you to come, Franz Brenner too.'

'And I'm sure I'll be delighted to attend,' said David Cromarty. 'Just tell me when. In the meantime, I will let Franz know the outcome of today's events as soon as I get back to my office. I hope this will work out well for Helen, for you both.'

'I'm quite sure it will,' said Sam.

'Helen, one more thing before I leave you. You have three sets of keys, the manse, the church and church hall.'

'Yes, I know.'

'Interestingly, there's another property. It's linked with the church deeds as part of an estate.'

'Oh? That sounds odd.'

'Very odd. The properties seem to have been combined together when the current church was founded. So it goes back a long way.'

Helen linked her arm through Sam's, squeezing it in tight to her. He grimaced slightly as the pressure fed across his body to the wounded shoulder. She smiled at David Cromarty. 'This is exciting. Sam, we have an estate!'

David Cromarty gave a little laugh. 'Well, don't hold your breath. It's a farm in Midlothian, not huge by any means. There's a tenant farmer; same family's been on the land for generations. It doesn't earn much in the way of rentals at all, I'm afraid. There's a steading and some acres of arable ground together with a good bit of grazing. The deed allows the tenants to stay for a peppercorn rent in return for protecting and preserving the adjoining woodland. That's yours too, ancient woodland, but it's not actually part of the farm tenancy. At a rough measure, the farm is around two hundred acres and the woodland a little less, perhaps a hundred and fifty acres. It's well over three hundred acres in total.'

'Well, it's always something and how fascinating,' said Helen.

'No real value to it I'm afraid. The farmland is committed for a very low income and parts of the wood are designated as SSSIs. So you can't even sell the timber, much less develop the land.'

'What's an SSSI?' asked Helen.

'A Site of Special Scientific Interest.' David Cromarty gave a little shrug. 'I'm afraid I haven't had the chance to look at the specifics in this case. Getting the main deal through fast was your express instruction and sole priority and, in practice, there is nothing you can do to the SSSI site in any event. The paperwork from Scottish Natural Heritage will work its way through to my office and I'll let you know as soon as I can.'

Sam nodded, understanding. 'It'll be interesting to see what's there. It could be anything; a breeding ground for a rare type of frog, endangered woodland flowers; anything. If it's ancient woodland, the land may have been untouched, that's really rare, especially in this part of the country. But the SSSI designation means it is protected.'

'Quite so,' said David, extending a hand towards Sam. 'Nice to have met you.'

Sam took his hand and shook. 'Whereabouts exactly is the land?' said Sam.

'It's beyond Bonnyrigg, just outside one of those little hamlets. Let me think, you know I actually had to look it up on the map when I checked the deeds; it's quite out of the way. What was it now? Yes, that's it, Temple. You have a parcel of land and woodland at Temple.'

David Cromarty extended his arm to shake Helen's hand and graciously allowed her to convert it to a light hug. Then he was gone.

Helen looked at Sam. They stood in silence for a long moment. 'We have land out at Temple,' she said.

'Yes, that's a name that's cropped up more than once, isn't it? And ancient woodland that may not have been touched for hundreds of years.'

'Perhaps seven hundred years.'

'Exactly. I think we will need to look at that woodland.'

'Agreed,' she said, linking her arm with his again, 'but for now, let's join the party.'

BOOKS IN THE SERIES

The Temple Legacy (The Temple Book 1) Published 2015

The Temple Scroll (The Temple Book 2) Published 2016

The Temple Covenant (The Temple Book 3) Published 2018

The Temple Deliverance (The Temple Book 4) Published 2019

Temple Legacy

(The Temple - Book 1)

Seven hundred years ago, in a time of war and betrayal, Europe's greatest treasure disappeared amidst a frenzied and brutal grab for power. The men who guarded it vanished into history.

In Edinburgh today, former élite British Military Intelligence officer Sam Cameron has turned to the quieter world of archaeology. Together with young church minister Helen Johnson, he leads his students on a field trip. What they unearth raises exciting questions. What are the mystery objects? What is their connection to the Knights Templar?

But others are asking the same questions and the thrill of discovery is quickly clouded by the brutal killing of a retired church minister and a spreading rage of violence and death.

Now Helen and Sam must race to unravel an ancient mystery, find how it links to the murdered minister, and fend off a very modern threat. Failure will cost their lives and the lives of many more. Success will answer the greatest unresolved mystery of the medieval world.

The Temple Scroll

(The Temple - Book 2)

A lost treasure, an impenetrable puzzle and a psychopathic killer: a deadly combination.

The Temple Scroll is a rollercoaster ride of danger, mystery and murder. From New England to the islands of the Mediterranean, it follows the deadly hunt for the Templars' lost treasure.

Archaeology lecturer Sam Cameron and church minister Helen Johnson thought their old problems were done. They were wrong. Killers are set on finding the Templars' treasure and they believe Sam and Helen hold the key.

As the psychopathic Cassiter directs his team of killers towards their goal, the calm of summer vanishes in an explosive bout of blood and suffering.

Under pressure from every side, Sam and Helen must draw on all their instincts and professional skills to stay alive as they attempt to crack the puzzle that protects the Templars' treasure.

As the search for the Templar hoard moves inexorably to a conclusion, Sam and Helen must risk all in a frantic bid to save their friends, the treasure, and the priceless holy relics of the early Church. Now there is no mercy and no escape - there is only win or die.

The Temple Covenant

(The Temple - Book 3)

A quiet sabbatical spent visiting archaeological sites in the Great Rift Valley offers Helen Johnson and Sam Cameron the perfect opportunity to unwind and put the violent climax to their recent adventures behind them. But where they go trouble isn't far away. Disturbing alarm bells start to ring when Helen attracts the attentions of the mysterious Bishop Ignatius of the Ethiopian Orthodox Tewahedo Church. He is desperate to meet with her and will not take no for an answer.

Elsewhere, news breaks that senior British Intelligence Corps Colonel Bob Prentice is missing in Nairobi and security chiefs have cause for concern. Concern turns to panic when it's realised an operational prototype of the British Army's latest super-weapon has vanished too.

In a last gasp attempt to retrieve the situation the British Government turns to former Intelligence Corps officer Sam, hoping that his civilian status can keep him under the radar and his old skills might just be enough to turn the problem round.

Meanwhile, Helen is co-opted into a role that goes against her every belief - a role that her patriotism demands she fulfil even as she struggles to evade the determined attentions of Bishop Ignatius and his men.

Far from the cloudy skies of Edinburgh, a frightening and bloody hunt plays out beneath the burning sun of the East African bush. Racing against the clock, and with scant support, Sam and Helen must risk everything to resolve the challenge of the enigmatic Bishop Ignatius while fighting to preserve the West's place in a dangerous world.

The Temple Deliverance

(The Temple - Book 4)

Scheduled for publication in late 2018.

Jolted out of their holiday season calm, Helen Johnson and Sam Cameron find they must play one last hand in a deadly game.

The final hunt is on to unpick an ancient code that hides the incredible nature of the Templars' greatest secret. From the depths of northern winter to the sun-kissed beaches of North Africa, Helen and Sam must hurry to piece together the final clues in a race against time to save themselves, their loyal friends and Christianity's greatest heritage.

ABOUT D.C. MACEY

D. C. Macey is an author and lecturer based in the United Kingdom.

A first career in the Merchant Navy saw Macey's early working life devoted to travelling the globe. In the process, it gave an introduction to the mad mix of beauty, kindness, cruelty and inequality that is the human experience everywhere. Between every frantic costal encounter was a trip across the ocean, which brought the contrast of tranquil moments and offered time for reading, writing and reflection. Those roving days came to a close, however, with Macey serving as a ship's officer in the North Sea oil industry.

Several years working in business made it apparent that Macey's greatest commercial skill was the ability to convert tenners into fivers, effortlessly and unerringly - a skill that ensured Macey had the unwelcome experience of encountering those darker aspects of life that lie beneath the veneer of our developed world and brought fleeting glimpses into the shadows where bad things lurk.

Eventually, life's turbulence, domestic tragedy and impending poverty demanded a change of course. As a result, the past decade and more has been spent in lecturing and producing predominantly corporate media resources, so allowing Macey the opportunity to return to the written word.

Throughout it all Macey is certain that a happy home and laughter have proven time and again to be the best protection against life's trials.

• • •

D.C. MACEY

For more information: contact@dcmacey.com
and visit: www.dcmacey.com